A FAINT ECHO

A FAINT ECHO

J A SEDLER

iUniverse, Inc.
Bloomington

A Faint Echo

This is a work of fiction. All of the characters, names, incidents, organizations, and dialogue in this novel are either the products of the author's imagination or are used fictitiously.

Excerpts from George Orwell used by permission of the estate of the late Sonia Brownell Orwell, Secker & Warburg (U.K.), and/or Houghton Mifflin Harcourt (U.S.).

iUniverse books may be ordered through booksellers or by contacting:

iUniverse
1663 Liberty Drive
Bloomington, IN 47403
www.iuniverse.com
1-800-Authors (1-800-288-4677)

Because of the dynamic nature of the Internet, any web addresses or links contained in this book may have changed since publication and may no longer be valid. The views expressed in this work are solely those of the author and do not necessarily reflect the views of the publisher, and the publisher hereby disclaims any responsibility for them.

Any people depicted in stock imagery provided by Thinkstock are models, and such images are being used for illustrative purposes only.

Certain stock imagery © Thinkstock.

ISBN: 978-1-4620-6636-0 (sc)
ISBN: 978-1-4620-6638-4 (hc)
ISBN: 978-1-4620-6637-7 (e)

Library of Congress Control Number: 2011960043

Printed in the United States of America

iUniverse rev. date: 01/27/2012

**To my family
and friends.**

PART 1:
FACTORY-MADE
REBELLS

CHAPTER 1

⌒

THE SUN BEAT DOWN ON my back like a man trying to break rock and rubble, my spine being the brace. The heat was only intensified through the heavy black jacket that I was wearing, making me wish that I'd found another place to stop and rest. The rock that I was using as a seat wasn't that comfortable either. The moss that grew on it didn't make that great of a cushion, but my leg was acting up again, and I needed to stop. Besides, a chair-sized rock by the side of this dusty road seemed as good a place as any to stop and take a breather. Glancing around the area, I looked for signs of civilization, of which there were none other than the fenced-off area just down the road. I hummed a bit to myself as I unloaded my backpack that was weighing me down on my trek across this unnamed area of country. A puff of dust scattered for safety underneath my backpack as it slumped onto the ground.

Weary eyes shaded by a worn hand scanned the horizon to see how far it was before I reached the next town. A small hill covered in grass, roughly a few hundred feet in front of me, blocked any attempt to see what was farther down the road. Other than that, there was an orchard off to the side. Apples grew on the branches, showing signs that they were not ready to be picked. Seeing the apples made my stomach rumble. Flipping open the well-woven fabric flap on the backpack, I reached into the sack and pulled out a few pieces of fruit and my water jug. *I guess I might as well have lunch*, I mused.

As the objects from the open pack were slowly removed, I took a moment to consider what a good purchase this was from the town before. Nestled against the side of the sack, another of my purchases caught my eye. It was more of an impulse buy than anything else. Setting the water jug down to my left, I reached into my pack and pulled out the cool leather-backed book. The gold lettering on the cover glistened in the heat of the bright midafternoon sun. A small, thin, red strip of fabric, cut like a serpent's tongue tasting the air, panted out of the top of the book. Setting the food down on a section of the rock, careful not to have them roll onto the ground, I brought my other hand to the book. I lightly traced the gold letters that bumped out from the leather forming the word *Journal.*

I sighed out loud, staring at the book and the work ahead of me. Grabbing one of the pieces of fruit, I crunched into the soft underbelly of a peach as I stared at the journal I held in my other hand. I reached into my jacket breast pocket to pull out a pen while holding the peach clamped in my mouth. The metal cylindrical contraption, any insignia that was once on it worn off from use, clinked as I placed it down on the rock. The peach in my mouth demanded my attention first.

The juice from the peach quenched my dry, dusty throat, which was exactly what I needed after all my walking. A twinge from my leg surged through the stiff appendage and showed off that I was in worse shape than I thought. I popped the peach pit into my mouth to suck off every last ounce of pulp from it, spitting it out onto the side of the road in order for a future peach tree to grow. Wiping my juice-stained fingers on my pant leg, I picked up my pen again and prepared to write. The leather covering the book crackled from unfamiliar use as it was pried open for the first time.

I had to readjust myself on the rock, making it so I had my back to the sun and giving my shadow the ability to shade the book so I could see what I was writing. This presented an even more uncomfortable position; my back was slowly cooking under the heat from the sun, and the sound of fat sizzled just under my skin.

"Ah, hell," I swore as I placed the book and pen on the rock in order to tear at the jacket to get it off of me.

Taking in a breath, prepping myself for the task at hand, I picked up the book again, reopened it where I had left the pen as a bookmark, and put pen to paper.

~

August 26, 2116.

My name is ...

~

My hand froze.

Doubt swam through my veins as I sat staring at the words. "My name is ..."

I closed my eyes and tilted my head back, stretching my weary back. A few clicks from my spine popped in the air as I stretched. A good minute passed as thoughts of all that had happened to me whizzed in the darkness. Images and memories flew across my third eye, blasting me with moments that I wish I could relive ... as well as points that I wished could be forgotten forever.

"No. This needs to be done," I pointed out, trying to convince myself again that what I was doing was right. If not for me, then for those who deserved to be remembered.

The written words stared back at me. Pen was set to paper once more.

~

My name is Thomas Haroldson.

To some who read this, that won't mean a thing.

To others, my name is a symbol of betrayal ... of a traitor to the cause.

Which cause did I betray first? Did I even betray a cause?

The purpose of this is not to ease a weary conscience but to set the record straight. Through my experience, I have found that the role of history is too easily manipulated by opinion, changed completely in order to suit the person taking it down, or is just a collection of lies. The book that you're holding is a recollection of what happened through my life: no figments of imagination, no expansion or deletion or fits of fancy, and no lies. What I have written down is, to the best of my memory, what really happened—a true dedication of events and people to better serve as a record of what happened and why. But before I start my personal compilation of events, a view of what happened that lead up to this seems to be in order.

The beginning, I guess, would be in the year 2035. A new chapter was opened up inside the United Nations. A new organization called the POLICE (which stood for "Planet-wide Organization Licensed in Crime Enforcement") joined forces with the UN to help establish order. Factions of the POLICE were open worldwide. A young man nicknamed the General, who first founded the POLICE, had equal authoritative power over the organization. They went out of their way to help out the world—feeding the hungry and the poor, ending the drug trades, stopping crime, getting medical supplies to those who were sick. They were miracle workers.

Then something went wrong.

The General claimed that the UN was trying to dirty the mission they started with the internal bickering of politics, while the UN insisted that the General was trying to corrupt the nature of the organization for his own will, making himself supreme commander. The POLICE then broke away from the UN, declaring independence. No longer holding the support of the UN, the POLICE had to fight hard to keep the organization alive during the next few months, fighting and forcing to get a foot on the ground.

The true disaster occurred at the final meeting between the General and the UN, when (on purpose or by mistake) a single shot killed one of the head speakers of the UN. The POLICE were blamed. Countries fractured under the strain of its populace showing support for or against the POLICE. The world was now at war with itself. Because there were POLICE stations all over the world, there was no safe haven for either side—no safe country to run to like before. Every street in every town became the front line.

Five long years of fighting commenced. The POLICE first seized full control over Germany, because the General wanted to secure that country as a center for control over Europe. He then ordered all efforts to focus on the capture of Russia. Once Russia was obtained, a group of officers who were ex-Russian secret service (I think they were called the USSR—the United Secret Soldiers of Russia, or something like that) broke into an old abandoned army bunker and fired the missiles that were stored there: planet-killers. These missiles were decommissioned after a peace treaty in 2016, but due to funding or scheduling, they were never actually deconstructed. Their target: the United States of America. Because of the peace treaty, there was nothing the United States could use to defend against them. The United States never had a chance.

The United States, the strongest force standing against the POLICE, was considered obliterated from the face of the map in one fell swoop.

After the United States fell, the remaining countries of the world were picked over and seized one by one. They didn't roll over easily, though. The remaining countries undertook a last-ditch effort against the POLICE by using the pieces of machinery orbiting the globe to emit an electrified magnetic pulse that shorted out all the machinery with electronics back on Earth. No longer being able to use their creations of war or means of communication, the POLICE still tried to move forward. The POLICE won World War III on February 24, 2041, when the last country opposing them surrendered.

Once the war was won, the real work began. Governments were dissolved. Religions were erased. Maps were redrawn. Places were renamed. All flags were immediately changed over to the symbol of the POLICE: a black background with a red circle containing a fist holding a nightstick high in the air. Languages were obliterated as well—only German remained.

After the victory, there were a few weeks of unrest as change was adapted into everyday life. Some groups rebelled against the new regime. Most of these groups were terminated with little trouble, but a small group that started up in what was once called France grew into an organized might against the POLICE. Thus, the faction Le Rebells came about, attacking through terrorist means—anything that might put a stop to the POLICE.

This is where I enter the records of history.

The year was 2112. I was sixteen at the time. I lived in Sicher Himmel, a small town in an area once called Germany. I was waking up on a Tuesday morning in order to go to work at the Factory....

CHAPTER 2

THE SCREECH OF THE FACTORY'S steam whistle invaded the air, breaking the silence of the morning. Eyes once immersed in sleep slowly started to open, peeling away the dust that had collected overnight. The muscles in my jaw stretched into a yawn as I raised my hands to my face. Rubbing the base of my palms into my eyes, I started to work my mind for the day ahead. The blankets rested at chest level, half on the ground from a night of tossing and turning. Without a second thought, I performed my daily curse toward the steam whistle's operator, hoping that he would develop some style of crippling disease.

Suddenly, the covers that were resting on my body just moments before were pulled away with an extreme force. Surprised by the motion, I scampered into a huddled position, pushing myself into the corner of my bed. There, at the base of my bed, rested the gray and brown blankets that had once covered me during my sleep. Holding them was a young man about my age, smiling brightly and showing off his white teeth. I relaxed upon recognizing my best friend, John.

John's hair was always a little messy, as was his general appearance. But despite his appearance and the fact that he worked in the mines section of the Factory, he prided himself for being extremely tidy and clean. Looking at his place, however, one would assume otherwise. He was bigger and stronger than I was (and rightly so, working manual labor six days a week), although I would never admit his superiority out loud. He was dressed in his usual Factory uniform: dark overalls with a deep breast pocket in the front, thick black boots, and a tan long-sleeved shirt.

His mother and my mother were friends, which made the early friendship mandatory. Over the years, though, that friendship had grown. We always had the greatest times when we were together; yet, for some odd reason, we were always running into some sort of mischief. The one fault I found in John was that he was a dreamer. He tended to go off regularly on some wild-goose chase, trying to find something that was not really there. We must have dug up half the town as kids searching for some sort of buried treasure or some other nonsense. It was either that, or he was sticking his nose into events that were not our business, helping out people as best he could, no matter what the reason. Because of this, the local authorities knew the two of us by our first names, which was probably not something to be proud of.

John gathered the blankets together in his arms with a cyclone motion and threw them back in a pile, which landed at my feet. "Gooooood morning, Sunshine! It's another beautiful day outside! The birds are chirping, the sun is just starting to peak its head over the horizon, the air is clear and fresh, and *you* have one hour to get ready for work or else the guards are going to have your ass!"

"You are such a jerk. You know that, don't you," I moaned, desperate to restart my failing heart.

John leaned over the bottom part of the bed frame, grabbed one of my ankles in his massive grip, and started yanking me toward the edge of the bed. My arms flailed about, trying to get my bearing and stop the slow assertion toward the edge of the bed and a short fall onto the floor.

"Come on, Tom," John prodded. "No snoozing today. We need to get to work on time."

I slapped at his hand, trying to get him to let go of me. "All right, all right, *all right*! I'm getting up. I'm getting up. You can let go now, John."

I stopped just at the cusp of falling off the bed as John let go of my leg, which was hanging over the mattress like I was fishing for some trout and my leg was the fishing pole. John smiled and motioned that he would be outside the bedroom waiting for me. Turning to leave, he mockingly skipped toward the door, humming some sort of bright and cheery tune.

I leaned back and grabbed for my pillow. Picking up the spongy sleeping apparatus, I arched my arm and gave it a good throw at my unsuspecting friend. It landed with a pluph, hitting him smack in the middle of his back. John, at being struck with my instrument of death, started to giggle at me. He hurried his pace out of the room, grabbing the door and closing it quickly behind him, leaving me alone to get dressed.

I dragged myself off of the straw-filled mattress that made up my bed and walked over to the small dresser that held all my clothes. A simple mirror was positioned on top. I stared hard into the reflective surface. Light brown hair, messy from a deep sleep, cropped the top of my head. Bangs too long for my liking crept out from the mesh of dry hair that sat on my head. A thin, sinewy frame helped carry the heavy head that housed my brain. The light cream shirt top and breezy black shorts didn't leave much to the imagination regarding muscle tone.

Opening the middle drawer, I pulled out a work shirt and pair of pants that made up the Factory's uniform and closed the drawer using my hip. Holding the woolen, scratchy tan uniform in my arms in order to examine it, I noticed that there was a small hole in the shirt that needed mending. Throwing the dirt-brown pants onto the bed, I took off the top that warmed me during the night and replaced it with my work shirt, careful not to jab my finger into the newly discovered hole. Once properly dressed, I walked over to my door and entered the other room.

John was standing in front of my counter in the kitchen slapping together a sandwich, a block of cheese, and a tube of sausage beside him. He glanced up over his shoulder. Holding up an apple, he mumbled, "Breakfast?" I raised my hand to decline, because I wasn't very hungry. Shrugging his shoulders, he returned to his work finishing up the sandwich and putting the unused food back into the cupboard. I scuffled over to where my boots lay beside the door and sat down on a nearby chair in order to put them on.

~

I locked the door to my two-room shelter—number 609, flat 4—and slid the key into my back pocket. This wasn't my first home. This was the place given to me to live in after I reached the sanctioned age of thirteen, being old enough to work and all. Before that time, I lived with a neighbor of mine, Mrs. Varse. She took me in when I was eight or so and cared for me after my parents' deaths. I can barely remember my parents now, which I guess is a blessing in disguise. The last days of the Fallout Plague were not exactly a pleasant time, and it did some horrible things to the body. At least my sister died quickly and didn't have to suffer like our parents.

John and I started walking toward the Factory as we always did, weaving in and out through the alleys and paths between the other shelter blocks, in order to get to the entranceway, or E-way as John like to call it, of the Factory faster. That's the one thing that took away from working at the Factory—the strictness for being on time. In order to make sure there would be no more missed shifts and to give all his employees a warning about getting to work on time, the owner, Mr. Freuhaven, put in the steam whistle about six years ago. At six in the morning, like clockwork, that cursed thing would blast out into the air, one hour before starting time. Along with the whistle, he put into work some heavy fines for being late. "Since there should be no more excuses," he would point out. Somehow John and I always managed to find a way to wriggle our way out of punishment for being constantly late.

John gave me a good nudge in the side of my ribs. "Penny for your thoughts," he remarked.

"What?"

"A penny ... for your thoughts."

"What the hell are you talking about?" I asked.

"It's something that my dad used to say to me when I was troubled by something. It means spill your guts. What's up with you? You've been moody all morning."

I forced a smile, showing off all my teeth. "There. I'm smiling. You happy? I can't have a problem if I'm smiling, right?"

"Fine. Don't tell me. See if I care," he mockingly pouted.

We continued walking down an alley toward the E-way in silence. John locked in his I'm-not-going-to-talk-to-you performance. The path that we were taking narrowed, the walls of the nearby housing squeezing us into single file. John took the lead. A few steps in, John stopped suddenly, his foot jerking straight in the air as if he was about to step on a nail. He stopped so quickly that I almost collided with him. John bent down slowly and picked something up off of the ground, cupping it in his hands. He turned around to show me. It was an earthworm.

After seeing that I had noticed what it was, he lightly brushed off the dirt that was clinging to the outside of the worm and gently scooped it into the breast pocket of his overalls. John always kept a damp cloth in his breast pocket to brush his brow with when he got too hot in the mines. My mouth parted slightly, and my eyebrows scrunched together, asking an unheard question to John as to why all this care and concern over an earthworm.

John looked proudly from his breast pocket and his new companion to me. Seeing my puzzled face, he answered, "I always wanted a pet."

John smirked his quirky smile, the one that he puts on when he's trying to be funny. He patted his pocket lightly, turned, and continued walking ahead of me. The utter insanity of the moment finally broke through, and I smiled at the idiot. The path widened up again so we could walk side-by-side once more. John was dropping pieces of bread from the sandwich that he had made at my home into the pocket with the worm. Glancing about, I noticed that we were almost at the gate that protected the E-way. The two of us were going to be early … for once.

John stopped walking, thrusting his arm out to block me from moving forward, his head raised slightly. "What was that?" he asked me in a hushed tone.

I stopped moving and listened to the air around me. The morning air was lightly soaring through the path between two sections of flats. A bird sang in the distance. The occasional person's voice was muffled through the walls of a nearby shelter—nothing out of the ordinary. I turned so I was facing John.

"Hear what?" I questioned.

He raised his hand, his index finger pointing up. His eyes scanned the horizon of the path, searching for a visible extension of the sound that he thought he had heard. "Wait for it," he instructed.

I waited and listened, all the while thinking that the gate was about ten minutes away and that we were going to be late because John's sixth sense told him a cat was nearby mewing for milk or something foolhardy like that.

wham

John whipped his head toward me. "That! Did you hear that?" he whispered, as if whatever made the sound would fly away if it heard him.

I nodded. "It sounds like someone hitting a hammer against a sheet of loose metal. So what?"

John tilted his head, giving me a you-should-know-better expression. "Metal being worked on outside of the Factory?"

John was right. Metal is rarely allowed off the Factory grounds, let alone to be worked on without the proper tools and supervision. There was something odd about this. I pointed toward one of the turnoffs the path was offering. "It sounded like it came from this way."

The path that I was pointing toward eventually led out into the market square and the houses that survived the war. Only the rich could afford to pay the town the amount of money required to live in that type of house. Squinting down the way, trying to see if I could see what was going on, I searched for reasons why someone would be beating on a piece of metal outside of the Factory grounds. Perhaps one of the shops needed a new wall, and some workers were repairing it. But the Factory hadn't started up yet, so there wouldn't be anyone working.

"Should we go see?" I asked my friend.

John chewed lightly on his lower lip, thinking over the options. With a nod, he said, "I'll go. You get to work. No reason why we should both get into trouble."

John took a deep breath and started trudging down the side path toward the strange sound and away from the Factory. I stood where I was, watching John grow smaller and smaller at each step, trying to work myself out of the moral dilemma that I was facing. Should I actually leave John to figure it out and go to work or join up with him and risk being late? With a sharp exhale, realizing that this was probably a really stupid idea, I started after him.

After two quick turns, we were deep onto the trail and walking along a path that we had never traveled before. The flats grew in height as we walked, covering the path in deep morning shadows that occasionally blocked out the sun entirely from where we stood. John looked around and noticed that I was walking behind him. John nodded toward me, showing a hint of relief at seeing that I had decided to join up with him.

I raised my head toward the noise. John motioned that he heard it too. The noise was getting louder, so we were obviously getting closer. It was a man's voice that came after the pounding of metal. The strange voice sounded like it was uttered through a cloth, mumbled and sore. John, slowly and cautiously, started walking forward again, stepping over his feet in a sidestep scissor motion, positioning his back against the wall of a nearby shelter as he moved.

Wham!

Both of our heads jerked up at the sound. The man that we heard gave out a wail of pain, followed by an eerie silence. John went into a sprint toward the sound, gravel kicking up from under his boots. I barely had time to react to John before he disappeared around a corner. Scrambling feet turned into a run in order to try to catch up to John, who was now a good length ahead of me. John was always a bit better at physical stuff, so it became a chore to keep him in sight as we weaved through the alleyway.

As we ran, John blasting out in front of me, a memory sparkled through my mind—one that hadn't come to mind in a very long time. It was when we were very young and my parents were still alive. John had come to my house and asked my mother if we could go play. John had heard about a festival happening at the opposite end of town and said that we would have to run in order to get there before it closed down for the day. That meant that we would have to cut through a few alleys to get there. My mother could tell that I wanted to go but gave me a stern warning before giving permission. She bent down to my level and stared directly into my eyes.

"Promise me that you and John won't go racing through the alleyways to get to this fair, Tom," she said. "Those are dangerous areas, and children have a tendency to get lost in those places. Not to mention that's where nasty people live—people who purposely hurt others."

We could hear the scuffle more easily as we got closer. There were three distinct voices that I could separate from the echoes of noise—all male. One was gruff and obviously enjoying the torment that was ensuing. The second was higher pitched, egging on the turmoil. The third was older and easily identifiable as the victim. By this time, John was an entire length ahead of me, kicking wide so that he wouldn't lose his momentum as he rounded the corners. It was all that I could do to catch a glimpse of the end of his shirt as he flew around the corner ahead of me. As I turned around the second corner, John was gone.

My breath was pumping out of my body hard; the blood was pounding inside my temples. It felt like my heart was a caged beast, banging against its prison for release. I could barely breathe in, taking the musty air into my lungs before forcing it out again in rhythm to my steps. My feet clumped unceremoniously on the ground now, leaving deep impressions in the dirt, reluctant to be yanked back into the air by my legs. Half collapsing against a back wall of a shelter, I turned the final corner at a slower pace and took a moment to take in what was happening.

The area was an old market hutch where grocers would sell food and baskets, which was usually found inside the business sector of town. Shelters surrounded the hutch, creating a mock arena, complete with alleyway entrances at each point of the compass. The arena was around forty or fifty feet across, giving plenty of room for the action occurring in the middle. By the looks of the walls on the shelters and the materials that they were made out of, we were just entering the rich section of town.

Two women were huddled in a corner; the older woman was trying to protect a younger girl, who was fighting against the older woman while attempting to enter the fray. A man who looked to be in his fifties was lying on the ground; his shirt and pants torn, and there was blood trickling out of his mouth. The man on the ground was struggling frantically to get to the two women in the corner. Three men were in the middle of the area standing over where the victim was scrambling, and that's where I found John. John was wrestling with the biggest one, firmly entangling himself on the guy's back. John raised his free hand into the air and would bring it down hard over and over again onto the head of the guy he was getting a piggyback ride from. The two other guys were trying to get a grip on John, desperately trying to pry him off of the big guy. The big guy was yelling at his cohorts: "Get this freak off of me!"

I recognized all of them. The first of the two goons was named Leon. He always went out of his way to treat everyone else like they were somehow inferior to him. Tall and skinny in frame, he made up for his stature with his mouth and wits. The second guy in the pack was named Ralph. He was the opposite of Leon—small, stout, and stupid. Thinking with his fists, Ralph grew up on the streets and became a force to be reckoned with. The two bruisers alone were enough of a reason to walk the other way, but it was the third, the one whom John was wrestling with, that made my blood run cold.

In the middle of it all was Vans Braun, the leader of this insignificant tribe. A few years older than I was, Vans was the perfect soldier: big, strong, obedient, and loyal. Even from a young age, all Vans wanted to do with his life was to be an officer inside the POLICE organization. All his life he's been unofficially training to become one of them. Unfortunately, through his personalized "training regiment," he's come to the conclusion that everyone else in this town is a law breaker and that everyone is guilty of some crime or another. On more than one occasion, I had been blessed with a meeting with this twisted idealist-of-the-cause nature, coming out of the scuffle with more than my share of bruises, cuts, and scrapes. In essence, Vans was the local bully for all the young kids around here, including me.

The worst part of it all was that some of the POLICE officers in this section of town had come to look at Vans as an informer and trained dog for them who would do their dirty work (through unofficial lines). Last year, I heard rumors that the First Sergeant, the guy in charge of the POLICE, was considering giving Vans special privileges by recruiting him into the training program early. Rather, he would become a SIT—a Soldier In Training. That never happened. He had clearly started his training, though.

John tightened his left arm around the tree trunk of a neck Vans had sprouting out of his torso to keep himself from being tossed off and landed a few more good rights onto the thick-headed brute. Ralph and Leon managed to unscrew John's legs from around Vans's chest and were yanking on each leg to pull John off of their leader. All this did was jerk Vans off-balance, and the four bounced from one side of the arena to another, swinging from side to side with each unanimous tug. Needless to say, the two goons were not being too successful with getting John off of Vans.

The man on the ground managed to get to the two women in the corner. The older woman cradled the head of the man in her arms. Leon and Ralph yelled at each other, giving incoherent orders within the mass of confusion. Vans managed to grab one side of John's face and was pushing against it in order to get him off of his back. John, his face in the web of fingers that composed Vans's hand, opened his mouth and bit down on the first finger that wriggled its way into the opening. A yelp of pain escaped Vans, and he doubled his effort to get John into a position where he could do some damage.

Leon, wrinkling his face at seeing their effort to subdue John was not going as planned, turned his attention to the ground and searched for something. Ralph took up John's leg and, using his own leg on the small of Vans's back as leverage, started to haul John off of Vans. Leon bent down and picked up a fist-sized rock.

"Vans, stand still!" he ordered.

Vans stopped swinging himself around the area and turned toward his teammate. Seeing the rock in Leon's hand, Vans turned away from Leon, exposing his back and a clear shot at John. Vans waved Ralph away from him so that he wouldn't get in the way of the blow. Ralph stepped aside a little, grinning widely. Leon prepped himself for a swing with his weapon, winding up for a pitch.

Craaack!

Ralph went down onto one knee, blood spurting out of his split lip like a fountain's spray. Spitting a mix of blood and saliva onto the dirt, Ralph slowly glanced up from his kneeling position at his would-be assailant, showing off his now-broken front tooth. I raised the board that I pried off of one of the shelters over my head a second time and brought it down again hard onto the skull of the stout young man.

Craaack!

As a marionette without his strings, Ralph collapsed onto the ground, sprawled out in the mix of sweat, blood, and dirt. The board cracked at the top from the impact against Ralph's head. I turned around, board raised, in order to re-enter the fray.

Vans had finally managed to get John off of his back, and John unceremoniously flopped onto the ground with a grunt. Leon stood a few feet away; a small patch of red now marked the gray-and-black rock in the assailant's hand. Both were still too focused on John to notice what had happened to Ralph. Vans had John stretched out in front of him, his huge hands firmly planted on either side of John's neck in a chokehold.

With board raised, I swung with all my might against the middle of Leon's face. The force of the impact threw him against one of the walls surrounding us. An explosion of blood cascaded against the wall from his nose, and Leon slumped back from the wall onto the ground in a pile.

Vans glanced toward me in shock, unsure as to what had just happened. From my position, I brought my right arm back up in a wide swing, the board now whistling in the air from the cracks and deformities that had resulted from the brawl. The wooden board connected with Vans's face, while one of the protruding splinters deeply cut into the flesh in his check. Blood flowed freely from the newly formed gash. John, free from Vans's grip, collapsed on the ground gasping for air and rubbing his neck. A screech of agony echoed from Vans as he clawed at his face in order to stop the flood of blood that was escaping. He started to twitch and spin uncontrollably, not looking where he stepped, his hands still desperately trying to protect his now-deformed face. Readying the board in my hand for a second swing against the perpetrator, I jabbed Vans in the stomach and knocked the wind out of him. Stepping on the rock that Leon dropped after being struck by the board, Vans lost his footing and plopped onto the ground.

Quickly glancing from Vans to John in order to check if he needed any help, I noticed that John had pulled himself into a standing position and was wobbling and weaving to get his balance. I returned my focus onto Vans. He was trying to get back up off of the ground, his blood mixing with the brown dirt and staining it a rusty color. His hands were now free from his face, and I could see that the broken section of the board had cut his face from the lower section of his left cheek to the bottom of his eye.

A flab of skin hung loosely from his face, flapping open and closed as he teetered. The blood from the wound, now mixed with the dirt from the ground, created a crusty formation on Vans's face.

Regaining his balance, Vans straightened his back so that he could stand at his full height, which towered over me by at least a good foot and a half. His eyes glowed red-hot with hate. His right hand slowly and meticulously raised itself to the fresh would on his cheek, brushing away some of the dirt that had gathered there. Vans winced inwardly at the sting of remembrance that the action caused. Moving his hand from his face into a jab at me, he pointed his finger out toward us all.

"You will regret that, you *mit eselsohren wegschnecke.* You all will!" he gurgled, cursing us from the pit of his stomach.

He took one step toward us, his footing still unsure and wobbling and his eyes curling into the back of his head. I swung wide. The board exploded into a shower of splinters as I drove the piece of wood across Vans's head one last time. No longer able to hold himself up from the rush of the fight, Vans crumpled in a heap on the ground in front of us. He was out.

The board that I was holding, blood speckling the splintered top, slipped out of my hand as I relaxed from the fight. John, gently nursing the wound on the back of his head, wandered to where I was standing. I hadn't moved since Vans collapsed onto the ground, my eyes still locked where he had landed. Adrenalin pumped through my veins with every pound of my heart, unsure if I was still in danger. I think the nerves in my arm had shut off; I couldn't feel it anymore—it just hung loosely by my side, unable to hold up its own weight. *I knocked out Vans*, I thought to myself over and over again. *I took out Vans.*

"Are you okay, Tom?" John wheezed, resting a hand on my shoulder.

I could barely make out John's voice from the pounding of blood in my ears. My head felt light, and my vision blurred slightly from the exhaustion that the fight. I never even looked in John's direction, too afraid to let my gaze off of Vans in case he stood back up and attacked again. I just nodded slowly, half to answer his question and half to get my head out of the fog that it had entered. He took a deep breath, which exited his body in a long sigh.

"Man ... what a mess," he mused.

A cough from behind us quickly brought back to my attention the three others in the area. John and I turned to face the three in the corner. They were slowly getting up, the older woman supporting the man as he got to his feet. Now that there were a few extra moments to actually look at him, his wounds didn't seem to be as bad as I first thought. The younger woman was hugging the man, draping him over her right arm to help him stand. They looked to be a family.

I raised my hands to the three. "We're not going to hurt you. It's okay now," I reassured them.

The older woman looked to be around forty. The younger woman looked about sixteen—around my age. The man wore a fine jacket and pants, now ruined from the fight, while the women wore comfortable dresses. From the style of clothes that they wore, despite the dirt and dust, I would assume that they were far better off money-wise than I was. After all, they weren't wearing the regular clothing that one would wear to a factory job or farming, but more so for an office job in the finance district. The man's hair was starting to gray in some parts, and he had soft wrinkles around his eyes. The older woman's hair was red, wild from the confrontation.

The man coughed, causing him to enter a moment of spasms. Both ladies tried to hold him together during the attack, concern crossing their ragged faces. He brought a hand up to cover his mouth and drew it away with a small stream of saliva stringing from his mouth. Looking up from his hindered position, he nodded toward the three grunts on the ground. "I think it would be best if we continued this conversation away from *those* people," he said.

I slowly moved toward the family, hands still in front of me. John decided to stay where he was, keeping his eyes on the gang. I went to the man and, showing that I wasn't going to attack them, took up the opposite side from where the young woman was holding him. Hooking my arm around his waist, I took up some of his weight, and the five of us trudged out of the area down one of the alleys.

As we walked, I glanced from the older man to the young woman. She glanced back over her shoulder to see if the three we left were following us, which they weren't. John, who now took up the man's weight alongside myself by replacing the older woman's position, did his best to take up the majority of the man's weight from me, because he was stronger. The five of us wandered through the alleyways for a few minutes.

"So, why was Vans attacking you three?" I asked as we walked.

The older man chuckled slightly, a spasm of pain registering at the movement. "That … might be a little complicated to explain," he answered.

"Well, we're not going anywhere fast," John grunted under the man's weight.

My eyes grew wide as my mind flashed through an internal schedule. We probably missed the closing of the Factory gate by now, making the two of us officially late for work—again.

"Um, John," I started, thinking out my words carefully, "we do have … pressing engagements that need our attention."

John shot me a disapproving look. "I'm not about to just leave this guy stranded in an alley, Tom."

The older woman came up from behind us where she was following and motioned down an alleyway that was leading toward the streets. "You've already done more than enough for us. We can manage from here," she briskly pointed out.

The older man cleared his throat. "Sherry, these two gentlemen just saved our lives. The least we can do is show some respect in return."

She glared at the older man, slumped between John and myself, hands planting on her hips. "William! I was not being rude. They want to leave; let them leave. I was pointing out that it's not their concern anymore. Besides, they don't want to get involved, so why bother dragging them into things? We don't even know them. They could be—"

William released himself from our grasps with a grunt and tried to stand, with extreme effort, on his own. Taking in a breath to counteract the shots of pain that this action caused him, he stood tall and proud and stared hard at the woman. "I'm not about to argue this point. Not here and not now. The very least we can do is care to their wounds and feed them a decent meal for their kindness."

William turned around so that he was facing us, his back to the street. He stuck a hand out to each of us. "My name is William Kenneth. This is my wife, Sherry, and my daughter, Dawn. I would like to thank you for saving our lives back there."

I took the hand that was offered and shook it. John did the same and said, "I hardly think that we saved your lives. Vans wouldn't have killed you. Beat you up—sure. Kill you—doubtful."

William waved off John's remark. "Who knows what those ruffians would have done if you two fine young men hadn't shown up when you did. Please, join us at our home so that we can take care of those cuts that you got and discuss a few things. Maybe have a bite to eat?"

I cleared my throat quickly, taking a quick glance toward John, and smiled toward William. "Uh ... we would love to, but we have to—"

A sharp elbow from John quickly made me stop talking. "What my friend was trying to say is that we would love to join up with you ... at a later time. Perhaps for dinner. Then we can talk about why Vans was attacking you."

I crossed my arms, knowing better than to argue with John once he got a thought in his head. John raised an eyebrow as he waited for a response from William, who was staring at the two of us. With a nod, William agreed. "All right, then. We'll meet you at the market in front of stall number 917 around seven tonight."

The old man turned and paused for a moment. "No ... best make it tomorrow. Meet us at the market stall; then we'll go to our home and have dinner."

John smiled. "Agreed."

John and I quickly said our good-bye to the small family and jogged out onto the street from the alleyway. After a quick survey of the surrounding area, I realized that we had backtracked a bit and were farther away from the Factory than when we started this rescue mission. Cursing softly at how far off we had veered, the two of us started jogging toward the Factory.

CHAPTER 3

We were late for work—a good hour late by the time we got to the Factory's gates. One way that the supervisors of the Factory tried to stop lateness was by locking the gates after starting time. Thus, anyone who was late would need to go to the guard on duty, report in, and ask to be let inside. The late employee then had to sign a form with the head secretary, complete with time he arrived and date of the occurrence. The POLICE took it one step further. If you got five of these forms in a short amount of time, then your job would be terminated, the late factor would become etched onto your permanent record, and you couldn't be hired at any other job for a month.

This was meant to deter you from doing something similar at your new job. And you would have plenty of time to think over your crimes as you starved, because most jobs paid monthly and rarely left enough money to cover expenses the following month. John and I had more than fifteen late accounts with the Factory. Thankfully, they were spaced out enough to avoid termination.

As we walked up to the closed gate, we started glancing around the courtyard to see who was on gate duty today. The courtyard was empty, with one or two advertising papers dancing from the slight breeze. This meant that the guard on duty was making his rounds around the gate in order to make sure no one was sneaking in. There was nothing left to do but to plunk ourselves down on the ground and wait for whomever that was on duty to let us in. John leaned up against the bars and used them to help him slide to the ground. A very small patch of greenish-brown grass looked inviting, and I eased myself into this sanction of nature a few feet away from John.

John leaned his head back to rest against the rusty gate. As soon as the metal made contact with his scalp, he jerked his head forward, bringing his hand up to where the flesh had touched metal. He pulled in a quick breath through clenched teeth, making a hissing sound, as he rested his hand against the back of his head. "Forgot about my goose egg," he explained to me.

The softness of the ground allowed me to get into a comfortable position, resting my back against the gate but also facing John. John faced forward, so I got a profile view of my friend. "I'll say one thing. Leon sure knows how to use a rock," he scoffed.

A grin etched itself onto my face as I leaned forward, resting my arms on my knees. "That's only because he hasn't evolved enough to discover fire," I mused.

John let out a hearty laugh, which caused him to jerk his head back. His head clanged against the metal bars of the gate once more, causing him to jerk forward as he cradled his wound. His laugh turned into a curse as he rocked back and forth, both hands around his head. With each breath, he softly hummed to himself a tune with no apparent melody, waiting for the pain to subside.

Turning my attention away from my friend so he wouldn't think I was laughing at him, my eyes scanned the area while soaking in the morning. The Factory sat on a small hill that overlooked the town, providing an outlook of shelter blocks five through eight. The POLICE Grounds, the section of town blocked off for all the POLICE buildings, could also be seen in the distance. Looking around the local area, I glanced over to a small section of the gate that was blocked off with security tape and a danger sign screwed into place. There were three bars missing from the gate, which the sign blocked so that no one could crawl through the hole it produced. A chuckle escaped my mouth, thinking back on how that hole was created.

A sharp pain exploded against the side of my arm. Letting out a yelp, I retracted from John, who had leaned over to give me a good slug on the shoulder. "Oh yeah, real funny," he pointed out, quite irate. "Let's see how funny it is when you get knocked on the head with a rock."

I rubbed my shoulder, trying to ease the bruise that would form. I turned so that I was facing John again. "I wasn't laughing at you," I explained bitterly.

John lowered his head but kept his eyes on me, raising one of his eyebrows. I simply shrugged at him. "Okay. At first I was laughing at you, but I wasn't laughing at you just *then*," I pointed out.

John didn't move. "So what were you laughing at, Chuckles?"

I nodded my head in the direction of the hole in the gate. John leaned out to see what I was nodding at and relaxed back into his sitting position, smiling. "I still remember that. It was … what … four years ago? Three?"

"Three," I agreed.

John shook his head. "Three years ago. Damn. And it was all because I dropped a load of coal on the head director's new shoes. Boy was his face red. He could hardly talk he was so mad. 'I … Bu … You … My … When … How … You're …' Finally, when he threatened to take me to a detention cell, that's when things went south," John mused, chuckling at the kaleidoscope of pictures that flew past his eyes.

Snapping his fingers, he turned to me. "It *was so* six guards that tried to pry me off the gate, not four."

I glanced back at the hole, studying the outline of the cut bars. *Oh … here we go again*, I thought to myself. John and I have been arguing about this incident for the past two years, at least.

"No it wasn't. It was four. One had your legs, two were wrestling with your arms, and one had the cutters to cut the bars you were clinging to," I pointed out to him.

"You lie," he scoffed. "Two had my legs, one on my arms, one was tugging from my belt—I remember that one distinctly—one to cut the bars I was gripping, and a final one to calm the head director down, insisting that I was not worth the bullet in his rifle."

"It was seven men," came a voice from behind the two of us.

Both John and I spun around. A kid about our age was leaning against the bars of the gate inside the Factory grounds just above where we were sitting and staring down at us. He was a regular looking kid—average height, straight black hair, and freckles. He wore the same factory uniform that John wore (which was a different model than mine, because I didn't do as much manual labor), except in front of his overall pocket was an ID badge and on his belt was a small baton.

I raised my hand to my heart. "Vlad! You scared the crap out of us."

John got up off the ground, brushing off the dust from his overalls. "How long have you been …?"

"Less than a minute," Vlad interrupted, still leaning against the bars.

Staggering to get to my feet, I grabbed onto one of the bars to help support myself. John was still brushing himself off when Vlad cocked his head to the side as a concerned look crossed his face. "That's quite a bump, John."

John, while slapping the dust off of his boots, chortled quietly, "Yeah, well, it was a gift from an old friend of ours."

Vlad pushed himself off of the bars and started walking slowly toward the entrance, shuffling in his pocket for the key to the lock. "Vans?"

We both nodded, walking in pace with Vlad on the other side of the gate. Vlad closed his eyes and lowered his head, stopping where he stood. "Crap. Now I have to write a report," he muttered quietly.

Vlad reached out with one hand and took hold of the bars that made up the small door built into the gate. With his other hand, he pulled out a ring of keys and started flipping through them. I cleared my throat to get Vlad's attention. "Yeah, but if you write that report, that would take up … what, how long?"

Vlad glanced upward to the sky in search of the answer. "About … half an hour."

"Right," I continued. "So, *if* you write up that report, you, John, and I lose half an hour filling out all the information. This half an hour will need to be made up somehow in the work that needs to be finished by the close of the day—time that John and I are already short on from coming here late, thanks to Vans. Now … since this report concerns an injury and an attack, it will need to be reported to the POLICE. They will have to come here and question us, taking even *more* time away from our work schedule. Not to mention, you will be questioned as to the conditions when we came in, which would interrupt your rounds and—"

"Yeah, I get your point, Tom," Vlad interrupted me with an agitated tone in his voice as he continued to flip through the key ring. "If I put in the report that it was Vans that beat the snot out of you, then they will ask *why* Vans had to beat the snot out of you. Then Vans will be called for and questioned. And because Vans is such a charmer, he will make up some story about how you're both part of Le Rebells and known terrorists. Then the Factory will be shut down for a few days while everyone is questioned. So, to keep everyone happy, I should just keep my mouth shut and let writing the report slide. Am I right?"

Vlad looked up in my direction, his hand maneuvering one of the keys into the lock with a quiet clank of metal on metal. I shrugged my shoulders sheepishly. The lock gave way to the key, and Vlad pulled the door open for us. Vlad closed the door behind us, again with a metallic clank from the lock. With the door once again secure and the keys in his pocket, Vlad turned around to face us and gave us a disapproving look. "Are you at least going to try to get here on time from now on? I can't keep covering for you guys forever."

A friendly slap on Vlad's shoulder was John's response. "You're one of the good guys, Vlad. Always have been and always will," John grinned widely.

Vlad had been our friend even before we all got jobs here at the Factory. We used to play all the time when we were younger. But as we grew, Vlad went in his own direction and slowly stopped hanging out with us. Now, he's trying to make security his career, pushing to become head security for the Factory.

Vlad shook his head at the two of us. "You're still gonna have to sign in, though. I have no power over that. What excuse are you gonna make up for that?"

John thought for a second, and then smiled. "The sky's falling."

Vlad stared at the two of us, finally giving in to nostalgia and easing his demeanor. "Get out of here before I change my mind," he threatened us through a smile.

John and I gave a quick wave good-bye to him as we started walking toward the front doors of the Factory. "That's another one you owe me," he called out to us.

The Factory loomed ahead of us, sitting proudly on top of the hill that we walked up. The two towers that bordered the main building, like two guards standing watch, stood proudly protecting the fragile old stones that made up the walls. Dark windows decorated the outskirts of the Factory, showing off the bars that protected the panes of glass. Thick black smoke belched out of the chimneys located toward the back of the building. All in all, it was a dreary sight to look forward to.

John gave me a quick nudge. "Hey, don't forget that we're meeting Lydia for lunch today."

"Oh yeah, I almost forgot," I blurted out sarcastically. "You only reminded me for the past three days about this lunch meeting with Lydia."

Lydia had been going out with John for the past year. A nice girl, she complemented John well. She worked inside the mines, roughly in the same section as John. She checked the gauges; John worked on the engines. That's where they met. A few days ago, John finally asked her to marry him; she said yes, and they immediately began working on the marriage details. They wanted me to help with the planning and to give Lydia away, since her father lived in a town by the edge of the ocean called Flor Del Condado and wouldn't be able to make it to the wedding.

"We're meeting at the usual place, right?" I asked John. He nodded.

The doors to the Factory stood closed to us as we arrived in front of them. The hardwood double doors that made up the entrance to the Factory were reinforced with bars of iron, which added to the intimidation of the building. The heavyset doors gave off the impression that they had some great mythical creature locked away, barring it from ever trying to escape. In reality, the purpose of the doors was more for the protection of what was inside the Factory from whatever might come and try to cause it harm. John reached out and grabbed hold of the handle, yanking hard on the doors for them to open. With a grinding creak, the oak eased open enough for the two of us to enter.

Inside, the main foyer scattered into five different passages, each leading to a different section of the building. One could tell which hallway led to what section of the building just by the general appearance and upkeep in front of each; there was no need to read the signs that hung loosely on rusty hooks. The hallway that led to the mines and refinery section of the Factory, where John slaved his day away, looked dusty and dirty from all the smoke and coal dust that had escaped through the iron doors at the end. No matter how many times they swept that floor (which was once after every shift change), the dust seemed to always creep back. The hallway floor that led to maintenance was larger and wider than the rest in order to make transporting bulky machinery easier. The tiles that ran along the maintenance hallway were also horribly scratched from years of machinery being moved back and forth from the different areas of the building.

The shipping wing's hallway had assorted shelves and packages of every size and shape. It was like walking through a maze of brown paper, wood, and boxes. The manufacturing wing looked just as bulky, except a wire fence at the end closed it off. A security officer stood on the opposite side, protecting the mesh door that allowed access into this restricted area. The hallway that I would eventually take, which led to the main office block, was the shortest of them all. It was a few echo-filled steps away from a winding metal staircase, leading up to the top floors where all the paperwork and filing was done.

The secretary's booth sat right in the middle of the foyer. She was surrounded by a C-shaped wooden desk, ornately designed from a time long gone, weighted with stacks of paperwork and files of assorted thicknesses. She was flipping through one of the files as we opened the doors and walked into the huge room. A clock hung from the rafters of the building, showing off the time in bright colorful numbers: 7:24. Her eyes iced over as she glanced toward us. Without blinking, she returned to the file she was busying herself with and with her free hand reached to her right where a clipboard rested. John and I walked calmly up to the desk of the secretary, knowing the routine that we were going to be subjected to.

"Hey, Bets," John smiled, trying to act casual with the fortyish woman.

Betty Nikle, or Bets as John liked to call her, had been the head secretary of the Factory for as long as I could remember. She squinted at the sound of John calling her his pet name, wrinkling her nose up at the two of us. Her graying hair was in a very tight bun, which pulled at her scalp slightly, making the squinting that much harder and more disturbing to witness. Thin-wired glasses hung low on the bridge of her nose. Her dark dress was also tightly woven around her, adding to the constriction she was under. She slowly swung the clipboard toward us, never letting her eyes escape the important information found within her folder.

"Name and reason for being late," she recited her script to us, well practiced and complete with a tone of irritation.

John took the clipboard from the woman's hand, resting it against one of the stacks of files that sat in front of us. With a pen that was chained to the desk, he started to scribble the needed information onto the piece of paper provided. Glancing up occasionally from his writing, he started making small talk with her, commenting on how her dress complemented her eyes and how he liked her perfume. I think John was doing it in spite, because she wasn't wearing perfume and she was wearing the same thing she always did. When he finished, John passed the clipboard and pen to me, which I took up and started filling out the exact same information. While I was doing this, John examined the files and papers on her desk, all the while continuing with his unsuccessful blathering.

Once finished writing, I handed the clipboard back to Betty. She took the board, glanced at it quickly to read what we had written down, put it back in its resting place on her desk, and turned her attention back to us.

"Jonathan, you're to report to your department head after checking in with the infirmary," she recited from the rulebook she had burnt into her head. John blew a kiss toward her in response to her "obvious concern" over him, and we turned to leave, each of us down our separate hallway.

I walked slowly toward the metal stairs that stood at the end of the hallway, thinking back on the events that happened this morning. *Should John and I have gotten involved in the fight?* I mused as I walked up the three floors to the level I worked on. Should we go to dinner with these people? It's not really any of our affairs. With Vans involved with all this, the POLICE will eventually get involved. What if Vans actually had a reason to attack those people? What is going to happen to us once Vans reports our involvement? He wouldn't attack someone like William and his family without proper cause. Right?

Arriving at the top of the stairs, I waved off the worrisome thoughts and prepared myself for another long day at work.

~

The day seemed to drag on forever while I sat at my desk and compiled order forms and finance statements. My supervisor, as an added incentive for me not to be late again, generously gave me extra paperwork that needed to be completed by the end of the day. He did this, I think, in order to establish the amount of work that this Factory does in a day and how important it was to show up on time. That, and he just doesn't like me—at all. He told me this little tidbit of information to my face once when he refused me for a promotion.

Mr. Burchanna, my supervisor, was generally an unhappy man. I don't remember ever seeing him smile. In fact, he regularly let us know just how unhappy he was or what exactly made him unhappy—being overweight, his thinning hair, new paperwork procedures, his wife—it was a new topic each day. Today, thanks to me, it was about the "lack of dedication that we hold to this Factory" and the fact that "there's a serious lapse in security." Then, once he got tired of badgering us on this topic, he piped in about how we should be thanking him for every day we work here, 'cause there are other people waiting for our jobs that he could hire instead of dealing with us deadbeats!

While I glanced over a report that was asking for extra power resources to be transferred to the maintenance section of the Factory, I thought about John and how lucky I was to land this position. I had a desk and a chair, which was a lot more than quite a few people who worked here were able to say. The hardest thing I had to do was hit a stapler, maybe move a stack of files from one desk to another. John got a daily workout fixing hot boilers or greasy engines.

The section that I worked for was Finance and Resources. I got to go through the mass of request forms from the other sections of the Factory and help decide who got what: loans, power, resources, purchasing, etc. It was quite a responsible job, especially for someone my age. Normally, people my age were shoved into the mines in order to work through their teens and early adulthood, because they were better adept at manual labor. Only after they were no longer fit enough for the mines were people trained and transferred to another section of the Factory, like shipping or something.

Mrs. Varse schooled me in both higher arithmetic and advanced writing techniques before I turned working age. This was above and beyond the standard education we all received through the mandatory schooling. Due to this, I was sent to finance instead of the mines. Everyone else on staff inside the financial department was at least twice my age. As Mr. Burchanna put it, we were the "brains and the wallet of the Factory."

The Factory's steam whistle bellowed out from the distance. With a heartfelt sigh of content at hearing the whistle, I closed the report that was stretched out on my desk and leaned back in my chair, scratching my hurting head. Lunch. Like cattle, everyone in the office stood up in unison and walked toward the doors that led to the stairs. I got up from my desk, pushing my chair back into its spot, and started walking to the stairs along with the others.

Everyone poured out of the Factory tired and hungry. People either looked for a place inside the courtyard to eat their meals from home or headed to the markets to eat something quickly before racing back to work. Mrs. Nikle was getting up from her desk as I walked passed her. I waved at her, trying to stay on her good side. She showed a crack in her defenses and a very small smile sprang to freedom before quickly being subdued and put back into the black hole she kept all of her other emotions in.

I eased myself away from the mass of people and started walking toward the spot where John and I normally met. About a two-minute walk from the E-way, there was a small patch of land on the Factory's property that was grass covered and sheltered by trees. John referred to this place as "the Hole" because of the contrast of dirt and rocks that surrounded the Factory. He had already stretched out under the apple tree in the Hole, resting his back against the trunk while waiting for both Lydia and myself. As I got closer, I noticed a small white bandage that wrapped around his head, probably given to him by the infirmary after this morning's incident.

"So, how badly did you get in trouble?" he asked me, tossing me an apple from the tree. It was not yet ripe; the skin still showing off a strong hue of green, but it was still edible.

I brushed it against the front of my shirt to clean it off as best I could and took a bite into the juicy fruit. Through the mouthful of apple, I sputtered out, "Not as bad as I thought I would."

John nodded and looked behind me, trying to catch a glimpse of Lydia. I shot a glance behind me as well, trying to pick her out from the mass of people still filtering out of the Factory's doors. Returning my eyes back to John and the small patch of grass and dirt he rested on, I glanced at the three trees that occupied the space. The apple tree was young and determined to grow, despite the poor conditions the soil provided. The other two trees were on the verge of dying, creaking softly in the light breeze, but too pigheaded to give up life just yet.

I motioned at the treed with my head. "I'm surprised more people don't sit here during lunch."

John looked up at the apple tree and the surrounding area and then back at me. "Hey, we don't have *that* long to eat and get back to work. If more people sat here, then we would be spending all our time fighting them for a decent place to sit down. Besides, I figure if everyone else that works here is like us, they want to spend the least amount of time on the Factory grounds as possible. Personally, I think the green scares them."

I shot a glance over my shoulder back to the Factory, half hearing John's explanation. "Yeah, I guess," I muttered out the side of my mouth.

Suddenly, from a mass of workers covered in black dust and soot, a hand rose into the air waving in our direction, and Lydia lightly jogged toward where we rested. Her black hair was done up in a ponytail, which bobbed and whisked right and left with each step. Full cheeks and pink full lips helped round out her face. She was wearing the same uniform as John, except she was lightly covered in soot. Her natural beauty still managed to shine through, the uniform showing off her figure. John got up from his resting position and walked toward her. She slowed down just before reaching John so as not to bowl him over and wrapped her arms around him, kissing him lightly on the lips. John returned her affection, giving out a surprised gurgle of sound.

"Hello to you too," he managed to blurt out once Lydia allowed him to catch air between kisses.

White teeth shone out from her soot-patched face as she smiled, kissing John again. I decided to examine the apple tree, the sky, the patch of grass I was standing on—anything interesting in order to avert my eyes from the two.

"Can I look now?" I asked, waiting a second after the smacking had finished.

John wrapped his arm around my head, bringing me into their lovers' embrace, squishing my head into his chest. "Aw, Tommy boy's jealous. You want some kisses too?" John cooed, smacking his lips into my ear.

A quick kidney tap made John let go of me. Bright energetic brown eyes matched up with mine, complete with that glowing smile that Lydia never seemed to get tired of showing off. Lydia hooked her arm in mine and started leading me toward the gate.

"Don't worry, Tom. We'll get someone for you. In fact, I know this cute little redhead in shipping who would be perfect," she giggled.

John tugged on her softly, knocking hips with her and getting her attention. "Oh no you don't," John warned. "We're not setting Tom up with Fireball Fretta. She'd eat him alive!"

Lydia snapped her head around at John, hissing out some air between her teeth in order to shush him. I reached over and patted the arm linked in mine reassuringly. Coal soot escaped from the folds of her clothing, dancing freely in the light air as we walked away.

"Hey, I'm young. There's plenty of time for me yet," I said.

John smiled at Lydia, giving her a slight tug to get her attention focused again. "So, my sweet apricot, where shall we eat today?"

Lydia nudged her forehead with his in a sign of affection. I could have sworn that I heard a hollow thud coming from John's head from the impact. "Oh, I don't know. Let's wander in the market for a place that we haven't been to yet," Lydia mused, picking up her pace toward the gate.

I laughed at the comment—not in a hurtful way but in a comradely way. "Yeah, that way we can be late twice in one day," I joked.

Lydia gave me a soft push at the remark but didn't let go of my arm. She led us in a direct line to the E-way. Even through an old, dried-up mud puddle was in our way, one which we usually wander around, she marched us through it determined to get to the E-way. I guess she had something to show us, perhaps a new restaurant she found in the market.

A bright light came from the Factory, which I caught from the corner of my eye. It was almost like a reflection of the sun off of a window or off a clean piece of metal. Out of reflex, I glanced over toward the Factory to see what it was.

What happened next was a blur of movement, color, and sound.

CHAPTER 4

THE GROUND SHOOK VIOLENTLY, KNOCKING the feet out from all three of us. White noise screamed through my head, filtering out anything audible from the action outside my cranium. Mud and dirt splashed up at my face as I landed on the ground, my hands barely outstretched in front of me in time to try to cushion the impact. Blood pounded in my temples, the veins no doubt pulsating with every pump from my heart. Sparks clouded my vision, along with the dirt from the ground inches away from my face. I blinked, trying to clear out the clutter, and tried to look around in order to gain a perspective of what just happened.

Rocks and brick were flying through the air, landing nearby and all throughout the area. People were running and falling around me. I couldn't tell who they were; they were rushing around so quickly. The speed and urgency of everyone else made me feel like I was moving at half speed. Everything ached when I tried to move to get up. I eased my hands underneath me to push myself off the ground, but for some odd reason, it was very hard to do this. I scuffled my foot under me in order to rest my weight on it and tried to stand up to my full height.

A strong sense of panic filled my being. Utter chaos filled the streets. Workers ran anywhere they could as they tried to find some sense of safety. Bodies were strewn all throughout the area—some moving, some not. A man, no older than twenty, was stretched out on the ground a few feet from me, reaching for a leg that was no longer there. It rested a few inches from his body, cut free by a piece of glass that must have flown through the air along with the debris. The white sound that filled my head and clouded my thoughts was now starting to slowly ease away, allowing me to hear things—things that I wish I never had to hear again. People were yelling at the top of their lungs, fragmented and filled with anguish, pain, and fear.

The Factory guards were either trying to organize the panicked and crazed or had joined in with the workers who managed to make it through the E-way and were racing toward town. They were waving at each other in some strange style of communication over the uproar of noise and confusion, or maybe they were grabbing people and pushing them out of the way. Confusion seeped through my mind. I must have been standing and glaring wide-eyed at all the horror for a full minute, unsure what to do. It felt longer.

I chanced a glance back at the Factory. One whole side of the building was just gone. It looked like a giant had taken a bite from it. Fire erupted from the opening in the building, reaching out to lick the sky and belching out thick, black smoke that blocked the sun. A dark shadow covered the area, which caused me to involuntarily shiver. I was numb from shock, not feeling the guards who brushed past me as they tried to run back to the Factory. The ones closest to the Factory were strewn throughout the grounds, which were now covered with charred remains from the explosion or punctured from flying debris. Brown dirt was now mixed with red from all the blood. It was a slaughter no matter where you looked.

Shaking hands covered unblinking eyes, but the images remained when they were uncovered. A person bumped into me, nearly knocking me over again, and I had to skip to reclaim my balance. The bump must have restarted my senses, for at that moment my thoughts went to my companions—John and Lydia. Whipping my head around frantically to find them in this barrage of insanity, I rested my gaze on John not too far away. He was covered in filth and sitting cross-legged. Lydia was sprawled out beside him, her upper body resting in his arms and lap and her head blocked out by John's body. He was rocking back and forth, whimpering something that I couldn't hear. I half stumbled toward where he sat, still trying to get a sense of things and froze at the image that met me.

I was now in a position to see John's hand brushing a strand of hair from Lydia's blank face, her eyes staring up into the darkening sky wide and expressionless. She was dead. A section of piping was gouged into the back of her skull, a small trickle of blood dripping from the exposed end. Ash, dirt, and flecks of the Factory were sprayed all over her face.

My foot rose to take a step toward John, but all the strength that resided in it escaped as I brought it back down. Ground rushed back up toward me as I collapsed hard onto the pebbles and mud, my left knee crashing into a piece of the Factory that had flown from the blast. Pain rocketed through my leg. Unable to stand back up properly, I crawled over to John who was still rocking Lydia in his arms. His breath escaped through clenched teeth, his words barely audible.

"It's go … going to be okay.… It's going to be … okay," he stuttered.

I raised my arm and rested my hand lightly on his exposed shoulder, the huge tear in his shirt probably due to the explosion. The bandage that had been wrapped around his head had been removed and used for Lydia's wound to try to stop the bleeding. John never acknowledged my existence; he just continued to rock back and forth softly, comforting his dead future wife.

"John," I whispered. "There's nothing you can do for her. She's dead."

John stopped rocking and slowly opened his eyes. He stared through watered pools toward nothing, stroking the loose hair from her face. I squeezed his shoulder with my hand.

"I am so sorry, John," I weakly choked out.

John didn't move.

~

The POLICE arrived at the Factory grounds about ten minutes after the explosion. Before this, someone had managed to make it back into what was left of the Factory and turn off the gas, which had fueled most of the fires. Small plumes of smoke pumped out from the opening; we could hear the death cry of the final fires clinging to life within the Factory. Workers and people from town walked in a daze from the overwhelming horror before them, trying to organize the dead into rows for better identification purposes. The sight was too much for most, causing men and women to break down crying at the sight of a loved one or friend lying still on the ground. John and I never moved from the spot where Lydia died, her body stretched out in front of us, arms crossed on her chest.

One set of POLICE officers went straight toward the Factory, disappearing through the wide-open oak doors. A few stopped at the entrance of the Factory and were talking to Mrs. Nikle, who was visibly shaken. A second set of POLICE officers made up of around twenty men went about to work within the surrounding area, some blocking off the entrance and exit route through the E-way. Suits of black with golden stripes on the right arm, distinguishing rank, wandered around the area giving orders to the fellow workers and townspeople.

A tall officer walked over toward where we stood. John kept his eyes locked on Lydia. The officer's hair was cut short and parted on one side. His uniform clung to his body as he walked, showing off a well-developed body underneath. His face showed obvious concern toward us, seeing Lydia's body at our feet. Stopping a few feet from us, he rested his hands on the equipment that hung off of his belt: a baton, two side pouches, and a holstered revolver. He sighed a heavy sigh, glancing from Lydia to the Factory to us. His face, still young but weathered with age and experience, scrunched a bit.

"Did either of you two see what happened? Anything out of the ordinary?" he asked us in a calm and even voice.

John didn't react to the officer's voice. I started to open my mouth in order to answer, but my jaw refused to work. He glanced at John and then me, burrowing his eyebrows together into one. "It's important that you tell me what happened," he advised, a little sterner this time.

I licked my lips, taking a moment to try to organize my thoughts, and told him everything that had happened that morning—our late arrival, work, meeting for lunch, walking toward the gate in order to go to the market, the explosion, and the aftermath. I didn't tell the officer the reason John and I were late. I didn't think he needed to know that little piece of information. Besides, if Vans hadn't talked or put in a report, I didn't want to raise any red flags. Instead, I told him that I just lost track of time and didn't make it before the start of the workday.

The officer took out a pad of paper from one of the pouches on his belt and a pen from his breast pocket and periodically wrote down what I had told him, nodding now and then after writing a piece of information. He was very interested with the fact that I saw where the blast originated and asked me to explain things like how big the explosion was originally, if it was a ball of flame or a pulse of debris from the building, and if anyone around the area gave an impression that they knew the explosion was coming.

After finishing up my debriefing, a lower-ranking officer came over to us from the direction of the building. The officer I was talking to turned around and greeted him. The new officer was covered in a bit of dust and debris from the building, which he tried to brush off while he talked. He was older than the officer I talked to by a few years, which showed both in how he held himself as well as the gruffness in his voice. Black hair, cut in the same style as the first, was slightly mussed up from the exploration he must have done in the Factory.

"From what we can see, the explosion was set," he explained to the first officer. "Source was right under one of the pipes leading from the main generator. No chance this was an accident."

The first officer shook his head at the news. He openly expressed his frustration and cursed under his breath as he finished writing something on his pad. I took in what the new officer said and stared toward the gaping hole in the Factory's side. Where two guarding towers once protected the surrounding area, only one bore the brunt of the blast. I shook my head.

"Who would do something like this?" I mused out loud to myself.

The officer who was interviewing me overheard my comment and turned his attention back to me. "First guess would be that the Rebells have something to do with this. It feels like something they would do," he sighed as he put his notepad back into his pouch.

"But there was no reason for blowing it up," I pointed out.

He scoffed, twisting one corner of his mouth into a wry smile. He looked down at me as a parent would a child trying to explain to them why the sky is blue. "All the more reason why they did it. They don't care about anyone or anything other than to cause as much havoc and death and disorder as they possibly can. Take a good look at the vision that they try to uphold," he said, waving his arm outstretched toward the misery that filled the area.

"I fail to understand their thinking, if, in fact, they think at all," he continued. "The Rebells insist on causing death in order to gain power and fear. And they do it through means that guarantees suffering. They say that *we*," motioning to his uniform, "disrupt the natural order and make society nothing more than slaves. *We* bring about peace and order. *They* are the ones going around raiding, terrorizing, and destroying things."

The second officer walked around the two of us and stood opposite John in front of Lydia. He stared down at her. John didn't move or raise his gaze.

The higher-ranking officer turned back to me and rested a hand on my shoulder. The sheer power in his hands became evident as he let the weight of his massive paw rest on my shoulder. He bent his head in an odd way, in order to lock his eyes with mine.

"You watch out for them, boy," he warned me in a soft but stern tone. "If you remember seeing anyone hanging around the Factory the past few days who shouldn't have been or have seen someone who wasn't acting right, you tell the closest POLICE officer as fast as you can. You hear me? We'll deal with them the only way they apparently know how to be dealt with."

He kept his gaze locked with mine, the weight of his hand on my shoulder driving home what he was saying. I nodded in recognition of his warning, unable to look away from the heat that radiated from his eyes. Accepting my answer, he eased his gaze and lifted his hand from my shoulder, standing up to his full height. "All right, then."

The second officer, the one looking at Lydia, raised his eyes to glance at John, a sly smirk on his face. "Damn shame about this one, eh? Looked like she had plenty of days ahead of her. Hell, if I knew a girl like this worked here, I would have asked to be reassigned, rather than hanging around all those old farts in the markets," he chuckled, winked, and clucked his tongue at John.

John slowly raised his head, looking from Lydia to the officer. Every muscle in his being tensed as he spoke through locked teeth, eyes echoing the fire that once erupted from the Factory's side. "Watch. Your. Mouth," he hissed.

The officer puffed out a bit at hearing the disrespectful tone from John. "You'd best be the one to watch your mouth, *citizen*."

I looked from the two glaring at each other to the officer I was standing beside. The taller officer started to walk over to the other one, a watchful eye on John. "Greg …" he warned.

Greg held up his hand to his superior, brushing off the warning or the support offered, and continued to stare down at John. "Well, there's nothing you can do about it now, is there? Nothing at all, except maybe bury her and find someone else to play with," he jabbed at John, a threatening and daring tone in his voice.

Greg shifted his gaze from John to Lydia and the ground around her body. He started brushing one of his feet in the dirt, creating a small hill by the toe of his shoe. John didn't move or speak, his fists tightening to the point that his knuckles turned white. The officer, once happy with his constructed pile of dirt in front of him, whipped his head up and cracked a wry smile at John. "Here. Let me start you off with the funeral details."

That said, he lightly kicked the pile of dirt onto Lydia's body with his boot. "Ashes to—"

I never even saw John move.

Officer Greg doubled over, holding his stomach, spitting, and gasping for air. John followed through from the first punch by leaping over Lydia's body and tackling the officer. The two landed on the ground a few feet from the taller officer and me, John gaining power over the toppled officer. A second and third fist flew through the air, creating a hollow thud as it connected in the chest and abdomen of the downed officer. The sound that came out of John as he wailed on the poor man was a sound that I never heard before. It didn't sound human. I couldn't begin to describe it.

The tall officer and I raced to where the two men lay—the officer trying to pry his fellow teammate free, while I tried to get a hold on John. John struggled and wriggled in my grasp, but I somehow managed to get him off the officer. He got a good elbow to my jaw to get me to back off, but I refused to let go. Pressing my weight onto his back forced him onto the ground. I held John there for a few seconds, heaving all my weight onto his upper body and whispered into his ear as he struggled against me.

"John, what do you think you're doing? Are you crazy?! You can't attack them! They're the POLICE. *Actual* POLICE officers, John! They have the power to throw you into a cell and toss away the key for what you did," I pleaded.

John tried to bench press me off of him, setting his arms for a push-up. "Get off of me, Tom! *Now!*"

My teeth clinked together as my head came crashing down onto the middle of his back, knocking him back onto the ground. Like a snake through the grass, one of my free hands wriggled to get a hold of one of John's arms. Grabbing a hold of a wrist, I wrenched it behind his back, pinning him. "Stay down, you idiot!"

I chanced a glance toward the POLICE officers to see what they were doing. It seems that the officer was having as much luck as I was trying to keep Greg apart from John. Greg weaved and scuttled about the area, trying to get past the officer in order to rip John to shreds. The officer ended up pushing Greg back whenever he tried to come forward. Pure hate glistened in Greg's eyes as he stared down at the two of us.

"That is enough!" came a clear, powerful voice from the right side of us.

Everybody froze. All of our heads swiveled toward the sound, because the tone of command was so impressed upon it. A single man stood near the E-way, arms crossed in front of his chest. His white teeth were firmly clenching a cigar that hung out of his mouth, almost with enough force to break it in two. A neatly pressed black uniform adorned his stature, complete with the golden stripes on his arm signifying his rank: three stripes up, three stripes down—first sergeant. Charles Buret, the head of the POLICE in Sicher Himmel, did not look happy.

The two officers, at the sight of their commander and chief of the POLICE Grounds, immediately released each other and stiffened into attention, offering a salute: right fist, knuckles out, planted over the heart. Their eyes became locked with the horizon, glassing over from years of training. The sergeant glared at everyone through eyes that felt like they could turn metal into liquid by sheer will alone. I got up off of John and stood off to the side, allowing him to scramble to his feet. He brushed himself off, giving me a dirty look, and looked over to where the sergeant stood.

Seeing that we were all giving him our fullest attention, the sergeant walked slowly over to our haphazard group and stopped directly in front of John and me, looking down from where he stood at the two of us, slowly puffing on his cigar. After three puffs, he uncrossed his arms and rested one hand on his belt, hooking his thumb in behind the leather. With his other hand, he took the cigar out of his mouth. "Name," he demanded, this time in a quieter tone but still a force to be reckoned with.

John and I both answered at the same time, spewing out our names to the overbearing man, our words intertwining into nonsense. He tilted his head to the side slightly, giving off the impression that he neither had the time nor the patience to deal with us. I shot John a quick glance, trying to make him understand that I would talk first and repeated my name. John repeated his name afterward. The sergeant squinted his eyes in order to examine the two of us, sizing us both up. He nodded and turned on his heals to face the two officers. They stiffened a little more at the sergeant's gaze.

"Name and rank," he barked at the two, a bit grizzlier than how he addressed us.

The taller officer returned his arm by his side and took a step forward, sharply snapping his heels together as he returned to attention. "Private First Class Henry Donson, sir," he shouted toward the sergeant. He stepped back in line with a motion of pomp and circumstance.

The officer who was fighting John repeated the same routine, announcing to the sergeant, "Private Greg Treble." His uniform was wrinkled and covered in mud, dirt, and blood from the tumble on the ground. His left eye was starting to puff out softly, which gave off the impression that he would be getting a black eye shortly.

The sergeant glanced from the two of us to the officers who stood before him. "Private First Class, would you mind telling me what the *hell* was going on here before I arrived?" he ordered, clearing his throat and shifting his weight.

The taller officer stepped forward a second time, eyes still locked onto the horizon. "We were gathering information and placing order on the Factory grounds as ordered, sir. I was interviewing these two workers, and Private Greg Treble was performing recon and damage assessment inside the Factory, sir. Upon gathering information proving that the destruction was deliberate, he exited the Factory to inform me, sir. After which, Private Greg Treble performed an act unbecoming a POLICE officer, sir. The workers under question responded to the private's actions, which is when you arrived, sir."

The sergeant put the cigar back into his mouth and recrossed his arms, letting out a long and heavy sigh. "Is this true, Private?"

Greg let his vision ease from the horizon toward John, a shot of invisible daggers flying toward him. "Yes, sir," Greg slurred under his breath.

The sergeant stepped abruptly in front of the private, nearly crushing his cigar into Greg's face. "What did you say?" he asked Greg.

Greg jerked back into full attention, flinging his eyes back into his head. "Yes, sir!" he shouted out to the sergeant, who stood less than a foot from him.

The sergeant then stepped back from Greg. "Return to the Grounds and wait for my arrival, Private," the sergeant ordered.

Greg took a step back, gave the sergeant a salute, turned on his heel, and started marching toward the E-way. The sergeant then turned his attention to the other officer. "Continue gathering your information, Private First Class."

The remaining officer stepped back, saluted the sergeant, and marched off toward a group of workers who had gathered to console each other. The sergeant watched the officer leave the three of us and turned around so he was looking at John and me. With a tired expression, the sergeant took back out the cigar that rested comfortably in his mouth. "What did he do, boys?"

John simply radiated frustration and hatred and was still pumped on adrenalin, so I jumped in with the explanation of how the officer made improper references toward John's recently deceased fiancée and how he kicked dirt on her as an attempt to bury her. The sergeant looked over to glance at Lydia, who was untouched by the scuffle other than the bit of dirt that landed on her. John just stared off into the distance, not taking anything in. His chest raised and lowered through his labored breathing, his fists still clenched with rage.

The sergeant, taking in the explanation, turned to John. He took the cigar from his mouth and carelessly tossed it off to the side, letting his hand rest on John's arm. John's gaze returned to the here and now, and he looked at the sergeant in front of him. The sergeant opened his mouth to speak, then changed his mind and looked away, in order to gather his thoughts together. A slight breeze wafted through the area, whistling and dancing as it passed.

After a moment, the sergeant said, "I'm sorry to hear about your loss. It's never easy to lose someone. I've lost over sixty people under my command, and it still hits me just as hard when I lose the next one."

The sergeant talked to us in a soft and quiet tone. He squeezed John's arm slightly, reassuringly. "I'm not going to press charges against you, if you're wondering. Not that I condone striking an officer, mind you, but it seems like he got what was coming to him. *But*, and I want to make this perfectly clear to you, both of you, you won't get this charity the next time. Hit another officer, and you will go down hard for it," he warned.

John nodded and thanked the sergeant in an almost inaudible whisper. The sergeant gave John's arm a second reassuring squeeze and let him go. He shot me a glance out of the corner of his eye, almost mischievously.

"I'm going to talk to your friend for a bit privately. You wait here, okay?" he offered to John.

John raised his eyes to meet mine, his eyes starting to glass over with tears again, and nodded unenergetically to the sergeant. The sergeant shot me a glance and tossed his head over toward the fence. Leaving John to his thoughts, the two of us walked over to where he indicated.

As we walked over to the fence that surrounded the entire grounds of the Factory, the sergeant reached into his left breast pocket and pulled out an open wooden tube revealing a fresh cigar, which he clamped into his mouth and pulled free from the tube. He then reached into his right breast pocket and pulled out a metal lighter. The end of the cigar crackled as it caught fire, gray smoke exiting his mouth in strong puffs. By this time, we had reached our destination by the fence.

He leaned his back against one of the iron bars that supported the fence and placed his lighter back in his pocket. I stood in front of him, unsure as to what I was doing with him. I mean, here I was with the most powerful person in our town, my friend was off to the side grieving over losing his love, and my job had just been blown to bits. My head was still racing with scenarios and questions when the sergeant took the cigar out of his mouth and motioned toward the Factory with it. "What a mess, huh?"

"What?" I asked, instantly regretting how dumb I sounded.

"This. Everything. It's a mess," he reaffirmed his last comment to me. He just leaned there against the fence, puffing away on his cigar. His blond hair was cut in strict military fashion, cut clean to the head. His face was starting to show his years, but his eyes were still sharp as a hawk's, scanning the scenery.

I shifted uncomfortably from one foot to the other and quietly cleared my throat. "Um, sir. Ah ... the private first class thinks it was the Rebells that did this," I informed him sheepishly, unsure as what to say to the guy.

He nodded his head toward my comment as if he had already come to that decision. His gaze was still locked toward the Factory. I figured I'd try a different tactic in our conversation.

"Was there something that you wanted to ask me, sir?" I asked politely, careful not to sound impatient.

He glanced down at me for a second, a hint of surprise in his manor. A small smile crossed over his face at my boldness. "Did you see what happened?"

I nodded.

"And you have already given your report to the private first class, right?"

I nodded.

The sergeant pulled the cigar from his mouth and studied my face as if he was looking for something. "You seem to be a smart kid. You've proven to me that you have a strong sense of loyalty and dedication, what with your actions concerning your friend over there. Most people would just let the officers deal with the situation, but you intervened and protected your friend, even when it meant getting involved and placing yourself in harm's way. You know you could have been charged for your friend's outburst, right?"

I swallowed hard and nodded.

He smiled again. "I want you to do something for me," he told me in a matter-of-fact tone.

He went on to explain, returning his gaze back onto the Factory and the events that were cascading around us. "Something like this is out of the ordinary for the Rebells. They mostly keep to small-time theft—the occasional disruption. Nothing to cause too much concern. But to blow up the Factory—this is too brash, too big, too noticeable. Something's not right about it all. There had to be more to it than just to cause a disturbance. There must have been someone on the inside, someone who knew the inner working of the Factory to cause this much destruction. I want you to keep your ears open for us. People will be talking about this for some time, pushing each other for information or general rumor. It's the nature of the beast. Eventually, the pressure will become too much for the person or persons involved, and something will slip out. If you hear anything, even if it's just a rumor, I want you to tell us immediately."

I stood there dumbfounded at the request. Slowly, my brain worked my head up and down to show I understood, and my tongue eventually freed itself from the vice it was imprisoned in. "Yeah, I can do that," I offered.

"I'm glad to hear it," the sergeant smiled and placed the cigar back into his mouth.

I turned to walk back to John but stopped as a thought crossed my mind. Glancing back to the sergeant, I raised my eyebrow questioningly. "What will happen with Lydia?" I asked him.

"Who?"

I motioned to the girl on the ground in front of John. He lowered his head, deep in thought. "She'll be buried along with the rest, I guess," he assured me.

I accepted his answer and started walking. A few paces away, the sergeant called out to me again. I stopped ad turned to face him a second time. He nodded toward John. "A word of advice. I'd watch out for your friend there. He might try to do something stupid again," he warned me, making sure that he was loud enough so John could hear as well.

I took his advice into account, waved a farewell, and walked back to John. He was kneeling beside Lydia, placing a blanket that he got from one of the other workers over top of her.

CHAPTER 5

... Once everyone in the area was interrogated and general clean up of the Factory grounds was concluded, the POLICE officers announced that the Factory would be off-limits to everyone while everything was properly documented and examined. This was going to take five days to complete. No one complained about this, despite the fact that being out of work for five days meant five days' less money to buy food next month. I think the reason why no one complained was because the POLICE told them what was happening, and no one argues with the POLICE.

The POLICE also mentioned that on the start of the sixth day, being next Monday, all the workers from the Factory would come back to take part in the reconstruction of the Factory. That got a mild reaction out of the crowd. It probably would have been worse if it wasn't the POLICE delivering the news. If we worked every day nonstop, we could probably have the Factory ready for reopening in four months—three if we worked during the night.

Since there wasn't anything left for us to do for the day, I decided to take John into the market and buy him lunch. We didn't have a chance to go for lunch because of the explosion, and I thought having something in his stomach would help cheer him up a bit. At least it would give us a chance to talk about what happened. The wagons used to carry off the dead arrived just as we were leaving, which was horrible timing on their part. John insisted on staying until Lydia was safely put into one of them. He even helped the person carry Lydia into the wagon when her time came. Once she was safe and secure on one of the wagons, I led him into town....

~

"Are you okay, John?" I mumbled through a mouth of cornbread, my spoon picking through the bowl of chili in front of me.

John was staring at the plate in front of him, a barely touched sandwich rested contently on his plate, mayo oozing from its side and mixing with the juice of a tomato. He was slumped over the table, not really focusing on anything. His head rested on his hands, his cheekbones cupped in the base of his palms, supporting the massive weight that was evident there. Dark shadows appeared under his eyes from the tilt of his head, the light of the sun unable to break through past his demeanor. After a moment, he shifted his palms to rub away at his eyes and lifted his face to mine.

"No, I'm not all right, Tom," he murmured, clasping his hands together to rest his chin on them.

The spoon made a wooden thunk as I dropped it into the bowl of chili; some juice spattered out over the bowl from the spoon's impact. I crossed my arms behind the wooden bowl, leaning on the table and over to John. "You want to talk about it?"

John's head bounced slightly as he shifted his head so he wasn't looking at me. His shoulders were slumped more, as if he were utterly defeated by the world, as an elderly man's shoulders would be.

"I can't believe she's gone," he finally managed to breathe out.

I reached out and took a hold of one of his arms. "There was nothing that you could have done to save her, John. It was a quick death."

John sat up in his chair, yanking the arm I was holding away from me. "That doesn't replace the fact that she's gone, Tom," he said.

"I know. I know," I repeated, unsure as to what else to say to him.

With a quick push on his chair that caused it to scuttle away from the table, John stood up. He reached into his breast pocket and pulled out the cloth that he stored there. The once-white fabric unfolded in John's hands, and he started placing his meal inside of it in order to carry it away with him.

I raised my eyebrows. "What do you think you're doing?"

John shook his head at me as he continued to place his food into the traveling package he created with the cloth. "I'm not hungry right now, but I will be later," he explained in a monotone voice. He stopped for a second and glanced up at me, a slightly agitated look on his face. "Is that all right with you?" he asked sternly.

I held up my hands in defense. "No problem," I responded calmly and softly.

Once all the food that was on the plate was secure inside his mock traveling sack, he tied the tips together, stepped away from the old wooden chair, and walked over to my side of the table. He rested a hand on the back of my chair so I couldn't pull away as well in order to leave.

"Look Tom, I appreciate what you're trying to do, really … but it's not helping. Not right now. I need to get my head straight, and being here isn't any good to me. I need to just … be alone for a while, you know? You can come by my place later on tonight, if you want," he offered, but it was the tone that told me he didn't mean what he said.

And with that, he turned and walked out of the open-air diner we were sitting at, leaving me alone at the table. People were walking hurriedly around the market, talking and pointing at different things, buying and selling odds and ends. He melted into the crowd quickly and was lost before I could open my mouth in protest. A few other patrons looked up to watch John leave but soon went back to eating their meals and talking to their guests. As I looked around the diner at the people eating their meals, I noticed Mrs. Nikle sipping on some soup at a table just behind me. Clinks from cheap metal goblets echoed emptily inside the tented area. I turned around in my chair, back to the meal in front of me, and tried to start eating again. I just ended up picking at my food. After talking to John, I just was not feeling very hungry anymore.

"Care for some company?" a voice above me chirped.

I looked up, and Mrs. Nikle was standing to my right, her bowl of soup in hand. Her hair was messed up from the chaos of that morning, and her glasses were slightly dusty, but she looked no worse for wear. I motioned for her to sit in the now empty seat across from me and continued poking at my food. She sat down in the sturdy and well-used wooden chair and gently released her bowl of tomato soup onto the table, sliding the plate that John had been using moments before off to the side. She smiled at me.

"What a day," she started off, nodding in the direction of the Factory.

"Yeah," I commented, not really wanting to talk. I was still worrying about John.

She took out her spoon from the bowl of soup, brought it to her lips, and lightly blew on it as she sipped the red broth. "It was lucky I was leaving to go into town for my lunch when it happened, or else I would have been blown to bits," she said.

I glanced up from my food. Irritation and confusion got the best of me as I tried to figure out why she was sitting at the table. It must have shown, because she put her spoon down to talk. "You seemed upset over something, so I thought I'd come over and talk. We really haven't had a chance to talk outside of work, so I thought it would be nice," she explained to me as she readjusted her glasses on her head.

I nodded and continued eating.

"So," she began, "have you heard anything as to what caused the explosion?"

I shrugged my shoulders at her question and stirred the chili inside my bowl a few times, mixing the meat and potato chunks in a swirl of sauce and beans before bringing a spoonful of the mixture up to my lips.

"Is John going to be okay?" she inquired, using a different tactic to get me to talk.

I stopped midchew and put down my spoon; my eyes shot up as I glared at the old woman. Swallowing the remaining food in my mouth hard, I reached out for the metal cup beside me and took a drink of water to quench my thirst. Still, my eyes locked with hers—unblinking. With a small gasp of air, I returned the cup back to its position and picked up my spoon again. She looked down the bridge of her nose, as she always did when John and I were late or in trouble, giving off a disapproving glare. "You could at least be more sociable," she scorned.

I dropped my spoon back into the nearly eaten chili in front of me, the wooden spoon making a whack against the bowl. "I'm sorry if I'm not being a great host, Mrs. Nikle, but my friend's fiancée died today. He's a total wreck right now. I'm a total wreck as well. Look … perhaps you should try sitting with someone else who's in the mood for idle chitchat, because I don't want to talk about it anymore," I rambled on with a hint of venom in my voice.

I wiped my mouth after my little outburst and sat facing her, waiting for some sort of reaction. She sat there, staring at me in disapproval at my minitantrum, slowly crossing her arms and closing her off.

"How dare you. I was there too, you know. I saw the death on the field as well. I was almost killed, along with the rest of you, so don't you take out your frustrations on me. I didn't blow up the building!" she scolded, waving a finger out toward me.

I leaned forward so that she could properly understand what I was about to tell her. "We're not friends, Mrs. Nikle. We never have been. We don't hang out after work or go out for dinner parties. It's always been *your* world and *our* world. You have always sat behind your desk and written up your reports, never once trying to reach out to us. You spew out the rules and the regulations whenever John and I try to ask for something work-related or when we come in late, never once asking how our day has been. You never once said 'hello'—ever! So what makes you think that by sitting here, sharing my table, and trying to make me open up to you after the Factory has been blown sky high, my friend's fiancée has been killed, and my job has been practically terminated that our relationship would all of the sudden turn into some kind of lifelong buddy-buddy bond?"

The two of us sat silent for a good moment, me staring hard at the older woman, Mrs. Nikle staring back at me with wide eyes of shock. Suddenly, the hard edges in my face melted away when I realized what hateful things I was saying to this old woman.

I refocused to take in her reaction. She sat there, hand frozen as she reached out for her spoon, mouth slightly open. She slowly leaned back in her chair and pulled her hands onto her lap, glancing around to see if anyone else in the diner had heard what I said to her. Biting her lower lip, her face turned a slight pinch of red in evident embarrassment. *I am a complete idiot*, I mused.

Letting out a louder sigh than I meant to, I rested my hands on the table and hung my head slightly in shame. "Look, I'm … I'm sorry."

"No, no. It's quite all right," she cut me off briskly, her voice like ice in the wind. "I deserved that, if that's how you thought I was treating you."

The tension at the table was chokingly thick. I shouldn't have let her sit here. Reaching into my front pocket for some money to pay for the two lunches—John's and my own—I blurted out a second apology as I pushed my chair out from under me and stood to leave. Mrs. Nikle didn't budge in her seat, her hands still cusped in her lap. I turned and left her alone to her lunch, walking up to the owner of the diner. The well-fed and balding man standing behind a small counter stood up from the stool that he was sitting on when I approached him. I quickly paid for the meals, declining my change. I had an overpowering desire to leave.

Free from the diner, I wandered throughout the market not having any real place to go. Patrons from their side-street huts called out their wares to me, trying to tempt me to take a look at their beads, breads, and fish. My head flew with the two conversations I'd just had with John and Mrs. Nikle. Feeling frustration with John and regret with Mrs. Nikle, I mentally replayed the event over and over in my mind, trying to think of a way that those two positions could have gone better.

Maybe I should have taken John to the fountain instead of a diner with other people, I thought to myself. Why did I cram John into a place where he didn't want to be? I should have thought about what he needed and just taken him home.

I caught a bench off to the side of the path that led out of the marketplace and decided to rest my feet as I churned the thoughts in my head. The bench was small, only big enough for two people, and only if they sat really close together. I took up what would have been both seats and stretched out my feet, being careful not to trip anyone that happened to walk past me.

Shaking my head in exhaustion, I tossed John from my thoughts, but I couldn't get Mrs. Nikle out of my mind. *Why did I take out my frustrations out on Mrs. Nikle?* I pondered, a sting of guilt clinging to my gut. *She just wanted to talk to someone.* I mean, she *was* there at the Factory along with the rest of us. She was probably just trying to find someone to talk to about the horrendous ordeal. Hell, if she wasn't going for lunch ...

I froze, eyes going wide. I threw my mind back to the diner and sitting at the table with Mrs. Nikle. Closing my mind to all other stimulus in order to concentrate better on the image, I walked through the entire conversation at a slug's pace, looking for a specific sentence. "It was lucky I was leaving to go into town for my lunch when it happened, or else I would have been blown to bits," she said to me. Then, I remembered something else that was told to me earlier on by the sergeant: "If you hear anything, even if it's just a rumor, I want you to tell us immediately."

I sprang to my feet and lunged into a sprint toward the Factory grounds. People whizzed past me in a blur as I weaved in and out between them. Some of the shop owners called out to me, insisting that I don't run so fast for fear of knocking someone over in such an in-closed area—that, or they assumed that I was a thief and just shouted at me.

I sprinted for all my worth back to the Factory. The POLICE were still there and were walking around the area, picking up different objects and pointing at the hole in the Factory. The gates were firmly closed and probably locked. Two officers were guarding the gate entrance on the outside. Both noticed me running up to them and yelled out for me to stop where I was. My feet skidded out underneath me as I slowed my dash to a jog and then to a walk. Panting and holding my side, which had begun to hurt from the run, I eventually came to a standstill. One of the officers started to hesitantly walk over to where I was, hand resting on his holster. I had no right being in the area, after all. Everyone was ordered away for the duration of the POLICE examination of the grounds.

"This area has been deemed off-limits while the investigation is under way," he explained.

"I ... have news ... for the ... first sergeant," I called out to him in between gasps of air, the chili not sitting right with me after the quick sprint.

The officer stopped for a moment and turned his head to check with the other officer at the gate. He too had his hand on his revolver and gave an insecure shrug to his partner. The officer who approached turned his attention back to me and motioned for me to come closer. I walked the twenty or so feet that separated us to stand in front of him.

The officer released his grip on his revolver and held out his hand to me. His partner at the gate was holding onto his revolver firmly but had not pulled it from its holster just yet. I paused, staring at his hand, a confused and flustered look on my face.

"Where's your message?" he asked.

"I don't have a written note for him. I have information that I have to tell him," I explained.

The officer took back his hand and, with a grumble, reached into his pockets for a notepad and pen. He pulled out a small black book and held the pen up to the paper inside it, posed to write down the message. "Name," he asked with a hint of irritation.

"Thomas Haroldson."

"Housing?"

"Shelter 609—flat 4."

"Job?'

"Office. Accounts and in-terms at the Factory."

He scribbled all my information down on the notepad, the pen waving back and forth in strict motions in front of me. "Message?"

"Well, I was having lunch, and Mrs. Nikle came and sat down at my table. She's the head secretary for the Factory. She said that she was leaving to go into town during her lunch break," I started to explain.

The officer that was taking down my information glanced up from his writing halfway through a sentence, a look of utter disgust painted clearly on his face. "I don't need your life story, kid. Just tell me your message and get out of here."

I took a breath and continued to tell the officer my message, trying to keep any outbursts in the back of my throat. "Mrs. Nikle stated that she was leaving for town. She never leaves the Factory for lunch. Not once, in all the years that I've worked there. She always has her lunch at her desk, because there's no one to replace her position while she's on break. Yet, today she left her post to go into town for lunch, moments before the explosion," I explained to the officer.

He finished his writing and raised one of his eyebrows. "That's it? That's your message?"

I nodded my head.

He clicked his pen closed and put the notepad and pen away. He stood over top of me, planting his hands on his belt. "You noticed the secretary leave for lunch? So what?"

I stared at the officer for a moment, not sure as to why he wasn't clueing into the importance of the information. "But she never leaves for lunch."

"Maybe she forgot her lunch. Maybe she was invited out for lunch. Maybe she wanted to forgo lunch and just go for a walk? Do you know *why* she left the Factory for lunch?"

I was about to say something when the words stalled in my mouth. "Uh … no."

The officer shook his head at me disapprovingly. "Look, this isn't some game, kid. We have a job to do here, and unless you have something solid for us, all you're doing is wasting our time," he scolded.

Okay, that's it. I've had enough, I thought to myself. I firmly planted my hands on my belt. "No, you look!" I started, shooting a finger into the officer's chest. "I've had a really bad day, and I don't need your attitude right now. The first sergeant—your boss—specifically asked me to—"

The officer's face grew to a beet red color. Without pause, he reached around my head, grabbed hold of my shirt collar, and turned to march back toward the gate. The sheer force of the pull threw me off balance, and I was half dragged back to the gate where the other officer was standing. He was laughing at my ridiculous and somewhat undignified escort. The officer who pulled me gave me a shove toward the other officer, who caught me easily, a hand on each of my arms.

"Hold him," he ordered and unlocked the gate to enter the grounds.

The old hinges grinded as they bore the weight of the gate once more. Once through the gate, the officer slammed it shut behind him. He stormed off in the direction of the Factory, passing by all the other officers nearby.

The officer holding me watched his partner march off and then turned his attention to me.

"What did you say to piss him off like that, kid?" he whispered.

The officer holding me shifted around, so he was facing the town again, still gripping my right arm firmly. I stared off into the Factory grounds. The officer I gave my report to walked directly up to the Factory doors, still wide open, and yelled incoherently at someone inside. A few moments later, someone walked up to the officer. I couldn't see who it was; the officer was in the way. He saluted whomever he was talking to and soon pointed in my direction. The two men started walking back over to the gate.

As the two men got closer, I was able to make out the first sergeant. The two men walked up to the gate but didn't open it to come outside. I waved sheepishly at the sergeant, acknowledging his presence. The officer jagged his thumb at me. "This is the kid, sir."

The first sergeant rested his arm on the fence above his head and leaned onto the cold metal frame. "You have a message for me," he ordered rather than asked, quiet and controlled.

I cleared my throat, feeling a little ashamed, and retold my story back to the Sergeant. After I finished, he nodded and tilted his head to one side. "So ... you think she has something to do with this? Because she left for lunch for a reason you were unable to find out or didn't bother to ask?"

"I just found it odd, sir."

"So what you're telling me, in essence, is that a fortysomething woman whose life has been stuck behind a desk for a company that doesn't pay her enough suddenly went berserk and blew the place up? Is that it?"

When the first sergeant put it that way, it did sound a little farfetched. The officer who was holding me in place softly chuckled to himself at the joke. I shrugged my shoulders, feeling kind of silly all of the sudden. "You asked me to—"

"I *asked* for you to tell me information relating to the destruction of this establishment—facts that you can back up with evidence. Not for you to catch me up on the local gossip between your friends," he boomed.

I started to panic. "But—"

"I also was just told about your flippant remarks to this POLICE officer!" he bolstered. The officer I gave the report to was standing slightly behind his commander. He crossed his arms across his chest and smiled smugly at me. He knew full well the trouble that I brought upon myself, let alone from the most powerful man in town—who happened to be in a very bad mood.

I started to bleat like a sheep being led to a butcher's table. "But you asked me to tell you, even if it was rumor, anything that I heard. I thought her leaving was out of the ordinary and that you would want to know," I pleaded with him.

The sergeant was about to say something but froze midbreath as I blurted out my comment and interrupted his reprimand to me. As I uttered the last sound from the last word of my last sentence, the realization of what I had just done squeezed through the cotton that compiled the majority of my brain. The officer who was holding me in position winced painfully at my outburst, giving out a whispered, "Oh no, kid. No, no."

I held my breath as the sergeant stood in front of me behind the bars, jaw locked in place, eyes bolted to my frame. I could almost swear small puffs of steam in the semichilled air blasted out from his nostrils as he stood staring at me. The sergeant stretched out one of his massive arms and grabbed hold of the gate entrance, giving it a good, solid yank. The door flew open, almost crashing off its old hinges from the force. I looked from the gate to the man who was holding it. Wasn't the gate relocked after it was closed? The officer holding me quickly looked in the direction of the sergeant, caught by the quick movement out of the corner of his eye. The sergeant pointed at the officer, half toward me as well.

"Get him in here," he ordered through clenched teeth.

The officer urgently pushed me onto the Factory grounds. The sergeant grabbed hold of my left arm, freeing me from the officer. He glared at the two in front of him.

"Return to your posts," he demanded. The two, without even saluting their superior, jumped at the command and leapt through the open gate door. The two of them fought each other to get hold of the gate to swing it shut behind them, both to relock it and to protect themselves from the sergeant.

He glared down at me, the pressure on my arm ever increasing. "You think you're in charge here? It that it, boy?" he barked at me.

"No, sir," I peeped.

"Well you must if you think that you can order my men around and spurt out your voice, giving your opinion when I'm talking. Do you know how long it took me to get the rank I have now? Command of *my own town?*"

"No, sir," I half-whispered.

He gave my arm a shake. "Speak like you mean it, boy!" he barked.

My eyes went wild. *"No, sir!"* I shouted at him.

He leaned over so his face was directly in front of my own, his breath beating down onto my face. "Twenty-seven years," he whispered to me.

He leaned back to the position he was in before, his grip on my arm constant. "Twenty-seven years of hard labor to get to where I am today. You can't appreciate that type of work yet, because you haven't even experienced twenty-seven years. Have you, boy?"

I glanced around the area, looking for someone to help me. All the other officers who were in the general area had stopped working and were watching the two of us. The sergeant shot a quick glance at the idle officers, who immediately went back to work. One officer, who didn't have an immediate job to go back to, started to frantically pick rocks off of the ground in front of him and held them up to examine them in the light, making faces as if he saw something interesting. Content with the reaction, the sergeant then continued lecturing me.

"You want to know what it felt like to go through what I had to go through to get to where I am now?"

I tried to adjust my arm a bit so that his grip wouldn't hurt as much. The blood flow pounded with each heartbeat in my chest. "No, sir," I responded.

He let go of my arm suddenly, which caused me to stumble backward slightly. He took a step toward me and smiled. "Oh, that's too bad, because you're going to. While this building is being repaired, I want you to come to the POLICE grounds. There, I'm going to personally train you into the best damn officer we've ever had. And you're *going* to turn into the best officer we ever had, even if it kills you," he hissed.

"But I'm not old enough to be a SIT," I tried to point out to him.

"Officers will speak only when permission is given or a question needs to be answered," he barked, giving me lesson number one.

He spent a second examining me. "How old are you?" he asked.

"Sixteen," I explained.

He shook his head and smiled. "Not anymore, you're not. As of right now, you're eighteen and legal age to join."

At this, he waved over to one of the officers. He dropped what he was doing and ran up beside the sergeant, saluting as he arrived. The sergeant jabbed a finger in my direction. "Make a note to fix the birth record of a—"

He snapped his fingers at me as a cue. "Thomas Haroldson," I responded.

"Thomas Haroldson. Make it so his birthday lands on this day. And make it so today is his eighteenth birthday. And you," he ordered, referring to me, "laps. *Now!*"

My eyes grew wide, my jaw opening to say what my brain could not fathom. The officer wrote the information down on his notepad, saluted, and turned to race off to the POLICE Grounds. Before leaving, the officer shot me a glance over his shoulder, an expression of pity on his face. "Happy birthday, kid," he called out to me.

CHAPTER 6

... I didn't meet up with John later on that day. I was too tired from all the running I did around the perimeter of the Factory grounds. The sergeant got one of the officers to keep pace with me, making sure that I wouldn't slow down. When he got tired, he switched off with another, and that officer would then race along with me, kicking at my heels when I started to lag. This was how it went until dinnertime when I was allowed to go home. I wearily went home and collapsed on my bed, not even having the strength to eat.

When I woke the next day, I realized that the Factory's whistle never went off, and I slept in. For some reason, I felt uneasy thinking about that. After getting dressed, I spent the day doing odd chores around the shelter. Around four in the afternoon, I decided to check in on John....

Knock, knock.

The window was shut tight, and the drapes were pulled. There was no evidence that he was in. There wasn't any sound or light inside. A moment passed, and John hadn't come to the door to answer. I raised my hand and knocked on the doorframe a second time, this time a little louder. Again, there was no answer. Looking around to see if anyone was in the area to see what I was doing, I tried opening the door. The knob turned freely, and the door eased open in front of me.

Stepping into the shelter, I stood for a second to allow my eyes to adjust to the darkness of the room. His kitchen area was a mess, half-cleaned kitchenware was strung about. A fly buzzed inside the room, jumping from one plate to another. I took a few steps into the place, glancing around for signs of life. His bed was slept in but not remade. Clothes were thrown about the place, clustered in piles. His water jug, complete with a small crack on the top of its lip, was overturned on his dresser. The occasional drip fell into the pond that was forming at the base of the dresser on the floor.

"What are you doing?" John's voice came from behind me.

Startled, I turned in the dark to face the open door, hand clinging to my chest. John was standing in the frame of the door, holding a bucket of water. He walked into his shelter and put the bucket on a counter, the water swishing back and forth. "Why was your door unlocked?" I asked him, letting my hand slump to my side.

He shrugged and carefully poured some of the water into his sink to wash his dishes. The cool, clear liquid flooded the stopped basin, creating a low moat in his sink.

"I figured I wouldn't be long," he explained to me.

I walked over to the door and softly shut it, cutting the light source from the room. Realizing what a silly move that was, I decided to leave the door ajar as I fumbled around the place for a candle or lantern.

"There's a lantern by the bed," John said, filling the basin with dishes to wash.

I walked to his bedroom. The lantern, an old metal mine contraption that he borrowed from work, sat on one of the pieces of furniture. I grabbed it and turned it on, clicking the springs and flints to spark up a flame. The soft glow of the lantern filled up the room. Careful not to step in any of the piles that cluttered the bedroom, I brought the light source back into the kitchen, resting it on the wooden table in the middle of the room. I pulled out a chair and sat down backward in it, resting my hands and head on the back frame.

"So, how are you holding up?" I asked him.

He had his back to me, so I couldn't see his reaction. He just worked on washing his dishes, placing the clean ones off to his right, stacking one on top of the other. "All right, I guess," he said.

"Did you still want to go to that family's place for dinner with me tonight?"

He shrugged. "I don't know."

I sighed loudly enough so he could hear my disappointment. "Come one, John. Don't make me go by myself," I whined.

Finishing the last dish, he reached over and picked up a drying rag from the side of the counter, still keeping his back to me. "I'm not really in the mood to go out," he said.

"Please," I begged, leaning forward on the back of the chair so the front legs were off of the ground.

John put the dish that he was drying down on the counter with a metal clank. Finally, he caved in. "All right, I'll go."

I smiled at my old friend, despite the fact that he couldn't see my smile. Suddenly, I snapped my fingers as a thought came to mind. "Oh, guess what happened to me," I started, changing the topic, trying to sound like the news was not important.

John leaned his head to the side, listening and drying the dish in his hands. I glanced over at the lantern, my eyes catching the dance of the flame inside the protective covering. "Turns out I'm not going to be working at the Factory anymore."

John turned to look at me. "Why's that?"

"Well, it seems that I'm … reassigned," I mumbled the last bit on news to John.

"Where?"

"I don't really want to get into it right now. I don't have all the details just yet. When I know more, I'll let you know. I just thought you should know that I'm not going to be working at the Factory," I reassured him.

"So, you're not going to help out with its reconstruction either?" he asked while putting the dish along with the other counterparts.

"No, I start my new position the same day."

He nodded and tossed the rag he was using to dry the dishes off to the side of the room. The cloth splattered against the wall, flopping lifeless onto the counter. "And you're going to leave me in the dark about this whole affair," he pointed out as he crossed his arms across his chest as if he was lecturing to a small child.

"I don't have all the information yet. I can only tell you what I know," I explained.

He looked about the room, trying to think of something to say. "What am I going to do with you?" he mused out loud. "Well," he sighed, "let's go to market, then."

~

"Where are they?" John asked me, staring out into the crowd.

The two of us stood outside the market hobble as we had been instructed. The stall sold exotic feathers, leather bags, necklaces, and other such knickknacks. The store owner, a burly man with a full beard, was trying to get people's attention as they walked passed his stall, waving a leather bag in the air and calling out what a great deal it was. They glanced over at the stall, picking over his wares, and then continued walking. I tried to stand on my toes in order to see past the heads.

The owner, growing agitated with the two of us standing in front and not shopping, leaned over his counter to speak. "If you two aren't buying, then go someplace else. You're scaring away the customers," he barked at John and me.

John shot a glance at the big man. "I don't think it's us that's scaring them away."

The owner harrumphed at the comment and went back to trying to sell his wares to the patrons. In my mind, I tried again to go over the instructions that the man we rescued from Vans gave us, trying to remember if this was the stall we were to meet at. Number 917. I shot the booth's number a quick glance out of the corner of my eye—917. Meet at seven.

A girl came running up to the stall, and I recognized her from the day before. She was wearing a simple tan blouse and a long black skirt. She stopped in front of us, slightly out of breath.

"Good. You're here," she smiled.

Upon seeing the young girl, the owner leaned over his counter again.

"Dawn, are these boys here your doing? Because if they are, then I'm not so sure that I'll have that satchel ready on time," he teased her, a smile brimming on his face.

Dawn whisked her head to look at the man, her corn stalk-colored hair flipping in the air from the motion. "Oh, Jerome. You know that it's not my fault," she giggled.

She turned back to John and me and picked up both of our hands. "Come on. Father's waiting," she said and started leading us both toward her home.

~

We took our time reaching the shelter. John didn't say anything to our guide but stared intently on the ground as we walked along. As we walked, I started some idle chitchat with Dawn in order to pass the time. She was also sixteen and an only daughter to William and Sherry Kenneth. They lived in the area where the housing survived the war. Her father used to work with books before he left the business. Now, he spent most of his time going off with his friends or talking to fellow colleagues—maybe doing a lecture on one book or such. Sherry used to work as a nurse at the local hospital, before the downsizing occurred. Dawn, probably due to the fact that her father would read to her every night, was incredibly smart and knew a lot about literature, the sciences, and other things. I told her a bit about my family but didn't divulge anything too personal. John just listened to the two of us.

After running out of things to talk about, I took a look around the area and noticed that that we were not walking on the street but in an alleyway. Also, the route was not a direct path. The housing district was only a half hour walk from the market in order to entice the families with money to shop there. The three of us must have been walking for a good hour by now. It was starting to get dark, so the light available between the buildings gave just enough radiance so we wouldn't trip over anything.

Huge towers stormed the air around us, composed of level after level of housing. Trying to get a bearing of where we were, I stopped walking and stared at the walls of the alleyway. John stopped walking and glanced up at me from his shoes.

"What?" he asked.

Squinting my eyelids in order to better concentrate, I came to the conclusion that I wasn't sure what section of the town we were in. I turned to Dawn, who had stopped a few feet in front. "Where are we?" I asked.

She casually pointed toward the end of the alley. "My house is just at the end. We're not far," she reassured us and continued walking.

I shot a glance at John. He was standing between Dawn and me, waiting for me to start moving again. I walked up beside my old friend and whispered into his ear, "This doesn't feel right."

John shrugged off my uneasiness. "You're being paranoid."

We continued the rest of the way in silence, Dawn leading the way in front. As we got to the end of the alley, she stopped by a metal door. Slight rust from the years of rain was easily visible on the doorframe and handle. She glanced past us, down the long, dark passageway that we had just wandered from and then risked a glance out into the street, whisking her hair back and forth as she flashed her head from side to side. Accepting that there was no one else around, she knocked on the door three times. Without removing her hand from the door, she gave a pause and then knocked twice more. I was about to ask Dawn why we were entering through a back door, when I heard the hard metal clank of a bolt from the other side of the door. The hinges, very rusted from the years of overuse, cringed from the force of moving, and the door swung open painfully slowly.

The older, red-haired woman was at the door. She smiled warmly at the three of us. "Ah, you made it. Come in, come in," she waved at us hurriedly.

I motioned for John and Dawn to enter first. John nodded to Sherry in a greeting and entered the house. Dawn quickly followed John, and I after her. Once we were all inside the house, she tightened her fingers around the handle of the door and gave a quick heave in order to give the door momentum to close. Again, the soft, shrill cry from the hinges called out in the darkening air, and the metal door clanked shut in front of us. Sherry reached for the mechanical contraption fused to the middle of the door and turned a switch. Two shafts of iron sprang from the cylindrical tubes attached to the contraption, sliding into place in the metal frame. The iron bars clanged into place, securing themselves again to bar the door closed.

The area we were led into from the alley was barely big enough to house the four of us. A small brass lantern hung from a hook on the wall. The paint was old and water-stained in places and chipping off in others. A second closed door, this one made of wood and very old, was to my back. Sherry turned from the metal door and reached out to pick up the lantern from the hook where it rested. Dawn, squeezing past John and me, opened up the wooden door. On the other side of the wooden door was a hallway that led to stairwells going both up and down. A small door stood off to the left, close to the front door. It was marked with some sort of protruding object on the front, but it was too dark to see what it was. Dawn motioned that we should follow her as she took the stairwell downstairs.

The stairs creaked quietly as they bore our weight down into the building. Dawn led, followed by John and myself, with Sherry and the lantern behind. At the bottom of the flight of stairs we found another wooden door, this one not as old. The copper-looking handle turned easily in Dawn's hand, and we all entered the room.

Once inside, the sheer atmosphere of the house nearly overpowered me. Rust-colored carpet and richly woven rugs covered the floor as far as I could see. A coatrack stood by the door, and an etched metal mirror hung by the entrance. The walls were painted a calming cream color, which added to the radiance of the place. As the small alcove where we stood opened up into the house, I could see four other doorways that led into different rooms. Pictures of the countryside hung on the walls in between the doorways, giving the house a pleasant and comfortable presentation. This place was huge! You could probably fit three of my shelters into this house, maybe four.

Sherry closed the door behind her and turned off the lantern, plunging us into a moment of darkness. A flickering of light and the crackling of a fire escaped the room directly to our right.

"Just a moment," she reassured us.

A click was heard, and the room filled with light from lamps that hung from the ceiling. The light fixtures were a lot like those at the Factory, except these were well kept and craftily made. Sherry put the lantern down on the floor beside the door and motioned that we were to enter the house.

"William should be waiting inside his den for you two," Sherry informed John and me, leading us to the doorway to our right where the crackling fire rested.

I quickly took off my work boots, so as not to get the carpet dirty. John, seeing what I was doing, also attempted to take off his boots. Dawn and Sherry walked past the two of us as we hopped from one foot to anther trying to get our boots off our feet and disappeared behind the second doorframe to our left. With a grunt, I removed my boots and walked to the doorway leading to where William was waiting for us, John a moment behind me.

William was sitting in a very comfortable chair directly in the center of the room, half turned toward the brick fireplace that nestled itself into the wall facing us. A metal bucket sat by the fenced-in fireplace, a bundle of wood resting inside of it. Two other chairs, smaller but also inviting, were off to the left of William. They were positioned so that he could face whoever was sitting there. In his lap rested an old book, which he was reading. A bookshelf covered the entire right wall, overflowing with any and every description of book possible. Books of multiple sizes and colors, leather-bound and not, lined the shelves. A small table sat on William's immediate right, in grabbing reach of a glass of water. Another light fixture hung from the roof of the room but wasn't turned on.

I cleared my throat, trying to get the man's attention. William glanced up from the book, smiled at seeing the two of us, and put a red cloth from his shirt pocket between the pages he was reading.

"Good evening, gentlemen. I'm glad that you could join us," he warmly welcomed John and me, motioning that we should enter the room.

I cautiously entered the den. John stood by the entrance, leaning against the doorway frame. William's smile grew wider, seeing our discomfort.

"Come now, gentlemen. Please, sit down," he offered, motioning to the chairs in front of him.

I moved over to the chairs and sat in the one closest to the fire. The leather covering the cushion of the chair crumpled as I sat down. John casually sat down beside me, almost throwing himself into the chair. William carefully placed the book he was reading on the table beside him, making sure not to knock over the glass of water, and returned his focus to us. From the light of the fire, I could see that the swelling of his eye had receded slightly, but there were still some cuts and bruises visible on his face. He was wearing a vest made of some style of fabric that I had not seen before. He leaned forward in his chair.

"I would like to thank you again for your timely rescue," he said.

I looked over to see what John was doing. He was looking around the place, sizing it up, and glancing out the doorway to see the opposite room we faced. He wasn't at all interested in what William had to say, so I guess it rested on me to respond.

"You're welcome," I stuttered.

He leaned back into his chair, the sly smile creeping onto his face. "It's okay ... Tom, was it?"

I nodded. He extended a finger toward my friend, a puzzled brow on his face. I smiled at his unasked question and repeated John's name to him. He continued. "It's okay, Tom. You can say whatever you want or ask any questions you want. We're all friends here," he encouraged, and I eased myself into my chair a bit more, feeling more relaxed at his words.

William turned his head and looked into the dancing fire. "So did you two boys get into trouble for being late for work?"

I was about to answer when John interrupted me. He was still looking into the second room when he answered. "Yeah, we were late. Not that it matters anymore, since we don't have a building to work at."

John's tone was deep and far away, as if there was something chewing on his brain, and he was trying to untie what it was. I could only guess that it had something to do with Lydia and the fact that she would have liked this place. William nodded, still staring into the fire.

"Oh, I take it you two worked at the Factory, then. Yes, I heard about that," he commented, casual and calm.

"*Used* to work at the Factory," John corrected the man.

William wriggled in his seat, trying to get himself into a more comfortable position. "Did a lot of people get hurt in the explosion?" he asked.

John looked from the other room to the floor. "Yeah, a lot of people got hurt."

William closed his eyes slowly. "I'm sorry to hear that. I really am. Did you lose anyone?"

John sat silent for a moment. I didn't feel it was in my place to answer for him, so I stayed silent until John got the nerve to say, "Yeah ... I lost someone."

William turned his gaze from the fire to John, whose head hung low. He brought his hands in front to his chest and intertwined his fingers, lacing them into a woven pattern of flesh and digits while he thought of the proper things to say. The fire crackled happily behind the wire mesh that protected the rest of the room from the beating of the fire. William took a breath and ended the minute pause of silence. "Fate can be cruel sometimes. I also lost someone I knew in the explosion. Even at my age, it's never easy to lose someone you care about."

John looked up from the carpeted floor at William. "What was their name?"

Just then, Sherry popped her head around the corner of the doorframe. "Supper's ready," she informed us and soon disappeared around the corner.

William shook his head. "Let's set our minds on happier things, gentlemen," he groaned as he pushed himself out of the chair.

John and I both rose from the leather cushioned chairs and followed William out of the room. He led us down the hallway toward the opening that Dawn and Sherry had walked through when we first entered the home. As we walked, I was able to get a better look at the paintings that adorned the hallway. One in particular caught my attention. It was an image of a landscape, complete with flowing fields of corn and wheat. A farmer and his wife were working on the soil, and a child was playing with a butterfly just off to the side. The sky, a deep shade of blue, covered the horizon. A cozy log cottage jutted out of the side of the frame onto the canvas.

The room that John and I walked into was again adorned with fine furniture. An oak table filled the middle of the room. White plates painted with little pink flowers on them and glass goblets were in front of each seating arrangement. The fact that these objects were not made of wood or metal, but china and glass, screamed wealth. A white, finely woven cloth covered the majority of the table, its ridges covered in beautifully ordained patterns and swirls. A cabinet filled with more pieces of ceramic plates and glassware rested in a corner of the room. In the middle was a vase filled with purple, yellow, and blue wild flowers, adding to the flowery design of the cloth.

Across the entire table, plates covered with food sat waiting to be gorged upon. There were deep purple grapes, a steaming loaf of bread complemented with a small dish of butter, a bowl of stuffing and mashed cranberries, a plate of sliced cheese layered in a winding motion, a mound of mashed potatoes, a cup of thick gravy, and a collection of steamed vegetables. The biggest plate had a polished metal covering, so I could only guess what was under it. Dawn was already inside the room, standing behind the second chair down from the head seat. She had changed into a blue dress, which flattered her figure quite nicely.

William walked to the seat that was at the head of the table. John and I each took a seat beside him. I sat beside Dawn, and John sat beside the empty chair that would probably end up being Sherry's. I looked around the room a bit more, overtaken by the glamour of the place. A pop came from a swinging door behind me, and Sherry emerged from behind it, carrying a bottle of wine.

I glanced at John. His eyes bulged out at the site of the wine bottle, his mind probably asking the same question that I was asking. *How did they get a bottle of wine?* Alcohol was forbidden for citizens to own. Only the higher-ranking POLICE officers could own it. Citizens were only allowed to drink alcohol on special occasions. Even then, the places that sold it were few, and the cost was staggering. Yet Sherry walked into the room with a freshly uncorked bottle of red wine and started walking around the table filling our glasses, as if she were pouring water into them.

Once Sherry had finished filling our glasses, she put the bottle into a finely crafted metal bucket beside William and sat down at the table. William picked up his glass, the red liquid swishing from the movement, and raised it in front of him. Dawn and Sherry repeated the action. Still looking at John, I motioned with my eyes that we were supposed to do this as well, and we slowly raised our goblets into the air. William scanned the table and smiled brightly.

"A toast," he announced, "to Tom and John. Let's hope that this is the beginning of a long and prosperous friendship."

Sherry and Dawn gave their glasses a slight bounce and repeated William's kind words before taking a sip from the wine. John and I thanked William and sampled the wine given to us. The rich and delicate flavor of the warm liquid danced on my tongue, filling the cavern of my mouth with its slightly tart texture. Delicious. John downed half the glass in one swallow. I wanted to savor the experience more, so I took my time with drinking it. William smiled at the sight of John consuming the drink and reached back to the bottle resting in the bucket to refill his glass.

After touching up John's glass, the velvet juice swimming in his goblet, William returned the bottle to its resting place. He smiled at us all, sweeping his eyes around the table while reaching out for the covered plate. "I hope everyone's hungry," he joked.

William took hold of the handle on top of the covering, and in one fell swoop, pulled it away to reveal a plump, juicy, mouth-watering turkey. My jaw must have dropped. To have turkey as a meal was a momentous event, because the bird had become quite rare in these parts. Even having a turkey sandwich was something to be treasured. Yet, like the wine, here sat a full bird basted and cooked for the five of us to eat at leisure.

As William picked up a strange type of utensil in each hand, he raised an eyebrow toward me. "How much would you like?"

Still in shock at the elaborate course of food John and I were presented with, I stuttered out that he could give me however much he thought I should have. The smell of the bird sitting in front of me was overpowering. Plates were passed around the table, food piling up on each. Eventually, each one of us sat with a heaping helping of turkey and other types of delicacies.

John and I dug into the food. The ranges of tastes were like nothing I have experienced before. The rest of the family started eating their meals as well but not with the eagerness that John and I had. One could almost compare our rigorous consumption of the meal as if we had not eaten for days. As we ate, William asked John and me questions about how we lived, what our jobs were like, and so on. We tried our best to answer his questions without choking on the food that never stopped filling our mouths. After each of our answers, he nodded as if filling out a questionnaire inside his head. I looked over at Dawn during our discussion and noticed that she had a concerned look on her face.

"Doesn't it get lonely living along like that?" she asked.

"Well," I tried to answer while swallowing the mouthful of turkey caught between my teeth, "there are times that it gets a little lonely, and I wish that I had someone to talk to. But, then again, John doesn't live that far off. I usually hang out with him. We spend a lot of time together. He's my best friend."

Sherry piped into the conversation with a question about my parents and why I didn't live with them. The conversation split off at that point, myself discussing my past experiences with Dawn and Sherry, while John and William delved into other things. Halfway through our discussion, I glanced over to see how John was doing. He and William entered a heated debate over work regulations at the Factory. The two of them were drawing diagrams with their fingers on the top of the tablecloth, each one trying to convince the other he was correct. Every so often, I caught a glimpse of the John I knew before the destruction of the Factory and the loss of Lydia—the lively John, quick with a smile and quicker with a snarky comment. A warm sensation came over me, like I really belonged. I was comfortable in this place. It was like I had a family once again.

Once the food was scraped clean from my plate, I decided to ask William some questions as well.

"Sir?" I interjected.

He glanced up from the table, the mock design of the refinery that John had sketched out for him fading from the table, and held up his hand to my request, a kind smile on his weathered face.

"Please, Tom, call me William," he answered.

"Well ... I don't mean to me rude or anything ... but how did you get wine?" I asked.

William eased himself back into his chair. The light mood of the room grew a tad more serious as he thought on the question I posed. "I have a few friends who were able to get me a bottle or two."

I further pushed for an answer. "Did Vans attack you because you knew how to get wine? I mean, you're not a part of the POLICE, or else he would have never attacked you. But the POLICE are the only people who are allowed to have wine. And the turkey," I mentioned, pointing a hand at the carved up bird that sat in the middle of the table. "Where did you get the turkey?"

John looked slightly shocked, as if he was unsure what I was doing. William stared long and hard at me, intertwining his fingers as he had in the den. I felt like a bug being dissected under a viewing glass. The table went silent as we waited for William to answer me.

Finally, he smiled. "Very astute questions, Tom. I'm impressed that you were able to come up with the courage to ask them."

Sherry glanced nervously between John, myself, and William. "Dear, are you sure that—"

William held up his hand to reassure his wife. "I think it's past that particular question, Dear. You know that as much as I do."

Sherry slowly nodded and stood up, collecting her dishes in her hand. Dawn also collected her dishes and left though the swinging door that attached the kitchen to the dining room where we sat. William brushed his eyes carefully with the base of his thumb, so not to irritate the one that was still healing. With a breath of air, William began to explain to us how he came to have the wine and turkey.

"The world was not always like it is today. You two must have realized this by now. No, it was quite different. It was an amazing time to live. You were able to do a lot more back then. But it wasn't perfect, mind you. Back then, there was always fighting and conflict between the different parts of the world. But now, that's all been removed—suppressed, rather. Now, there is only one form of government: no conflict between parties, no fighting between leaders, and no more wars. This is good, of course."

William sat up in his chair, gently placing his hands on the table. He looked from John to me as he continued talking. "The way in which we are being governed now, though, is not the idealistic view that we are lead to believe. The POLICE treat everyone as subservient to themselves. That means that the regular person is below the POLICE in both power and voice. We've become nothing more than slaves to the POLICE force. Some believe that a way to take revenge against their mistreatment is to try to punish the POLICE by holding riots and other forms of outcries. These riots are not necessarily all violent. Sometimes, these riots are targeted to take away those things that the POLICE hold dear in order to level the playing field—such as turkeys and bottles of wine."

William spoke the last sentence very slowly, so we were able to get the full implication of what he was saying. He didn't have to do that. I understood exactly what he was saying. The secrecy getting to his home, why Vans attacked them, why he had a turkey and a bottle of wine for dinner. With a chill rolling up my spine, I understood it all. William and his family were Rebells.

Quickly shooting a glance over at John, I was able to witness his face turning from confusion to understanding, his hands curling into fists. He understood as well.

CHAPTER 7

"You're part of Le Rebells?" John asked, making sure that he understood what William was telling him.

William smirked at the question. "I prefer the title—"

He didn't get a chance to finish his thought. John jumped out of his chair, knocking it back loudly onto the ground, and grabbed a hold of the front of William's shirt. He yanked on the shirt, almost pulling William out from where he was sitting. "How could you! You killed my fiancée, you bastard! You killed her!"

William grabbed a hold of the hands that were wringing the shirt he was wearing, trying to pry them off. "Who? What?" William managed to stammer out.

I exploded out of my chair, a screeching sound coming from the ground where the legs ran along the floorboards as I pushed the piece of furniture away from me. Running around to where the two men wrestled with each other, I tried to aid William by also attempting to remove John's hands from his shirt. "John," I yelled out at my friend, "what do you think you're doing?"

William managed to slap John's hands away and scampered to a standing position; his chair clattered onto the ground. He clutched his shirt and neck, trying to get a grip as to what had just happened. John tried to lunge at the older man again, but I was able to restrain him. Taking a few deep breaths, John stopped pushing against me, allowing me to relax my grip on him. I still stood ready to block another attack, though.

Sherry and Dawn stood in the doorway, holding onto each other's waist inside a secure embrace. Sherry, armed with a rolling pin inside her right hand, glanced at William. A worried and concerned look blanketed her face. William's strong, deep breaths labored from the excitement, his eyes ricocheting from myself to John.

"I had nothing to do with the Factory, John," William tried to explain, an uncertain expression across his face.

John snorted. "Why should I believe your lies, Rebell?"

William, his breath slowly regaining with his composure, turned around and picked up the chair that had fallen when he escaped John's grasp. "I'm sorry that you feel this way, John, and I am truly sorry about your departed fiancée, but there's nothing you can do about the situation now."

John just shook his head. "We should have left you to rot. Because of you and your kind, my life is ruined. I've lost my love. I've lost my job. I've lost everything that I hold dear."

William rested his hand on the now upright chair, his fingers tracing the deep grains inside the wooden panel that formed the backing. As he brushed the chair affectionately, he smiled slightly. "I'm sorry. 'Our kind,' John?"

John glared at the older gentleman. "Yeah, that's right. *Your* kind. Tom and I, we're nothing like you."

William's smile turned into a shot of pity. "You don't understand the seriousness of the situation, do you?" he stated more than asked us, a sigh escaping his breath with the realization that he now had to sit us back down and try to explain the importance of understanding the scenario.

I shot John a quick glance to see if he knew what William was talking about. John's expression went from anger to confusion. I then glanced at Sherry and Dawn, who were still standing in the doorframe. Realizing that there was no reason to stand by, that things were calming down once more, the two of them went back into the side room. A creak from the hinges eased the air as they went through the well-used door, creating a slight breeze within the room.

"What are you getting at, William?" I finally asked.

William shook his head disapprovingly. "You should have been able to piece it together, Tom. You're quite bright, and the answer is blatantly obvious if you're looking. When you entered the house, didn't you notice the security that was taken to make sure you were not discovered? That's why I put off this little get-together for a day, so that you could think and come to the realization that your life as you knew it … well … was over."

John and I exchanged quick glances of confusion and returned our attention back to William. He wandered tiredly to the base of the chair and, with a puff of air, plopped onto the frame with a thud.

"When you helped me and my family back there in the alley," he started to explain to us as if he were talking to children, "when you attacked those ruffians, you became labeled as Rebells yourselves. After all, think back on what you did: aiding and abetting, causing a disturbance, publicly attacking and causing physical harm to an officer of the POLICE—"

I opened my mouth to start to speak, but William beat me to the punch. "Yes, even a person in training is under that law. You see, that's why I invited you here. I showed you where I live in order to give you a safe house. During dinner, I tried to make sure that you understood where I stood in the whole scheme of things, so I could be viewed as an ally, especially since you tossed everything aside to come to my rescue. I thought you realized this before you even stepped through my front door. Obviously, I was wrong. Needless to say, you two lads are now Rebells, whether you like it or not. 'Our kind,' as John aptly put it, is in fact 'your kind.'" He finished by waving at his house and all that was in view and then brought his hands together pointing at us both.

The full weight of the situation hit me full in the face like a cold, hard slap. How could I have been so stupid not to realize this before! My jaw grew slack as my mind raced through the details of the situation, playing them out over and over again.

Vans, a popular go-to understudy of the POLICE, was assigned to make an example of this family of Rebells. John and I got involved and rescued William and his family, thus tying us to the Rebell faction. Vans wrote his report, probably spicing up our involvement, and it was distributed throughout the POLICE organization. John and I were now marked as "wanted for questioning" or fugitives. Eventually, the report and my name would go to the sergeant. He would probably put out a priority warrant for the two of us, because we were there when the Factory blew up and there was evidence that the Rebells were involved. We would become the main suspects!

I had already made the sergeant mad at me once; this would push it over the top. What's worse, the first sergeant was going to be expecting me for training. John and I couldn't stick our faces into the street anymore or else we would be caught. Because of this, there was nowhere we could go and no one who would take us in. No one, that is, except the other Rebells—*our* kind.

I felt like I was going to throw up.

John, on the other hand, merely sputtered out a scoff and folded his arms at the accusation, shaking his head in disbelief. "Nice try, old man. It takes more than a report from a local bully to be labeled as part of Le Rebells. They will have no reason to hunt us. You, on the other hand, freely admitted that you're part of the organization. What makes you think that we won't just turn you and your family in?"

William smiled a knowing smile. "That's an empty threat, and you know it. It's not in your character, John."

John regained his rage and took another step forward toward the older man sitting in the chair. John stopped in front of him, towering over him like an interrogator, and stared icily down at his captive.

"You don't know anything about me," he spat out.

William leaned back against the wooden frame. A small crick echoed from the wood, resenting the pressure William placed against the back frame as he stretched against it.

"Untrue," he said. "First, it's your nature to help people. You showed that fact by coming to my family's rescue. Secondly, by turning me in, you prove that the thug you and John have been tormented by for who knows how long was right. Pride alone will stop you from resolving this point. Third, even if you do turn me in, your reputation for residing with a known Rebell will tarnish any chance of gaining status inside your company. You will be shown as untrustworthy and a risk to security."

I took a step over to the table, looking for a goblet with wine still in it. Finding one, I downed the tart red wine in one gulp, letting the fluid burn my throat as it passed down into my stomach. The glass clanked loudly as I carelessly plunked it down onto the table from where I grabbed it. John carefully glanced back to where I stood, still looming over the man in the chair.

"Tom?" he asked, emphasizing that he wanted my opinion on the situation.

My two hands reached out and lightly rested on the table in front of me. My head, feeling like a lead weight, finally caved in from the stress I had put myself under from the past few days. A pounding—like a hammer forming a hot, burning bar of iron on an anvil—beat with every heartbeat against my temples. I winced on every throb, trying to form my mind around the situation I was thrust into.

"I don't know, John. I just don't know," I answered quietly.

John scampered from where William sat and ran to my side. His hand grabbed hold of my arm, and with a force that he probably didn't mean, he threw me around to face him. His eyes searched mine for any sense of reality; his own were caught in a feud of anger and panic.

"What the hell is wrong with you, Tom?! You're not actually buying what this guy is saying, are you? He has no power over us. There's no way that the POLICE will try to convict us. Besides, think about what the Rebells have done to us! Do you actually want to join them now, after all the crap that they've done?!"

I pinched the bridge of my nose, squinting from the sheer energy that it took to get my head clear. "I can't ... it's too hard to think," I apologized.

John whipped his head back at William, who was getting up out of his chair again. "What did you do to him?" he demanded. "Was the wine drugged?"

William walked over to where the wine bottle rested inside the bucket and removed it; the bottle clanked against the base of the basin as it was removed. "You need to relax. Your emotions are getting the best of you," he tossed out while he filled up a goblet that sat empty on the table.

With a flash of his hand, John knocked the goblet off of the table. The wine splashed against the wall, forming a red splat like one would see if an overripe tomato exploded. The goblet crashed onto the ground, exploding into a cascade of tiny pieces. William yanked the bottle back toward his body, splashing a bit of the wine on himself in the process. John glared at the old man again, still holding onto my arm. "I have had enough of you and your petty words," he snapped.

"John," I winced quietly.

"I've had enough of your recruitment and your wine and your turkey," John continued. "I've had enough of your lies and your mind games."

The grip on my arm tightened even more with every passing syllable from John. "John," I spoke, a little louder to try to get his attention again.

"I've had it with you and your Rebells, always destroying those who mean no harm! What did she ever do to you?! Tell me! What did she ever do *to you*?!"

John's grip tightened to the point of breaking bones. My hand was starting to go numb. My hand slashed out, grabbing hold of John's wrist, and forcefully yanked his hand from my arm. John, shocked stone cold from my reaction, stood silently and frozen. I held his hand out in front of me, my grip clamped hard onto his wrist. The pulse of John's heart was bumping softly underneath my fingers. I took a few breaths; the warm air inside the room filled and exited my tired lungs.

"Stop this. It's not helping," I finally whispered.

John, still locked in surprise at my sudden force, stood dumb at my words. Realizing that John wasn't going to do anything, I threw his hand back at him and turned away. Taking a few steps from the two of them, trying to clear my thoughts, I leaned against the doorframe that lead out into the hallway. My back was firmly planted to them both.

"We're not going to turn them in," I blatantly told John.

The force of my words unlocked the spell that John was under. "What did you say?" he asked, his words nothing more than a hiss.

Quickly turning around, my eyes bore through John. "We are not going to turn them in," I repeated, my voice never wavering.

John took a step forward. Quickly holding up a hand to stop John, I continued, staring at William as I talked. "We saved your family's lives,

William. You now owe us. To repay us, you and your family will use your connection through the Rebells in order to find the ones who are responsible for the Factory. Once you know, you will tell us so we can deal with them. After that, your debt is paid. From that point on, we don't know you, and you don't know us. Life returns back to the way it was," I explained.

John squinted at me. "That's it?" he asked, unsure if I was serious.

I folded my arms across my chest, resettling my feet on the ground. "Dead serious, John."

John waved a hand at William. "But they are—"

"No longer your concern, John," I finished his sentence for him.

"But they killed Lydia!" he finally burst out.

William, at hearing John finally say his fiancé's name, gave him a quick double take but said nothing. I lowered my head and scowled at John. "William and his family were in no condition to plant any bomb or whatever caused the explosion of the Factory. Thus, they didn't kill Lydia. Someone else did."

"How can you stand there and say that we're going to let them go, especially after what they did to us … to me," John asked, quiet and unsure.

Turning on my heel, no longer wanting to be inside the house any longer than I had to, I walked out of the room.

"We should be leaving, John," I called out.

~

The door clicked behind us as John and I left through the back door of the house, which led us back onto the alleyway. John, uneasily glancing at me and standing to the side a small distance, hugged himself in order to warm his body in the cold night air. I pulled my shirt collar up in order to block the slight breeze whispering through the area. The two of us, not bothering to talk, turned and wandered out onto the street off the alleyway.

Sicher Himmel was a fairly big and prosperous town, especially with all the shelters, the Factory, the huge market, and the other wealthy businesses that crowded the many streets. The town was segregated into different areas, each with its own classification—most often wealthy to poor. Everything had its place. And, like all the other major towns, there were plenty of restricted areas within it and Fallout Zones surrounding the outskirts—areas I had never dreamed of going into. Looking around, I didn't immediately recognize what section we were in.

John and I wandered the streets, trying to find an area that we were both familiar with. The stars gave off little light to brighten our paths. Even the moon, caught in a half crescent shape, gave off little to no light. We walked in silence for a while, John occasionally glancing in my direction over his shoulder. The houses that bordered the streets, remembrances of days long gone, blinked and fluttered with the occasional echo of light from the windows. There was not another soul on the street, just John and myself, so our footsteps resounded off of the houses back to us in a hollow, empty clop. We must have wandered around the town for half an hour before the houses started to turn into the less desirable shelters that both John and I live in. This was the first clue that we were going in the right direction. The second piece of evidence was more distinct.

The two of us turned a corner and found ourselves in view of the one landmark that made Sicher Himmel unique in comparison to the other cities around the country: the fountain. The fountain was created prewar and was untouched during the battles that ensued during the cross-street feuds. This creation was probably the only piece of architecture that was untouched during the war, which made the fountain that much more special to the people of this town. We had a living piece of history untarnished by the POLICE or the Rebells or by time itself.

The fountain was a wide circular bowl constructed of rock and cement with a podium sprouting from the middle. It filled with water every morning through jets and old tubing from the local water supply. When he was given control of the town, the sergeant purposefully made sure that this was to continue, despite protests of wasting water.

In the middle of the fountain, perched forever on the podium, was a huge statue of a man sitting on a horse. The horse was rearing back, its two back legs fused onto the podium. The man wore a suit, perhaps an old uniform, and was wielding a sword above his head. The metal statue was leached with bird droppings and discolored from the rains. Even though it was in poor condition, it stood proud and strong, the look of determination etched firmly on its quite visible face. When we were younger, John and I used to come to this place all the time to play or to talk. Seeing the fountain again brought back a few memories of a much easier and happier time.

John focused his eyes on the fountain and then shot me a glance, jabbing a thumb in the fountain's direction. I nodded, showing that I saw it as well. John picked up his pace to wander over to the fountain's side. He rubbed the rock and concrete with his hands. It was almost like he was trying to wake a small child, letting it know that he was back from wherever he'd one off to. I had to smile a bit at the image and walked up beside John.

"Do you remember when we were younger and the two of us would sneak out of our shelters at night and come to this place?" he asked in a casual tone, as if everything that had happened just hours before had never happened.

I thought back to our misadventures in this area. Playing POLICE and Rebells and hide-and-seek, talking about whatever topic happened to be important until the sun rose over the shelters—we'd had some good times here. I sat down on the edge of the fountain; the cold rock seeped through my pants, causing me to shiver slightly.

"Yeah, I remember," I answered quietly.

John sat down beside me on the fountain's ledge. Kicking his feet up from under him, he swung back onto the fountain's lip and stretched out fully on the rock and concrete embankment. "We would play and talk and laugh ... and we would tell our deepest, darkest secrets to each other. Just you, the stars, and me. Just us three against the world. And we knew that no one would tell. Not you, not me, not the stars—what we said would be locked away in time, just like the fountain," he mused, resting his head on his right arm as he stared out onto the stars and moon above.

I glanced over the area trying to retrace our previous lives here. We used to have so much fun beside this place. Before we went to our jobs at the Factory, we would escape from our homes every night when the sky was clear and meet here. We would spend hours and hours out here, playing in the spring and summer night air. I'm surprised that we never got caught, considering that there were shelters off to the side. I guess the sound of the water helped conceal our activities. Even after getting our jobs, we still popped out here occasionally. John and I hadn't been here in a year and a half. *Had it really been that long?* I thought to myself.

"We had a lot of fun here." I sighed as the lives we used to have raced across my eyes.

"What happened to us, Tom?"

I chuckled a bit at the thought. "We grew up, I guess."

"Did you know this was where I proposed to Lydia?" he said, more telling me than asking me, his voice distant with the wash of history.

"John—"

"What the hell are we going to do, Tom?" John asked me.

"I don't know, John."

We sat for a few moments in silence, the seriousness of our situation hanging over us. I glanced up to the man on the horse. He stared off into the distance, unblinking, not offering any advice.

"Whatever happens, I'm sure it will turn out okay. No one's going to believe Vans, no matter what he tells people. Even if he does put us in a report and the POLICE take notice of it, they probably won't do anything about it. They have other things to worry about right now."

I turned in my seat so I could face John, one of my legs folding underneath my body to help steady myself on the fountain's lip. John rolled over onto his belly, careful not to fall into the still water, and rested his head on his hands.

"Do you remember that one night when I told you my deep, deep, deep secret fear? The one that I made you promise to go to work naked if you ever told a single person?" he asked.

The sudden question took me back a bit as my mind raced to the moment. John and I had just started working at the Factory a few months back. There was a crack in the hallway that led to the mines, and hot steam would puff up out of it, usually scaring the hell out of anyone who happened to stand beside or above it. The older workers whispered that it was a pit that led straight into the Earth's middle and that any young lads who got into trouble would be pitched down it. John was deathly afraid of that crack and even more afraid of falling in. He would have to walk past that crack every day, normally hugging the opposite wall for dear life.

I laughed out loud at the thought of John stretching out against the far wall so he wouldn't fall into the crevasse.

"Yeah, I remember. And I haven't told another soul about that. I can't believe that you bought the whole idea of hot liquid lava boiling out from that small crack in the flooring."

John shot me a good hit against my leg. "It was not small! I saw a kid fit his entire lower torso into it."

I smiled at my old friend. "Well, I can't remember a day you looked more relieved than the one when they plugged up the broken pipe underneath it, which was causing all that steam to spurt up. And then they got around to fixing the flooring."

John rolled onto his back, resettling himself into a comfortable position. He chuckled for a moment, thinking back on our past lives. Staring off into the sky once more, he said, "I lied, you know."

"Lied about what?"

"My fear," he explained as he pushed himself up off of the ledge of the fountain. He continued talking as he wandered around the rock foundation that held the water inside the fountain, balancing himself and being careful not to fall in. I got up and followed him around the fountain base walking on the ground. "The crevasse was just a childish phobia I had. It wasn't *the* most secret fear I had."

I walked in silence, watching my friend as he waved his hands in the air, trying to keep his balance on the rock base. John continued his confession as he wandered. "Your mom and my mom were good friends when they were both alive. I can still remember my first party. That's when I first met you. You remember that? Your mother brought you over in that dopey looking suit. What was she thinking? It was hideous!"

I stopped walking, jabbing a finger disapprovingly at John. "My mother made that suit," I reproached him jokingly.

He smiled and continued. "The two of them pushed us outside to play while they talked and made lunch. Once we were outside, I laughed at your suit. Laughed long and hard at that ridiculous thing you were wearing. You started crying."

I picked up my pace so I could face him. "I was not crying."

"You were crying."

"I was not!" I insisted, smiling broadly.

John waved off the point. "Well, if you weren't at the start, then I turned you into a little puddle of whining, crying goop by the time I was done with you. You have to admit that."

"It didn't make me look like a duck," I pouted quietly.

"And then Vans happened to pass by. He saw me making fun of you and decided to join in on the fun—threw a mud ball at you."

I stopped in my tracks. "Why are you reminding me of this again?" I asked him, careful not to start chuckling at the whole thing.

John ignored my comment. "Me making fun of you was entertainment. Vans making fun of you was just plain mean. I yelled at him to stop. He threw a rock, and it hit you in the arm."

John stopped walking, his eyes staring off into nothing. "Then I said something. Something that I can still remember as if it just happened yesterday. I said, 'Don't hurt my friend.' It's funny ... one moment I was poking fun at you and making jokes at your suit. The next moment you were my best friend in the whole wide world, and I was defending you against a guy who could easily beat me up."

He sat down directly where he was standing, his feet kicking out from under him and bouncing harmlessly against the rock base of the fountain. I took a few steps back toward John and sat beside him, shuffling around so I could get comfortable on the hard rock surface. John's eyes were still locked into the darkness that surrounded us.

"I picked up a rock, probably the one he threw at you, and threw it back at him. It hit Vans in the chest and knocked the wind out of him. He ran off, wheezing and crying. Once he was gone, I helped you wipe the mud off of your suit, and I think I said it wasn't that bad looking or something. I can't remember."

John hung his head low, switching his sight from the oblivion to the ground around the fountain. "When your parents died, my mother took it upon herself to help raise you. Maybe it was a request from your mom, or maybe she just felt bad about the situation. I don't know. Truthfully, I always felt that we had adopted you."

I nudged him softly. "Great, now I'm the family pet," I joked.

"When my mother died, and we were both of age to start working and get our own places ... that was one of the worst days of my life," John confessed.

John looked away from me as he continued speaking. "My biggest fear is that I'll lose the people I love. That one day they will all be gone, and I will be left alone—like you were with your parents, like I was when my mother died and I had to live alone."

He didn't move. I didn't move. We both just sat there on the edge of the fountain, listening to the water bubble and swish. The gurgle of the water echoed off of the shelters that surrounded the fountain. My hands started to feel the cold of the night.

"John?" I asked quietly, barely a whisper.

He didn't respond.

"Do you remember what you did the day my family died?" I asked.

He didn't move.

"Do you remember what you did for me?"

He turned his head slowly to face me. "What did I do?" he asked, his voice cracking softly.

"When my family died, I felt like the world had come to an end. Emotions ran very high inside me. I didn't know what to feel or what I could do. I felt useless in the situation. In fact, I could have sworn that I would have gone insane with grief if you didn't come by and help me out."

John smirked, glancing away from me. "Oh, yeah, sure. How the hell did I help?"

I lifted up one of my hands and rested it on John's shoulder. "You listened," I explained. "I cleansed myself of every emotion I thought I ever had, and there were still more waiting to be expressed. I talked about how I felt about their deaths, how I felt inside, what might happen to me, what might happen if … anything I could think of," I trailed off as I remembered that horrid event.

John sat there, staring off into the darkness, listening to how I felt after talking to him. "Tell me about Lydia, John," I asked him quietly.

There was silence.

I tried to catch John's eyes. "Please?"

More silence.

"She … she was going to marry me.…"

CHAPTER 8

The screech of the Factory's steam whistle invaded the air, breaking the silence of the morning. I jerked my head up, eyes bolting open. At the end of the whistle, I slammed my head back onto the pillow, rolling over onto my side. "Why did they have to fix the whistle first?" I whined out loud as I tried to hide my head from the coming sun.

John and I didn't leave the fountain until very late into the night—or very early in the morning, depending on how one looked at it. We talked about the first time John met Lydia, how they grew to love each other, the day they agreed to get married, what she was like, funny stories that involved her ... the list went on. The two of us told stories and lived out our memories beside that fountain. Eventually, the night pressed down hard on the two of us, and we both agreed to go home. In fact, I had to help John back to his shelter, because he was so tired and emotionally worn out from our talk. After dropping him off, I wandered, half-dazed due to sleep deprivation back to my own shelter. I didn't even change into my sleeping clothes. I think I slept for two hours between lying down and hearing the whistle.

Readjusting myself on my bed, I curled up into a ball and hid myself from the world outside, trying desperately to reenter the field of dreamland.

"Oh, get up you lazy ass," came a voice from the kitchen.

John was sitting down in one of my chairs, leaning it back on its hind legs and eating an apple. He positioned it so he could look in on my bedroom. I rolled around in my bed so I could continue lying down and look at my old friend. He was in the same clothes as the night before as well, stubble covering his face.

"Didn't I take you home?" I asked him, trying to reaffirm that I actually did and didn't just dream it.

John took another bite from the apple. "Yeah, but I never went to sleep. So, when the sun came up, I figured I'd come over here," he told me between bites.

I pulled the covers up over my head, trying to block out the world from my very tired eyes, the corners of my eyelids pinching my face in pain from the lack of sleep.

"Come on! Get out of here and go to sleep!" I yelled through the warmth of the blankets.

There was a thump from the kitchen area, but I didn't stick my head out from under the blankets to see what it was, not wanting to bare myself to the day. John walked over to where I was and sat down beside me on the bed, the mattress sinking slightly under his weight. He nudged my feet under the blanket, trying to get my attention. Receiving only a grunt of reluctance, he nudged my feet a second time from above the covers.

"I ... uh ... I wanted to thank you for what you did last night," John said softly, as if he didn't want me to truly hear what he said.

I poked my head up from under the covers in order to look at John better. His head was downcast, staring at my boots beside the bed. The lack of a good night's sleep had visibly taken its toll on him, the dark circles around his eyes sticking out strongly.

"What?" I asked, still trying to focus from my half-sleep daze.

John glanced over shyly. "The fountain?" he reminded me.

I smiled weakly. "Just repaying my debt," I explained.

He looked back to my boots stretched out on the floor. "Yeah, well ... could you do me a favor?" he asked me, growing a bit more serious.

I raised my arm out from under the blanket to cushion my head in order to get comfortable. He took a breath, and let it roll out from his lungs in a prolonged sigh. "I was wondering if you could apologize to William for me for my actions."

I pulled myself out of the covers at hearing the request, the blankets crumpling into a pile by the base of my legs. I slowly sat upright on my bed and stared at John hard, shocked that he would ask me such a thing.

"Wait a minute. What?"

John sighed deeply. "I was wondering if you could apologize to William for me."

I stared at my friend for a second. "Where is this coming from?"

John started to pace the room. "I've been up the entire night running the whole dinner thing through in my mind. The way we left things, how I treated him … he's not going to search for whoever actually destroyed the Factory for us. Why would he? If anything, he'll put his effort toward planting evidence that we did it. But if I said I was sorry, that we didn't mean to treat him like we did, then it might smooth things over a bit. Y'know … help motivate him to help us discover who actually did it. I'd go over and apologize, but—"

"But you think they would be more receptive toward me. Is that it?"

Wringing his hands at the thought, John shrugged his shoulders. "I did try to strangle the guy. And you are so much better with words, Tom! You could word things so William can see that I wasn't in a good frame of mind last night," he pleaded.

I reluctantly got up out of my bed and walked over to my dresser where my clean clothes sat. I grabbed hold of the knob that would open the drawer for my shirts but paused before I opened the drawer.

Turning to look at John once more, I paused for a moment and mused over the situation. Suddenly, like a bolt of lightning, I thought of the true reason why John didn't want to go over to William's home.

"You want me to go over for you because you're still angry over the whole Rebell thing with the Factory. Isn't that the real reason?" I interrogated rather than asked.

John squirmed on the bed under my question but reluctantly answered. "Kind of. I want to say the actual words that I'm sorry for the whole thing last night, but I don't think I can personally do that just yet."

I nodded my head and turned around to open the drawer that held my clothes. "Are you *actually* sorry for what you did? Is the apology legit?"

John didn't say anything.

"All right, I'll go for you," I called out.

As I sorted through my clothes to find something presentable, I could hear John getting up off of the bed. He walked over to where I stood and rested a hand on my shoulder, which caused me to turn around to face him a second time. He was smiling, giving off the slightest glimpse of a John that I used to play with as a kid. "Thanks," he said simply.

He turned and started walking toward the door out of my bedroom. As he walked out of the room, he walked a bit taller than before, like there was a weight lifted off of him. As he was closing the door, he glanced in for the last time. "You know, I wish I were smart like you, Tom."

The door closed behind him with a soft click of the bolt fitting back into place inside the frame. I set my clothes out in front of me, still staring at the now-closed door where John once stood.

"So do I, John. So do I," I whispered.

~

Knock, knock.

The air was crisp in the early morning, which caused me to shiver slightly. People were wandering the streets, leaving their houses to go to the marketplace to gather what they needed for the rest of the day. The sun peaked through the scattering of clouds, shooting a blast of heat onto me as I stood out in front of the main entrance to the house where William and his family lived. Curious to see if anyone inside heard me, I placed my ear up against the weathered door to hear if there was any movement from inside. Nothing.

Knock, knock, knock.

A muffled female voice came from the other side of the door telling me to "wait one moment." The grinding of metal against metal slid through the door as I stood outside, all the while the woman's voice was muttering away about how her arms hurt and how "one of these days, this beam will fall onto my foot, and then where will I be?" The door slowly opened, and a plump little woman presented herself. She had on a simple dress made of some flowery fabric that must have been very colorful at one time. Her hair was done up in a bun behind her head, the gray in her hair showing off her age, along with the wrinkles around her eyes and mouth. There was still color in her cheeks and a sparkle in her eyes, which showed off liveliness in her as she scanned me over for a moment.

"What 'n who might you be?" she asked, turning her nose up at the sight of my presence. As she spoke, a thick accent filled her words, which told me she wasn't born in Sicher Himmel but moved here late in her life.

She raised a finger up at me, still squinting her nose and glaring at me. "If you're tryin' to sell somethin', I ain't interested," she scolded, shaking her finger at me.

I took a step back from the woman and held up my hands in my own defense, trying to protect myself from the waging finger. "Whoa, whoa. I'm here to see Mr. Kenneth."

She slowly relaxed but still examined me with her deep, piercing eyes. "He expectin' you?" she asked.

"Umm ... no."

She raised her head up and down, as if she already knew the answer to the question. The two of us stood on either side of the door for a few moments more, the old woman trying to come up with a decision as to what to do with me. Finally, after what felt like an eternity, she gave a nod.

"Wait here," she instructed in a tone that meant no funny business. And with that, she closed the door once more.

I looked around the street once more to double check and make sure that I was in the right place. I followed the route that John and I had wandered the night before when we left their house to the best of my ability, even passing by the fountain again. I wandered the streets, trying to remake my journey to the house under question, only getting lost for a moment. After a good morning's hike, I had arrived at the iron door that we'd entered the night before. Instead of knocking and entering through this door, which I thought would look a little odd, I decided to walk to the front door and use that. After all, it was morning, and no one would take a second look at someone trying to get in touch with someone through the front door. The same could not be said with me trying to use the back door, lost in the darkness of the alley.

The door in front of me jerked open quite quickly and revealed the pudgy woman standing on the other side once more. She was still in a disapproving mood.

"Not home. Go 'way," she ordered. With that, she tried to close the door just as quickly as she opened it. Out of reflex, I reached out to catch the door barreling quickly toward my face. The tips of my fingers scraped across the wooden frame of the door, skidding across the old, peeling paint, and wrapped themselves around the edge of the door. Unfortunately, my actions were either not quick enough or not seen, because the door continued on its breakneck pace to close.

Wham!

Pain shot through my arm as the fingers that were once wrapped around the edge of the door were now pinned between wood and frame. My eyes bulged out of their sockets, and the burst of stress screaming through my brain emphasized that I was in pain and needed to do something to stop it. My second hand, the one not caught in the doorframe, leapt to force the door back open. My tongue, nearly bitten off from the force of my teeth smashing together, welled out of my mouth, followed by a low grunt of displeasure as I whispered and begged for the woman to reopen the door.

The woman opened it slightly to see what was wrong. The release of pressure on my captured hand allowed me to jerk the now-pounding-with-pain fingers away from their wooden cage. I thrust my hurt hand to my chest, cradling it between my stomach and other hand. She peaked out from the crack created between the frame and door, studying my stance and pain-filled expression. She shook her head. "Tsk-tsk. Now why you go 'n do that, then?"

I tried to compose myself. "Could I wait inside for them to return?" I asked as politely as I could, gritting through the pain.

Her face softened a bit as she looked from my hand to my face. She opened the door wide for me. "Well, come in then, you stubborn mule. Let's get a look at that hand 'o yours."

As I walked into the house, she reached out, took me by the elbow, and directed me into the open door off the right while closing the main door behind me. The door that the little woman led me through was the one I had seen when I'd first came to visit this place. On the doorframe rested a picture frame holding a letter of ownership signed by the POLICE. She must be the homeowner, I mused as the graying woman reattached the metal beam back across the front door.

I stopped a moment to glance around the room. Like William's rooms, the room I was standing in was richly ordained with paintings of open fields and knickknacks of all sorts, but it didn't match the sheer size. In fact, this place was no bigger than my shelter, just cluttered with more things. There was a comfortable chair positioned so that whoever sat in it could watch life go by outside a wide window, which was temporarily draped closed with some blinds. A small tea tray sat near the chair, the top well stained from use. A rug covered the majority of the room, layering the place with a warmth and coziness that escaped most places I had been. The older woman, swishing into the room behind me, gave me a nudge to move farther into the room and closed the door behind her.

"Let's get some ice for your hand," she muttered softly as she continued past me into a tiny kitchen.

"You sit in my chair 'n get yourself comfy there," the woman called out from the kitchen to me. I did as she asked. A few moments passed while I further examined the room and waited for her to come back from the kitchen with whatever she was searching for.

"Here now. You put this on your hand," she ordered, turning around one of the corners of the chairs and thrusting a well-used cloth bag full of ice into my lap. I was not entirely prepared to have a bag of ice thrust onto my lap. The sting of cold ate its way through the fabric bag and found a certain area of my body that was not used to having freezing cold pressed against it. Passing off the mild shock, I did as I was ordered and rested the ice bag in between the armrest and myself.

"Now then. You be nice 'n comfy?" she asked, taking a few steps back in order to get a good look at me.

I nodded.

"Right. How long have you known the Kenneths?" she continued to question.

"Um … not that long," I responded, glancing at the ground and the carpet in order to avoid her piercing eyes.

Suddenly, she was bent down in front of me, inches away from my face. Her breath was stained with old tea and vanilla cookies, probably from the meal that I interrupted when I knocked. "You look at me when I'm talkin' to ye. You hear me?" she barked. "What you want with 'em?"

She kept her face mere inches from mine, waiting for my response, as if my words were the air she was allowed to breathe. I squirmed on the very padded chair. A few moments passed … then a few more. Neither of us moved an inch during this time; the old woman crouched intently in front of me as I pressed pressing into the backing of the chair I was seated in.

Knock, knock, knock.

The two of us turned and glanced at the closed front door. The knocking was faint and echoed inside the hallway, as if it wasn't on her door but on another door. She slowly raised herself into a standing position, still glancing toward me with eyebrows raised as if she were warning me not to try anything foolish. The old woman slowly wandered to the window that faced the street and flicked aside one of the wooden beams so she could peep through them. The stern gaze slowly melted away to a more pleasing smile as she saw who was standing outside the building. Giving me a wry smirk, she started to walk toward her closed front door.

"I guess we'll just have to ask the Kenneths, then."

She opened her door wide, making sure that the door didn't close behind so I could be visible from the hallway, and shuffled out toward the front door. The sound of the metal beam grinding against the metallic posts caressed the air around where she disappeared. All this was out of view from where I sat. A few clinks and clanks later, the door was open. Air from outside blew in, and the soft glow of light illuminated the hallway slightly.

"Hello, Luv. Good day at the shoppers, then?"

"Hello, Mrs. Roget. How are you doing today?" piped Dawn's voice from the entrance of the home. The sound of rustling and fabric could be heard, and Dawn let loose a quick sigh as she put something on the ground, the weight of the package making a soft thud onto the wooden ground.

Mrs. Roget's harsh whisper scratched the silence once door shut—her attempt at being subtle, I suppose.

"There's a strange lad lookin' for your pap, I wager. He's sittin' in my chair," she explained to Dawn.

There was a brief moment of silence. Dawn's unsure face peeped around the doorframe leading to Mrs. Roget's apartment in order to see who was waiting for her father. Dawn's hand rested against the old wood to help her keep her balance as she snooped around the corner. Seeing her face, I smiled and waved with my good hand, trying my best to seem friendly. Dawn's face scrunched up as one would at smelling a burnt cookie, and she disappeared back into the hallway to lift up her packages.

"What do you want?" she called out from the hallway to me, a point of annoyance in her tone.

Sliding out from the chair, I placed the bag of ice that once rested on my injured hand back in the seat. Slowly, I made my way into the hallway. "I ... um ... I was wondering ..."

A package of groceries suddenly leapt from Mrs. Roget's arms and into mine, a sly smile in her eyes. "Go 'n; make yourself useful, now."

Scrambling to get my arms under and around the bag of food and supplies that was popped into my possession, I stumbled about for a bit. A piece of celery that was sticking out of the bag smacked me in the face as I tried to secure the package from falling. Dawn, giving the bags she was carrying a soft jolt to better rest them in her arms and on her hips, shot past me, not bothering to give me a second glance. I watched her streak past me, the groceries Mrs. Roget forced upon me still crumpled in my arms.

Dawn continued her trek down the hallway, not stopping to see if I kept up with her, her stride strong and sure. Mrs. Roget, still standing in the hallway by the closed door beside me, cleared her throat to get me moving again. With a short jolt, my legs regained movement, and I scuffled to catch up with Dawn. Dawn had put one of the bags of supplies down in order to reach into her front pocket and pull out the key for the door, sliding the metallic instrument into the lock and turning it to a click.

With the door open to allow her entrance, the key still secure inside the locking mechanism, Dawn stepped over the bag on the ground and entered her home. She went about to add some light into the place. I stood firm, staring at Dawn, the bag given to be by Mrs. Roget still clinging to my arms awkwardly. Finally, Dawn turned to me while standing in the hallway that branched off to the different rooms.

"Well? Are you coming in?" she asked rather annoyed.

Bending down quickly to scoop up the bag that Dawn had left behind, I stumbled my way into the place. An orange popped its head out from the top of the bag that was on the ground as I yanked it up and made its way across the floor out toward Dawn, who just shook her head at me and walked out of sight into the dining area. With one bag secure in my arms and the other bag carried loosely in my fingers, I hunched my way into the dining area as well to meet up with Dawn, who had disappeared once more into the kitchen.

I tried to rest the bag that barely clung to my fingers on the table where we'd eaten dinner the night before. Trying to maneuver my eyes around the bag clutched to my chest in order to see the other bag so that I could find the edge of the table, I must have attempted to put it down three times with no success before Dawn banged through the swinging door once more. Seeing my pathetic attempts to put the bags down, she quickly walked over to where I stood and grabbed the loose bag from my hands. Dawn then stormed back out of the room in a huff, leaving me alone in the dining room once more. I stood transfixed on the swinging of the door that led to the kitchen, the swoosh of the air from the door the only thing heard from the whole home.

"Dawn?" I called out questioningly. "Are you mad at me?"

Dawn almost pushed the swinging door off of its hinges, the door creating a rather big bang against the outside wall, when she burst back into the room in response to my question. In her hand was a single carrot, which she waved around the room as she talked, using it as an extended finger or as a dagger as she sparred with me.

"Mad? *Mad!?!* What on *earth* would I have to be mad about? You only threaten my family after pretending to be our friends. You practically attacked my father after saving him from those bullies. And ... and ..."

She glanced around the room in a rushed, flustered state, the carrot in her tight fist shaking as she pointed it at my face. Finally finding what she was looking for, she shot the carrot out toward my feet like she held the power to strike me down with her vegetable. "… and you're tracking dirt over my floor!"

I tried to open my mouth to respond to Dawn's outburst in order to point out that she had yet to take off her shoes as well, but again my tongue would not allow sound to escape. With no response from me, she puffed a huff and tore the bag of food and supplies I was carrying from my arms, turned on her heel, and stomped back through the swinging door leaving me alone in the room once again.

Well this is going well, I mused to myself, letting my arms flop to my sides.

Dawn exploded from the swinging door once more, this time holding a jar of beans. "What are you doing here, anyway? Are you here to arrest us? Huh!"

I opened my mouth to respond. Dawn waved the jar around the room. "Are you here to pick out the things you're going to take with you when we get arrested? Is that it?"

Dawn didn't wait for the response to her question, retreating back into the kitchen, the swinging door flapping behind her as she pushed her way through it.

"Dawn," I called out to her through the flapping of the swinging door.

Dawn appeared back into the dining room, still holding the jar of beans. "You made it very clear last night that you didn't want anything to do with this family, and now here you are—not even half a day later."

"Dawn."

"Was the attack on my dad staged? Was it? Was it set up so you could get in close to my dad, find out where we live, and arrest us all?"

"Dawn."

"And where's your friend? Is he outside with a patrol of POLICE officers waiting for your signal to storm in here and destroy the place, taking everyone off in handcuffs?"

"*Dawn!*"

I grabbed her by both shoulders in order to make her stop buzzing about the room. The quick action caused her to lock eyes with mine. She was taken aback from my directness. Her muscles tightened up under my grip, ready to buck if I tried anything. I took a breath, still keeping my eyes glued with hers as they searched frantically in mine, and calmly relaxed my grip on her. Half leading her to one of the chairs, I eased her into a sitting position, her hands gripping the chair for support. With Dawn finally sitting, I released her and bent down on my haunches to better talk to her. Dawn, leaning away from me, refused to leave my stare, her eyes wide and doe-like.

Quickly brushing my palms across my cheeks and face to help clear my mind, I let out a breath of frustration. "Dawn, will you just shut up and listen for a second? I'm not here to hurt you or your father or to pick out stuff for when you get arrested or anything like that. I'm here—"

I stood up from my crouched position and started to walk away from the seated girl. I stared hard at the floor in front of me and tried to come up with a better way to explain what I was doing. Turning around to look back at the confused and scared young lady, I took a deep breath to help clear out and organize my thoughts.

"Dawn, the reason why ... I want you to understand that ... You see ... I'm here because I ... John and I want you and your family to know that ..."

I turned around again, swearing within at my lack of control over my ability to speak. Raising my hand to my forehead, I rubbed my scalp and closed my eyes softly. "You have to understand where we're coming from," I started to explain.

Dawn, getting up from her chair, slammed the jar of beans still inside her hand down hard onto the table beside her, the thick, chunky, hollow thud of the juicy produce reverberated inside the can.

"I have to understand?" she shot back. "We invited you to our home, Tom! We risked way more than you did!"

I turned around to face Dawn once more, annoyance at being interrupted rising in my voice. "Yeah, I get that. I get the fact that your father put himself on the line by bringing us into the fold, so to speak. But also understand that my best friend—the guy who's closer to me than any brother I could have had—lost someone very close to him yesterday because of you damn Rebells. And then your dad turns around and tells us that we're now going to be associated with these people who killed his lover—that we're going to be working side by side with these murderers ... these—"

The words failed me and trickled away as I realized that this wasn't working. Shaking my hands and head to start over, I started pacing about the room, keeping my attention out toward Dawn.

Dawn folded her arms across her chest. "These ... what?" she asked me in a very dark tone.

"I'm not doing a good job explaining myself," I sputtered out, more to myself than to Dawn.

"I'll say," she smirked.

I noticed that we had somehow managed to get the table between ourselves—myself on one side and Dawn on the other, with her close to the swinging door that led to the kitchen. Leaning over the table and resting my knuckles on the hard finished wood, I smiled at the girl.

"Can we start over here?" I asked.

Dawn, still giving me a wide birth, waved for me to talk. I stood back up and straightened out my shirt. "Okay. I came over here today to talk to William and explain to him that John and I were in a very bad place last night. We might have overreacted a bit, but we were not ready for him to tell us that we were inducted into the Rebells just like that." I snapped my fingers to further emphasize the quickness.

Dawn simply nodded.

"All right." I smiled, happy with how things were now moving along. "Now, for as long as we can remember, we have been told that the organization Le Rebells was evil, that they were terrorists, that they were the scum of the Earth."

Dawn opened her mouth to respond, but I quickly raised my hands to stop her from speaking. "Please, let me finish."

Dawn, slowly and softly, folded her arms back up and stood listening to my explanation. I nodded to her and continued my speech. "Before John and I found out that you and your family were Rebells, we thought you were just a simple group of people who were at the wrong place at the wrong time. Then, we find out that you're all Rebells, and suddenly there's a conflict of interest in our understanding between this kind and loving family and what we've been told day in and day out about the Rebells."

Dawn, listening contently, nodded her head at me.

I continued. "After we left this place, John and I ended up talking, and we stayed up pretty much the entire night."

Dawn leaned her head to the side, her hair swishing from one side of her head to the other. "What did you talk about?"

I smiled at the recent memories. "What *didn't* we talk about? Look … long story short, we're not turning you guys in. Not now, not ever. John wanted me to apologize for his actions last night, but he wasn't ready to look at you people yet in the face. His feelings are still quite raw."

"And what about you, Tom?" came a voice from the entrance of the dining room area.

I turned around to face the voice. William was leaning against one of the walls. He was wearing a simple and casual faded burgundy shirt; the top three buttons were not done up and gave a peek at his white undershirt. His light brown traveling pants, complete with long pockets along the side of the pant legs, showed many days of wear. A satchel hung loosely from a strap in his hands and swung carelessly in the air by his legs. Dawn turned her attention from me to her father and smiled. "Hi, Dad."

William smiled at his daughter and turned his gaze back to me.

CHAPTER 9

"HELLO, WILLIAM," I ACKNOWLEDGED.

William nodded toward me, a strong smile on his face, and wandered into the room. The satchel that he was holding swung heavily as he made his way toward the table and us. The bruises from his beating a few days ago still caused him visible strain as he gave a light grunt while resting his satchel on the table. Something within the satchel make a distinct clunk as it found a resting place against the wooden planks of the table. Opening up the leather and canvas bag, William pulled out a bottle of wine with an image of a house and a large field on the label. Handing the bottle of wine over to Dawn, he instructed her to put it into the kitchen with the other wine bottles. Dawn took the bottle of wine, gave me a quick glance over her shoulder, and wandered back out through the swinging doors. Once Dawn was out of the picture, William's expression grew a bit darker as he focused his attention back to me. He nodded outwards toward the hallway.

"Let's speak in the den, Tom."

William led me back into the den where we had met him yesterday. There was no fire in the fireplace this time, so instead of being greeted by a warm glow, I was introduced to a semidark and cold atmosphere. William walked over to the switch on the side of the wall and gave it a quick flick, turning on the gaslights that hung from the roof of the room. William went to his chair and eased himself into it, the groan of aged wood wheezing under the man's weight as he released himself into the soft cushions. I stood in the room in front of him, unsure as to whether I should sit or stay standing. William readjusted himself in the chair into a more comfortable position and stared hard at me.

"This is a bit of a surprise," he finally said.

I looked around the room nervously. "How so?"

William folded his fingers together so that he was able to rest his chin on his knuckles as he continued to study me from where he sat, his tone calm but questioning. "I figured that last night was the last time we were going to see the two of you. Especially after how you made it very clear to us that you wanted nothing more to do with this family or the organization. What was it you said? 'We don't know you, and you don't know us.' Was that right?"

"Yeah ... about that. Ummm."

William leaned out toward me, motioning for me to take the chair directly across from him. "Why are you here, Tom?"

I walked calmly over to the chair but stood behind it instead of sitting down. Leaning hard against the back brace of the chair, I stared down at William. "John and I ... well, mostly John ... he ... well ..."

This was not going at all how I had planned it. For some odd reason, it was harder than I had imagined. How do you put into words the thoughts and feelings that John had been forced to face and put up with in the past two days? All the misery, the aggravation, and the death that was caused by a group that this sweet family had to be a part of?

William leaned back into his chair. His tone lowered and grew a bit more concerned. "So, how is your friend?"

I started to pace the room, choking back what I really wanted to say to the man about the state of John. "He ... he's going to be okay, I guess. He was just really shaken up with the whole ordeal. He should be all right, but he's going to need some time to grieve and all."

William nodded his head. "Of course. Losing someone that you love is always a hard thing to deal with. In truth, you never really heal. It's always there with you."

I stopped my pacing and looked over at William. The shadows from the lights above us gave off deep, dark shadows on the man's face, making him look very old and tired. "Could you tell John for me that I *am* sorry for his loss."

I nodded to the request. At that, William got up and turned to his bookcase. As he brushed his fingers along the spines of the multicolored covers of his books, he talked over his shoulder to me. "Before you left, you told me to use my connections to find out who caused the explosion. 'You now owe us,' is what you said. At first, I was just going to warn everyone to blacklist you and pretend that I knew nothing of the Rebells in case you decided to throw me to the wolves. I thought, 'How dare this punk come into my home and do this to me? I open my arms up to this boy, and this is how he repays me? I presented him my home and an open hand, showing that we're his allies since the POLICE will now be hunting him when they find out it was him that aided me.'

"But today, as I was getting that bottle from my sources to replenish my stock, I spent some time asking around for information about the Factory explosion: who did it, how they did it, why they did it. More so for curiosity than to pay back an imaginary debt that you put on our heads. You know what I found out, Tom?"

He turned around and faced me once more, leaning against the bookcase. "No one had a clue as to what happened up there. Not one rumor, not one fact. That got me thinking. Something that big must have been planned out months in advance, blueprints had to have been designed, favors pulled in, supplies bought. You can't keep something that big so tightly wound that nothing was mentioned to anyone—even Rebell to Rebell. If anything, there should have been a general warning in the area to avoid the Factory at the time of the explosion. There was nothing, Tom. That means only one thing. The Rebells had nothing to do with the destruction of the Factory."

I took everything in. The Rebells had nothing to do with it? Then what ... how ... but the Factory? The POLICE's analysis of the explosion— there's no way that it was just an accident, a freak moment of fate. John would never accept that. He would need someone to blame for the Factory. If there was no one, then he would find someone even if they didn't actually participate in its destruction. I sighed loudly as I tried to come to terms to this discovery.

"Sorry to be the bearer of bad news, Tom," William scoffed sarcastically as he returned his attention back to the books behind him, tossing his back to me. He continued over the side of his shoulder, his eyes searching the shelves for some sort of mystery selection.

"You must really think that the Rebells are monsters, don't you? That there was no other reason for that place to go up, never mind all the explosive material that was stored haphazardly inside that rotting building. No, it *had* to be the Rebells. If there's a shortage in water, it must be the Rebells! Ran out of bread at the market? Rebells! Snowing? Gotta be the Rebells!"

I raised my arm to stop the man. "Okay, you made your point."

William turned around quickly, a fire churning in his eyes, a single book latched inside his hand. "No, I don't think I have, Tom. The Rebells are not the monsters here. The POLICE are! The POLICE have always been the monsters. The masses just don't realize it. They either don't remember how things once were or never knew what life was like before the POLICE seized power. That's where the Rebells come in—to remind them what we lost. We just want to live how our ancestors lived—free of depression, free from oppression, to live in a proper democratic society. And the more we strive to bring back those days, the harder we have to fight for those ideals. It's not like we want to do what we do. It's a matter of looking at the two evils and figuring out what's worse."

"Dad? Are you okay?" Dawn stood at the door, a pitcher of water in her hands. She looked in at the two of us with a worried look on her face, the corners of her mouth turning and twisting with concern. William, seeing Dawn, relaxed his stance. He glanced down at the bundle of collected papers and half-smirked at himself. "Listen to me. For a moment, I sounded just like Duncan."

Dawn nodded her head at her father in agreement, her hair bouncing in the light that cascaded from the room. I, on the other hand, stood puzzled at the remark. I know that name—Duncan. The name buzzed around in my brain. Where had I heard that name before?

Dawn looked down at the pitcher of water in her hands, remembering the reason why she came into the room. Walking quietly, her feet barely touching the ground, she put the container down on the side table, turned, and left. William returned his focus back to me, leaning back against the bookcase. He folded his arms together slowly.

"Tom, can you read?" he asked me.

I looked from William to the bookcase directly behind him, the tomes resting in silent judgment against me. "Kind of. I could read most of the things that were given to me when I worked in the Factory, but there are still some things that I have trouble with."

William softly pitched the book that he was holding; the pages ruffled quickly and tried to take flight in the air as it soared toward me. I cupped my hands outward to catch the wounded bird that fluttered awkwardly in the air. The book thumped in my hands, the pages slowly coming to a rest from the hectic travel. I looked at the thing that sat in my grip, not sure exactly what I was supposed to do with it. The cover was hardened paper, well worn and used. The corners of the cover were torn away from years of abuse, lost to the ravages of time. The words written in it were soft and faded, the pages smelling of age.

William gestured toward the book he threw me. "What does it say?"

"Pardon?"

"The title. What's the title of it?"

I turned the book over so I could see the front cover. On the cover there was an image of a pig with a windmill off in the background. An angry-looking chicken looked off into the distance in the corner by the spine of the book; the other top corner was long gone. The total presentation was almost childish in its manner. Why would William have a child's book in with his works of art? I shot William a glance under my tilted brow signaling the unasked question to him. William just brushed off my inquiry and waited for me to respond. I returned my focus onto the title of the book. The letters were easy enough to read, and yet, they were in the wrong order. The words were gibberish. I flipped the book over to see if my eyes were just playing tricks on me. Lo and behold, all the words that were written on the back were also out of order and all over the place. The pages inside revealed more and more of this backward language.

"I … I can't," I said finally, a defeated tone to my voice.

William gave himself a slight heave off of the bookcase and walked back to his chair, collapsing into its embrace. "I'm not surprised," he added as he adjusted himself to a more comfortable position. "It's written in English."

English?

"What does it say?" I asked him, holding out the mysterious edition.

"It's called *Farm*. At least, that's what it says on what's left of the cover. The full title, the author … who knows."

I looked the book over, quickly brushing the pages with my thumb in a stream of words and paper. "So … what's it about?"

William smiled at my question. "It's about a group of farm animals that overthrow their tyrannical farmer. They take over the farm, and for a while, things are good. Unfortunately, it slowly falls back into the state that it first was in—under a tyrannical rule. The reason this happened is simple: the animals were raised inside that style of environment. And when they were given true freedom, they didn't know how to properly wield it. That eventually led to their downfall. One animal took power over the others, that power grew, and then in a blink of an eye—tyrannical rule. This is why it's so important to bring back the old ways that existed before the war before it's too late. Soon, very soon, there won't be anyone around who remembers how things were before the POLICE took over. There won't be anyone around to instruct us on how to live with true freedom—with democracy. Soon they'll be gone, and all we will have left is the POLICE."

I looked from the book in my hands to William, who was sitting forward in his chair to speak more directly to me. "But what was so great about the old ways that they need to be brought back? I mean, this was one of the main reasons there was the war, wasn't it? The old ways weren't working, so the POLICE stepped in and made things better."

William waved around the room to help demonstrate his point, an exasperated tone in his voice. "You call *this* better? Look around you, Tom. We're literally hiding in a basement so that the POLICE can't hear us talking about stuff that we're not supposed to. When you walk the streets, do you not smell the fear in the air? They don't want anyone educated on things that happened before the war, because they're afraid that people will see how they're treated now versus how they used to live. The farm would revolt against them. The Rebells have been trying to educate everyone as much as they have been trying to stop the future progression of the POLICE. In some ways, we've been successful. Others, we haven't. But the point is that we at least try. We try to do what is right. I'd figured you would understand that."

With the book still in hand, I moved around the chair I had been leaning against and plunked myself on the cushions. "Understand? Understand what?" I questioned.

"Well, for example," William smirked as he reached over to the pitcher of water to get himself a glass, "you and John came to my aid against that brute. Without thinking of consequence. Without concerning yourself with the reason why he was coming after my family and me. You saw someone who was in trouble, and you reacted. You did the right thing; you helped someone in need. Ninety-nine percent of the populace wouldn't have done that, Tom. They're buried in their fear and doubt, because that's how the POLICE like it. Because of the POLICE, they would have ignored my plight and just kept on walking, head down, looking at their feet. That's why I invited you here in the first place, Tom. Because I knew that there was hope with you. Because I knew that you would listen to what I had to say and that you would keep an open mind. And, with the proper education, you might be able to help us again. I thought I explained all this last night."

As I leaned back into the chair at the weight of the words, I could also feel the weight of the world press down against me. I still had doubts about it all, but this time around, it made a little more sense somehow. "You seriously want me to join the Rebells?"

William smiled and shook his head. "You're one already, Tom. You just don't realize it yet."

I sighed out loud. "Yeah, yeah, yeah, so you've tried to tell me."

I suddenly stopped and jerked my head up out of the fog I was in. William said that I needed the proper education to understand why the

POLICE were wrong. What was so incorrect with the education I had received through the public schooling? What was it that they were not telling me?

"Wait a minute. What type of education? And how will this new information help you out? What are you going to do? Train me to become some sort of assassin for Le Rebells?"

William leaned back and laughed. "Is that what you think? That we're going to stick you up to a machine and just pump in a bunch of information into your head against your will? Or send you off to some secret training camp and turn you into a hit man?"

I shrugged sheepishly at the question. How was I supposed to know what he meant by education?

William pointed to the book still in my hands. "That book. It's written in English. You've probably never even heard of that language. Odds are there aren't that many people left who openly speak that language. But, once upon a time, English was spoken all over the world. More importantly, it was the major language of the people who once lived across the sea. These people strived to live their lives through the concept of democracy. Democracy meant that the people *chose* the leader of their government and that he or she was responsible to represent *their* wants and needs."

My hands fluttered in front of me in an attempt to stop the speech for a moment. "Wait, wait. What island across the sea? There's no island across the sea. There's nothing across the sea—just the other side of the country."

The sigh that escaped from William sounded like an air vent that had sprung a low leak. Once again, the weight of the world seemed to sit heavily with him. He got up and slowly walked over to where I sat. With a simple gesture, he reached out and took back the book that had rested in my hands for so long. As he made the small trek back to the bookshelf to return the paper tomb back to its home, he spoke to me over his shoulder. "I knew that the POLICE had doctored the education of the young in order to wipe out the world that existed before the war, but I didn't realize how far off the education system was until now. This is going to take some time."

William took a second and brushed his hands across the row of books that were in front of him. With a nod, as if agreeing to whatever argument was going on inside his head, he turned around and gazed back down at where I sat. "Okay, here's what I would like you to do. When you can, I want you to come by, and we will start your *real* education. Dawn," William quickly nodded toward the entrance of the den, where Dawn was leaning against the door frame listening to our conversation. I hadn't noticed she was there.

William continued. "… and I will teach you the *true* history of the world. I'm talking about what went on prewar and beyond—the stuff that you missed out on. We will also teach you to read these books. That means learning French, English, Spanish—the other languages that used to exist in the world prior to the POLICE taking over and making German the one and only language. This is going to take a very long time, Tom. Most importantly, everything that you do here or learn here, you can't tell anyone about. Not even John. That means you're going to have to start coming up with excuses, lying, whatever it takes. Are you willing to give it a go?"

I thought hard for a second at the question. "John isn't allowed to come?"

William shook his head. "Having the both of you here would raise too many questions. We can probably get away with just you. Both, doubtful. Besides, he's … not ready yet. You said it yourself. He knows it, and so do we."

I got up from the chair. There was a strange energy inside the room that I couldn't put my finger on. It was kind of a mixture of hope and fear—like a guy would feel just before talking to a girl he liked for the first time, but not quite. I looked from Dawn, hair coming down in soft steams beside her face and smiling in a friendly manner, to William, who was back to leaning against the bookcase and awaiting my answer.

I stuck out my hand for William to take and shook.

"All right. I'm in."

CHAPTER 10

... With a handshake, I sealed my fate with William, Sherry, and Dawn. During the next few days, prior to the start of the repair of the Factory, I visited William's home and continued my education. During those visits, I spent my time evenly between the three: Dawn and Sherry worked with me on the reading and writing of English, so I could read that Farm book on my own, while William and I relived real history. My five years of public education never taught me anything about the Americas, freedom and slavery, that there was a World War I and II, not to mention what the POLICE really did during the last war.

"The POLICE did what?" I asked William.

William sat across from me in his chair and simply shrugged at my surprise, as if this was common knowledge. "The POLICE didn't take too kindly to prisoners during the war," he explained. "And there was nowhere to put them, really. Any prison would have been an immediate target for commandeering, and the POLICE had neither the manpower nor the time to bother with it. The commanders often used the excuse that the prisoners were 'misguided' and that they simply needed to be 'reprogrammed to better serve society,' which of course would take a very long time. They did this in order to ease the conscience of the populace and not have them turn against the POLICE when the parade of prisoners entered huge warehouses and never came out."

I leaned forward in my seat I, putting my upper body weight on my arms and legs. "So what exactly was this 'reprogramming'?"

A deep voice from behind my chair roared to life. "They dragged them into buildings with massive furnaces in them, shot the prisoners' brains out, then tossed the bodies into the fires—alive or dead. There was usually a lot of pain in the process, I heard."

William, looking up at the owner of the mystery voice behind me, shot a wry smile at the stranger. I tried to swivel around so I could see past the backing and glance at whoever was speaking. A single man stood against the far wall of the den, hiding contently in the shadows that were created from the chairs and the fire. The shade barely made the figure visible, but I could pick out the main features: tall, powerful, I'd say in his fifties with dark hair tied back into a ponytail. He was well dressed, wearing a tight-fitting shirt, work pants, a dark-colored vest, and boots that showed off a world of walking. By his side, a rather large knife hilt was visible.

"Please, come in! Welcome," William addressed the man warmly.

The man took powerful strides into the room and stood in front of William, who got up to address him. After a quick handshake, the man shot me a steely glance out from the corner of his eye and gave a gentle nod in my direction to William. William, resting a hand on the shoulder of the man, turned him in my direction and gestured with his free hand as if he was presenting a prized piece of art to me.

"Tom, allow me to introduce you to Duncan. He's going to be staying with me for a couple days."

Duncan gave me a good, hard stare and nodded his greeting to me. The gaze that came off the towering goliath made me wither into the chair ever so slightly. He just radiated power—almost like that of the sergeant when I first met him at the Factory. William continued his introduction. "He—how best to put it—helped establish the Rebells in this section of the world."

Duncan shot William a quick glance, as if he just called him something inappropriate. "You helped," Duncan pointed out, a hint of disappointment in his voice at not adding that important piece of information.

William merely shrugged playfully at the comment and returned his attention to the task at hand. "Perhaps you would like to take over for me for a second with Tom as I get some refreshments for us all, Duncan?"

Duncan took a quick pause and smirked. "I wouldn't know where to begin."

Was I just insulted?

William wandered past me on the way to the kitchen and gave me a reassuring pat on the shoulder. Once William was out of view, Duncan folded his arms and stared down at my sitting form. The silence between the two of us was deafening. He bore down on me from his standing presence. I couldn't look away. Duncan, after a long time, finally spoke. "So, you're the kid who helped them out with that SIT, huh?"

His stare was like a jackhammer. I looked away for the briefest moment, not being able to take his eyes any longer. That was a mistake apparently, because Duncan was quick to jerk his head down to my exact level, staring again into my eyes. His hunched body was mere inches away from me, which caused me to jerk back into the chair a bit. Duncan's eyes were wide and searching, looking for some style of deception or hint of suspicion.

"When someone asks you a question, it's only polite that you look at them when you answer and answer right away. If you don't, it makes the other person think that you're hiding something. You're not hiding something, are you?"

Duncan's eyebrow rose by a mere hair as he asked me his question, almost as if he was daring me to lie right to his face. I had no reason to be nervous, but for some odd reason, Duncan just made me uneasy.

"No, sir," I answered simply.

Duncan slowly released his gaze and returned to his standing position in front of me, arms still crossed across his overbearing chest. The knife that rested in its hilt on his side made a single clink against a piece of metal on his belt. "I've known William and his family for a very long time. I'd hate for anything to happen to them."

Duncan's voice was low and quiet, but every word was poignant and emphasized. Somehow I got the impression that the last statement was more of a warning than anything else. I cleared the lump that was building in my throat and took a reassuring breath. "Mr. Duncan, sir. I have absolutely no desire to put them in harm's way."

Duncan thought for a second and then grunted once as he took over William's chair facing me, adjusting his knife so it wasn't uncomfortable by his side. I got the impression that this was a natural reflex for the older man, showing off just how long he had been at war with the POLICE.

"Well, kid, you sure got the wool pulled over their eyes. Me ... I'm not that trusting. You understand, of course, if I do a little looking into you—see if you're on the up-and-up."

I stayed on track with my defensive demeanor. "I've got nothing to hide."

Duncan nodded, a small smirk escaping from his stern gaze. "Good. This will make things easy, then."

We watched each other for a moment; I studied Duncan, and he studied me. His immediate intimidation on me faded into a contest to see which one of us would buckle first. Duncan casually looked around the room, taking in the comfortable environment as he tried to settle into the role given to him by William.

"So, what has the old man told you so far in regards to the whole fiasco that's been going on? Wait, let me guess. The masses are just 'misguided,' and it's up to the Rebells 'to tell the truth about the POLICE so that they can make their own decisions and figure out which path to follow: the POLICE or Le Rebells.' That sound about right?"

I nodded. Duncan, lost in his own world, smiled at William's attempt at trying to educate me. "Like a broken parrot," he mused quietly.

At this, Duncan leaned forward in the chair and waved me closer, giving the door to the den a quick glance to see if William was coming back anytime soon. I gave my own glance to the door and leaned forward, curious to hear what Duncan was so afraid William might hear.

"All right, kid," Duncan started off, his voice softer than before, "if he wants me to give you an education, then that's what I'm going to do. I'm going to give you a dose of reality. I've been friends with William for years. He's a good guy—a smart guy. Would trust him watching my back for any mission. But he likes to sugarcoat things. He's a bit of a dreamer on one aspect. William, for all his strengths, somehow thinks that the regular person can still choose which side to be on. Well, he's wrong. They can't choose! They're sheep. They're cattle. They can't think for themselves! That's your common man—so brainwashed by that POLICE regalia that he can't put a single original thought into his mush up here!

"Me, I've been on the front lines for a long time. I've seen the POLICE at their worst. I know better, and you should too. The POLICE aren't going to change. As far as they're concerned, they won the war a long time ago; we're just a couple of cockroaches that need to be stepped on. *That's* where their weakness is, kid: overconfidence. The Rebells have been exploiting it for years, but they're starting to catch up to us."

Duncan slowly leaned back into the chair, his gaze lost in his vision of the future. "We need to get a break—something that will really put a dent in the confidence of the POLICE. Something … big."

I was about to point out that the destruction of the Factory was fairly important when William reentered the room and looked at Duncan in his chair, a hint of mild annoyance in his stare.

"Comfy?" he teased his old friend.

Duncan readjusted himself in the chair in a rather flamboyant presentation and smiled up at William. "Yes, I am. Thank you," he teased back.

William put down the tray and three drinks on the small table that rested beside his chair and started handing out the steaming liquid to each of us. The smell of a strong, bitter mixture wafted past my nose as I took my drink. William, looking around the room briefly to see where he would sit, blew into his cup to cool down the concoction. With a sigh admitting defeat, he resorted to leaning against the bookcase as the lesson progressed.

"So," he started up, taking a brief sip from his cup, "where did we leave off?"

"You were explaining about the prisoners during the war and how they were treated," I answered.

William mumbled quietly as he tried to remember the point he was trying to get across. As the lesson went on, I listened contently, absorbing the information that sprouted from the man's lips. William described in explicit detail things that I never imagined possible. Duncan nodded his head in agreement now and then to the information and facts that William presented. He even corrected William on the occasion, which usually led to a brief argument over the facts, with neither side wanting to lose ground over the matter. Whenever I looked over at Duncan, I noticed he was watching me the entire time the lesson went on.

~

It was getting close to dinnertime, which meant it was time for me to go home.

"Good-bye, William. May I come back tomorrow?" I asked him as I was just about to head out the back door.

"Not tomorrow, Tom. Duncan and I will be … working."

The two men could see that I was a little shocked and a little disappointed at the news. *Working on what?* I wondered to myself.

"You can stop by if you want," offered Duncan, "but *not* before three in the afternoon. We can't stop his education now, William. It wouldn't be fair to him. Not when there's so much to teach him. Besides, I'm here for a good week. There will be plenty of time for … work."

With a quick glance outside the metal door to see if anyone was in the alley, I waved good-bye to the two gentlemen and headed home. As I walked down the now somewhat familiar path, I shot a glance upward at the sky. The sun was still shining, but it was late enough in the afternoon that the warm rays of light were too high up on the buildings surrounding me to even attempt to bask in it.

The walk home from William's gave me a chance to properly think about what I was doing over there and what I had learned. With Duncan coming over today, we spent more time talking about the old days, rather than splitting my time up between the other languages and history.

Based on what William had told me about the war, I could understand how some people didn't trust the POLICE fully. But with Duncan—well, he was programmed to hate the POLICE. From what I'd heard through rumor, hearsay, and the lessons I'd learned, Duncan's entire family had been a part of Le Rebells since they had started.

His grandfather was a part of the French division of the United Nations and had fought and died in the war. After his death, Duncan's father had taken over the reins and formulated the whole Rebells against the POLICE, right there in La Tower. When Duncan was old enough, his father sent him all over the place, trying to organize little factions in every town he could find. In essence, they were doing exactly what the POLICE did when they were first starting out. There was even a rumor that he cut off the head of a high-ranking officer with his knife. Seeing the knife up close, I could believe it.

But what kind of person does that environment raise? I asked myself. Knowing nothing but hate, nothing but mistrust. Looking out at everyone as some sort of possible enemy. Never knowing if the person you're talking to will betray you when things get too intense. Trying to get a single foothold against a very slippery slope, desperate to start something that will hopefully blossom into an organization that could attempt some sort of rebellion against the power on hand. Does this world even have room for friends?

With my eyes lowered and my thoughts lost inside my head, I barely realized that I was almost back at my place. A few more turns and a hop across one or two alleys, and—boom—I'd be back at home. I wondered if I should stop by John's and see how he was doing. After all, he would be going back to the Factory soon to start the repairs, while I—

Oh no.

My feet stopped in the dirt as if hands were reaching out from under me and grabbing hold of them. A cold shiver ran through my spine. How could I have been so forgetful?! The Factory … the POLICE … the sergeant … the recruitment. I was supposed to start my POLICE Soldier In Training work tomorrow. That's what the sergeant had said. When everyone else was fixing the Factory, I was to report to the POLICE Grounds and become a SIT. How could I possibly do that after everything

I have learned from William and the others? How could I willfully go there? *Because if I don't, I'm dead. That's why,* came the answer to my own question, smacking me point-blank in my forehead in order to get through the empty void between my ears.

The tread stuck on the bottom of my shoes started to give way, and my trek toward my shelter began again. The playful musing of Duncan was long gone now, replaced with worry and regret. What if the POLICE found out about what I had been doing with William and his family? A small puff of dust rose with every heavy thump of my feet as they moved my deadened body toward home. As I was about to turn the last corner and escape from the alley, a simple thought crept into my mind. A single ray of hope broke through the fog and gave me the briefest glimpse of release. *Maybe the sergeant was just trying to get under my skin,* I mused. *After all, I embarrassed him in front of the other officers. Right? He was just trying to come up with an excuse to punish me—to scare me. You can't really change a person's age in order to make them train as a SIT. I'm still sixteen! I'm not old enough to start.*

With a sigh that erased all my worry and doubt from my ragged form, I exited the alley and made my way home with a renewed vigor, safe with the knowledge that I was in the clear. As I headed to the shelter, I started to whistle a little tune that popped into my head.

"Stop!"

I froze in my tracks, the song that had been momentarily floating alongside me now gone. I slowly turned to see who it was that shouted the order, not recognizing the voice offhand. There behind me stood two POLICE officers, complete in proper uniform: dark gray shirt with shiny buttons, a strong leather belt holding a nightstick to one side, black pants with a red stripe down the outside of the legs, and black gloves with the POLICE symbol on the back of them. The major difference between the standard POLICE officer and these two was that they were wearing boots normally worn for riots—heavy and spike-riveted along the front toes. One of the officers was leaning against a wall, while the other one was standing out in the street and was pointing directly at me.

"Can I help you?" I asked politely, not sure what else to say to them.

The one against the wall eased himself up and started walking toward me; the other officer stood firm, hand slowly reaching out toward his nightstick as a precaution. The officer who walked toward me looked a little annoyed for some reason, his eyebrows scowling over his dark, weathered eyes. Before he reached where I stood, he nodded out toward me.

"You Haroldson?" he snapped.

I felt the eyes of everyone standing around the area watching me with great intent, both with curiosity to hear what I had done to deem the POLICE presence and fear over what they might do. I quickly adjusted my clothing, not sure what to do with my hands and desperate not to show off their nervousness.

"Um ... yeah," I replied.

The officer finally reached where I was standing. He was taller than I was but not by much. Even still, he easily outweighed me with sheer muscle that could be seen through the shirt. His skin was tight and well tanned, obviously used to being out in the sun. The bars on his broad, strong shoulders showed off that he was a private first class—one stripe up, one stripe down. He hooked his thumbs into his belt, the nightstick jostling slightly with the jarring movement. The officer gave me the once-over with his eyes. He gave a simple grunt to clear his throat.

"You know you've kept us waiting for a good hour?" he asked.

"Uh. I'm ... sorry?" I stuttered.

The officer, scoffing at my reply, turned around and gave the other officer standing in the middle of the street a quick nod. The other officer kicked at the ground a bit, clearing off something on his boot, and started walking to where the two of us stood. The officer in front of me returned his attention to where I was, giving the street behind me a general stab in the air with his thumb that he managed to pry out from behind his belt.

"The first sergeant wants to see you."

CHAPTER 11

THE SERGEANT STOOD BY THE entrance to the Factory, going over a clipboard that another officer was holding out in front of him. The officers working around the area didn't give me any notice. They were too busy finishing up their tasks and cleaning up the workspace they were assigned to. I walked up the path to the E-way of the Factory, right where the sergeant was standing, both POLICE officers that came for me on either side. The sergeant, hearing someone walking toward him, gave a quick shot out the corner of his eye to see who it was. Seeing the three of us, he gave the papers on the clipboard a quick scribble with the pen he was holding and shoved the clipboard back toward the officer who was holding it. As we got closer, he stretched his back a bit and calmly waited for the three of us to reach where he stood.

The officer whom I was talking to in the street gave a sharp salute to the sergeant, who saluted back. "Sir, I present Haroldson, as ordered, sir," the officer barked to his commander.

The sergeant simply nodded to the officer, giving them the impression that they were dismissed, and looked down at me with a disapproving glare. "I sent those officers over an hour ago to come and get you."

I opened my mouth to answer but then thought it better not to say anything. The sergeant clicked his tongue and softly shook his head. "Now, since an officer is trained to obey a commanding officer's order to his fullest and to complete that order as quickly as humanly possible, I can only assume that the fault is not with my men. Am I correct in that assumption?"

His eyebrows rose playfully at his question, daring me to answer him. I said nothing. The two officers who had escorted me were now gone. It was just the sergeant and me. Everyone else was either working far away from us or purposefully not trying to give us any attention.

The sergeant simply shrugged. "Nothing to say, eh?"

Turning on his heel, he started walking away from me toward the outer rim of the area. After a few steps, he turned around to see if I was walking beside him. "You coming?" he offered.

Not sure exactly what was going on, I skipped up to where he was standing, and the two of us started making a slow pace around the area of the Factory. Looking from his men working to me walking beside him, he smiled to himself. "Last time you were here, you were definitely more talkative. I guess that bit of running you did sealed in some manners," he mused as he reached into his coat pocket and pulled out a cigar and a lighter.

I nodded, again not risking saying anything too conspicuous or upsetting the man. He put the rolled cigar to his lips, and with a casual flick of his fingers, a flame roared to life from the small metal box he pulled out of another pocket. His face was half-covered with a mist of sweet-smelling smoke as he puffed on the cigar to keep the flame alive. Giving the burning coals at the end of it a soft blow, tiny embers flew off the burning tube from the light wind that escaped from his lungs.

The sergeant, content with the state of his cigar, put it back into the corner of his mouth so that he could both puff away and talk.

"You have that friend who lost his fiancé in this ... debacle, right? How's he doing?" he asked.

There was a sense of calmness to his voice, quite unlike the last time we'd met. There was even a tone of sorrow and pity. The sergeant stopped walking and waited for my reply, looking down at me through the haze between puffs on his cigar.

I paused as I thought long and hard about what I was about to say. "He's still broken up about her death, but with enough time to grieve, I'm sure he'll be okay."

The sergeant nodded at my reply and continued his trek along the outskirts of the Factory's gate. I followed alongside him. His gaze was now locked firmly on the horizon, as if he were trying to see something off in the distance that only he could see. "Based on the overseer's reports before the … incident, your friend's work habits were starting to slip a bit. It seems that there was something that was making him lose focus. I can't say exactly what was causing this based on the man's scribbles. Perhaps you could shed some light on the subject?"

I looked up at the man, a swell slowly growing in my throat that caused me to gulp hard. *Did he consider John a suspect with the Factory?* I wondered as we walked. What evidence could there be besides the fact that he was starting to slow down a bit? There could be any number of reasons why—increased workload, planning his marriage—it could be anything. Was it because he attacked that officer?

I stumbled and stuttered, trying to come up with a believable answer. The sergeant, after I stumbled over a few words, held up a hand in my direction.

"You can stop now," he said. "If you don't know, then you don't know. Admit it and move on. Don't bother trying to come up with an excuse; it just weakens your position. I'd rather get a firm yes or no to a question, no matter what it might be about. One of the things that I can't stand is to be lied to by my officers. It's degrading to both you *and* me."

I looked away toward the city in the distance. The sun was close to setting, giving the shelters that dotted the distance a soft glow of yellows, reds, and orange.

The sergeant continued. "The point I was trying to make was that, with the investigation finishing up, the repairs would be starting up tomorrow. He will be expected to show up and help out with the work. If his work habits continue to slip from where they once were, no matter what the reason, he would be let go. If he's let go, despite the fact that his now-founded grief might be aiding to his downfall, I seriously doubt he would be rehired anywhere for quite some time. That could prove … disappointing to your friend."

The sergeant took a long pull from the cigar and let the smoke roll off his tongue; the steaming stream of fumes strolled out of his mouth into the open air. "I can't remember if you told me or not. Where were you that my men had to wait?" he asked me, giving me a knowing sideways glance.

"I was at John's place—my friend we were just talking about. He wasn't home, so I waited outside for a while for him to get home. When he never showed up, I came back to my place," I half-lied. I was going to go to see John after coming come from William's—eventually.

He paused for a second, then gave the Factory beside us a quick glance to check on the status of the officers still working. Most were either getting ready to leave or had left the area already. He turned back toward me. "Well then, let's go see John. By the looks of things, we're just wrapping up here. Perhaps *he* can explain why his work habits were recently going south."

"Uh … sure." I smiled.

He started walking toward the road that leads off to the town. Suddenly, he stopped and turned toward me. "Coming?"

I was about to interject and say something like John still wasn't home or anything to stop the man, but I knew that it would just get me into deeper trouble. With a nod, I started walking out toward the sergeant and off to where John lived. When I got to where the sergeant was standing, he waved for me to lead.

"Take me to him," he gestured out in front of him.

The two of us walked in silence until we left the Factory grounds, me leading the first sergeant to my best friend's home. A pit in my stomach grew with every agonizing step. I felt like I was going to throw up. I carefully checked behind me to see where the sergeant was in relation to me. He was just off to the side, but what unnerved me was that he wasn't watching where we were going. Rather, he was staring directly at me, looking for something.

Why is he looking at me like that? I asked myself. *Does he suspect that I just came from a Rebell's house? How could he tell? Does he think I'm lying? Is that why we were really going to John's place?*

"So, enjoying your little holiday from work?" he asked, again the playfulness from before could be detected in his voice.

I slowed a bit so that he was walking beside me once again. "Um ... sure. It's giving me time to learn about ... new ... things."

I quickly looked away from the man, scrunching up my eyes and swearing at myself internally. *Why did I say that? Why?!*

The sergeant looked over at me with interest. "Such as?"

Think, damn it, Tom! Think!

"Numbers! I work in the accounting section. I'm learning about new number figures from a tutor. That way, when I start working again, I can do my work better and more quickly," I blurted out, my answer sounding a little too desperate for my own taste.

He looked from me to the path we were walking. "Smart lad," he clicked, puffing away on his cigar.

You don't know the half of it, I mused to myself.

The sergeant cleared his throat a bit, getting my attention once again. "Do you know why I wanted to see you today, Haroldson?"

"No, sir."

"I wanted to talk to you a bit more about that tip you gave us the last time I met with you. You *do* remember that, don't you?" He spoke as if to hint strongly to me to think long and hard about that particular point in time.

My legs sure do, I mused. I nodded my head to confirm that I did.

"Well, for the past few days, we've been piecing together what went on at the Factory before, during, and after the incident. We've been sifting through everything—every brick, piece of plaster—trying to figure out if it was simply an accident, or ... something more." He said that last part with strong hesitation and distrust, like he wanted to say something else but chose not to at the last second.

"When you told us about the main secretary, I handed it over to one of the other officers to look into further. You want to know what he found?"

"Sure," I said simply, trying to pass off simple interest. I didn't want to seem too eager in case it was bad news and the whole effort would blow up in my face.

The sergeant paused before speaking, purposefully drawing it out. He was enjoying this little game.

"You were right to be suspicious of her," he finally pointed out.

I half-turned my head to look at the sergeant, who was looking back at me.

"That's all I can say officially, you understand," he explained.

I nodded, still unsure what he was driving at.

"Still, despite all that," the sergeant went on, more to himself than to me, "there are too many unanswered questions about what really happened up there. Nothing we can pinpoint with hard evidence.

"But that's not the point of why I called for you. I called for you because you were the only one, despite all the manpower I had pouring over the books and asking questions, the *only* one that picked up on her leaving for lunch on that day."

As we talked, I started to veer off the street to make our way through one of the alleys. I wanted this little adventure to end as soon as possible, and if we had to cut through a few alleys, so be it. Also, I didn't really want anyone to see me walking with the sergeant. What if someone saw us together—someone who *shouldn't* see us together—and it got back to William. How would I explain that one? A turn of a corner here, a turn of the corner there, and the two of us entered the open area where Vans and I had the fight—the one when I saved William, Sherry, and Dawn. This was the first time I'd come back to that place since the fight. When we entered the area, the sergeant stopped walking suddenly and looked around the area, as if trying to remember something. I mentally pleaded with him to continue walking.

"Have you heard about what happened here?" he asked me without looking toward me, more like he was asking himself in order to remember whatever it was on the tip of his brain. His eyes scanned the area ferociously, picking out every detail and replaying some hidden image out in front of him. Before I could reply, his eyes grew wide. He turned his head toward me slowly. "Wait a minute. What's your full name again?"

"Tom ... Thomas Haroldson."

Uh oh!

He turned to face me, staring into my eyes the entire time. I was locked in the embrace of his gaze. I could see the pieces fall into place inside his head. The answer slowly materialized as he realized who I was. He snapped his fingers, the final piece clicking into place with the soft repeating of my name. "That's what has been bugging me about you. That's why your name sounded so familiar. It was *you*, wasn't it? You and your friend were the ones that attacked that SIT … ummm … oh, what was his name? Vans Braun. You gave him that scar?"

At that moment, my imagination took over. I could feel the bars of the cell where I would be spending the rest of my life closing in around me. I was going to be sentenced to die in one of those cells. I was going to die by one of those POLICE toys that killed the other prisoners during the war, just like Duncan said. I was going to be tied up against a pole, and Vans would be allowed to take his revenge out on me.

The sergeant walked straight over to where I stood, his hand outstretched to grab me from running. *This is it!* I thought. *I'm doomed!*

With his outstretched hand, the sergeant grabbed hold of my hand and started shaking it. "It's about time someone stood up to that *sardelle!*"

The sudden shaking of my hand slowly pulled me back into reality. "Pardon?"

"That boy is nothing but trouble. Always has been. Acting like he's big stuff 'n all. Just because he's in good with a few of the local officers and just started his training as a SIT, he thinks that he can get away with anything. You have no idea how many complaints I've gotten over that one trainee and the shenanigans he's done. Humph. I'm surprised that it took *this* long for someone to smack him good."

The sergeant, suddenly realizing what he was saying, paused and leaned forward so that I could hear him better. "I never said that. You never heard me say that, and I'll deny ever saying that," he chuckled.

Leaning back to a standing position, still shaking my hand, he looked down at me with a sense of pride. "It's nice to see you standing up for yourself against that bully. You got guts. In his report, it says that you started it. But meeting you and knowing him, I highly doubt that to be the case."

With one hand still shaking mine, he rested his other hand on my shoulder. "You're POLICE material if ever I saw it. In a few years, who knows how far you could go."

All this flew over me like a wave. I'm POLICE material? He let go of my hand, which fell limply to my side, but still rested his other hand on my shoulder. This was happening too fast for me to contemplate. What just happened here?

Smiling, the sergeant nodded knowingly. "I knew straight off that I was right to start your training up early. Yeah, I know I said it out of anger and frustration at the time, but I was going to do it anyway. I knew there was something different about you, right from the get-go. Right from when I first met you at the Factory."

And then, my heart sunk. He was serious. He was *serious* about me training. A wave of panic smacked the wind out of me. My throat was clenching up and running dry, my tongue freezing up in my mouth. I could feel my heart pounding against the ribs that caged the roaring beast within me. *William! I'm supposed to meet with William and Duncan tomorrow*, my head screamed. *What if William found out that I was asked to become one of the POLICE? Would that mean he wouldn't want me around anymore? What about my "real" history lessons? Will Dawn or Sherry want to talk to me ever again? What if the POLICE found out about William because of me? Will they punish him? Would they punish me?*

"I can't do anything after two—no, wait—that's ... fourteen hundred hours," I told the sergeant blatantly. An hour should give me enough time to change and get ready to go to William's.

"Why not?" the sergeant asked.

Well, I'm going to a Rebell's house, and I don't want to embarrass him by wearing a POLICE uniform, I thought to myself sarcastically.

"That's when I go to my tutor," I half-lied to him again.

The sergeant took it all in and then nodded his head in agreement. "Fair enough! I'll let you go off early this time just so you can inform your tutor that you're going to stop going to him in the future. With your training, there's no need to get lessons for a job that you're not going back to. Meet me at the POLICE Grounds at seven thirty. You do know where the Grounds are, don't you?"

Who *doesn't* know.

"Yes, sir!"

"Tell the officer at the gate your name, and he will take you to me."
With that, he held out his hand in order to affirm the deal. I shook it.
"Agreed," I said, signing over my fate once again.

CHAPTER 12

"He said *what*?!"

John looked at me like he had just swallowed a cherry whole.

"He wants me to train to be a POLICE officer. He's going to train me personally. He said so himself," I said out loud, no inflection in my voice at all. It still felt alien to me; even saying it out loud didn't sound right somehow.

"You're serious? I mean … I knew something was up when you got to my place with the first sergeant in tow, but this? When does he want you to start?"

"Tomorrow at seven thirty."

John sighed. He reached behind him, dipping his hand into the water sprinkling inside the fountain. John then brushed his hand through his hair, allowing droplets of water to run through his hair and down his face, trying to wake himself up a bit. "Man … that's big."

"Tell me about it."

John chewed his lower lip a bit as he thought to himself about the situation. "What about William and his family? What do you think they're going do when they find out about this?"

I gave John a quick glance. I hadn't told him about the deal I'd made with William, just like William had asked. But, in order to keep John offtrack, I instead told him that I would be helping William find out about the Factory through the Rebells. It would only be a matter of time before John figured that something was up, anyways.

"I don't know," I said, a little doubtful.

I got up and started to wander in front of the fountain, quickly thinking about how I would try to break the news to William and what his reaction might be. And then a thought popped into my head. I turned and look at John. "Who says he has to know?"

John looked at me as if I should have known better than to suggest such a thing. "Oh come on, Tom. You know as well as I do that he's going to find out about this one way or another."

I raised my hands to my face and pressed the base of my palms into my eye sockets, grunting out my frustration. Finally, sighing loudly, I dropped my arms and blinked away the stars that were shooting across my vision. John scratched his cheek; a very early shadow of a beard could be seen in the very dim light.

"Look, Tom," he started. "I'm your best friend. I know you better than you know yourself. Now, for some odd reason, you've decided to make this special bond with that family. I mean, it takes everything you got just to stay away from them recently. They're nice and all, but this is something more. It's only fair that you tell them about … this. If you don't, it's just going to eat away at you until you go and do something stupid. By that time, it will be too late."

He got up and started walking away. "Gotta tell 'em, Tom. Besides, maybe it will let him know how it feels to have someone snuffed out from under him and not be able to do a damn thing about it."

"That's rather cold," I yelled out after John.

He stopped and half-turned toward me. "So is the truth."

I watched him go. Once he was gone, I concentrated on the matter at hand. John was right about one thing: I had to tell William. But how? *By the way, I've joined the POLICE in order to be trained as an officer. Oh, don't worry, though. I've put aside time to be taught by you too.* I shook my head.

I slowly leaned out toward the water in the fountain. I dipped my hand into the deep running cool water and with a quick jerk upward, splashed myself in the face. My superior at the factory used to say, "Worry about a cure only when there is a disease." Yet, how do you cure a disease like this without hurting the patient? Or the doctor?

~

The screech of the Factory's steam whistle invaded the air, breaking the silence of the morning. I opened my eyes and slowly tried to roll out of the warmth and security of my dream state when I stopped and realized the importance of the day. I would be going to the POLICE Grounds to start my training as a POLICE officer today. The weight of that sat heavily on my chest as I lay there, staring up at the ceiling. There was no way of getting out of it—I was stuck. William's possible reaction to this bit of news kept rolling in my mind and wouldn't let me be.

Am I betraying him? I asked myself. *Betraying the trust that he put in me? But what is he exactly to me, anyway? A few days ago, he was just another stranger on the street, someone whom I passed by with no cause of alarm. Now, he's my friend and teacher—and a Rebell. His family? Sherry is a nice enough woman, always ready to give me something to eat or drink as we go through our lesson. She's kind and warm in her ways. And then there's Dawn ...*

I shook myself out of my gloomy demeanor. *C'mon, man. You gotta get ready,* I tried to convince myself as I threw the covers off. My hands eventually found my face and ran long forgotten fingers through my straw-strewn hair to try to make it presentable. *All right,* I mused with a stronger determination, *let's do this.*

~

All towns have restricted zones. The POLICE Grounds, or Grounds for short, were but one of them. This made it so the POLICE could go about their daily routine without having to run into anyone else. It was kind of like having a smaller town inside a bigger one. Some areas, however, were put up in order to protect the everyday person from harm, like the Fallout Zone. No one goes near the Zone even after all this time since the war. Radiation from the nuclear power plant still lingered there. Those who do wander into the Zone and stay too long in its confines often don't live long enough to regret their mistake.

The Grounds were just on the outskirts of town, out toward the farming areas. I had never actually been there personally, but I knew exactly where it was. If you took a nice, brisk half-hour jog south of the fountain, you would eventually get to the POLICE restricted area gates. Past the gates, roughly a five-minute run, would be the Grounds. John would often joke and call this area "Vans territory." All of a sudden, that joke didn't seem as funny.

I reached into my pocket and took out a semisweet apple to munch on as I walked. I let the fresh juices roll over my tongue as I calmly made my way down the street, past the fountain, and to the Grounds. The apple was no comfort on this trek, because my thoughts locked on what it was the training would consist of. Tactics, body training, education, weaponry, and field work were only a few examples of the courses that I could think of the POLICE would make me take. Yet, despite my trying to imagine what it would be like to take these courses, all I could think about were of my memories of running around the Factory with an officer right behind me barking orders and chasing after me with a stick.

Casting a quick glance around to make sure I was on the right route, I took in the area that I was walking through. The sun was pretty much up and shining through the morning clouds, lightly spraying the area with light. The shelters were in need of a new layer of paint, but they looked like any other style of shelter.

After a few turns, I managed to reach the gates that separated the Grounds from the rest of the town. The bars that guarded the Grounds were made of a thick metal, thicker than that of the Factory's E-way. It stood tall, strong, impenetrable—and closed. Just past the gate, row after row of buildings of every size and description lined the sky inside the Grounds, each one there for a different purpose. But first, one had to get inside. Luckily, I had a ticket.

I leaned against the bars, looking in at the world that existed just beyond my grasp. There was an officer with the rank of private just inside, leaning up against a small booth and facing away from me. I called out to him to get his attention. He glanced toward me, a look of both annoyance and surprise on his face, and started walking toward the gate. He wore the regular issue POLICE uniform and had a gun holstered on the left side of his belt, which flashed in the morning light.

He glared down at me. "What do you want?"

All of the sudden, I was nervous. "I … ahem … I want … I would like … Well, I was told …"

"You're not allowed here," he barked.

"But—" I started up, trying to plead my case.

"This is a restricted area. Leave, or I will be forced to report you—or worse," he added, his hand reaching for his holster.

I just stood there, staring at him. My eyes stuck to the holster, which he rested his hand on. With no reply from me, he turned and started walking back toward his post.

"But I was asked here," I called out to the back of his head.

He turned to face me again, arms crossed. "Look, no one is allowed in without clearance, and I doubt you have any, so get lost kid!"

"Look, the first sergeant said that—"

He uncrossed his arms. All of the sudden, I had his full attention. "Name," he demanded.

I stopped talking.

He didn't move. "Your name. What is it?"

"Thomas Haroldson."

The officer walked back toward his post and picked up a clipboard that was resting on a short nail inside. He flipped a page and then looked back at me. He put the clipboard back and walked back toward the gate, reaching for his breast pocket. He found the key and opened the lock that held the gate closed. The officer pulled open the gate, which smoothly swung open without groan or resistance, and stood holding it open for me. The officer opened the gate just enough to give me room to enter.

"The first sergeant is expecting you. I have been instructed to take you to the Guardhouse as soon as you arrive."

After I entered, he swung the gate closed and relocked it.

Clank.

I was in.

CHAPTER 13

THE GUARDHOUSE WAS APTLY NAMED. There weren't any windows I could see, the door was made of steel, and the walls were brick. I found out later it was originally created to hold supplies for shipping during the war. Now, since the war was over, it was used as a small lounge for after-hours brandy and cigars for the top officers.

The officer and I walked up to the foreboding iron door, and he led me into the building. Inside, we stood at the cusp of a well-lit room, despite the lack of windows. Beside the iron door, hanging up on the wall, was a telephone. The telephone was old and well used, but it still had a shine of importance to it. There were two small hallways, one on each side of me, leading off to a single wooden door. Against the wall facing me, a comfortable-looking couch and a chair sat invitingly. In front of the couch was a table with a small wooden box on it. Pictures of the war lined the tops of the walls. A lamp was hanging from the middle of the roof, providing the light in the area.

The officer pointed to the chair. "Sit."

I did as I was told. The officer went over to the phone, picked up the receiver, and punched in three numbers. While waiting for the other person to pick up the line, he looked over at one of the pictures on the wall. I looked at the picture he was focusing on as well. It was a small group of officers, all huddled around a really big gun. The photo looked like it was taken a very long time ago, probably during the end of the war.

Signatures in black ink scattered the base of the picture. Suddenly, he pulled himself out of his gaze and turned toward the wall, speaking softly into the receiver. A few muffled yeses and an "of course" were all I could really get out of the one-sided conversation.

The officer hung up the phone and returned to where I was sitting, not uttering a word or giving me a second glance. He silently stood beside me at attention, just to my left. Deafening silence filled the air between us.

"What's your name?" I asked, trying to start up a conversation while I waited.

"Greg," he reluctantly answered.

I scrunched my eyebrows, trying to remember where I had heard that name before. He caught my expression out of the corner of his eye and turned to look at toward me. "Something wrong with my name?" he demanded.

"I think I've met you before," I told him.

He didn't seem too impressed. "I don't remember."

I stared hard at the iron door, letting the events of the past few days flash before me in a parade of images and sounds. There was the fight, work, the explosion, the aftermath, and ... the fight that John got into with that officer!

I glanced back up at the officer beside me to verify it was him. There was no doubt. Greg saw that I had remembered where I knew him. "Well?" he asked me impatiently.

I answered him in a low voice. "The Factory explosion."

Curiosity turned to confusion, and confusion slowly turned to fury when his mind clicked in realization of who I was. His face was slowly turning red. Little veins started to poke out from under the skin in his neck. "Now I remember you. You had that brat friend with you. You two are the reason why I'm pulling security for the main gate for the next two months."

He looked like he could have pulled my head from my body right then and there, his body towering over me. With a realization of what he was doing, Greg stiffened his back and returned to his stance, glaring out at the void between him and the door. Quick intakes of air through his nose

A Faint Echo   141

swallowed his anger. He didn't say or do anything after that. I guess, since
the sergeant had invited me, I was under his protection. The chair I sat in
suddenly felt a bit more comfortable after realizing that.

"How long have you been an officer?" I asked him casually, trying to
show that there were no hard feelings.

He looked straight ahead and answered me through clenched teeth.
"That question is irrelevant," he spat out.

"Why?"

"Because I will be spending the rest of my life in the POLICE service.
What are a few years compared to a lifetime?"

I guess not that important, I sarcastically mused to myself.

He gave me a quick glance and asked me, "Why are you here?"

"To get trained," I answered him.

He snorted and returned to gaze out in front of him. "Then all of your
other questions will be answered by your trainer," he smiled knowingly.

In other words, shut up and sit there, I thought to myself.

The door clicked and opened wide, letting in the sun along with the
figure opening the door. It took me a second for my eyes to adjust to the
extra light that flooded in.

"Ah, there you are," the sergeant remarked casually.

The sergeant walked proudly into the room to greet me. He still wore
the same uniform that he wore when I talked to him yesterday, except for
a change of boots. Today, he wore regular design work boots. Another man
followed him. He wore a uniform similar to the sergeant, except this man
was a special rank of sergeant: three bars pointing up, one pointing down.
He had jet-black hair, combed straight back to show off more of his face.
The thing that stuck out the most was a faded scar racing across the left
side of his face, running from midcheek straight through his eye, which
was covered by a patch, to the middle of his forehead. On the patch, the
symbol of the POLICE was evident.

Greg stiffened up his position upon their arrival and saluted them
both. I quickly got up out of the chair and stood before it. Greg held
out his hand in front of me in order present me to the two men. "Here is
Haroldson, as you requested, sir."

"Good, good. Dismissed," ordered the sergeant.

Greg saluted the two superiors again and then nodded toward me as if to say, "We'll meet again." Making his way quickly past the two other officers, Greg left through the iron doors and closed it behind him. The sergeant walked over to where I stood and put his hand on my shoulder, his other hand grabbing my hand from my side and shook it.

"Welcome, Tom. Come forward. I would like to introduce you to someone."

Releasing his grip on me, he turned and waved his hand to present the new officer. "This is Staff Sergeant Victor Fürl. I consider him to be my right-hand man around here. I'm going to be sending you to him quite a bit, so I figured it best that you meet him now."

Fürl bowed toward me. "I am pleased to meet you."

His voice was as cold as his hand, which he offered to shake with mine. It sounded like he was talking through a throat full of gravel. Fürl turned to the sergeant after greeting me, his body stiff with duty and respecting of rank. "Now, if you would excuse me, sir, I have urgent work that needs my attention."

The first sergeant nodded to the lower-ranking sergeant and dismissed him. Fürl nodded toward me as a farewell and turned to leave. A chill went right down my spine as he walked past me. That man was creepy—100 percent creepy. Once Fürl was gone, the sergeant walked to the table and opened the box that was upon it. Inside the box were rows upon rows of cigars; the sergeant took one and closed the lid behind him.

He then turned toward me and chuckled. "I'd offer you one, but you're not old enough just yet."

He reached into one of his pockets, pulled out the metallic lighter he had on him, and lit the cigar. The tube of tobacco fired to life in the open flame, the room quickly filling with the smoke. I coughed slightly at the smoky air. It was then that I realized what a stupid move it was on their part to have a drinking and smoking room with no windows for ventilation. Once content with the level of flame on the end of the cigar, the sergeant turned toward me and started walking toward the iron door.

"Come, Tom. Let's take a walk."

As we walked around the Grounds on the grand tour, the sergeant seemed to be more relaxed than the previous times I was with him. Given, he still gave off the gruff and superior stature, but there was a softer demeanor to him now. He pointed out each building and what happened inside. First it was the barracks, a huge building that screamed into the sky where all the officers had a place to call home. There was a mess hall where everyone would eat on the second floor and later enjoy a small recreation room in the basement area, I was told. Then we went by the generator area. This was something that the sergeant was quite happy with. He informed me that it was under his reign, the first year to be exact, that the generator that powers all the lights with electricity was rebuilt. Quite an accomplishment, he told me. The soldiers who hung around the doorways of the buildings stood at attention and saluted as we walked by. They all looked happy enough.

"Do you understand the importance of control and order, Tom?"

"If you don't have order, rules, and laws, then there is only chaos, and chaos leads to destruction," I quoted to the sergeant a line I learned—rather, that they drilled into all the students' heads—when I was in school.

"Text book answer," he complimented me while taking long drags on the cigar. "Do you fully understand *why* we need rules and laws? And no help thinking back to what the teacher said during your education—your own words this time."

I walked in silence for a second or two, thinking this one over. "It is needed toooo ... obtain order?"

"Close," noted the sergeant. "Rules and laws are needed in order to keep people safe. That's our job here. That's what we do. We make sure people stay safe and protected. Before the POLICE came to power—hell, before the POLICE were even thought up—there was chaos! Whoo, was there chaos! Corrupt governments, countries fighting each other, neighbors killing neighbors, taxes, and racism, not to mention there were two world wars! Bet you never knew about that."

I simply nodded, trying my best to hold off from smiling. I thought back on the things I learned from William about the two previous wars, trying to filter out the facts from opinion. The sergeant took another long haul on the cigar and continued his thought. "That was something that your regular schooling never covered because, well, no one really needed to know about it now that we're here to protect them. The point of all this is that back then wasn't a good time to live in."

At this, the sergeant shook his head. I looked toward him and saw a hint of pity.

"Sir?"

"Such a waste it was back then. But the POLICE removed all that."

He held out his arms to the Grounds and the town just on the outskirts as he walked. "Now, everyone lives in harmony. Everyone is looked after. Everyone is able to live their lives as how they want. No one is discriminated against. That means that everyone is treated equally."

Then, all of the sudden, the mood changed drastically. "Unfortunately," the sergeant said with a sigh, "no type of control is perfect."

I perked up at this point.

"I admit, some officers in the POLICE take their jobs a little too seriously, and they start … enjoying their power. You saw evidence of that, I'm sure, with your Vans friend. Even before he was a part of the SITs, there he was … being the ever-loyal soldier and going around terrorizing the countryside. Boy, some of the officers really ate it up. When he wrote up that report against you, some officers that predeputized Vans wanted to go after you right away and arrest you. I mean, how dare some *civvies* go and attack one of their own like that. He was a little unclear on the report as to what started the whole shebang, but I'm positive that he started it.

"Anyway, there's that … or else they become careless and worthless to the uniform. They forget the reason they put on the uniform and just let things slowly disintegrate around them. They stop chasing after a thief when he gets too far ahead, they ignore protocol, and they start taking in kickbacks from the civilians. These officers are lowered in rank until they are eventually discharged. Then, wanting revenge or their power back, they start endangering the public. Of course, we have to turn around and— ahem, arrest them. This doesn't happen too often, but it does happen.

"And then ... there are the Rebells," he trailed off.

The sergeant clicked his tongue at the thought of the Rebells and what they'd done over the years. When he spoke next, his voice was low and his words were clearly spoken like they were chosen very specifically.

"Those damn Rebells! I don't understand their thinking at all. We save a world from the brink of utter destruction, and they want it back the way it *was*?! They don't care about safety. Look at what happened at the Factory! It was obviously them! Look at the other 'protests' they gave and the deaths that uprooted from those events! They say that they are saddened by the deaths, but they were necessary to fulfill their *cause*?!' They say they're doing it for the benefit of the people? They care *nothing* about these people! The only thing they care about is their cause and causing as much chaos as they can!"

The sergeant spent the rest of the walk cursing the Rebells and talking about all the previous examples of disorder they'd caused in the past years. At the end of the tour, we arrived back outside the Guardhouse and stopped just outside the iron door. The sergeant looked down at me.

"So, now that we've ended the tour, what is your general opinion of this place? Before you answer, I want you to understand that just because I run the place don't mean that you can't be completely honest. Speak your mind."

He leaned forward a bit to drive home a point. "It might be one of the last times during the next little while you can freely say whatever you want to me."

He leaned back and waited for my response. I looked at my feet to help organize my thoughts. What should I say to him? I took my time before I opened my mouth. "I can say whatever I want, and you won't get mad?"

He waved his hand at me. "Give it to me straight. I can take it," he smiled playfully.

I took a deep breath and cleared my throat. "This place is nice and all ... but ... I didn't choose to be here. I know that's a horrible thing to say, but you want me to be honest with you. I'm being forced to do this. *You're* forcing me to do this. You made me come to the Grounds to be trained as an officer after I tried to do exactly what you wanted me to do at the Factory. I know the way I went about it was wrong and I disrespected your authority in the matter—and for that, I'm sorry. But it wasn't *my* choice to join. You said that the POLICE helped everyone get to the point where they could live their lives how they wanted, right? Well, you *are* the POLICE in this area, and you're not letting me live my life as how I want to. If I'm going to become a POLICE officer, then I should have the right to choose to be one.... Right?"

And with that, I felt better. After spewing out everything that had been weighing on me for the past few days, a certain euphoria came over me. I was able to relax my shoulders a bit. Wow. I really needed to get that off my chest. The sergeant, however, wasn't expecting that to be my answer. His demeanor went from jolly to very, very serious. He didn't say a word—didn't move an inch. All of the sudden, staring back up at the sergeant, a thought came to mind. *I think I should have just kept my mouth shut.*

The sergeant looked off to the side for a second; a serious, disapproving scowl was ironed onto his face, showing off exactly what he thought of my little outburst. Looking back at me, he gave his back a quick stretch to work out the muscles and took in a long hard breath.

"Okay," he said.

Wait. Okay? I thought to myself. *That's it? I'm not in trouble?*

The sergeant still had not moved from where he stood, still had not unfolded his arms, still had not bothered to change his outlook at me. His voice was still quiet and calm, despite his outward appearance of being ready to explode.

"I knew you were a smart one, Tom. Didn't realize until now how smart. But you're right. You're absolutely right. It wasn't your choice. It was mine. It would be hypocritical of me to go back on everything I said on this tour about the POLICE if I were to make you train against your will. So, I want to change that. As of right now, it is all on you. The choice is yours. If you want to leave, you can leave—no hard feelings, no repercussions. If you want to stay, then you can stay, and we can start up your training in earnest."

Was he kidding? Really? I could leave? Just like that? The sergeant rested one hand on my shoulder in order to make sure that I understood everything he was about to say.

"Tom, I want you to think long and hard on this one, okay?" he began. "I can see in you a damn fine officer. You leave, and what's waiting for you? Really? To go back and continue working in a little office crunching numbers for a boss who doesn't appreciate what you have going on up here?" he tapped the side of my head as he spoke.

"If you stay, then you would be making a true difference around here. With enough time, you could be making policies that would greatly improve the lives of the people in this town. You could be a great example to everyone of what the POLICE are capable of. Think of all the good you could do if you were a part of this place, if you had the resources of the POLICE behind you. Think of all the lives you could save. I'm just trying to make you reach your full potential. But," he sighed loudly, "it's up to you to decide."

He reached into his pocket and pulled out a piece of black cloth, still neatly folded. "I'll expect your answer tomorrow. Until that time, I want you to wear this," he said simply as he held out the cloth to me.

I took the cloth from him and unraveled it to see what it was. Resting in my hands was an armband made out of a soft fabric. On it, stitched with red thread, was the symbol of the POLICE.

"This will tell everyone who sees you that you're a SIT. It's so you can get a feel of what life is like when you join. Hopefully, it will help you choose. So tomorrow, if you're here, then I'll assume your answer is a yes. If you're not here by noon or if you return the armband early, then I'll take your answer as a no. Is that fair enough for you?"

I didn't know what to say just then. I just stared at the armband, thinking over what the sergeant said about me making a difference in the POLICE. About me saving lives. It was the saving lives line that really stuck with me. What could I really do with the resources of the POLICE behind me? Which lives could I save? I took the armband and put it on, adjusting it so that the symbol was resting outward for all to see.

"Tomorrow," I said.

CHAPTER 14

IN THE SHORT AMOUNT OF time I spent walking away from the Grounds, I noticed what a difference wearing the armband made. Before, when I walked somewhere, I was one of the crowd being pushed along to my destination—a simple sheep bleating. That was one of the main reasons why John and I started using the alleys to skim between places—so we could skip the crowds and being tossed around. Now, as I walked through the streets, everyone gave me plenty of room. They said polite things to me and allowed me to go around corners before they did. Everywhere I went there was a smile. It was as if I were a full-ranking POLICE officer. And as I walked, I saw in their eyes, even if just a little, awe and respect.

I opted to take the long route to William's place, just in case. As I slipped into an alley that would eventually lead to William's house, I peeled away the black fabric from my arm. I didn't want to add any unwanted attention going to William's, especially with the recognition I had gotten wearing it for the little while I'd had it. After I took off the armband, I looked around to see if anyone was watching me. The alley was empty.

Quickly stuffing the fabric into my pocket, I thought about what had happened that morning. The tour replayed itself inside my head, but it was the sergeant's last bit of advice that got stuck inside my skull the most: the weight of his hand on my shoulder, the look in his eyes—soft and reassuring—the tone and inflection in his voice, but more importantly, his words.

"If you stay, then you would be making a true difference around here.... You could be making policies that would greatly improve the lives of the people in this town.... Think of all the good you could do if you were a part of this place—if you had the resources of the POLICE behind you.... Think of all the lives you could save."

I smiled inwardly.

William's house popped into view. Instead of going through the front door, I decided to go through the back. This was the moment of truth. What would I tell him about my idea? Would I tell him right away? How would I tell him? How would they react? What would I say to the sergeant tomorrow? Did I really want to join the POLICE?

"You think he'll believe that, Duncan?!"

A voice carried itself through the metal door, soft but still understandable. It was William.

"What else are we going to tell him?" asked Duncan, anger clearly inside his voice. "Think, William! As soon as we tell him the truth, he'll run out and tell that friend of his who was going to wed Lydia. From what I've heard from you and the others, that boy has a wicked temper. When he hears about this, that kid will come hunting for us! Probably with a few hundred POLICE officers in tow. No, William. No matter the amount of guilt you may have, we absolutely cannot tell either Tom or John the truth. She was just in the wrong place at the wrong time."

I eased my head away from the door after Duncan's speech. What won't they tell me? What has it got to do with Lydia? Don't they think I would do the right thing? Don't they trust me after all this time? If there were something bad that would upset John regarding Lydia, then of course I wouldn't tell him the news. Not right away, at least. The way he is now, whatever they found out about Lydia would just destroy him more.

"Hi, Tom."

I was so focused on listening to the conversation beyond the door that I didn't hear someone walk up behind me. I jumped into the air while waving my arms in a pathetic rendition of a bird's first attempt of flight. Then Dawn jumped into the air waving her arms, yelling in fright. The bag she was carrying dropped to her feet, spilling the odd fruit and can out into the alley.

"Why did you do that?" I asked her, trying to get my heart under control.

"I thought it might surprise you," she wheezed, bending down to grab her groceries.

"It worked."

"Dad not home?"

"I don't know," I lied. "Didn't knock yet."

She waved at me as she started walking around to the front. "C'mon," she offered. "Best to go through the front, just in case he's not in."

We walked from the alley to the front of the house and went inside. Going from bright and sunny outdoors to the darker hallway meant my eyes needed a bit of time to adjust. Closing the door behind me, I rested my hand out against the wall as I blinked a few times in order to kick-start my vision. Dawn was ahead of me.

"I can hear them inside," she said. "Come on in."

As we went down the stairs and entered the home, I could hear that the two men had stopped their conversation. The door was open to William's part of the house, and Dawn yelled out to them that I was there.

William called from the den. "Come in, Tom. We've been waiting for you."

I walked into the den. Duncan was standing by the bookcase, scowling and visually upset about something. He wore a leather vest over a white shirt, rugged pants, and work boots. His knife was not on his belt this time. William sat in his chair, a big smile on his face. He gestured to the chair opposite of him. I sat down, and the lesson for the day began.

I didn't tell them about my involvement with the POLICE during the session. It didn't feel right. *Besides,* I thought to myself, *if William and Duncan can keep secrets, so can I.* Overhearing Duncan and William through the door earlier sealed my decision. Tomorrow I would tell the sergeant that I would like to join the POLICE and start my training. That way, I would be able to get the best from both teachers.

It was late when we finished. I said good-bye to Duncan and William as I went out the back door. William pointed out that, if I were to come by tomorrow, I should arrive after fifteen hundred hours again. I waved as I went on my way, the metallic door closing behind me. While exiting the alley and entering the regular street on my way home, it quickly hit me just how tiring the day had been. My feet felt like the raw materials that John had to work with inside the Factory.

Just as I reached the turn that led to my home, a hand appeared from out of the darkness, grabbed me, and pulled me into a separate alley. It was dark, so I couldn't see who had grabbed me. I tried to struggle free, but a second pair of hands grabbed my feet, and the two of them picked me up and carried me away. Screaming was useless, because a gag was shoved into my mouth, blocking any chance to yell for help.

These two mystery men carried me through the alley for some time. They had me turned upside down, my face bouncing mere inches from the ground, so I couldn't see where I was being taken. There was little to no light from the rising moon, so the alley was close to utter darkness. Of course, my interest at that particular moment was not so much trying to see who had me but rather on escaping. I tried jerking my hands free and kicking my feet. Whoever they were, they had a firm grip and were not letting go. As I traveled in this awkward way, I got the impression that they had done this before.

We entered an opening, and they started to slow down. I managed to take a quick look around, the light filling up the area enough so I could at least catch a glimpse of where they might be taking me. I recognized the area almost immediately. It was the same place John and I had fought Vans. *Why here?* I thought to myself. The two dropped me unceremoniously onto the ground. My face hit the ground hard; a small pebble jabbed itself into my forehead. The bigger of the two men started kicking away at my midsection, knocking the wind out from under me.

"Just butter him up," the other one laughed.

Blow after blow came crashing down on me. Boot after boot soared at me, landing with excruciating effect. I tried to yank the gag out from my mouth, but every time I would reach for it, I got a fist across my cheek for my effort. After the big one was done "buttering me up," he stood back to better examine his handiwork. I cradled my stomach, almost as if it would have fallen out if I didn't hold it back. Based on the way I felt, it just might have. I coughed against the gag and rolled it out of my mouth with my tongue. The piece of fabric spat itself out from my mouth and rested just in front of me. There was blood on it.

"Don't feel so high and mighty now, do ya, vermin?" exclaimed the one who was standing off to the side watching the other beat me senseless. There was a bit of light from the moon that occasionally cracked through the clouds that hung overhead. The light illuminated his face—just enough to show a stitched-up cheek. The stitches crawled up his face from his chin to his right eye.

Vans.

"Leave me ... alone ... or you're ..." I sputtered out, still trying to catch my breath.

That just got me another kick in the face.

"Do *not* tell me what I *may* or *may NOT do!*" Vans yelled down at me. "Just because the POLCE haven't gotten around to dealing with you for what you did, doesn't mean I can't make sure you never get in my way ever again."

I started to see flashes before my eyes. Chest on fire. Stomach in knots. Tasted copper. He towered over my crumpled form, his hands in fists. He had the power to destroy me at that moment, and we both knew it. It was just a question of time. Quickly, he threw his own face in front of mine, brushing his hand over the stitchwork that covered the right side of his face. "I still have to repay you for this."

"Pick him up," he ordered to the other guy who was in the clearing with him. There was a hint of disgust in his voice, as if I were a heap of garbage covered in moss ready to be thrown away.

The big guy lurched over me without question. He grasped me in his massive paws and yanked me to my feet. I couldn't feel the ground under me. I just hung there like a rag doll in the guy's arms.

"It's time to have some fun," Vans laughed.

As I was jerked up from the ground, Vans noticed something lying underneath me in the dim light of the moon that shone in and out of the cloud breaks.

"Hold him," he ordered to the brute and reached down to pick up the object. He held it up to the available light in order to see what it was. A quick gasp came from Vans, immediately followed by a very low growl. He pushed the big guy out of his way in order to get into my face. In one solid motion, he managed to throw me against one of the walls that made up the square and held up the object directly in front of my nose. "Where did you get this?!" he bellowed into my face.

I tried to focus on what he was showing me, but my eyes saw nothing but a dark, blurry nothing. Vans's breath was hot and quick on my face and neck. Slowly, it came into focus before me. Vans was holding a black piece of cloth, ratted with mud with a distinct red symbol on it—my armband. It must have fallen out of my pocket during the beating. At that moment, even though I was in great pain and Vans could have hurt me even more, I couldn't help but smile. I smiled a very big smile.

"I got that the same place that you got yours," I spat out of my mouth in a calm, clear voice. "I am now a trainee under the teaching and protection of the POLICE First Sergeant."

His mouth hung open. His grip on me loosened, and the pressure he put against me to keep me up against the wall lessened. "N ... no," he whispered.

And then he let me go. Very slowly.

"You do know what the punishment is for attacking a POLICE officer in training, don't you?" I teased, my ribs reeling from the strain of having to put up with the beating moments before.

I knew that he knew. I figured he would know, because he would have used the same clause in his report against me when I stopped him from attacking William. I only wish that I knew what it was. It would've been nice to threaten him with it specifically.

Vans's face hardened. "Are you going to report me ... comrade?" It sounded like Vans was swallowing pure fish oil and spitting out venom with each syllable he spoke. I couldn't have been enjoying myself more—if only I wasn't in so much pain.

"Why not? You reported me," I flatly pointed out as I tried my best to sound tough and in control, when in reality I was relying on the wall to stand up straight.

Vans started to back away from me. He reluctantly gave me back my armband and stiffened up in front of me. Vans shot out his fist in front of himself. I flinched at the motion out of reflex as the big youth stood there and saluted me. Vans was saluting me. *Me!*

"I … I apologize," he mumbled under his breath. That said, he turned on his heel and started to make his way out of the area, the other big guy in tow asking if he was going to get into trouble over this.

Once Vans was out of view, my legs couldn't bear my weight any longer, and I collapsed onto the ground in order to catch my breath and relax. Bed looked better and better by the second. A sigh of pure relief escaped my empty chest, immediately followed by excruciating pain. Whoever that was with Vans, he sure knew how and where to hit someone. I brought my hand up to the corner of my mouth and wiped away any blood that had tried to make an escape. I just sat there, taking a mental tally of all the parts that were either damaged or in some sort of pain. I think I lost a tooth.…

After taking a much-needed breather, I forced myself up with great help from the wall I was leaning against. If I was going to make it back to my shelter before passing out, I had to get onto my feet and start moving. Every step I took toward home was an effort, both because of my exhaustion from the long day and my wounds. As I stumbled through the darkness, I came to realize that my balance was off. The major tip-off was my crashing into walls and the constant tripping over my own feet. Inside my head, I kept repeating over and over, *Just make it home.… Just gotta make it home.*

What am I going to tell the POLICE tomorrow when I go to the grounds? There's going to be obvious indications that I had been in a fight sometime between leaving today and showing up tomorrow. The swelling around my black eye was going to be giveaway number one. The sergeant will want to know what happened. I can just imagine what he would be thinking. I just got the armband, and I was attacked. He'll probably blame the Rebells. Who else would dare attack someone wearing the POLICE symbol? Do I just tell them about Vans? No. That wasn't an option. Vans would be punished, but that could lead to me being punished for attacking him, which started this ugly circle in the first place.

My head jerked up a bit at a thought—one that didn't sit well with me. With me being attacked—or rather an officer being blatantly attacked in the street and with the immediate blame going to the Rebells—the sergeant would probably start a crackdown on Rebell action in the area. I mean really put the squeeze on them. It was one thing to have a strong assumption for the destruction of the Factory, but this is more personal. Either that, or he'd have someone follow me around to make sure the person who attacked me didn't get another chance. That meant I could lead them to William accidentally. Or worse—Duncan.

As I opened my door and shuffled inside, my head was a whirl with possible excuses as to why I looked the way I did. Mugged? Would that work? No direct association to the Rebells or cause for extra security. They were after whatever I happened to be carrying on me—wrong place, wrong time. They didn't see the armband right away—too dark. Only after jumping me did they see the symbol, and they ran. Wasn't able to get a good look at them. Yeah, that could work.

I carefully sat myself down on the edge of the bed in order to take off my boots, the weight of the day crashing down upon me. In order to even reach my boots, I had to grab the cusp of my pant leg and pull upward on it, dragging my foot toward me. There was no strength left in my body. I was done. The act of pulling on my pant leg was more than I could manage, so I simply let go. My foot, having made it halfway up my leg, crashed back down to the ground with a resounding thud. Giving in to the exhaustion, I eased my weary body onto the full length of the bed and closed my eyes.

I let out a long sigh of relief.

Knock, knock.

"You gotta be kidding me," I mumbled out loud.

My eyes opened slightly at the sound of someone knocking—probably John. Rolling over so I could use my arms to help aid my effort in standing,

I heaved myself back into a sitting position, the strain not helping my wounds. I gave a loud exhale as I got myself standing, holding onto my side to help keep my bruised ribs in check.

Knock, knock.

"I'm coming," I called out.

The distance between my bed and the door seemed to go on forever. My feet, hardly working the way they should have been, clumped on the ground with each step. Resting against the side of the door, I reached out, took hold of the handle, and pulled it open. The door opened a sliver so I could see who it was. Dawn stood behind the frame holding one arm in another; her hair was down and covering one side of her face completely.

"Tom? Can I please talk to you?"

I pulled the door wide and stepped to the side to allow her entrance. What was she doing here? How did she know where I lived? My head was pounding with each heartbeat. It was hard to think straight. Dawn cautiously came into my home, not sure what to do or what to say. She looked around for a moment and then turned around.

"I never realized you lived in such a small place," she commented politely. When she saw the state I was in, her face went from shock to concern to worry. "Tom! Are you okay?"

My head started to spin. I was ... trouble balancing ... room ... door closed ... Dawn ... fading ...

And then there was darkness.

CHAPTER 15

I WOKE UP ON THE BED. My head was still pounding, and I still felt every inch that was battered and bruised, but somehow I felt a little bit better after my unexpected nap. There was a damp cloth resting on my forehead that smelt of tea leaves. I could feel something around my waist. I risked a glance toward my chest, knowing that it would cost me a moment of pain. My shirt was off and was hanging up off to the side. Wound around my lower chest and stomach was a tight bandage. My boots were off.

I removed the cloth from my face and slowly propped myself up to take in what was going on around me. There was a light on in the kitchen, and I heard someone working on something in there. I cleared my throat to indicate that I was awake, seeing if that got the person's attention. Dawn poked her head around the corner, a smile on her face at seeing me up.

"Good morning, Sunshine."

I rubbed my eyes, careful not to poke any of the areas that were trying to heal. "What happened? How did I get to my bed?"

Dawn made her way into my room, a bowl of some sort of steaming liquid in her hands. She sat down just to the side of me and put the wet cloth back onto my forehead.

"I put you here," she answered. "I also helped bandage you up. You gave me quite a scare, you know."

I leaned back onto the bed and let Dawn care for me. "How long was I out?" I asked meekly.

Dawn merely shrugged, stirring the concoction with a spoon. "Dunno. An hour or two maybe. Wasn't keeping track."

Taking the spoon out of the mixture she had prepared, she lightly blew on the broth that was settled on the spoon and held it out to me. "Eat it," she ordered.

"What is—"

"Eat," she ordered a bit more forcefully, like I was a child not wanting to eat his beans.

A smile cracked its way through my busted lips, and I opened my mouth as ordered. Dawn carefully drew the spoon closer and put it in my mouth. My gag reflex kicked into overtime as I tried to choke down the vile, sour syrup that she tried to force-feed me. My eyes started to water as my attempt to keep it down worked against me. Once I was able to breathe again, I started coughing and choking to try to get some sort of sense back. This only caused me to clench my side as I held together my broken frame underneath the bandages.

Dawn stirred and mixed the sludge again with her spoon, not daunted by my reaction, drew another spoonful, blew on it, and held it out for me to devour. "It will help you heal quicker," she said.

Not being in any shape to put up a fight, I reluctantly opened my mouth again, crushing my eyes together in an attempt to help block out the sensation. The spoon reentered my mouth and poured the poison down my throat again and again. If this was what it took to get better, perhaps it would have been better to just let Vans have his way with me.

Finally, after what felt like an eternity, Dawn scraped the last of the molasses up onto the spoon and force-fed the oil to me. Taking the last swallow, I gasped for air. *I probably won't be able to get the taste out of my mouth for a week*, I thought.

Happy seeing the empty bowl, Dawn set it off to the side and turned her attention back to me. "So, care to tell me what exactly happened to you?" she asked as she brushed a piece of her bangs out of her face and tucked them behind her ear.

She took the cloth off of my head and dabbed it in a small bowl beside my bed. Wringing it out, she held it in her hand and waited for my response. Running my tongue around my mouth to rinse out any leftover residue of the sauce she fed me, I cleared my throat once again.

"I … ah … was jumped by Vans before I made it home," I stammered. "He took me to the spot where I first met you and your family and then beat me within an inch of my life. Once he was done, he left me there. I somehow made it back home, and then you knocked at the door."

Dawn, listening contently, nodded her head to me. "Well then," she started up calmly as she reached into her front pocket and took out a black piece of cloth. She dangled it out in front of me like bait to a fish. "I guess that explains this."

My breath caught inside my throat. My eyes grew wide. I slowly took the armband from her, being careful not to move too hastily. Dawn looked from it to me, a half-knowing glance in her eyes. "You took it off him, I suppose?"

"No," I whispered.

When I reopened my eyes to look at Dawn, I could see that she was a little shocked at my answer.

"No?" she repeated, leaning forward and tilting her head in order to make sure she heard me correctly.

"Someone … gave it to me. They thought that if I had it, I would—" I started to explain, but the words felt hollow.

"Who gave it to you?" she asked me.

I hesitated.

"Who?!"

She pounded the mattress with her hand. I couldn't look her in the face; I felt so ashamed. I could barely put voice to the words. They came out as a breathy whisper.

"The *sangria* of the Grounds."

Dawn sat back. A very somber look crossed her face. "You joined?"

I raised my hand to meet with hers, but she pulled away like I was going to attack her.

"You joined the POLICE?" she asked again.

"It wasn't really by choice … at first." I tried to explain to her simply the whole long event that led me to getting the armband: the Factory, the officer who attacked John, me trying to tell the sergeant about Mrs. Nikle, the meeting with the sergeant at the Factory, going to the Grounds, and receiving the armband from the sergeant. Dawn seemed to take it all in stride, or so I thought. I think she was still in shock.

"How could you join up with the POLICE after all that you had learned? After all you've done? Why, Tom?"

I squirmed a bit under her gaze. "One of the reasons was for protection."

She threw the wet cloth she was using to help my wounds onto my head with little care. It slapped me on the forehead; water saturated with tea splashed and stung my eyes a bit. "That obviously didn't work, now did it?" Dawn bitterly pointed out, arms crossed.

I looked toward her, head still hung in shame. "Another reason was because of something that my mother told me: before passing judgment, know both sides."

At that, Dawn got up from the side of the bed where she was carefully taking care of me and started to walk away into the kitchen in a huff.

"Is that such a good reason to throw your life away?! Just so you can live up to something your dead mother said to you many years ago?" Dawn exclaimed. Her quiet disbelief was evidently starting to give way to anger and hurt.

She disappeared around the corner of the kitchen entrance. I tried to prop myself back up to a sitting position, being careful not to stretch any parts of my body that were not yet ready to stretch.

"Oh, I know!" she continued. "You're just trying to place your bets. That way, if we get caught, you can turn your back on us and just walk away. If the POLICE happen to fall, then you can say you had a part in that as well. I can't believe you! I can't believe how stupid you are!"

Dawn screamed from the kitchen. A clay pot flew through the air from one side of the kitchen to the other. It crashed against the opposite wall with a loud crack. Pieces of the pottery could be heard clanking and scattering among the ground. A plate splattered against the ground soon afterward and blasted into pieces. Sounds of other pottery being devastated in Dawn's rage could be heard.

"Also," I called out to her from where I sat on the bed, "I chose to join the POLICE so I could warn William and you about projects the POLICE were working on."

Dawn stopped whatever she was doing inside the kitchen and slowly crept out from her hiding place. A jug was in her hands—or at least the handle of one. Her face was no longer hurt and angry, but confused.

"What did you just say?" she asked.

"I'm going to join the POLICE so I can warn you about things," I explained again.

Dawn cautiously stepped back into the bedchamber, hugging herself in her own harms in order to give herself support. Her hair was a bit wild with her recent outburst in my kitchen. "You're going undercover for the Rebells?" she whispered.

I held up my hand to stop her. "Not the Rebells—for you ... and Sherry and William."

She looked a little worried now. "Did Duncan put you up to this?" she asked, jabbing the broken handle in her hands. "'Cause if he did, I swear I'm gonna—"

I adjusted myself on the bed again to get into a better position to talk to her, the facecloth flopping off of my forehead. "No no no ... Duncan had nothing to do with this. And for the last time, I'm not going undercover for the Rebells. I'm doing it for you and your family. If the POLICE are going to do anything against the Rebells, I don't want any of you there. Your family has treated me with love and respect. It's almost like having a family of my own again. For years, it's just been John and me. Now I have you. I haven't had something like this for a long time. I don't want to jeopardize that."

Dawn made her way back to my bed and sat beside me once again. She stared me straight in the eyes. "Do you know what you're doing? If you get caught—"

I grabbed her hand quickly, pain be damned. "That's the thing! No one must know about this. You can't tell anyone about this—not even your father. Not yet, at least. I'll be fine. It's for everyone's own good that no one knows."

Dawn didn't pull away from my grasp but lightly held onto my hand with hers. Her hand was soft and warm in mine. "How are you going to keep this a secret? Someone's going to see you entering and exiting the Grounds when you go to train. And what about when you come over for the lessons? What's going to happen then?"

"I don't know. I'll think of something."

Those words burnt inside my mouth as I spoke them. I was ready for Dawn to get up and storm out or start beating on me herself. Instead, she leaned closer to me. "I believe you. I know that you won't turn us in and that you'll do everything in your power to protect us. Okay, I promise not to tell—on on one condition: as long as you don't get hurt again. If I see one cut, bruise, or scratch on you, I'm going to march right out to the market square and announce your dual loyalty to anyone who can hear."

I smiled at her empty threat. "Thank you."

We stared at each other for a few more seconds, hand touching hand. The only illumination inside the room came from the lantern that sat on the opposite side of my bed. Her eyes glowed in the dim light. The light shone on her smooth skin. Her hair fell freely down her back. Her lips … she was beautiful. I started to lean toward her.

Dawn jerked out of the way suddenly. "Oh! Um … I almost forgot the reason I came here. There was something I was supposed to give you."

She pulled her hand free from mine and stood up facing away from me. A little flustered, she quickly brushed back her hair from her face and, once composed, turned around to face me once again.

"After you left, Father asked to talk to Duncan alone for a while. Whatever they talked about, Father was not happy. Neither was Duncan. Soon afterward, Duncan stormed out of the den and said that he was going for a walk and left. I was doing some work at the table, so I saw everything that happened. Father came out of the den with an envelope in his hands. He gave it to me and asked if I could deliver it to you."

She reached into her side pocket and pulled out a simple envelope. On it was my name. Dawn looked at it for a second, turned it over in her hands, and presented it to me. "I'm guessing this is what the fight was about," she pointed out as I took it from her.

The envelope was simple enough, sealed with just a piece of wax at the very tip of the opening. I ran my finger around the wax seal and cracked the letter open. Inside were two pieces of folded paper; the words on them looked like they were written quickly. Dawn sat back down on the side of the bed, curious as to what was on the letter she was asked to deliver.

"Well?" she asked me.

I moved the letter closer to the light and began to read it aloud, so that both Dawn and I could hear what was written....

~

Dear Tom,

Duncan insisted that I don't tell you this, but I have to. Before I tell you, you must understand that this is for your eyes only. I don't want you to tell John—please! I can't see how he would properly understand what I'm about to tell you, and he might do things with this knowledge that would jeopardize everyone. Only you may know this. After reading this, I want you to burn this letter.

I lied to you.

I lied to you about my knowledge about the Factory's destruction. I lied to you about my involvement with the Factory's destruction. I'm now ready to tell you the truth. The Rebells did have a hand in the destruction the Factory.

Duncan thinks that I have this overwhelming need to tell you this because I must ease my conscience. Why does he think this? Because I sent someone you knew to destroy the Factory. For some reason, I didn't connect the dots right away. I didn't see how she might have known you or how you knew her. But, after looking at the facts, there was no possible explanation as to why she wouldn't be.

I don't know how to gently say this, so I'll just say it. Lydia, John's wife-to-be, was part of the Rebells. Worse was that I sent that poor girl to her death. But the thing that worries me the most is that I sent her to her death in order to save *my own life* and the lives of my family.

I guess I do have a guilty conscience, but that's still not the reason why I'm writing this letter. I'm paying tribute to her. One would think that John should be the one reading this, but after the display that he gave to us regarding his emotional stability over the matter, I thought it best that you should hold this burden along with me.

Where do I start? The beginning is always a good place. Duncan and I have been friends for a very long time. He visits my family and me every three years or so in order to keep me in check with what's going on in the different countries and what other factions are up to. On his last visit three years ago, he brought someone along with him—a girl about thirteen years old. It was Lydia. It seems that he adopted an orphan girl when he was last in Flor Del Condado. Didn't say what happened to her family. I can only assume it had something to do with the POLICE.

While Duncan and I talked and planned what was going to happen with the general Rebell revolts and POLICE destruction in the area, because that's what our actions would turn out to be, Lydia and Dawn would play. During this visit, Duncan told me about an old storage room/bunker inside the mine section of the Factory inside town. He said that the bunker was being rebuilt and fixed for a hidden POLICE project. He didn't know exactly what this project was, but he knew it was set toward the destruction of the Rebells. He had received this information from a very reliable source.

So he asked me if I knew anyone who worked inside the Factory, preferably inside the mine section. I told him I didn't. He then asked me if I knew anyone who could take up a job inside the factory in order to supervise the construction. I told him that there were few Rebells in town who did not already have POLICE suspicion on them, my family being one of the groups remaining. I volunteered to go, but he declined my offer. Something to do with my age or such rubbish. I say he just didn't want me to get into any type of trouble.

Since there was no one to qualify for the mission, he did the unthinkable. He asked his new daughter to come into the den. He then told her that she had to do it. I protested long and hard against this, but he didn't listen to a word that I said. He went to work designing her backstory and paper trail.

Once Duncan left, she stayed in town and joined the factory after a few months, showing them particular interest inside the mine section.

She never came by the house again after that first visit. She did, however, send me messages every second week or so to keep me updated on what she found out. Duncan was right. The bunker's purpose was something to do with the destruction of the Rebells in the area. They were setting up a Rebell Watch, or whatever it was called. They had monitors and files all over the room, complete with a set of spies who followed possible Rebells in order to find who they came into contact with. Everyone that the Rebells visited or talked to or even nodded at became a suspect. Once a group was found and verified, those unfortunate people were bagged and tagged, as Lydia put it. Lydia found out about all of this during one of her tours of the factory. She had been working for about a year by then. According to one of her last reports on the Watch, the system would be operational soon.

From then on, I assigned her to try to find out who was tagged for the targeting, so we could warn the poor souls. She would send me a note with a list of names, and I would touch base with them through all sorts of mixed routes to put them into hiding. This went on for a couple weeks.

The POLICE were going crazy. None of the tagged Rebells were giving the POLICE any of the identities or the positions of other Rebells. In fact, the ones they had tagged were disappearing off the face of the map soon afterward. The POLICE gave up on the idea of tagging after another month or so of this. I believe this was around the time when John was starting to see Lydia quite seriously.

Then, one week before the bombing, one of the last Rebells to be tagged by this system came to my house for a drink, and we talked. Unfortunately, one of the POLICE who used to work at the bunker recognized the Rebell entering my house. A very cautious officer, he was. For the next two days, he followed the Rebell. During both of these two days, that man came to my house. We were having a very interesting conversation, and I had asked him back so we could continue.

The POLICE officer, after seeing this, went back to the factory to check on an old file that was in the database inside the bunker. Lydia was getting off work when he entered the building. She recognized him and decided to follow him to see why he had returned after so much time had passed. He entered the bunker. Lydia stayed back a bit but looked inside. The room was clean and still in use. The POLICE hadn't closed the project down after all but just kept it on as a side project for the officers who were either looking for a promotion or for those who were being reprimanded.

The officer opened up a file cabinet and checked on the tagged Rebells who were there. He then began to search through his files on any information about my family. He wrote some things down inside the file and put it back. When he was gone, Lydia snuck into the bunker and grabbed my file to see what he wrote. He updated my personal file as a "possible Rebell" and selected me for observation because of "suspicious behavior."

Without delay, Lydia contacted me, saying that we had to meet face-to-face. She informed me what she had seen. When I found out what had happened, I told her that the all the files needed to be destroyed before the officers brought anyone to see my file. Maybe the entire bunker, so no future endeavors could be taken. With my name now tagged, it would endanger Duncan when he visited. Destroying the bunker would also release the other Rebells who were tagged. She told me of a plan that she was thinking about for the past little while in order to get rid of the bunker, but she told me that it was quite risky. It might not even work, and there was a good chance that she might get caught. I told her to do it without a second thought for her welfare. At that moment, all I cared about was trying to keep my family safe.

The next day, she took an instant-light gas lantern (it had been inside the family for generations, that old thing), some rope, and a brick that she found by the factory and put them inside a knapsack. Her plan was to go to one of the gas chambers that routed all fuel to the factory, and when the coast was clear, she would crawl behind one of the pipes and make her bomb. She said that she would set the lantern to on but make sure it wasn't on just yet. Then, using the rope and brick, she would create some sort of pulley system to create a timer for the ignition switch on the lantern. Lastly, before leaving the room, she would open one of the pipes to flood the room with a very flammable gas. She said that she would wait for a time when the majority of the workers were out before the explosion occurred. She couldn't wait too long, though, or else someone might have asked about the supplies she had, or worse—found the bomb.

Obviously, it worked.

The POLICE officer must have met up with Vans two days before the explosion and, probably through a little persuasion, told Vans what he had found out about me. The next day, Vans and the other boys met up with me while my family and I were going to the market before they opened. You know the rest.

I don't know what happened to the officer who became suspicious of me. Worse, Lydia didn't tell me what the officer looked like. From now on, keep your eyes open for the POLICE when coming near the house. If you see one, walk right by the house and don't look back. I don't want you in any more danger than you already are from being in contact with me. You can't trust anyone now.

Take care of yourself, Tom.

William Kenneth

~

I folded the pieces of paper back to their original state and lowered them to my lap. Dawn held her hand up to her mouth, trying to hold back her sobs. I was struck dumb by what I had just read. Lydia was a Rebell. She caused the explosion. William knew about it. That meant he lied to me when he said he didn't know what had happened. William lied to me. Lydia lied to both me and John. I couldn't believe it.

There was an officer out there who knew William was a Rebell as well. With the Factory destroyed, there was no way to prove it, but that wouldn't stop them. Who else, besides Vans, did he tell? Had he been watching William's house while the investigation was going on at the Factory? If he had, then he saw me go into William's home when I had used the front door.

Dawn, brushing the back of her hand at her eyes to wipe away the tears, took a cleansing breath to help compose herself. "I can't believe that he would do such a thing," she choked. I'm guessing that she had never seen this side of her father before—someone who would order a bomb to be set.

My mind raced with the possible scenarios this news caused. William was right—John couldn't know. The news would destroy him—utterly. To know that her own bomb killed her, even if it was a fluke that some wild debris hit her. I can understand Lydia trying to destroy the bunker alone. But to destroy the entire Factory just to cover up the destruction of a small section that held sensitive files on possible Rebells? How many other people died in that explosion? Everyone who worked there—their livelihoods just thrown out the window for who knows how long just for the sake of William not wanting his name on that POLICE file.

"Tom?"

The POLICE knew that there was something odd with the Factory explosion when they first arrived there. I overheard them. Did they know that it was the bunker that had been targeted? During the five days of sifting through the debris, were they trying to gather up any clues, or were they just focused on pieces of the files that may have survived? Were they trying to make sure that no one else would find out what they were doing there? I mean, they were using a civilian institution for an undercover POLICE activity. More importantly, they were actively spying on the community and hunting down anyone with even a hint of suspicion. If people knew, they would revolt against the POLICE. Was that what Duncan wanted all along? Would he actually go to this length to bring about the downfall of the POLICE—the death of one of his family?

"Tom?!"

Dawn's voice jerked me out of my stupor. She sat on the edge of my bed. Her eyes were red and puffy from crying as she looked at me. "Tom?"

Dawn looked like she was ready to break down. I couldn't tell if her state was from learning that it was her father who caused the ultimate destruction of the Factory and all the deaths associated with it or the knowledge that he willingly sent people to die in order to save her. I reached out to console her, once again resting my hand on hers. Dawn slid into my arms and started to cry on my shoulder. She wrapped her arms around me and held me tightly as she sobbed uncontrolled tears. Her embrace was warm, and her hair smelled of cherry blossoms. I helped hold her to give her support.

"It's okay. Let it out," I assured her.

She wept openly for a while, her chest convulsing with every gasp of air between sobs. I simply held her—nothing more. No words needed to be said. No actions needed to be made. She just needed someone to hold her. That was my job. Slowly, she pulled away, wiping her eyes and cheeks with the base of her palm.

"You must think we're monsters now," she quietly whispered.

I shook my head. "No. I don't think William's a monster. He did what he felt was necessary as a father and a husband in order to protect his family. Unfortunately, a lot of people paid the price for his actions—some with their lives."

I took Dawn's hand back into mine and held it up so that we were both looking at our enclosed fingers.

"But it didn't have to be this way. Dawn, this is what I've been talking to you about. You asked me why I joined the POLICE. *This* is why. I have been put into a position that can directly help you. I can now protect you, Sherry, and William without the bloodshed. I can stop any reports, remove any suspicion, and blind the POLICE toward you and your family without the loss of life.

"When the sergeant approached me, he said, 'Think of all the good you could do if you were a part of this place, if you had the resources of the POLICE behind you. Think of all the lives you could save.' He was referencing my actions against the Rebells, but I took it a different way. I will have complete access to make sure that the POLICE don't hurt anyone else. And because of that, the Rebells won't have to blow up another building. Both sides win."

Dawn sniffed and brushed the last of her tears away. Removing her hand from mine, she reached over to the side of the bed and took the bowl she had recently used to feed me. What leftover oil there was inside the bowl had started to dry in the night air. Putting the bowl out in front of her, she nodded toward the lantern on the opposite side of me. I reached over with the pieces of paper and gently maneuvered them so that the corner would touch the flame. There was a flicker of life, and light crept up onto the paper, the flame licking at the parchment—the letter was on fire. With one hand underneath the letter so that it wouldn't set my bed on fire, I let the flames consume the pages. Holding it as long as I dared, I dropped the ash and smoldering paper into the bowl to finish off. The letter was no more.

Dawn smiled shyly at me. "I … should get back. Dad is probably wondering what's taken me so long. Just … just be careful, Tom."

And soon she was gone, leaving me alone with my thoughts and my wounds. I put the bowl back off to the side, being careful not to disturb the ash that slept inside the pottery. Easing myself slowly back onto my bed, I stared up at the ceiling. Closing my eyes, I started my venture off to a much-needed sleep.

I hope I know what I'm doing, I mused to myself.

PART 2:
IN THE ZONE

CHAPTER 16

THE RAIN WAS COMING DOWN hard and fast, the droplets crashing onto the now muddied path as I tried to bounce from tree to tree for cover. Puddles formed all around me, making the path of clear patches between puddles of muck a maze. The stick I was using as a mock cane during my travels was doing me no favors as I tried to waddle through the thunderstorm. Admittedly, I didn't need that blasted thing as much recently, my leg almost at the end of its mending, but I still couldn't put my full weight down on my leg just yet. The contents inside my canvas backpack were throwing me off balance a little as I raced to get to some sampling of cover. The sky was darkened by the gray clouds and the setting sun, but I still had enough light to see the farm just off in the distance—my eventual destination.

I took a quick glance behind me at the path I was traveling just to see how far off the road it was and if I would be able to find my way back in the dark if I had to. With the times being what they are, it was a good idea to have an escape route in case things went bad.

A quick sprint to a tree on the opposite side of the path caused me to lose my footing for a single second, but it was long enough to land square on the ground. My cane flew into the air and off to the side of the path, muddy water splashing up around me in the explosion my body's impact created. There was something hard and jagged in my backpack that drove home the point that lying in the middle of the path was a bad idea.

"Who's there?" called out a mystery voice above me.

I turned my head around so I could look toward the farm. From my view, the world was turned upside down, but I could still make out the scene. There was someone with a lantern standing in the middle of the path, their free hand covering their face to help them see who was out there. I raised my hand to show that I heard them and tried to right myself, which took a try or two due to the awkward positioning and the weight of the stuff in my backpack. The stranger stood still, not bothering to come to my aid.

My black jacket, now drenched in both mud and water, did nothing but weigh me down. It offered no help in trying to protect me from the cold and rain. As I put my hands on the ground to get myself righted, I could feel streams of cool water trickle out from the sleeves. This was not going as I had hoped—not at all. With a heave on my good leg, I got myself back into a standing position and took a moment to look over the result of taking a mud bath in the middle of the path. I was a mess.

Trying to get back some level of composure, I gave my jacket a solid flick to get some of the rain and mud off of it. The person with the lantern still had not moved. I raised my hand to my face in order to brush off what water and mud had rested there and started walking toward the light. I raised my free hand again to show I was aware of them and had no weapon to speak of.

"Excuse me," I called out, "but would you be able to help me?"

"Stop where you are. What do you want?" was the reply.

I stopped where I was in the middle of the path. I raised both hands up in an effort of good will. "Ah ... I'm just looking for a night's worth of shelter from the rain." I smiled, trying to show off my good intentions.

There was a long pause where neither one of us spoke; the only sound was the rain pummeling the trees and the ground. I kept my hands up the entire time, just in case. Finally, the lantern light that was floating in midair in front of the body I was talking to started to lower.

"Can't. Full up," they yelled back and turned to go back to the farm.

I took a step forward in desperation. "Please. Just for the night," I begged.

The stranger stopped and turned back to look at my pathetic form, drenched to the bone and muddied from my spill. I shrugged a bit in an effort to display the ridiculous situation I was in, hoping that some sting of pity would aid my cause.

"Full up," they repeated and went back to walking toward the farm.

I lowered my hands in defeat. I simply watched the person make their way back to the farmhouse and the open door waiting for them. The door closed.

And that was that.

I took a quick glance around the area, trying to size up my situation. I was in the middle of a mud path in the pouring rain. The cane I was using to help me with my leg was nowhere to be seen. I was drenched and filthy from the fall. There was no solid piece of shelter other than the farmhouse and the barn that stood off to the side. The trees were too sparse to give any relief. There were no coverings or rock abrasions that would be big enough to hide in. I was, simply put, out of luck. Smacking my lips together at the defeated moment, I gave out a sigh and started my way back down the path that led toward the road.

I turned around one last time. The door to the farmhouse was again open, and this time a woman stood in the light. She was arguing lightly with the person whom I'd originally talked to. Their words were not clear enough for me to hear what they were saying, but I could tell by her tone that she wasn't happy with the guy. I waved back toward the two once again, showing that I saw them.

"Hello. Please. I'm just looking to spend the night out of the rain. That's all. Look … I don't have that much money, but I would be more than happy to compensate you."

The two looked over at me, and then returned to their whispered argument. The man, pointing off toward my direction, kept waving his hand in front of himself, showing off that he didn't want me there. The woman, however, waved at me and then toward the barn, bobbing the lantern in her hand to demonstrate her point. Clearly there was some disagreement regarding my predicament. I didn't budge, not wanting to scare them into retreating back into the house once more.

Finally, after much deliberation, the man relaxed as he stared off at my soaked form. Giving her a frustrated brush off, he went back inside and left her alone standing in front of the open door and the light that cascaded from within. The woman closed the door slightly, shutting off the source of light that shone freely, and directed the lantern out in the direction of the barn.

"You can stay in there for tonight," she called out to me.

Thankful to get out of the torrent, I started to jog over toward the barn. The woman quickly started to make her way to the front of the wide doors in order to let me in. The barn that was just off to the side of the home was quite substantial. At least two levels, the wooden structure looked to be well constructed and somewhat old, the peeling paint telling its age. Two huge doors, heavy and secure, stood out in the front. As I got closer, the woman unlatched the locking mechanism in front and started to heave at one of the massive doors. It was reluctant to open, but it slowly started to give way. There was enough room for us to enter by the time I arrived where she stood.

The two of us made a hurried dash to get inside from the rain, the lantern weaving in her hand once more. The smell of hay and animal was strong in the barn. The light, like a single firefly, floated in the air and gave off just enough light to illuminate the immediate area around us. A ladder was just off to the left, leading off into the darkened second floor. There were a few stalls, each full of hay strewn on the ground. The one at the far end was occupied by a young mare. The horse gave off a snort at the two of us for disturbing its slumber. Supplies and so forth were spread about the area, each in its own designated place.

With the light, I finally got a chance to look at the woman who was kind enough to offer me shelter. She had on a very simple dress, long and well made, that covered her from her neck to her ankles. There was a patch or two sewn into the dress, showing off that she was not used to finery—not that she needed any. There was strength about her that one could just feel—like she had no need for jewelry or makeup or anything like that. An apron covered her front, still covered with a light dusting of flour or something from the night's dinner. Her hair was up in a ponytail, allowing her face full view. She looked young, but the way she held herself showed off age and wisdom.

She pointed off toward the first stall, using the lantern to guide us. "You can stay there," she offered.

"Thank you, Miss—"

"Gertrude. My name is Gertrude."

I smiled at the pleasant woman. "Thank you, Gertrude. My name's Tom."

The two of us made our way toward the stall that was to be my home for the night. There was a small gate that blocked off the stall, which she opened for me. I took a few steps inside the small room, giving it a quick look over. There was no evidence that the stall had recently been used by anything, which gave promise for a good night's rest. Taking hold of my backpack, I set it down onto the hay with a strong sigh of relief.

Gertrude hung the lantern on a nail near the gate. "Here, now. You'd best give me your wet things so they can dry overnight."

"Thank you, again," I offered as I took off my soaking jacket and handed it to her.

She nodded and grabbed hold of the jacket that I offered her, giving it a quick once-over as she wandered away. There was a piece of rope that hung between two support beams in the center of the barn, which she walked skillfully toward in the mild darkness.

"Your jacket's ruined," she flatly pointed out to me, giving it a toss over the rope so that it could drip-dry.

I plopped down onto the hay with a soft crunch as I started working on the laces of my boots. The mud that covered the edges of the laces made getting a grip on the thin strings a little difficult, but somehow I was able to manage.

"Is it just the two of you?" I asked, trying to start up a conversation with the quiet woman.

"You mean is there anyone on the farm besides my husband and me? There's our boy, and there are two farmhands that help us out," she started up casually, moving the jacket on the rope so it was in a better position to dry, but then gave a quick pause. "And a neighbor that comes by every morning with milk and eggs, who checks to see that we're safe if that's what you're wondering," she finished, giving me a suspicious glance over her shoulder.

I held up my hands in defense from her glare, a sopping wet sock in one hand. "Not what I was getting at, I assure you. Your husband just mentioned that you were full up here."

She made her way back toward me and reached out to take more of my wet things. "Not a lot of space for the ones we have here, let alone strange men walking up our way in the middle of a rainstorm—at night," she tossed out as she took my socks.

I gave a quick chuckle at the situation as I watched her wander away once again toward the rope. "I thought I would be able to make it into town before night, but my leg was slowing me down too much … and then the rain hit … and I saw your barn from the road," I tried to explain to her as I struggled to take off my shirt, the wet sleeves turning into a second layer of skin and not wanting to part from my body.

"Well, you're lucky that I got a kind streak, or else you'd be stuck out there in the rain with all the rest of them," she called out behind me, setting the socks up and over the outstretched rope.

I finally managed to pull my shirt up and over my head. "The … rest of them?"

She returned back into the light and took up my shirt, which I had placed over the gate between us. "Considering what's been going on lately, with all the commotion and all, we've been mindful of strangers. If it weren't raining so badly, I probably wouldn't have given you a second glance."

I started to get a little uncomfortable. "I understand all too clearly," I mentioned in a soft tone.

"How long have you been on the road?"

Working the belt that held up my pants, I turned away from the woman. "I … ah … I've been wandering for some time now," I sputtered as I tried to come up with an appropriate answer—one that wouldn't give off too much information as to where I'd been, or rather where I came from.

"Oh, fer crying out loud," she scolded from behind me.

I glanced over my shoulder toward the woman to see what the matter was. She stood at the gate that marked off the stall, her hands planted on her hips in disapproval. I gave a quick glance around, trying to figure out what had upset her. She impatiently waved for the rest of my clothes.

"C'mon—all of it," she scolded me.

I gave the little room a glance over for cover—there was none. "Um—"

She gave a scoff and rolled her eyes at me. "I told you. I have a husband. I have a son. Now, unless you have a third testicle or something, there's nothing you have that I haven't seen already. You're going to catch your death in those wet clothes. Off with it."

I had to smile at her determination and her obstinate nature. "Yes, ma'am," I retorted as I dropped my trousers to the hay-filled ground. Working my legs out from the leggings, I passed my drenched and muddied pants to the woman. After she grabbed them and had them securely in her arms, she snapped her fingers and pointed toward my boxers. "Them, too," she ordered.

With a sigh, I removed my boxers. With nothing left to remove, I stood there in the stall staring off at the back wall while Gertrude wandered away to set up my clothes for drying. Standing there, naked to the world, I could only imagine what anyone must think had they happened to enter the barn at that particular moment.

"There's some horse blankets in the next stall to wrap up in for the night," she called out to me as she adjusted my pants on the rope so they could drip-dry for morning.

Making sure I didn't snag anything important, I opened the gate and quickly made my way into the neighboring stall. There, as mentioned, were two blankets sitting on a wooden box. They didn't exactly look too comforting against my bare skin, but they certainly looked thick and would definitely keep me warm during the night. Taking one in my hands, I swung it around my body to make up for the lack of clothing. The wool fabric rubbed and tugged against my moist skin, but it did its job.

I slowly made my way out of the second stall and started to wander back to the first one, where I'd left my backpack and supplies. She was just finishing adjusting my clothes on the rope that stretched between the two support posts.

"There," she smiled, "that should allow you to have dry clothes when the sun comes up. They won't be clean, mind you, but there's nothing we can do about that right now."

I stood in the opening of the first stall, the horse blanket wrapped around me like a cocoon. "Thank you again for all that you've done."

Without even giving me a second glance, she walked back toward the heavy door. Stopping just short of leaving the building, Gertrude looked back at me standing in the stall. Giving her apron a final swipe with her hands, she smiled.

"Now, I'm expecting you to be a man of your word with your offer for compensation for the roof over your head. If you take off on us as soon as the storm lets up, I swear I'll never hear the end of it for letting you in."

I smiled back at the woman. "I promise."

She nodded. "We wake close to dawn, so don't expect to sleep in."

She stepped out through the open door and grabbed hold of the handle on the opposite side. "Once the day starts up, we can negotiate your offer of compensation. Nice thing about a farm is that there's always something needing to be done."

The door slid close, leaving me alone inside the warm building. With the place left to myself, I sat myself down on the hay and started to prepare myself for night. Suddenly remembering the jab in my back when I fell in the middle of the path, I reached out and grabbed hold of my canvas backpack in order to check the contents to see if anything had broken or been squished. Tossing the flap to the side, I started to unload the well-packed carrying case of supplies—still good, traveling material, nothing broken, and my journal. I gave the cover of the book a quick wipe with the corner of the blanket, making sure that no moisture that might have entered the backpack from the tumble managed to make its way onto its golden pages. I gave the book a quick flip through to see where I had left off my writing....

⁓

... The next day, I joined officially with the POLICE. The sergeant was a little curious as to what had happened to me, my bruises still

fresh from the night before, but I stuck with the mugging excuse. That seemed to go over as I expected.

～

Right ... the beating from Vans, the letter from William ... I remembered.

I tapped my pen against the journal as I tried to gather my thoughts into some sort of format that I could put into written form. My training had just started ... ummm ... what to write, what to write. I chewed my lower lip for a bit as inspiration escaped my grasp, the tap-tap-tap of the pen against bound paper my only means of tracking the time it took for me to come up with something to write. It wasn't so much a basis of writer's block that struck me; it was trying to put into words the next three years of my life in a way that actually made sense. There was so much that happened, and yet, there was nothing really significant to it. It wasn't until that one day when I uncovered ... but how to get there on paper?

Tap-tap-tap ...

～

The next three years were a blur of activity, which started day one with my training ...

For the first six months, my life revolved completely around the POLICE and their training program. No time off for good behavior. It was train, train, and train some more. I found out at the end of my training that the sergeant brought about a special training program just for me. What normally happened was a group of SITs were trained under the lowest ranking sergeant on the grounds. Yet with me, he ordered Fürl alone to be responsible for my training. Not only that, but Fürl was under specific orders from the Sergeant to beef up the stakes. If a SIT was allowed 40 minutes to complete a training run, I was given 30. If a SIT needed to shoot a target with a chest shot, I had to get a head shot. And if I didn't make the cutoff time, then I wasn't allowed to rest or eat until I got it right. You get the idea....

Since I was working for the POLICE, I no longer had to live in my shelter. I now had a room on the Grounds. Not as big as my shelter, but I didn't complain much. It was closer to walk to William's. I also no longer had to work for the Factory. The look on my supervisor's face when I arrived at the Factory, complete with two officers behind me, to tell him I was no longer working for him was breathtaking. I guess he thought I was going to take out my revenge on him for all the horrible things he did to me over the years.

Because I was stuck on the POLICE Grounds for six months, I didn't get a chance to visit William like I had before. Didn't have the time. If I actually had a moment when I could steal myself away for a few hours, I didn't want to risk going too far. Fürl had a bad habit of finding me, no matter where I might have disappeared. I only ended up visiting on my days off, of which there were few.

I did get letters from John during the time I was in training, though. He was quite cryptic in his writing, but based on his letters, I found out that Dawn was covering for me as best she could, saying that the work I was doing to help rebuild the Factory took a lot out of me. If something needed to be sent to me or asked of me, Dawn would pass it by to John, who would then give her my answer ... or what I probably would have said, at least. He then gave me the head's up as to what it was about, so when I got a chance to visit, I would be able to cover. He even started to visit William on my behalf, he said, to help hide the fact I was in training. Didn't say what they talked about. Also mentioned that the repairs of the Factory were taking more time than expected, but he was doing well. He was put in charge of a small group of workers during the rebuilding, so when the Factory reopens, he will be given the rank of supervisor. Good for him!

At the graduation ceremonies, I was placed with the group that was in training at the same time I was. There was the occasional stare from the other recruits trying to figure out who I was and what I was doing at the party, but I tried my best to ignore them. Based on my scores, due to my enhanced training requirements, I graduated top of the class. Shortly after my graduation, Fürl was promoted to sergeant first class. I can assume it was for the great job he did with my training.

With my training done and my place in the POLICE confirmed, I was put to work immediately by the first sergeant. It seemed as though every assignment I was given was linked directly to my advancement. I flew through the ranks in record time. I was a private for about four months. Private first class lasted about ten months. Corporal was a full year. With my rank of corporal major, I was able to hang out with the first sergeant in his office quite a bit.

Allow me to explain the significance of the office. On the first day of training, the first sergeant would go down to the training area, and inform the SITs in true sergeant fashion, "The only reason you go into MY office is to find out that your family is DEAD or to discuss your performance. Either way, you will walk out with your HEAD BETWEEN YOUR KNEES AND YOUR LUNCH ON THE FLOOR!" Needless to say, because of that introduction, the officers would then lovingly refer to the office as Hell's Gate. The soldiers, when called in, walked in bleach white with their knees knocking, always prepared for the worst. The sergeant always allowed me to sit in whenever Vans was called down. For some odd reason, he was always a little more intimidated whenever I was in there … go figure.

As I went about completing assignment after assignment for the first sergeant, earning my rank up to corporal major, I tried to keep my ears open around the Grounds. Kept myself visible in the barracks … stayed in the middle of the pack at lunches and dinners. Read every report and made friends early with those in communication. Anything to hear about what moves there were against the Rebells. When something was uncovered, I would determine if it posed a great enough threat. Simple raids were easy enough to cover for. The Rebells would get wind of it early enough via an anonymous tip. They would then set up a mock stash of inventory. There would be just enough contraband to make it worthwhile for the POLICE, so they would think it had been a success, but nothing too expensive or rare to cause the Rebells harm. If lives were going to be lost on either side, then I took a more personal role in its disablement, either through Rebell or POLICE engagement.

I did eventually get around to talking to William about my POLICE involvement. I went to his place the second day after graduating. He welcomed me warmly and barraged me as to where I had been. Dawn stood by me as I then explained what was going on. He … took it in stride. First, he kicked me out of his house. Then he refused to talk to me for a month. Honestly, I wasn't surprised. Dawn was in my corner during this to-do, trying to get William to stop being so foolish. It wasn't until my first attempt to veer the POLICE off the path of the Rebells through my anonymous tip routine that William started to warm up to the idea of me being part of the POLICE.

The first couple months were rough going, but we warmed up to each other once again, and my visiting rights started back up after close to a year's hiatus. I would pop by on the weekends mostly, and the two of us would discuss the events going on between the two factions. My history lessons started to veer off course to planning sessions.

It was during this time that I talked to William about telling John about Lydia. I figured enough time had passed that he would be able to cope with the news. It was time for him to know. John surprised everyone by taking the news quite well. In fact, when John went to visit William that next day, he asked to take over Lydia's job of touring the Factory for the Rebells. Granted, the bunker was long gone and the POLICE weren't stupid enough to attempt that again, but John would be our eyes and ears inside that place. William thought it was a great idea, particularly with his position giving him free access to the Factory and how it would be a good way of preserving Lydia's memory.

Dawn and Sherry still kept up with my language lessons, despite William trying to squeeze me for information on POLICE rounds or POLICE targets. French was easy enough to learn, Spanish was a bit harder, but it was English that was the hardest. I don't know if it was through Sherry's influence or not, but she started to spend less and less time with my lessons and put more and more emphasis on me being tutored by Dawn. Eventually, she stopped tutoring me completely and spent her time trying to stop William from pestering me and interrupting the lesson.

The more time Dawn and I spent together, the stronger our relationship became. Soon, we started to date each other, much to Sherry's approval. Over the years, our love for each other blossomed into a strong romance, one that gave me both strength and courage to do my duty to protect this family. It also gave me a perfect cover for the POLICE to go see William—I was going to see my girlfriend. I tossed a few bribes here and there inside the communications building in order to make sure that the background check on William was first-rate. Didn't want any surprises popping up.

It was around the beginning of the year 2115 when things started to get complicated....

CHAPTER 17

Even though I had moved into the barracks about two years ago, I still hadn't gotten used to the whole change if it all. Instead of the two rooms I was allotted in my shelter, I now had one single space to deal with. I still had all the necessities, like a dresser and bed and such, but there were quite a few new things to play with. I had electricity. This meant that instead of that old lantern I had beside my old bed, I could simply flick a switch to fill my room with unending light. No more canisters to fill, no more risks of fire. I missed not having a kitchen readily available, but with the mess hall on the second floor, there was no need for one in my room. Probably the best part of the new abode was, thanks to the electricity, I could turn a tap and have fresh, preheated water any time I wanted. There was a huge basin full of constantly red-hot metallic bars that the water would flow through in the basement. The electricity that shot through these bars kept them at a constant burning status. No more wasting time trying to heat up the water in buckets under a flame—now it was instant hot water. The first night in my new place, I must have stood under a steady stream of steaming water for over an hour.

I was in my room polishing my boots when there was a knock at the door. The rag I was using, stained black with many previous uses, fell limply to the side as I put the boot down beside the one that was already finished.

"I'll be right there," I called out to the person behind the door.

I opened the door to my room, number thirty-three on floor nineteen, to see who was knocking. The officer who stood waiting for me to answer was a private in rank. Young, brown hair, average height—nothing out of the ordinary. I didn't recognize him from anywhere before. He must have been one of the new graduates, I guessed. He had a satchel off to the side that was full of letters and folders of all sorts. Mail. I nodded to the young man, and he saluted back. Reaching into his satchel, he produced a letter from the first sergeant and presented it to me. I took the letter and thanked him.

"Very urgent news," the officer told me with a serious look on his face. When the first sergeant sent a letter marked urgent, it was never a good sign. I thanked him, saluted, and started to close the door, all the while searching the envelope for some sort of clue as to what this was all about.

Walking over to my desk, I grabbed a letter opener that was carelessly thrown on top of it. The metallic dull knife slid through the paper concealing the message with ease, and I was able to pull out the letter. In the envelope, there was a single piece of paper with a single sentence: Come at once.

I quickly put on my boots and straightened up my appearance before leaving my room, the door automatically locking behind me—another feature that had taken some time getting used to around here. As I walked down the hallway to get to the stairs that lead to the ground floor, I started to come up with ideas as to why he would want to see me so early. Maybe he finally had that new assignment for me that he had been teasing me about for the past week—one that would "make my career," as he put it. As I passed the occasional officer walking down the stairwell, I nodded a greeting or said a general hello, my thoughts focused elsewhere.

It always took a lot of self-control not to burst out laughing when I saw everyone's reaction of me walking into the sergeant's office. Based on the reputation of Hell's Gate, they must have thought I was constantly getting into trouble. It seemed that I was spending more and more time there. Not so much to deliver reports or get new assignments, mind you. I still managed to do that on a regular basis. It was just that with my rank as corporal major, I didn't have that many small jobs left to do—they were all assigned to the lower ranks. When I wasn't working on some major project, I had time on my hands—time I then spent with the first sergeant. We would play chess, work on honing my abilities regarding POLICE rules and regulations, or just talk about whatever. The two of us came to an unwritten understanding with each other. Inside the office, we were just two guys hanging out. Outside the office, however, the sergeant was still the commander in chief and someone to be respected and feared. I was never to confuse the two.

Eventually, I made it to the building that housed all the offices for the higher-ranking officers. It was a building like all the others, not too tall and not too wide, but it held two very distinct differences from the other buildings, which made it stand out. The most obvious difference was that it was right in the middle of the Grounds. All roads and paths led to this one building. It was also positioned just right so that it could see, and be seen from, every other building. I guess this was so that the first sergeant could look out his window at everything going on around him and his office would be within running distance no matter where you were on the Grounds. Whatever the reason, everyone knew this building by association with the first sergeant's office—and all knew the fear of going anywhere near it.

The second major difference between this building and all the others was the small courtyard it housed. There was this minipark plopped right in the middle of the building, brick and mortar guarding it from all sides. When you first saw it from one of the windows, it just seemed odd and out of place. Surrounding the courtyard was concrete and stone and empty windows looking into stark gray offices. But in this small section of land locked away in hiding, there was green grass, yellow and red flowers when the season permitted, and trees that sprouted brown and orange leaves in the fall. On good days the higher officers would sit outside on the benches that lined the courtyard and have their lunches, talking about the different events of the day.

I quickly made my way through the front doors to the offices and off toward the first sergeant's wing. The hallways were well lit and adorned with pictures of previous first sergeants that had come and gone before the sergeant currently in charge. Some of the men in the pictures were standing behind desks, while others were in front of banners or flags or looking off to the future—but all of them were saluting. The last photo at the end of the hall was the first sergeant whom we all knew. He was the only one who wasn't saluting. The sergeant was instead holding a huge wrench and standing in front of the generator that he had managed to get working. I guess he wanted to show off his contribution to the Grounds more than being locked in the standard pose.

Turning around the corner, I was greeted by the lobby to the first sergeant's office. A desk sat directly in the middle of the room, the first sergeant's secretary working away on paperwork and whatnot. There were very comfortable chairs that lined the walls. It was what you would expect. But what immediately grabbed your attention were the two officers placed on guard duty on either side of a closed door. Armed with high-powered rifles, these two giants stood at attention on either side of the door frame that led to the sergeant's office. Their uniforms were pressed and shined to perfection; not one hair was out of place. Their eyes were locked on the horizon. No emotion dared caress their faces. They were a presence of pure intimidation. I smiled at seeing the two officers, knowing the real reason they were there.

The secretary, looking up from her paperwork to see who had interrupted her routine, returned her gaze to the duty at hand and waved nonchalantly to the two officers for me to go through. The soldiers saluted me and opened the door. I saluted back and entered the room, having the door closed behind me by the guard. The first sergeant looked up from a sheet that he was working on when I opened the door and entered.

"Ah, ya made it. Good," he smiled.

The first sergeant was sitting at his desk, working on some general paperwork. A soft, woven chair was open and waiting on the opposite side of the desk for guests. The wide window behind him, opened slightly to let in the fresh air, showed off a picturesque view of the courtyard. The bookcases were filled with knickknacks and memorabilia of all sorts from the years of service that he had provided to the POLICE. A map of the town and the surrounding countryside was adorned by a picture frame against one of the walls, showing off the border of the area he was put in charge of. A small chessboard was off to the side, two empty stools on either side. The board was in midgame. *We have to get around to finishing that game*, I mused as the board caught my eye.

I walked into the room a bit so the guards wouldn't hear me talking to the sergeant. "Sir, you really gotta get rid of those guys protecting your door." I smiled, jabbing a thumb at the closed door and the guards standing outside.

The sergeant leaned back against the old wood that made up his chair. "How many times do I have to tell you—it's all about image," said the sergeant in return.

When I was private first class, during one of my assignments, he confided in me their true purpose. "There's no real need for the security outside," I remember him whispering to me when I asked him about the two. "I just do it to scare the hell out of everyone who has to come see me. The guns they're holding don't even work. They know it too, but they all have signed a paper stating that they will not tell anyone under pain of reprimand. I got a whole slew of 'em on rotation, so the officers don't get too bored just standing there. But, when a private has to come to my office and sees them, it makes it all worthwhile."

He offered me the chair that sat in front of the desk. "Besides," he added while reaching for a cigar inside the box on top of his desk, "I don't see you complaining whenever Vans gets into trouble and comes here, looking like he'd just seen a ghost or holding his stomach like he's just been stabbed."

I eased myself into the chair opposite the desk and leaned back. "Touché."

The sergeant, while lighting his cigar, looked across the desk at my relaxed posture with a discouraging glare. "Whatever happened to saluting a superior officer?" he mumbled in a hurtful tone.

The sergeant and I had both agreed when I turned corporal major that we'd pass on the saluting each other strictly inside the office. When someone was watching us or if we were in the Grounds, then of course we would salute each other—but never in private. Too much pomp and circumstance, we'd both decided. Actually, if I remembered the exact words that the sergeant had said, it was something like, "With the amount of times that we see each other a day, if we keep saluting each other every time, we're going to flap ourselves airborne, and I hate heights."

I smiled coyly at the quick stab from the familiarity we had developed around each other. I jumped out of my chair, snapping myself into a sturdy attention, clicked my heels, and proudly stomped my chest in a salute. "Yes, sir, officer, sir! Please forgive this unworthy soldier of the POLICE, sir. It will never happen again … Charles."

The sergeant's eyes bugged out a bit at hearing his first name. "Hey! I told you—quit calling me by my first name. You know how much I hate that name, ya little—" he warned me jokingly, sticking a particular finger out at me to emphasize his earnestness.

I waved off the gesture, but when I returned to my chair, I did sit up more. "So, what's this urgent news you asked me here for?"

Charles put the paperwork in front of him off to the side. "I finally came up with your new assignment."

"Oh boy, more work," I teased.

Charles started to open up a side drawer on his desk. "Ya know," he started his debriefing being careful not to let any ashes from the cigar clamped inside his mouth fall into the open drawer, "I feel I've done a bit of a disservice to you, Tom."

I adjusted myself in the chair in an attempt to get more comfortable. When Charles started a lecture with a "ya know," it meant that it was going to be a long one. Charles continued his rant as he searched his desk for whatever he was looking for, tossing papers and whatnot off to the side as he talked. "When an officer gets to a certain rank, he's placed inside one of the departments as a base of operations."

"Yeah, I know this already," I pointed out.

Charles glanced up from his mad search to stop me from talking, waving his hand up in front of him. "Ah ah ah—listen."

I held up my hands in mock defense and let the man continue. "As I was saying, most officers get placed roughly around when they become a corporal. You, on the other hand, did not. I've been having you bounce from department to department, filling every role I could possibly think of in order to advance your career as quickly as possible. In one way, this greatly helped you, since most don't get a chance to go up the ranks unless the prime assignment happens to fall into their lap. With you jumping between departments, you went where the assignments landed."

Charles smiled as he finally found whatever he was searching for inside his disorganized drawer, his teeth half cloaked by the smog that crawled out of his mouth from the cigar. Grabbing hold of the object, he respectfully took it out of the drawer. Being careful not to show me what it was, Charles let it rest inside his lap. With the mad treasure hunt completed, he closed his drawer and returned to addressing me directly.

"Well, that's about to change. I'm going to officially assign you to the communications department, more specifically the quality control wing, along with a major assignment," he continued to smile at me.

"Quality control?"

The sergeant smiled. "I'm not surprised that you haven't heard of it. It's a small unit inside the communications wing, but it's a very important one. It's in charge of going through all material destined to hit the open market and be seen by the regular populace in order to make sure that it follows … well … proper POLICE guidelines. That includes material both recently written or found and uncovered from the war. If it follows the philosophy of the POLICE, then it can be released. If it needs editing, then it's edited. If it goes against POLICE doctorate, if it suggests ideals that were purposefully removed after the war or leads to undesirable effects, then the material will be removed or destroyed altogether."

I sat waiting for the bomb to drop. "Um … okay?" I answered, unsure exactly what the big deal was.

Charles leaned forward, took the rolled cigar from his mouth, and gently put the smoke-spewing tube into an ashtray on the corner of his desk. "I think this will be right up your alley, Tom."

With that, Charles reached into his lap and took out the mystery object that he'd spent the past few moments searching for, placing it on the desk in front of him. The old, ratty pages of a well-loved book splattered on the hardened wooden desk as it came to a rest. The cover was gone, the binding was close to collapsing, and the pages were falling apart. Charles grinned at me.

"Well?" he asked me, excited to hear what I had to say.

I stammered while I tried to come up with something to say. "Uh ... it's ... a book ... that looks like it's about to collapse under its own weight."

Charles waved his finger in a mock reprimand as he picked back up the pages and presented it to me in a more prestigious manner. "Not just any book, Tom. Take a look at it and tell me what you see."

I took the book from the first sergeant, handling it like one would when given a newborn. I turned it over a few times in an attempt to better examine its worth, being careful not to break it. Again, I saw nothing directly out of the ordinary. It seemed like any other book that was close to dying from old age. Yet, upon closer inspection, I finally glanced at what Charles was so adamant on showing me. The first page, since the cover was long missing, showed off in big, dark letters the year that it was written: 1984. This book was close to two hundred years in age. That explains the state it was in.

My head jerked up at the realization of what I was holding. "1984?" I asked Charles, in order to clarify what it was that I had just read.

Charles leaned back into his chair. "Yep. From what others have been able to determine, this book is prewar."

I started to quickly flip through the pages to properly study it in more detail. The writing was not as smudged as I'd first thought, but reading it was still difficult. The yellowing of the paper added to the difficulty of deciphering words. Taking a bit of time to decipher a paragraph lost somewhere within its pages, I mouthed the words as I tried to read them silently. It was written in English.

I slowly eased myself back into the chair, an uneasy feeling creeping over my body as I held onto the book. Taking a risk at glancing up at Charles to gauge his response, I cleared my throat. "I ... am having trouble reading this," I lied.

Charles scoffed at my response. "Of course you are. It's written in one of the old languages. I don't think anyone can read it now."

I breathed a quick sigh of relief at this. The last thing I needed to do was give away my ability to read the old languages. Then there would be a lot of hard questions to answer, such as how I learned these things. The POLICE would take a much harder look at those I associated with—like William and Dawn. Things would turn ugly very quickly.

I put the aged collection of paper into my lap. "Has anyone attempted to translate it yet?"

"Nah, not really. The kids in quality control tried to take a crack at it, but their minds were just too small for the task. They worked on it for about a day or two, but the best they got was three pages—and those were unreadable. I don't know if it was their translation abilities or the topic of the book. It would take too long to translate the entire book properly at that rate. Besides, it could be instruction on how to properly grow potatoes, for all we know."

I picked back up the book, curious to see what it was concerning. Skimming through the first few pages, I tried to pick out distinct words that would help lead me to what it was about. There was mention of a brother who was looking out for everyone—probably due to his siblings always getting into trouble. I flipped page after page back and forth, trying to get a sense of what the book was trying to say. Finally, ready to close the thing and dismiss it as Charles has done, I came across something written on the inside of the first page. It was the copyright portion of the book, listing off the publisher and such. According to the copyright, it was ... hard to read ... but I thought ... thought it said ...

"America," I whispered.

"What?" asked Charles.

"This book was written inside America!"

Charles tried to look at the book in my hand from where he sat. "How can you tell?

I pointed at the page I was reading. "It says so right here. See? There it is in black and white: America."

Charles took the book back from me and started examining it himself. After a few moments, he gave it back to me. "This book came from a crate we uncovered a few days ago inside the Zone about thirty kilometers outside of town. Now, I'm not allowed to say officially what we were doing out there, but what I can say is that we were checking on a rumor.

While there, the officers came across a bunch of crates inside a destroyed warehouse. They managed to open one of them and found a bunch of stuff, like this book here. The officers then decided to bring the crates back to the Grounds, and all were put into decontamination. Now, since they're clear of the possible radiation left over from the Zone, we have all the crates in storage inside a bunker beside the communications building.

"This leads to your assignment: You are to lead a team to take stock of the contents of those crates. I'll set it up so those you work with will be best suited for the task. Since the contents of the crates are from, or possibly from, America, this assignment has taken on a whole new meaning. If there is any other material or books like this one, go through them first and take note of anything that seems important. The important stuff will be broken up between quality control and research, while everything else has to be destroyed. This is high priority, Tom. We can't let it get out that the contents from these crates came from America. Who knows what type of gossip that could create. Get the report to me as quickly as possible."

"It might take awhile to go through everything inside these crates. How long do I have before the report is due?" I asked him.

"As soon as you finish, report directly to me," he told me, a hint of excitement in his voice.

With the tattered book in hand, I got up from the chair and saluted Charles. "I'll start work on it right away. Who knows, we might actually manage to get a better translation of the book for you too."

Charles smiled at me. "I'd expect nothing less. Dismissed."

I walked out the door and went on my way toward the communications building. All I could think about was the possibility of discovery, trying to figure out what lost treasures were nuzzled away inside those crates. What if one of the books had pictures of America? To see another part of the world now long gone, prewar documentation of life before ... what William wouldn't do to get hold of some of those books. Realizing that I was still holding onto the book that Charles gave me, I opened up the pages and started to translate/read as I walked on my way.

"It was a bright cold day in April, and the clocks were striking thirteen...."

CHAPTER 18

THE BUNKER WAS A SMALL, one-story shed attachment of the communications building composed of rock and mortar. It had absolutely no redeeming qualities to it whatsoever. It looked much older than the other buildings. It was probably one of the original structures on the land, and the POLICE created the Grounds around it. No windows adorned the outside, making it look like a solid brick. Moss grew in the cracks that formed in the rocks and mortar, like the building was bleeding green ooze. Small air vents encircled the top parts of the walls, just out of reach of hands that happen to be looking for someplace to put unwanted garbage. As I walked toward the bunker that housed these mystery crates and my future home for many hours to come, I couldn't help but feel a slow sense of dread. This place didn't exactly scream out a happy environment.

There were two officers on guard duty at the building's entrance. They were leaning casually against the wall, talking about the last night's poker game and laughing. One soldier was a tad bigger than the other, but neither jumped out at me as recognizable. It's amazing just how many officers the Grounds held. Every time I turned around, I saw some new person wandering around the Grounds. It was like there was one officer for every four townsmen.

As I walked toward the guards, one took notice of me walking in their direction and gave the other a quick jab to the side to stop him from talking. The two officers quickly shuffled into a guard-like position in front of the door and saluted me once I got close enough. I saluted back, making no reference to their previous behavior.

"Is this the bunker with the materials that finished quarantine?" I inquired, making sure that I'd found the right place.

The officer to my left stepped forward. I reached into my pocket and pulled out a single folded sheet of paper—the orders I was given from Charles that allowed me entrance into the bunker. The officer who had stepped forward took the sheet from me, looked it over, and then gave me back the sheet.

"Sir, yes, sir. All contents are here for your inspection, sir," the officer stated proudly, as if the two beat away roving packs of thieves and cutthroats to protect the crates safely locked away inside the bunker. I smiled at the image as it formed inside my head.

The officer to my right opened the door that lead into the bunker and held it open for me. The door opened without a sound, which was out of place for the state of the building. He swept his arm inside the room and bowed low, presenting the inner bunker to me. The other officer lit a small lantern and held it out for me to take. I grabbed the handle in my free hand, my other hand still holding onto the book that I'd taken along with me from Charles's office.

Once I was inside, the guards closed the door and firmly locked it, enclosing me in the building and preventing any chance of escape. It was a good thing that I had the lantern with me, because the bunker was pitch black. There was no other light source inside the building. No windows meant no natural light. Also, there was an overpowering musty smell, probably due to poor or no air circulation. I guess that was because the bunker was not used all that often. There was a fine mist of dust and dirt covering the cold cement floor, showing off just how rarely the bunker was used. A single corridor flowed in front of me. At the end of the corridor was an old, heavy, reinforced oaken door. It looked like the bunker was broken into two compartments—the one I was currently in and the one just beyond.

As I walked toward the oak door, a small glint of metal happened to catch the shaking beams of light that were scattered by the lantern as it wobbled to and fro in my hand. It caught the corner of my eye and could have easily been overlooked, this small shrapnel on the ground. The piece of metal was half-buried in ages of dust and dirt, barely able to be seen by the naked eye, but it somehow managed to grasp the light briefly. The object was no bigger than my thumbnail. Honestly, I'm surprised I saw it with the little amount of light available to me. Bending down to uncover the long lost hidden treasure, I pulled a golden ring out from the ground—an identification ring.

There was a name engraved on the inside of the band. I squinted my eyes to strain against the darkness in order to read the tiny imprinted words—Albert Schontzheir. Pausing for a moment to weigh my options with this uncovered discovery, I opted to put the ring inside my pocket so I could study it in more detail later on. Who knew—there might be a reward. I continued to the door that blocked my path and opened it.

There was an officer, ranked private first class, sitting on the ground by an open crate. He was looking at a list in his hands and was writing something on it when I entered the second compartment. The room was dimly lit from second and third lanterns that were hanging from hooks in the ceiling, but my lantern added generously to the much-needed light. The room was very plain. The seven or so crates that lined the walls were all opened, each one with different odds and ends hanging out or around them. One crate, in the very middle of the room, was still closed and nailed shut. A chair was placed off toward the wall facing me. A crowbar was on the seat.

The officer, shocked at the extra light inside the room, looked up toward me as if I'd just caught him playing hooky from school. The clipboard that he was writing on fell to the ground. He threw his head up toward me so fast that I was surprised his head didn't continue swinging around. Upon seeing who I was, he scrambled to his feet and gave me a hurried salute. I saluted back to him. The lad relaxed a bit afterward, but not by much, quickly reaching down and scooping up the clipboard he'd dropped. He must be the last officer of the group that brought in all the crates.

I say lad because he was very young for an officer. He might have been the same age as me, but he looked younger. Looking at his face, it was hard to tell. I'd say he was no more than twenty. Then again, I broke a few rules and records when I got my corporal bars. His black hair cut in the proper POLICE style, average build, deep brown eyes—he would do well in a fight, I wagered to myself. He must do just as well with the women.

"Name and rank, Officer," I ordered, trying to impress against the lad that I was in charge.

He stiffened a bit, shoving out his chest. "I am Private First Class H. J. Madison. Serial number 96—"

"Your name was quite enough. So, Private First Class H. J. Madison … anything to report?" I asked him, taking a quick glance around the room and the opened crates. As I glanced around, I put the book I was carrying onto the chair with the crowbar, being careful not to damage the already decaying binding and casting paper all over the ground.

"N-no, sir!" he bellowed, as a SIT would when answering the sergeant on the field. With the closed-in walls, our voices echoed off of them easily. If either of us even whispered, it could probably have been heard from the opposite corner.

"Please, you don't have to yell. I'm right in front of you."

I lowered the lantern and let it rest on the ground by my boot, rubbing my ears to help stop the ringing.

"No, sir," he answered again, looking for approval at the volume of his voice.

I stretched out my hand to him for the list he was working on, not moving from where I stood. After all, lower-ranking officers deliver to the higher ranking, not the other way around. "What's your assignment here," I questioned him.

He didn't even blink. The officer took the three steps toward me and presented the list that he was working on. "To take inventory of the contents inside the crates, sir. I have one more crate to go through," he nervously spat out as he showed me his clipboard.

The list covered the contents of the crates. Clothes, food (gone moldy from the age), soap, towels, and other useless materials covered the indexes of the list. Nothing that I found particularly interesting. I looked up to the top of the list and noticed that the filename wasn't filled out. I lowered the clipboard and returned my attention to the officer. "So ... who asked you to start working on inventorying the crates before the ranking officer arrived?"

"Um ... sir?"

I crossed my arms. "Answer the question, Private."

H. J. lowered his eyes in shame. I think the dark and enclosed environment added to the horror of the inquisition. "I assumed, sir, that since I was a part of the group that found the crates, I was responsible for logging the contents once they cleared decontamination."

I unfolded my arms at hearing his answer. He wasn't assigned to the ... he just walked ... I didn't believe it. A small fire ignited in my stomach as I turned and walked back toward the oak door, yanking it open with a bit more force than was needed. The lantern that I once carried was still exactly where I had left it, and the light from the room with the crates was the only stream of light as I tried to make my way down the dark corridor to the front door of the bunker. Arriving at the iron door that led to the outside, I kicked at it to get the two officers standing outside to open it. There was some quick shuffling just outside, a grinding of metal, and a blinding flash of light as the door swung open. I immediately raised the clipboard to my eyes to protect them from the explosion of light.

"Is there a problem, sir?" the officer holding the door asked me.

I took a quick shot behind me to see if H. J. was within earshot, the dark, inner workings of the building cast in shadow. H. J., from where I could see, was still standing in shame in the room just visible through the open doorway and the little light that shone from the lanterns. Returning my gaze to the two officers outside, I gave a quick jab at H. J.'s direction.

"Why is there an officer inside this secured building?" I demanded.

The one off to the side took a glance at the other officer, who was holding the door still for me, as if to say "I told you so."

"He ... uh ... said that he had permission to enter. He was part of the group that first brought the crates here, so I assumed—"

"You assumed?" I blurted out, my anger over the situation getting more and more riled up as each event presented itself.

The two officers shuffled their feet under my watch, gulping hard to swallow their shame. The officer who was doing all the talking licked his lips as he uneasily shifted his weight from foot to foot. "Well, sir, he's been coming here for the past two days, and no one said anything about it, so I thought that—"

I held my hand up to stop the officer from talking. "Wait wait wait ... you mean to say that he's been coming in here for the past two days—to a locked down and secured building holding possible valuable material—and you never once checked his clearance with anyone?"

The two officers, each taking a long breath, looked like they were about to list off a bunch of reasons as to why they did what they did in an attempt to defend their actions. I raised my hand to cradle my head; the blood pounded with every heartbeat, causing my head to throb with the start of a migraine as I thought about the situation I was suddenly thrust into. Behind me, I had an officer that willingly violated a secure area, thinking he was doing a good thing by breaking into classified objects and creating an inventory of them. Then, I had these two officers posted as guards in order to protect the classified objects; only they allowed an officer, who had no right being there, through without a second thought and then failed to report him. I sighed deeply at the paperwork I had ahead of me, trying to explain the situation and the reason for reprimand.

I dropped my arms to my sides and stared at the two, exhausted at the sight of them. Taking a cleansing breath, I gritted my teeth and started to go through the motions.

"Okay," I smiled calmly at the two, trying my best not to lose my temper, "obviously you two didn't get the notice stating that the objects inside this building were of great importance, or else you wouldn't have let anyone through. How you two missed that piece of information is beyond me, but apparently it happened. Fine! That's no excuse for not telling anyone about someone going in unsupervised for the past two days. Your carelessness will be noted in my report. Now, just so we're clear, under no circumstances are you two to let anyone else inside this building without direct orders from the first sergeant or myself. Is that clear?"

The two officers stiffened up and stood at attention while I reprimanded them, gazing off into the distance.

"Now, let's try to rectify this situation," I said more to myself than to the officers. I stared off into the sky as I tried to come up with a solution to this debacle. With H. J. working for the past two days, the majority of the inventory had already been documented. Based on the quick scan of the sheets on the clipboard, most of the materials found within the crates were worthless junk. Charles wouldn't be too happy with a list of expired food and scattered knickknacks. There was the one last crate left, but based on the materials found already ...

Turning to the officer who had been doing all the talking, I put my hands on either side of my waist to make myself look like I meant business. "All right. I want you to go to the first sergeant and give him a message for me."

"Sir?" he asked meekly.

"Inform the first sergeant that I will not need the team that he is in the midst of organizing for me. I already have all the officers I need for this assignment," I pointed out, glancing over my shoulder into the building at H. J.

The officer saluted urgently to me and then took off into a sprint toward Charles's office. Once he was out of sight, I turned around and reentered the building. I stopped just inside and turned back toward the officer still holding onto the door for dear life.

"Close this behind me and don't disturb me for any reason," I ordered.

The door locked behind me, plunging me back into a mild darkness and the musty stench of age and dust. *Now ... for H. J.*, I mused to myself, walking quickly back into the room with all the crates. H. J. hadn't moved from the spot where I'd left him. He was still locked in attention, waiting patiently for my return. When I reentered the room with him, he stiffened up his stance and stared straight ahead in true officer's training. I closed the oaken door behind me and then leaned up against the door, crossing my arms while I stared down at H. J.

"Do you know why I was ordered here?" I asked.

"To check on the materials of the crates, sir," H. J. replied.

I nodded. "That's right. Now, imagine my surprise when I found you here already going through them. I was told that there would be a team dedicated to helping me do this, so I naturally assumed that you were a part of this team. Still, I was just given this assignment, so having you here before I got here was quite a shock. I mean, how did you get orders to come here and start this up before I even had a chance to gauge how many officers I would need for my team?

"So, here I find an officer going through all the crates by himself, taking inventory of all the things inside of them. More importantly, this same officer was tossing around the contents of two hundred year old materials like they were yesterday's dinner scraps!"

H. J.'s eyes grew a bit at my last statement. He shifted his gaze toward the opened crates and the lack of care that was apparent in his handling of the contents. I gave myself a little internal push to get myself out of the leaning stance I was in and started to walk toward the flustered officer.

"If I find out that you inadvertently ruined something because of your lack of care, I will move you back down to private and have you on gate duty for the rest of your POLICE career. Do I make myself clear?" I threatened him, lowering my voice to a soft growl.

"Yes, sir!" he shouted.

I winced at the echo inside the room, adding to the pounding headache that I had been faced with due to this incident. H. J., noticing my reaction to his outburst, gave a silent apology through his facial expression.

I circled around the frozen officer as I continued my rant. "I can only assume you pulled this little stunt to further advance your career. A show to your immediate superiors that you are able to go above and beyond the order originally given. A display of self-motivation. Well, good news. I've informed the first sergeant that I will no longer need that team he was building for me. I've got you, after all. You're going to be my team. You are going to painstakingly separate, label, mark, package, and catalog each and every object that we discover inside these crates. And you will do this without question, without quarrel, without issue, and without breaks."

I stopped just behind H. J. as a thought encircled my mind. Smiling a sly grin, I continued my pace around the officer. "You will need to go and get a cot from storage, because you are going to stay in here until this assignment is completed. These contents are far too important to just leave around, and you have blatantly proved that the guards outside are too incompetent to leave them unguarded."

H. J. groaned softly at that last bit, his vocal protest not careful enough for me not to hear it. His eyes went wide when he realized what he had just done. He had just complained about his issued job, even thought it was just a sigh, with a superior right beside him. In training, you learned very quickly to enjoy the exact amount of work you were given. After all, there could be more given to you—a *lot* more. I stopped my winding march around the slightly smaller officer, and looked into his face.

"You have something to add, Private?" I asked.

H. J. bit down on his lower lip. "Permission to speak freely, sir?"

This kid is seriously just digging himself into a bigger and bigger grave. *Oh, this is gonna be good*, I thought to myself and waved for him to speak. H. J. relaxed his stance into an at-ease position.

"I fail to see the importance and the high security for a bunch of old clothes and some really moldy food."

I stopped him then and there. "One—we had no way of knowing that the crates held the clothes and food, as well as the other things. They could have housed more delicate objects, things that needed particular care when handling. Because of this unknown factor, we had to assume the worst and follow protocol. Two—we found that," I pointed to the book that was sitting beside the crowbar on the chair to H. J., "inside one of the crates that had already been opened inside the Zone. Do you recognize it?"

H. J. looked over at the book. "Yeah, it was the book that we found in the first box. We couldn't decipher it, so we marked it for quality control."

I walked over to the book and picked it up, handing it over to H. J. He took the poor collection of pages from me and glanced it over while I continued. "The reason why you were not able to decipher it was because it's written in one of the old languages. More importantly, it was published in America."

H. J. looked up at me, a confused expression crossing his face. "You mean that island that was bombed during the war? So what?"

I picked up the crowbar from the chair. Walking toward the crate that had not been opened yet by H. J., I jabbed the flattened metallic bar into a groove between the nailed-shut lid and the base of the crate. The crate was as tall as my waist, strong, and well made.

"So what?" I responded. "So, hopefully this last crate will have more of those books in it. Who knows, there might be printed material that could give us a better way to water our fields, to increase productivity in the Factory, or maybe even tell us what life was like before the war. That is, if the books survived the barrier of time and the process of the decontamination."

With a low grunt here and a heave there, the lid came crumbling off the crate into a dusty heap on the ground. H. J. cautiously walked up to where I was standing and looked into the crate. "What's inside, sir?"

Jackpot.

Books upon books. Of every description: big, small, red dyed, leather casing, but mostly paper-covered. Unfortunately, based on the condition of the books inside, the crate was never tested for waterproofing. Only the well-protected books in the middle of the pile could have survived the wet onslaught from the decontamination process. The books on the top, the sides, and I'm guessing the bottom were all but destroyed.

H. J. saw the amount of work ahead of us and let out a sigh, again reacting quickly to his mild outburst to the task at hand and my reaction to it. He took a quick glance toward me, which I caught out of the corner of my eye, in order to see if I heard him sigh. I could just imagine what was going through his mind at that moment. A smirk crossed my face. I couldn't help it.

"All right," I breathed as I pushed myself to full height and stretched out my lower back, "wait here while I order our dinners to be brought here."

Since we were going to be spending quite a bit of time together, I might as well make the best of it.

CHAPTER 19

... For almost a week, H. J. and I worked on the contents of the crates. He was more focused on the categorization of the other material, the stuff that he had already discovered from the other crates. I, on the other hand, was fully engrossed with the books. Eleven books survived the voyage intact. Nine of the eleven were fully readable. The other fifty-six books found within the crate were destroyed and were, for all intents and purposes, considered firewood. What a waste!

In order to go through the books and mark which ones were to be translated fully into German, I had to requisition a German/English dictionary from the archives of the communication building. Normally, that would be close to impossible, but Charles's assignment letter helped with the process. After all, I had to give off the illusion that I needed it to help me with the translation.

The first book that I was able to work on was one by Charles Dickens, called *Hard Times*. The book had already been translated long ago, so I had no need to delve into it further. It was an easy enough read with nothing drastically important regarding prewar documentation. I was about to pass it along, but there was a section that caught my attention, and for the longest time, I couldn't get out of my head:

"You are to be in all things regulated and governed," said the gentleman, "by fact. We hope to have, before long, a board of fact, composed of commissioners of fact, who will force the people to be a people of fact. You must discard the word FANCY altogether. You have nothing to do with it. You are not to have, in any object of use or ornament, what would be contradiction in fact. You do not walk upon flowers in fact; you cannot be allowed to walk on flowers in carpets. You don't find that foreign birds and butterflies come and perch upon your crockery; you cannot be permitted to paint foreign birds and butterflies on your crockery. You never meet with horses going up and down walls; you must not have horses represented upon walls. You must use," said the gentleman, "for all these purposes, combinations and modifications (in primary colors) of mathematical figures which are susceptible of proof and demonstration. This is the new discovery. This is true. This is fact."

During this time, I tried to break the ice with H. J. As we talked, I got to know him better. His father worked inside a bakery cooking bread. H. J. couldn't emphasize enough how good his father smelled after coming home from work. His father also ground cinnamon at the bakery, adding to his pleasant aroma. His mother died when he was very young. The only reason he could remember what his mother looked like was because of a picture he had hidden inside a locket, which he carried around with him around his neck. He showed her to me. She was a very beautiful lady with flowing black hair. H. J. was a fast talker as well. What I meant was that he enjoyed talking, as well as his use of words. He had a real knack with talking. Something he said he picked up from his grandfather, among other things ...

The bunker, now full of lamps, was quite a bit changed since the first time I had entered it. H. J. had managed to pull in a table for me to use as a desk while I worked with the books that had survived. The crates were flipped over to create a mock assembly line for his inventory documentation. All sorts of objects were labeled and piled into different configurations. Things were running smoothly, for once. I sat at the table and had my nose firmly stuck inside one of the books that had been found within the crate, the English/German dictionary in close reach. The books that I had finished sorting through were in two neat piles at the end of the table— one for future translating and one for books that didn't need much more examination. H. J. was in the midst of writing something on a clipboard regarding a pile of boxed up crackers long gone and was telling me some tale of one of his many adventures.

"… Rebell … three … surrounded."

"Uh huh."

"… threw … ground …"

"Uh huh."

"Sure … die."

"Uh huh."

"Then … meteor … creature … tentacles."

"Uh huh."

"Sir … listening?"

"Uh huh."

A tap on my shoulder pulled me out of the written log that I was hard at work trying to translate into German for the sergeant. H. J. stood to the side, his head tilted in question. "Sir?"

I blinked out of my stupor, realizing that I hadn't heard a single word that this poor man was trying to say. Embarrassed at my lack of manners, I pushed the book away with my notes and translation of the book resting in front. "I'm sorry," I said, wiping the stress from my eyes, "that was rude of me."

H. J. smiled at me in his young, energetic way. "That's okay, sir. You were focused on your work. I was just about to say that we should call for lunch soon."

I leaned back in my chair, the muscles in my back creaking and stretching from lack of movement. I hadn't realized how stiff I was. Perhaps a quick break was in order, after all. I got up from my chair, pushing it back to the table once I was clear, and looked about the room to see how H. J. was progressing with the cataloging.

"Yeah, you're probably right," I agreed, weaving my arms around my body in an attempt to stretch out the kinks. I nodded out toward the front door. "Give the guards our order for lunch."

H. J. nodded and went out toward the opened oak door, leaving me to my weary body and my thoughts. Taking in the view of the semiorganized room, I tried to figure out how much more time it would take to complete this task. I was almost done flipping through the books that had survived, marking the ones that were to be translated completely. By the looks of things, H. J. was close to finishing his cataloging as well. Maybe another day or two, but no more than that. H. J. popped back into the room, an apple in his hands. "They said that it shouldn't be too long before one of 'em returns with lunch. Said it was beef sandwiches today."

I nodded, glancing around the room at all the stuff within it. "So," I thought out loud, summing up the room, "I'd say we got about another day's worth of work. What do you think?"

H. J., who was sifting through one of the piles of books I had off to the side, looked up at me and then to the room. His seemed to be crafting a mental chart in front of him, checking off the things that had been completed and those which still needed to be done. "Yeah, about a day," he summarized and then turned his attention back to the books.

I turned and walked over to where he was standing. H. J. picked up one book in particular, a leather-bound book with yellowing pages within it. On the leather binding was a simple image of a huge weather balloon and a basket hanging just underneath it. Above the image were the words *"Around the World in 80 Days* by Jules Verne." He glanced my way, showing off the book that he was holding with little care.

"Never did like this one," he shot out to me, putting the book back onto the pile that didn't need to be translated. He then saw a second book: *Peter Pan* by J. M. Barrie. "Didn't like that one, either."

I smiled. "Why not?"

"I don't know. Just couldn't get into 'em, I guess."

I leaned up against the table as we waited for lunch to arrive, my thoughts elsewhere than the books for once. "So where in the Zone did you find all this stuff, anyway?" I asked H. J.

H. J. looked up from the books, thinking. "Uh ... I think we grabbed them in some sort of warehouse. Or maybe it was an indoor market square. Dunno where it was, exactly. We were checking a lot of big buildings around the outskirts of the Zone. Wouldn't go near the hot spot. Too much radiation left from the power station when it went critical."

I nodded, a smile growing inside me. "Odd to check for supplies and materials now. Didn't think we were in need of any," I continued, inadvertently trying for him to divulge the reason for going into the Zone.

"Oh no," H. J. corrected me. "We weren't looking for supplies. We were—"

H. J. suddenly stopped talking, realizing he was about to say something he wasn't supposed to. Quickly, he turned back to looking over the books, picking one up and then another, flipping through the pages without reading them. I smiled at H. J.'s restraint.

"Above my rank?" I asked him, shooting him a smirk.

H. J., not looking up from his attempt to look busy, didn't say anything. I eased myself up off of the table and stood in front of the lad. He stopped sifting through the books and looked up at me.

"Look, if you can't say, then you can't say. I understand. I do, really. Orders are orders."

"We weren't ordered," he spoke softly, unsure.

"So?"

H. J. squirmed a bit under my gaze and took a breath. "Don't tell anyone I told you this. This is supposed to be top secret, or something ... I think."

I held up my hand in a silent promise. And with that, H. J. started his tale.

"Awhile back, I was in the barracks' common room playing poker with a few of the guys. I wasn't doing too hot that night. Anyway, all of a sudden Sergeant Fürl walked through, saw us, and then walked over to where we were playing. I thought he was going to join us. Instead, he told us that he had a mission for us—real top secret and stuff. He needed a few brave officers to do something for him, something that would put us in harm's way. That didn't go over too well with the guys and me, but since Fürl asked us—I mean, c'mon—this is a guy who fought the Rebell leader Duncan one-on-one when he had just gotten the rank of sergeant, took a knife to the face, lost an eye, and still managed to send Duncan packing. He's not the type of person you say no to, right?"

"Anyway, he led us to his office, and we all piled in. It was late, so no one really noticed us. Once we're inside his office, he takes this map of the town and lays it on his desk. We all crowd around the thing, and he starts to tell us about how he needs us to go in the Zone outside of town and size up all these different big buildings. He points to them on the map, saying that these are the most likely targets so we know which ones he's talking about. One of the officers asked him what it was exactly we were looking for, but that just got Fürl in a bad mood. Said that we weren't looking for anything in particular, just to take an estimate of the size of the building. It was almost like he was planning to hold a convention or a massive party for all the POLICE officers in one of them. I'm standing there listening to all this and I'm thinking, 'Why would anyone want to have a massive gathering in the Zone?' But, that's what he wanted … just for us to gather intel and to return—that's it. So, we left that night. Got to the Zone, took a look around, saw the crates in one of the buildings, and figured, 'Hey, while we're here. Might as well make our trip worthwhile, right?' Found a cart. Brought them back."

I stood in silence, taking in the story that H. J. had just churned for me and tried to make sense of it. What was Fürl up to? What was he planning? Charles said that they were sent to test out a rumor. A rumor of what, and why would it need a really big building? And why in the Zone? Sure, the radiation has depleted enough so that one wouldn't get the Fallout Plague like before, but only if you stayed on the outskirts of the area. There was still enough radiation there to make you sick if you stayed too long. And that was just on the outskirts. If you went too close to the old power station, then you were risking serious harm. It made no sense. Why risk it at all?

Knock, knock.

One of the guards stood beside the oak door, a tray of food in his hands. I looked over to the table, a nice clear spot opened up from my work being pushed off to the side, and waved for the officer to put the tray down there. He did so without a word and left right afterward. On the tray were two plates, each with a steak sandwich, some general greens or celery, a couple slices of fruit, and a piece of cake. There were also two cups and a jug of some sort of liquid. H. J. took up one of the plates, poured himself a drink, and wandered off toward the opposite end of the bunker, easing himself down onto the ground to eat. I took the sandwich from the second plate.

While I did so, my eye caught the book that H. J. said he didn't like. At first, I just stared at the picture on the cover—the weathered leather cracking and breaking the image in some parts. But then I noticed something … something that was out of place. I slowly turned back toward H. J., an uneasy feeling starting to creep over me.

"Mind if I ask you something else, H. J.?" I asked while wandering over to the oaken door left open by the officer who brought in our lunch and closing it gently.

"Sure," he said, his mouth choking down a bite of sandwich.

I wandered back over to the table and pointed with my sandwich to the pile of books on the desk beside me. "This is just out of curiosity, but what about the book didn't you like?"

"Which one?"

"Either, I suppose," I shrugged, tossing off the question as casually as I could.

H. J. adjusted himself on the ground so that he was leaning on one of the crates that were set up around the bunker. He chewed his sandwich carefully, formulating his words inside his head before he spoke. "Well, I didn't like *Peter Pan*, 'cause it was too far-fetched. An island where you never grow up and pixies with dust that makes you fly? Ridiculous. And *Around the World*? I guess that one because it was too dry."

I nodded, taking a slow drink of the fruity drink inside my cup. "How did you know the titles of the books?"

H. J. looked up at me, confused as to what I was trying to ask exactly. "They're on the covers?" he answered slowly, not sure as to what I was driving at.

I nodded and started to eat my sandwich, taking a firm bite into the meat and bread. H. J. raised one of his eyebrows to question where that came from and took another bite.

"It's just that," I continued, covering my mouth with the back of my free hand so not to spit out any bits of sandwich I was still chewing. My eyes locked on H. J.'s position. "I would have figured you'd have trouble reading the title and recognizing the book, them being in English and all."

H. J. froze for a second, his mouth in midchew. Neither of us moved. I looked down at H. J., and H. J. locked his eyes with mine. "I recognized the pictures," he finally pointed out.

I smiled a bit. "Only the one book has an image on the cover. The other one was only words."

And with that, he was caught. H. J. knew it, and I knew it. He slowly closed his eyes and cursed silently at his carelessness. The relaxed environment that we had created inside the bunker put him squarely into a trap that he couldn't escape. An awkward silence crept in the area between us, neither of us quite sure what to say or to do regarding the situation. I couldn't exactly punish the kid over the fact that he knew English. I knew English. To punish him would make me a hypocrite. But, the law was quite clear on the use of the old languages, and the punishment was really severe.

I clicked my tongue in an attempt to make some sort of noise to break the silence in the room, my mind still churning as to what exactly to do. H. J. still did not move or say anything, but he did lower his face to the ground. I can only imagine what horrors were going through his mind at that point. He was probably envisioning being dragged through the street by an angry mob, imprisoned, and then killed by the death squad—maybe even being tortured right before the death squad.

After what seemed like a lifetime, I grabbed hold of the chair that was parked by the table and pulled it out to sit down. The wooden frame made little sound as it scraped along the floor, the dust that once covered the area swept clear earlier on. I collapsed into the chair, sitting out toward H. J., arms resting on the end of my legs so I could look him in the face better.

"So ... what are we going to do about this?" I asked, searching for an opinion from the kid on what was fair. I looked at him with a somber expression. You have to give him credit for taking it with honor. No attempts of bribery, no fits of anger at the discovery.

H. J., lost in his own world of destruction and despair, started to mumble to himself about how stupid or how careless he was. I'm not sure which one, because I couldn't hear him correctly. I got up sharply from the chair and started to pace a bit in the little room available. As I wandered the room, I started to weigh the options available to me: option A—I follow the law and the POLICE procedure as per my rank and submit the kid for reprimand for having knowledge of a forbidden language in accordance to ancient decree. By doing this, H. J. would be stripped of rank, severely punished, and probably put to death—I thought. Or, I go with option B—keep my mouth shut with regards to reporting him, possibly let him know my *own* knowledge of English, and further the Rebell's hold within the POLICE grounds by planting the seeds of discontent regarding the laws and the harsh rules we abide by.

If only I could flip a coin ...

"Sir?"

I blinked for a second, regained my sense of the situation, and looked over at the voice that called out to me. H. J. was standing behind me, trying his best to look brave. His shaking hands, however, gave him away. I guess it was time to deliver my answer.

"Well," I started up, trying my best to sound as calm as possible, "I have to say that I'm a bit disappointed in you."

Walking over to one of the piles of books on the table, I grabbed a random one and tossed it to H. J. He caught the book with a flutter of fingers, the spray of pages calmly coming to a rest within his chest as he pressed the precious cargo to him.

"Do you realize how much time we wasted in here?" I sarcastically asked him, shooting him a quick smirk. "If I had known you read English,

I'd have made you do the analysis. It woulda been done in a day!" I gave a good wave at all the work I had done for emphasis.

"Uh ... sir?"

I leaned back up against the table and tried to get him to sit down in the chair, which I pulled out for him to use. H. J., still clutching onto the book, softly plopped himself down into the chair. Half-sitting on the table, I smiled at the kid.

"You can relax, ya know," I assured. "Just so there's no confusion, I'll say it out loud. I'm not going to turn you in. You're a good officer, and it would be a shame to get rid of you just because of this. You shouldn't be punished for learning something when it betters you. Yes, in my opinion, knowing more languages betters you. It allows you to look at things in a different perspective, which is important, especially as you go further in the ranks. Now, with that being said, we need to take a look at the more serious points of this issue. Since my viewpoint on the matter is, for all intents and purposes, breaking the law and thus could be viewed as treason, I will flatly and utterly deny ever saying it if pressed. Considering it would be your word against mine, I feel safe with that.

"But, also so there's no confusion, there *will* be a price for my silence. Odds are, in the future, I will eventually need a favor done. Don't know what for ... don't know when. Could be big, could be small, but it will probably need to be done by someone I can count on and trust. If I ever ask you to do something, and I emphasize that it's to be done as a favor—no matter what it might be—you *will* do it for me, no questions asked. Deal?"

I felt kind of bad for what I was doing to the kid, backing him into a corner like that and all and then threatening to expose him. But one thing I had learned working with the POLICE for the past three years was that you always needed to have your back covered. That, and it was always good to have dirt on someone that you could bring back up for a favor.

Favors were like the transparent currency inside the POLICE Grounds. If you didn't have a favor owed to you, then you had nothing to barter with. I'd had to do a few favors for other officers in exchange for sneaking out of the Grounds to go see Dawn after hours. A few more favors for the cost of being let back in. This eventually led to me doing extra kitchen duty, filing extra paperwork, letting a report slide, covering for patrols, and having to return the favor of letting officers sneak out to see loved ones—stuff like that.

H. J. took in the whole speech. I could actively see the gears working behind his eyes within his head, trying to come to a decision. He finally put the book he was cradling onto the table and held out his hand to me. "Deal."

I took his hand and gave it a shake, confident that he would honor the deal we made if the option came up. I motioned for him to take the chair by the table. "Just out of curiosity, where did you learn English?" I inquired.

H. J. took the chair in front of me, a puff of relief easing from his weary body. "My grandfather taught me. Actually, I taught myself, but my grandfather gave me a good start on my learning. He would read me a story. I sat on his lap as he read, so I saw the words as well. I was pretty young at the time. He went line by line with painstaking precision to emphasize each syllable. He died soon afterward. I got the book through inheritance. It was the only thing I got from him. Each night from then on, after I went to bed, I stayed up about half an hour later than I should've and read the book over and over again. I emphasized each word, just like my grandfather had. One day, I found that I could read the book so well that I tried to find another book. The bookstore owner slapped me in the face for asking for a book in this language. I kept the fact about me reading English to myself from then on. Of course, by that time, I found out that reading or speaking in anything other than German was against the law."

"What book was it?"

H. J. smiled. "*Robin Hood*."

CHAPTER 20

We managed to finish the paperwork section of the report for Charles that day, but we both agreed that it would be best to give it to the first sergeant after we did some final prep for it. That way, we could really impress him. For the next three days, H. J. and I went about searching for the origin of the crates. We had nothing but the name of the company that was written on the side of the crates, the cargo waybill that was found inside the last crate we opened, and some general detective work. Apparently, the crates belonged to an American shipping company that traveled to Spain. The shipment was made during the war, but the boat was raided and destroyed. The crates, after being dragged out of the water, were placed under security in Italy before being shipped here for storage. It's quite funny, really. The group that attacked the ship opened a single crate, to see what the Americans were shipping to Spain. It was pure luck that they opened the one crate that held the weapons that Spain had asked for from America as opposed to the fifty or so other crates that were packed with useless stuff to help cover for the one important crate. I found this out through some hunting inside the weapons department's archives.

On the day that we would have completed everything, I got a surprise urgent request to see Charles in his office. Figuring that this might take some time, I sent a quick message to H. J. that we would be taking the day off from the report and then made my way to see Charles.

~

The guard opened the door for me, and I wandered in. Charles was at his desk, muttering to himself over a letter in front of him. Apparently, Charles was not too thrilled about whatever was written on it—his grumbling and mumbling was never a good sign. He brushed aside the paper for the briefest of moments to look up and see me entering the room. He impatiently waved at the chair in front of the desk and returned his full attention to the paper. I nodded to the guard who held the door open, signifying that I would be fine and that he could close the door.

"Wow," I smirked as I eased myself into the chair, "what's got you in a good mood?"

Charles let out a frustrated sigh. Brushing his temples, he closed his eyes and took deep breaths.

"It's this requisition for resources that Fürl managed to whip up for me. According to this," he spat as he slapped the paper, "he wants to pull an entire battalion for some sort of specific training that he's going to govern over. And then there's the request for the use of the training grounds for half the year—which would knock out the spring recruit drive completely—the equipment that he wants to train with, the special medical attention he wants allocated for this.... All for a rumor that he's gotten from one of his sources. If it's legit, then this could be a major break for the POLICE force, but if it turns out to be just a rumor ... what a waste of time and effort."

I adjusted myself in the chair as I listened to Charles complain, thinking over the past month or so. "This wouldn't have anything to do with the run into the Zone and the acquisition of the crates that you have Private First Class Madison and I going through, would it?"

Charles guffawed at my question, picking back up the request that Fürl had submitted. "The worst of it is that it all lands on my desk. If it turns out that the rumor is false and I give the go-ahead on all this, or if I say no and it turns out to be true, then I look the fool and my superiors will berate me for years. On the other hand, if I give the go-ahead and this little rumor is legit, woo, boy—good times for me."

I crumpled my brow and leaned forward. "Charles, what is going on? What is this rumor that's going around? What is Fürl planning?"

There was a light rap at the door, which brought us both to attention. Charles, leaning out of his chair to get a better look at the door without actually getting up, called out to the mystery person to enter. The door opened slowly, the base of the door brushing the carpeted flooring slightly and making a shushing sound. One of the guards popped his head around the door, looking both apologetic for interrupting our meeting and earnest to inform the first sergeant of the news he held.

"Sir?"

Charles, not wanting to move from his chair, motioned for the officer to speak. The officer, still clinging onto the doorframe, stepped into the room a little bit so he wasn't fully hidden. "You wanted to be informed when Fürl was leaving to go to his meeting outside the Grounds? Well, he's now leaving, sir."

Charles grew somber at the information that was delivered. Obviously, it had something to do with what Fürl was planning—whatever. it was. Charles nodded to the officer, who then saluted and left us alone, closing the door behind him. Charles sat for a moment, unmoving. I cleared my throat softly in an attempt to remind Charles that I was still there.

"So, regarding my previous question about what Fürl—"

Charles suddenly snapped his fingers and jabbed a finger out toward me, a sense of urgency exploding out of him. "Oh! I forgot. The reason why I called you over here. I swear my mind has been all over the place for the past day or so."

It looked like I wouldn't be finding out what Fürl was up to. His little performance for my account was an inadvertent attempt to let me know he didn't want to talk about it. Charles had a bad habit of doing that. When I asked him something that he either didn't want to talk about or couldn't talk about, he would flip the conversation onto some other topic.

"I called you for two reasons," he mentioned simply as he reached into a drawer inside his desk and pulled out a single envelope. He continued his explanation as he offered the opened letter to me. "First was to see how you're doing with the report."

I took the letter from him and leaned back into the chair I was sitting in. "The private and I should be finished in a day or so."

"Good," Charles smiled. "Secondly," he nodded toward the letter, "I received this first thing this morning. It arrived special delivery."

Taking the folded paper in my hands, I flipped it over in order to see the front of it and who might have written it. The letter was adorned lightly with the symbol of the POLICE in the corner, proving that it was POLICE issued. There was no mention on the outside who wrote it, where it came from, or the purpose of the letter. It simply had "To First Sergeant of POLICE Grounds 104" written on it in fine penmanship.

Charles nodded to the letter in my hands. "Read it."

I opened the broken seal that kept the letter inside the envelope and took out a single piece of paper.

⌒

Dear First Sergeant Charles Buret, Head of POLICE Grounds 104.

Look down at the name before reading any more of this letter. Now that you know it's from me, you can believe that everything I'm about to say is true. The reason I'm writing is because I owed you a favor. A big favor. One which I didn't think I was going to be able to repay. I think I just repaid it.

As you know, next year will be the seventy-fifth anniversary of the victory of the war. You've probably been wondering why there hasn't been any news regarding the festivities trickling down to the local areas. That's because there's not going to be as big of a celebration as there was during the fiftieth anniversary, although something important *is* being planned. The General thought it would be a good idea to take a grand tour of the world that has remained from the war, and the anniversary would be a perfect time for it.

I'm sure that you would have found out about this from someone, sooner or later. My repayment to you is to inform you that he is taking a special, unappointed visit to your Grounds to see you. He has a new opening inside his elite guards. Through some string-pulling and some serious pushing on my behalf, YOU have been nominated for that position. You have no idea how many other favors I had to pull in for this, but I figured that my debt was too big to let this one just pass by, and this was a good way to repay you.

You are going to move up to Sergeant Major in one year's time. Use this year to start getting yourself and the Grounds ready!

Enjoy!

Your friend and colleague,
S-M Fran Vasover., Comm.

~

I looked up from the paper in astonishment. "Charles!? Is this true?"

"As far as I know, it is. Fran wouldn't write something like this if there wasn't a shred of truth to it," he smiled.

I got up from my chair, reached over the desk, and grabbed his hand. "Congratulations, Sergeant."

Charles raised one of his eyebrows. "'Sergeant?'"

"Sorry … Sergeant *Major*."

He nodded his head and smiled even wider. "Say it again. I like the sound of that."

"So," I asked, bringing him back to solid earth, "when does the general supposedly arrive?"

Charles leaned over and reopened the drawer that held the letter. The now mildly disorganized drawer was full of all sorts of paperwork that Charles liked to keep on hand for easy access. One such thing inside the drawer of importance was a map of the overall area, covering the land that once made up the country Germany. He grabbed the folded collection and traded it for the letter. Careful not to crack and peel off any more of the wax seal that adorned it, he lightly placed the letter into the drawer and closed it. Charles, with a flourish of unfolding and stretching, spread out the map on the desk in front of us. The two of us leaned over the collection of squiggly lines and dotted towns to better investigate the question.

"Well," he said after a few moments of study, "if he's leaving from Hauptstadt and going south from there, spending *probably* ... three to four days inside each town that he passes—not to mention that he wouldn't be leaving until the end-of-war anniversary date—I'd say a good five months. Maybe six at the most. That would mean toward end of August or beginning of September next year. But, then again, this is just speculation."

"That will give us plenty of time to get the Grounds in shape and ready for his visit," I nodded.

"Remember," warned Charles, as he folded the map again to its former state, "this is supposed to be a surprise. So don't prepare too much. We don't want to look like we knew that he was coming."

I looked over Charles's shoulder at the huge window behind him that displayed the courtyard in all its glory as I tried to take it all in. The general was coming to Sicher Himmel, the first sergeant would be leaving us, and that would mean ... uh oh. I looked back at Charles, a concerned feeling growing in my gut.

"Charles, when you become a sergeant major and leave with the general, who—"

"Will become the next sergeant and have control over the Grounds?" interrupted Charles.

I nodded.

He gave me a sly smile and raised his hand up to his heart in a mocking attempt to pretend he was just stabbed by an invisible blade. "You just can't wait until I'm gone, can you?"

"Well, it would be a good idea to start thinking about that, so when you leave, there won't be a huge fight to get your old position," I pointed out.

He leaned his head back and stared hard at the ceiling. "Umm ... how did it go? Once the head officer leaves the POLICE Grounds by transfer, promotion, or other ... ummm ... the next highest-ranking officer stationed on the POLICE Grounds becomes the next official head officer. This can only be superseded by—oh, what was it—superseded by the head officer's personal recommendation for replacement. In this case, approval, proper rank, and any additional training by a first sergeant or higher must be obtained before transfer of POLICE Grounds will become official."

Charles, quite proud of himself for remembering in such detail his little quote, smiled to himself and reached for a victory cigar. "The next highest ranking officer is Fürl, being sergeant first class," I pointed out.

Charles nodded, cigar between teeth, as he searched his shirt pocket for his lighter. "Fürl would be the first candidate."

I thought for a second on this, trying to imagine what the Grounds would be like with Fürl being in charge. Images of my time being trained by Fürl, reporting to Fürl, and just spending time with Fürl summed up the experience—torture. Any sense of fun would be yanked from the Grounds, turning it into a gray pit of sucking emptiness. Fürl would improve the overall numbers and stats the Grounds gets—that was sure. But it would be at the cost of its personality.

Charles looked over the bridge of his nose at me. "Buuut ... he wouldn't get the position. Unfortunately, the POLICE official needs to be a poster boy representative for the town—a sign of perfection that shows no flaws, mental or physical, to the other soldiers. With his—how best to put it— beauty mark and his failing health that tends to hamper him from extreme exertion, he's pretty much out of the running. He knows this already and has come to terms with it."

"Well, if that's the case, the next is Staff Sergeant Gustaff, Fürl's right-hand man," I pointed out.

Charles nodded his head. "Correct. Gustaff would be next on the list."

I leaned forward in my chair. "But he's irrational and irresponsible," I added. "Fürl is always restraining him from going half-cocked on his ideas."

Charles put the cigar to his lips. "Not to mention he has been looking for my chair ever since he became a staff sergeant. He is rude, annoying, and a pain in the butt! That disallows *him*!"

I rested myself against the arm of the chair. "We could go on with this for hours. There are quite a few people with the possible qualifications for this position. Who do you feel would make the best candidate?"

Charles puffed on his cigar, not letting his sight move from where I sat. "Yes, there are a few people with qualifications. Yet, strangely enough, when

I called for you, your very question entered my mind. All the candidates I could think of bounced back and forth while I sorted them down on paper. Near the end of it all, I got this invoice from Fürl and it totally distracted me—I stopped writing and sorting. Through all these officers, there was only one man who I felt content with and happy with passing the Grounds on to."

I threw my arms up into the air. "You mean you already had someone picked? Why did we just go through all of that nonsense then?"

"Curiosity. I wanted to see who you would come up with," Charles smiled.

"Who did you pick?"

Charles smiled.

"Congratulations … sir."

~

Dawn was ecstatic. "Do you know what this means!? Having you in charge of the Grounds?!"

I risked a quick glance around the alley we'd snuck into to see if anyone heard Dawn's rather loud outburst. No one was in view. I smiled and returned my attention to Dawn, holding her close to me. "Yeah. I get the joy of making up the rules and yelling at people," I jokingly said.

Dawn nudged my playfully. "No. What it means is that the Rebells will have power for once in this long battle. We will have secret control over the POLICE in our town through you. You could ease off the attacks. Not to mention the fact that no one will have to hide anymore. No one would *dare* accuse the family of the head officer of being Rebells, no matter what evidence they gathered."

I looked into her eyes. "You know that I wouldn't be able to just turn the Grounds around and say 'Okay, everyone. No more hunting Rebells. It's duck season now.' Even though I would be in charge, my hands would be tied in some places."

She locked eyes with me and stuck out her lower lip, pretending to pout. I smiled, tilting my head. "Although, I could put in a word here or there as to having the force concentrate on other things … if properly motivated."

We kissed.

Dawn was beaming with joy. "I have to tell father!"

I grabbed her arm as she was just about to leave the alley. "No, wait!"

She looked at me, confused. I motioned for her to come back away from the street. "Let me tell him," I offered.

"Why?"

"I want to see the look on his face when he finds out that his prize Freedom Fighter is about to be crowned head of the POLICE Grounds."

She giggled and pulled me into a hug. We held each other for quite some time, lost in the warmth of the embrace. Slowly, I pulled out of the hug and gave her an inquisitive look by raising one of my eyebrows playfully. "Wait a minute … 'No one would accuse the family of the head officer?' Since when did we become family? I thought we were only dating."

Dawn gave me a solid shove at the remark, mouthing an "Oh you." Entwining our arms together, we quickly made our way out of the alley and toward William's place.

CHAPTER 21

"You're going to be *what*?!" William sputtered out, nearly choking on the words.

This was not going as Dawn and I had hoped it would. I took a deep breath, trying to figure out how best to explain the situation without having William bite my head off any further. "Once the general comes and promotes Charles, I have been asked to replace him as head officer of the Grounds."

Dawn gripped my arm protectively. We both stared at William, who was sitting in his chair in the den. "When will this happen?" he asked me, his voice not registering any tone.

"As I said, when the general visits the Grounds. Charles thinks that it won't be until after the anniversary, and even then it would take another five or six months."

William got up from his chair and walked right past Dawn, straight toward the bookcase. He stood before it, hands crossed behind him. "Year, six months," he muttered.

Dawn looked concerned about her father. "You're not pleased with the news?" she asked him.

William snorted, keeping his back to us. "Pleased?! Am I supposed to be pleased?"

"Well, we thought you would be," I answered him. "We thought you might be … proud of me. I'm pushing quite a few higher ranking officers out of—"

William turned toward the two of us, spinning quickly on the spot. "Proud?!" he mimicked, anger rising inside his voice.

He closed his eyes and gave a sigh, releasing the pressure that he was carrying slowly through clenched teeth. With a simple gesture portraying he was giving up, William walked back to his chair and collapsed into it.

"You just told me that you're going to control the POLICE in this town inside the next year. Fine. You just told me that, with you in command, the Rebells wouldn't have to be as afraid anymore. Great!"

He looked at Dawn. "This, I don't see a problem with. I'm sure Tom's going to make a great leader."

He turned his gaze to me. "Here's where the problem lies: the POLICE officials tend to look very thoroughly at the records of officers who are applying for such a high status. That's what always happens. They look at education, work records, POLICE training records, and relations. Since you're courting Dawn and you have no living relative, that makes *us* your relatives. That means that the POLICE will be looking very closely at *us*."

Dawn said, "But people wouldn't dare accuse the family of the head officer of being Rebells."

"True, they wouldn't," commented William, rubbing his face. "They would be too afraid of the consequences. But what about *before* he becomes the head officer? People will start asking questions. Also, what about the complications we would have after you become the head officer?"

"What complications?" I asked.

William looked soberly at me as if I should know. "We would no longer be allowed to visit known Rebells as easily as we could before or have them visit us as regularly. Everyone will know you; thus, they will know *us* by association. If we did do anything with the Rebells and someone found out, that information could put everything and everyone into jeopardy. Besides, how do you think the other Rebells, the ones who don't know you as well as we do, would react to having you become head officer? They would think that you were a spy for the POLICE the entire time. They'd probably try to have you assassinated."

I looked toward my feet. William's words planted a deep cloud over my thoughts and hopes. Worse, he was right. "I guess I didn't think of all the scenarios."

William nodded. "It's always better to know what you're agreeing to before you sign your name. You might end up a gravedigger—or worse, in the grave yourself."

Dawn looked downcast. I felt horrible. "So, what do I do now?"

"Maybe we could find some sort of solution at the meeting. A suggestion or an idea might come up that could allow this to work after all," William pointed out.

The meeting?

"What meeting?" I asked William.

"The corporal isn't coming," a deep voice behind me boomed.

I turned around to see who was speaking. Duncan stood in the doorway of the den, a huge frown on his face.

"Hello again … corporal," Duncan hissed as he frowned.

~

"You joined the POLICE in order to spy on them?!" asked Duncan, his voice rising.

I stood my ground. "That was one of my reasons."

"Was the other one *stupidity*?!" he yelled at me.

I stood perfectly still a few feet away from the wall opposite the bookcase. William and Dawn sat in the seats available, watching this little drama unfold in front of them. Duncan continued his pacing around me, as if he were trying to interrogate me.

"How long do you think they will keep a blind eye to you? How long do you think they will put off testing your loyalty to their cause? Did you even think and *all*?!"

Duncan was going red in the face. My patience was wearing thin as well. "I thought this decision through," I calmly explained to the leader of the Rebells.

I stood at ease. If I was going to be drilled, I might as well be comfortable. Duncan just stared through me, glaring from where he stood. "For how long?"

"Roughly twenty-four hours," I answered.

"One. Day. You threw you life away to the jackals after *one day*?!"

Duncan calmed himself down a bit, or at least tried to, rubbing the bridge of his nose in an attempt to come to terms with what I was saying to him. Dawn got up from her chair and stood in between Duncan and me.

She spoke to us in a quiet, calming voice. "I knew about his dilemma before he made his decision. We talked about it, looking at all the pros and cons. At first, I tried to convince him against joining."

Duncan turned to Dawn. "Obviously, you didn't try very hard," he pointed out.

"Watch your mouth!" I barked at Duncan.

He turned his full attention back to me, eyes flaring. He jabbed his finger at me. "I don't listen to empty POLICE threats."

He pushed the words *empty* and *POLICE*. I was just about ready to deck Duncan in the face, if not for William's interruption. "Gentlemen, please! This is going nowhere! Use your energy for more productive issues, like the meeting."

Duncan jabbed his finger at me again, arm outstretched so not to get close to me. "*He's* not going," he further emphasized his first statement.

Dawn walked over to where I was standing and rested her hand on my arm, offering me her support. I gladly took it. I looked to where William was sitting, a look of complete confusion across my face. "What is this meeting that you keep talking about?" I asked him.

Duncan lowered his hand. "It doesn't concern you. It doesn't matter. You're not going."

I shot Duncan a glance. "I didn't know I had to ask your permission."

Duncan ignored me and turned to William. "Everyone there, excluding your family, would riot as soon as they heard that a POLICE officer was attending the meeting."

"As long as no one tells," said Dawn, "no one will know."

Duncan choked on the words. "'No one *tells*?!'"

He pointed at me again, as if I was a pet being trained obedience. "He came here in his *uniform* for crying out loud!"

I had been coming here in my uniform ever since I was given my corporal bars. I failed to see the importance. Duncan stared at me like I had no understanding of the language he was speaking. "How many people see you a day who are not POLICE officers?"

I decided to play with Duncan's game. "I don't know. A few, I guess."

He walked toward me until he was right in front of my face. "How many of those few people who see you do you think are Rebells?"

"I have no idea!"

Duncan was almost whispering to me now. "So, what makes you think that those people who have seen you in your uniform will either not come to this meeting or keep quiet about your smug, little secret if they see you there, hmmmm?"

"That's pure speculation," I shot back.

Duncan had hit a nerve with me, and he knew it. "Admit it. I'm right," he teased.

My hands clenched. Dawn could feel the tension in my arms. She eased away from my side and went in between Duncan and me again, trying to break the two of us apart. "Stop it. Both of you. You two are acting like children."

We both stared at each other, listening to Dawn as she continued to put sense back into our heads. Duncan broke free of my gaze and walked to the bookshelf. I stayed where I was. Dawn placed my head between her soft, warm hands, and made me look at her. Her eyes were deep and loving. My anger and annoyance with Duncan melted away in Dawn's hands like ice inside a drink—slowly but continuously.

"Thomas, love," Dawn said, "Duncan is just worried that if you did go to this meeting, something bad might happen to you."

"Yeah, he might get killed. Damn shame if that happened," Duncan added sarcastically from across the room.

"Hush, Duncan!" Dawn scolded him. She gave him a quick glance, which told him not to say anything more. She returned her attention back to me. "Because of this, he's just trying to frustrate you and make you mad, so you won't want to go. Also, he doesn't know what side your loyalty is on."

"Got that right," Duncan mumbled.

Removing Dawn's hands softly, I returned my attention to Duncan. "I can end that problem right now," I said.

Duncan turned and looked at me. Our eyes locked. "Duncan, my loyalty is where it has always been—with the Kenneth family."

Duncan threw his arms up into the air. "There you go. All my problems are solved," he said sarcastically.

Obviously, not the answer he was waiting for. He turned and walked to the opening of the den, leaned against the doorframe, and stared at the ceiling. "I still say he shouldn't go. You would just be asking for trouble."

"Maybe I wouldn't even want to go to this meeting if someone would be so kind as to tell me what the hell this meeting is and what was happening in it," I pointed out to everyone.

Duncan cleared his throat. "No."

"Why not?"

"Your 'loyal POLICE training' might consider this traitorous," he teased me, yet again.

William got up from the chair. He looked at Duncan. "Tell him."

William looked like he had aged twenty years during the fight. He walked right past all of us and headed toward the kitchen, talking as he walked. "I'm growing tired of this tedious argument. Tell him and be done with it."

Duncan sighed and stared at the floor. "Fine. The Rebells in the nearby towns are going to have an emergency meeting soon. Due to the amount of people gathering and the sensitivity of the topic, everyone involved agreed that it needed to be somewhere the POLICE wouldn't suspect, so we've searched and found ourselves a nice covert place in the Zone just outside of this city to be the center of operations. On the day of the meeting, we'll go into the Zone and discuss ... battle plans."

And with that, everything fell into place. The rumor that had been floating around. The searching of the Zone by the POLICE. The huge amount of secrecy. Fürl trying to get a battalion of officers properly trained to deal with the search. It all made sense now. All this effort and panic because a bunch of Rebells are going to meet somewhere in the Zone and talk about … something regarding the POLICE.

I walked toward him. "What plans? For what?"

"For a raid."

"Against the POLICE?" I asked.

"No. Against the chocolate company around the corner. I heard that they're putting fake nuts inside their bars. Who do you think I'm talking about?!"

"This meeting … it's just going to be a few key Rebells?"

Duncan shrugged, not defining exactly if I was correct or not. I thought for a second on this. If it's only going to be a few people—probably ten at the most—then that means Fürl is going about this all wrong. He's searching for some massive meeting place, probably thinking that it's going to be every Rebell in the area coming together. That's why he's focusing on big buildings and convention areas. Instead, they're going to go into a small house or shop to plan this. So even if Fürl goes ahead with all the planning and training, odds are they will never find the meeting after all. Good. That means I don't have to tell them about Fürl. No point adding to the stress.

"What have you planned so far?"

"Be content that I'm telling you this much."

I was getting tired of this game.

"Where will the Rebells be taking this raid?" I asked him, pushing for an answer.

Duncan fumed over that question for a good minute or two. Dawn stomped her foot in frustration. "Duncan. Just tell him."

"Hauptstadt," he mumbled.

My face never changed. "The general?"

Duncan covered his expression so I couldn't gloat at getting the answer right.

It was now my turn for the interrogation. "When do you plan on leaving?"

"As soon as we're ready."

"Which is when exactly?"

"By my calculations, it will take a year to prepare for the attack, another couple months to get to Hauptstadt, and then four months to properly deploy the plan. That could change, or maybe it won't. The meeting will help finalize the scenario."

Dawn stepped into the conversation. "Well, why not just wait?"

Duncan gave Dawn a tired look. "Wait for what?"

"Wait for the general to arrive here," she told him.

Duncan's eyes grew at the news. This got his attention. "He's coming here?" Duncan asked us both.

We both nodded our heads in agreement. "He's coming on a tour to help celebrate the anniversary of the war. He will arrive here six months or so into the tour. Once here, he'll promote Charles to sergeant major and make me the new head officer of the Grounds inside town," I explained.

Duncan smiled.

CHAPTER 22

Duncan didn't say much after learning of the General coming to visit in a year's time. He just mentioned in passing that he would have to take this new information under consideration and left. Dawn and I spent the rest of the afternoon together, talking and having dinner with William and Sherry. William said nothing during dinner, his focus elsewhere. Sherry, worried about William, didn't say much either. I left shortly afterward.

The next day I met back up with H. J. and managed to finish up the report for Charles quickly. H. J. offered to come with me when I presented the report, but I suggested that I should deliver it by myself. He was a little put out by this, but I didn't want H. J. in earshot in case more discussion of the General came up.

I opened the door to the sergeant's office, holding onto the report that H. J. and I had finished just moments ago. The sergeant was not in, so I left the folder on his desk for him to look at when he got back. Popping my head out of the door, I got the attention of the receptionist, who was busy working on her nails.

"When do you think the first sergeant will be back?" I asked.

She glanced up from her nail file, a hint of annoyance as I interrupted her from her "work."

"The sergeant has stepped out for the moment, like I told you when you got here. He didn't say where he was going. He rarely tells me anything. He'll get back when he gets back, I assume. You're welcome to wait in his office."

That didn't help at all. I gave a short wave at the women behind the desk as a thanks and returned to the room that was Charles's office. It would probably be best if I waited and went over the report with him. Closing the door behind me, I gave myself a chuckle at the thought of me getting a new receptionist when I took over the position of head officer.

The office was as same as usual, albeit a little messier than the norm. The map that was beside the door had a bunch of little red flags poking out of it, marking certain areas that were under stricter surveillance due to increased Rebell activity. Taking a moment to check, I noticed that William's place was not marked by a flag—good to know. Continuing my short tour of the office, I also noticed that the chessboard that was off to the side no longer housed any pieces. Instead, the board was used as a stand for a collection of files and other business material. I could only guess that since I hadn't been able to play a game with Charles, he opted to put the board to better use.

The door opened behind me, and the sergeant walked in with Fürl behind him. "Ah, Tom," Charles smiled. "Thanks for waiting for us. Is that the report from the assignment I gave you? It's done already?" he asked me while pointing to the fresh folder on his desk.

I nodded and saluted them both. Charles gave me a face when he saluted. Victor didn't notice it. Charles walked over to his desk and sat down in his chair. He grabbed the report and quickly skimmed it over.

"I would usually go through this with you in more detail, but the sergeant," he opened his hand to Fürl, not raising his eyes from the report I gave him, "and I have some pressing matters to attend to."

He dismissed me. I saluted them both again and left the room, closing the door behind me. *Well, that was odd*, I thought to myself as I walked away from the office and back outside. Charles was in such a rush to get me onto this assignment and to complete it as quickly as I could. Yet, when I presented him with the report, he took it as if it wasn't that big of a deal. What has got him so preoccupied that he would do that? Something to do with his attempt to organize some sort of brigade to invade the Zone, perhaps? Fürl following up on another rumor? Perhaps he's now planning on setting up a guard station in the Zone so there's a twenty-four-hour watch.

I shook my head at the attempt to supersede Duncan's little meeting. The POLICE know nothing; they're chasing ghosts. They only know that something is planned, but they don't know what or where or even when. And if they do find out about it, what is it really? A few ranking Rebells sitting around an old table plotting an impossible dream that they would have no hope of succeeding at?

I started to cross the field that made up the wide expanse between buildings, the grass sweet smelling and slightly damp with the morning dew. The sun wasn't quite warm enough in the late winter sky to burn away the wet, cold water off of the grass. As I wandered, pondering the events from the office, my stomach gave off a low growl in order to remind me that I still had not eaten anything. Looks like it's a quick run to the barracks and the mess hall for breakfast.

"Hey, Corporal!" H. J. called to me across the field.

He was sitting on the stairs to the entrance of barracks, talking to another officer whom I didn't recognize. Seeing that he'd gotten my attention, he got up, said something quickly to the officer, and jogged over to where I stood. I made my way over to where he was coming from to ease the distance H. J. had to run.

"How did the sergeant like the report?" he asked me once he was close enough to talk.

"He didn't get a chance to read it fully while I was inside the office with him."

H. J. looked a little disappointed at the news. In all honesty, so was I. I wish I had something better to tell him, considering how much time and work we put into preparing the file.

"Well, he'll read it soon, I'm sure." he mused.

I nodded toward the barracks. "Have you had breakfast yet?"

"Well ... actually—"

Uh oh. I knew that sound. That was the start of asking for something that you knew you shouldn't be asking or telling someone something that was not good news. H. J. was leading up to something; I was sure of it. Somehow, it just screamed that it wasn't going to be good. A hopeful look crossed his face. *Here it comes*, I thought to myself.

"Can I say something? Off the record? Like, in confidence? That no one else will hear about?" he asked.

The kid looked like he was going to explode unless he told me what was going on in his mind. "Sure. I guess," I agreed, letting my words slide slowly out of my mouth.

"You're not what I expected you to be."

I took a step back. "How am I supposed to take that? Compliment or insult?"

H. J., realizing how it must have sounded to me, quickly covered his tracks. "What I meant was that based on what I heard about you before I got a chance to meet you, I thought you would be this perfect officer quoting the POLICE's handbook everywhere you went."

At this, H. J. stiffened up and started puffing out his chest in a mock representation of what he thought I would be like. Swinging his arms with every phrase, he started croaking out catch phrases pulled out of the POLICE manual in a deep voice. "Unification is truth. Strength comes from purity. Obey and survive." The presentation was more than ridiculous.

"Okay, I get the point. Why did you think that I would be like that?"

H. J. let go of the super soldier persona and returned back to his friendly self. "Because you're the youngest corporal major ever. You must have followed that book to the very last word and lived it. You must have been the greatest officer ever to get this high in such a short amount of time," he smiled, almost as if he were proud of me.

That's when it hit me. He didn't know about my early enrollment. Still, I was quite literally a copy of the first sergeant when I was training, mimicking everything that Fürl did and covering all the extra training that Charles gave me. I observed and absorbed any and all information that I could get my hands on back then. Anything Charles said or did, I copied with skill and precision. It's not surprising that I'd become corporal major so soon—I had the teacher's notes.

"So let me get this straight. You're saying, now that you've actually met me, that I'm not some sort of super soldier?" I half-teased.

H. J. apparently hadn't developed a sense of humor just yet. "*No!* No, it's just that … you're human too."

Okay, I was confused again.

"You may be the perfect officer, but you don't act like one. You're more down to earth than the other officers. You're more comfortable to talk to—almost like a big brother."

I watched him as he talked. He seemed sincere. He wasn't just trying to get on my good side by saying these things. "I just have a different outlook. That's all." I smiled and saluted to H. J.

He saluted back. "I'm glad that I finally got a chance to tell you that. I meant it."

"I appreciate it."

H. J. started to walk away from me. He then stopped a few paces away from me and tried to get my attention again. "After hours, a few officers and I are planning to go into town. Do you want to come along?" he called out to me.

I smiled at the soldier. "Not tonight. Thanks anyway."

H. J. rammed his fists onto his hips, not happy with my answer. "Oh, c'mon! It will be good for you to get out. We're going to the hall by the market. Dancing, girls—"

H. J. started to gyrate his hips to some unheard music, trying to entice me to join.

I simply pointed to myself. "Girlfriend. Remember?"

"Bring her along. I'm sure she would love a night out dancing." H. J. exclaimed, the groove moving from his hips to his entire body.

I watched the private continue his exotic tribal dance. A few officers who were by the entrance of the barracks started to hoot and holler in a show of appreciation for H. J.'s crazed performance. That only encouraged him to break out even more moves. Waving his arms and kicking his feet, H. J. was a whirlwind of dance fever. I waved my hands at the kid, giving up at the display.

"I'll think about it—but not very hard," I called out to him.

H. J. finally stopped dancing, a little out of breath, and smiled toward me. He pointed out at my direction. "I'm gonna hold you to it, sir."

I gave a simple wave to the kid as I turned around and started making my way back toward the entrance of the barracks and the mess hall. The officers standing around on the stairs gave me a wide birth as I walked to the door. One officer, a private first class by the looks of it, gave H. J. a quick nod. "Hey, sir, what was that all about?"

I smiled at H. J., looking back at the happy officer as he made his way across the Grounds. "Oh," I lied, "he's just happy about a really sweet assignment I gave him."

The smile I had on my face quickly erased itself with the sudden startling realization of something I'd forgotten to do. The sweet assignment! I completely forgot to put H. J.'s recommendation for his next assignment inside the report for Charles. I couldn't believe I'd forgotten. I rolled my eyes at the thought of the trek back to Charles's office and disturbing him to add the final note inside my report.

So much for breakfast, I whined inwardly.

~

It didn't feel like it took as long to get back to the office as it did to get to the barracks when I first left. Perhaps it had something to do with an empty stomach as motivation to get this done with quickly. Turning the corner to enter the reception area, I made my way back to where I'd just been. The receptionist was still working away on her nails, the guards were still just standing there protecting Charles's door—same old, same old. The receptionist glanced up briefly from the nail she was busily scratching away on with a small rough board.

"He's still in a meeting with the staff sergeant, Corporal Major."

"That's okay," I mentioned, looking around the room for somewhere to wait. "I don't want to disturb them."

I made my way over to where the guards were standing, thinking that they would want someone to talk to. After all, their entire job was to just stand there and protect a door. I stood by one of the guards, an older recruit with bad hair.

"So, how are things?" I casually smiled, trying to get the guard to open up.

Nothing. He stared off out into nothing, totally zoned out and focused on something only he could see. Seeing that my attempt at a conversation was hopeless, I twisted myself around so I was leaning up against the wall in order to wait for Charles to be finished with Fürl. Humming softly, I tapped my foot in beat with the song that I was working with. The guard, whom I tried to start up a conversation with, slowly turned his head and looked at me, a most disgruntled look upon his face. Noticing the guard, I started to slow and then stop my whistling, which then caused the guard to return to his regular stance at staring into nothing.

Okay. Note to self—no whistling, I reflected.

As I stood there, waiting and doing absolutely nothing, just as the guards were, I realized I could faintly hear the conversation that was taking place inside the office. I could hear Charles and Fürl talking about … something. Suddenly, I had a new appreciation with the peace and quiet that the guards silently demanded as I strained to hear what was being said. I guessed that meant that everything that had been spoken inside the office was heard by the guards—every piece of conversation, every secret discussion, and every crack at their expense.

"… but my source has never been wrong," Fürl pointed out, a little indignant due to some sort of protest that I had not heard previously.

"Be that as it may," Charles calmly pointed out to Fürl, probably from sitting behind his desk, "I can't do that."

"But, sir, I must—"

"Look. This argument is pointless, Sergeant. You have no proof. Now, I'm willing to assign a rather substantial resource of men for you to train for your special assignment. It's always beneficial for the men to get some training in, no matter what it's for. But I just can't consciously hand over the entire Grounds to you based on a rumor."

"Sir, I'm not asking you to give me the entire Grounds," Fürl explained.

"Oh no?" Charles quipped. There was an exaggerated rustle of paper, and the sound of Charles clearing his throat in preparation to read. "Perhaps this sounds familiar? 'In order for the mission to be successful, I will need the following: a battalion of officers under my strict control, the use of the training grounds for an unknown and extended period of time in order to train the officers, the full use of the medical wing and all medical equipment wherein to help prep the officers for their assignment, enough high-caliber weapons to arm all officers under my command, special all-black uniforms for night movement ...' I mean, the list just goes on and on."

"And every word on that list is justified inside the description below," Fürl pointed out to Charles with assurance, clearly refusing to bend.

"That may be the case, but it's all wrapped around a rumor—a guess—from one of your sources. You say that this person, who you refuse to disclose, has never been wrong. Well, there's always a first time. Besides, what exactly has your source told you? 'The Rebells are planning to have a meeting in the Zone in the next few months.' That's it. No mention of roll call, strength, topic, importance, exact date, and let's not forget the sheer size of the Zone. It would have been nice to find out where in that mess they were having this meeting."

"My source didn't have that information at the time."

"Here's the deal, then. You get me the hard facts of this supposed meeting, and I will sign off on everything on your list. You can have your invasion party, but only if I get it all in writing and it is verifiable."

"But ... But, sir."

"Dismissed, Sergeant."

There was a general moment of silence. Then the door opened, and Fürl appeared from behind the door. The guards, standing on either side, straightened into attention out of an automated reaction they had developed over time. Fürl, obviously not happy with the outcome of his meeting with Charles, walked out of the room with steam in his strides and a scowl etched on his face. He didn't notice me standing off to the side. He just walked right past the receptionist's desk and disappeared around the corner. I risked a glance into the office to see the state that it was in. Charles sat in his chair, staring out into the reception area, shaking his head at Fürl. Seeing my head bob into view, Charles perked up a bit. "Corporal?"

I pulled myself into full view. Charles stood up from his chair. "Were you outside waiting this entire time?"

I carefully glanced toward the path that Fürl had taken to see if he was really gone.

"Um ... not really. I just forgot to mention something inside my report, and I thought it best that I come back and tell you."

Charles waved me in, and I entered the office, closing the door behind me. He offered me the chair opposite him and sat back down inside his own. I didn't take it.

"What was that all about, if I may ask?" I asked him, pretending not to know.

Charles merely waved it off. "Don't worry about it. Just head officer stuff. You'll get used to it soon enough," he smiled.

Stretching back in his chair and working his tired muscles, Charles got himself more comfortable. "So, what was it that you wanted to add to your report, Tom?"

"I just wanted to recommend the private first class whom I was working with to the future assignment of translating the books we found inside the crates. I figured that since he already knew of their existence and he saw what I was doing in order to translate them, it wouldn't be as big of a security risk to have him work them into German."

Charles sat there, staring at me. "That's it?"

"That's it," I affirmed.

He clapped his hands together. "Done. There—simple enough."

"Thank you, sir."

CHAPTER 23

One month.

One month of peace and quiet. No surprise assignments. No word from Duncan. No further information about the meeting. It almost felt like things were getting back to a low sense of normality—if such a thing existed.

H. J. was assigned to the team from quality control that was asked to translate the books we'd found within the crates in order to make them appropriate for viewing by the general public, as per my recommendation. H. J. mentioned to me at lunch one day that before starting up the assignment he had to sign a piece of paper swearing him to secrecy regarding the origin of the book or what language it was originally written in. I heard through the grapevine that he was always first in translating his section, which really impressed his superiors. I can only imagine why.

During this time, I was given light duty doing general chores for the communications building between assignments. That consisted of sorting folders, writing up reports for other officers, and updating officer files. Not too exciting, but I wasn't complaining. It gave me time to think about other things, like what was going on around the Grounds.

The Grounds was a buzz in activity, or at least certain areas were. Fürl was working the officers who had been put under him for his project into a sheer frenzy, training and testing and doing all sorts of strange activities. Once I saw a group of them trying to scale the wall that surrounded the Grounds using grappling hooks and ropes. Another time I caught a group of them crawling on the grass across the entire training ground field. It was like Fürl was preparing them to take on an invading army.

It was nice having an entire month to myself, not having to worry about anything. Unfortunately, it wasn't to last....

Charles smiled at the chessboard as he grabbed hold of his knight and moved it to take my rook. "Ah ha! Thought you'd get past me."

I watched as Charles peeled away the rook in victory, clasping the small ivory piece inside his hand as he took it away and put it beside my lost bishop and three pawns on his side of the board. I clicked my teeth at the loss of the piece, staring hard at the board as it was laid out in front of me. Time to think of a new strategy. Charles was in a strong defensive position—his king was locked behind a row of pawns, his queen was loose on the board but not in a position where I could risk taking her, and the rest of the pieces were strategically placed so a direct confrontation was out of the question. I could try to bring up a pawn and go for a mad dash to the other side, but the risk of losing it would be too great. He had me cornered, and he knew it.

I took my time and scanned the board, looking for some sort of weakness in his plan. I searched and planned and thought my way across the board. Move after move played itself out in my head. One move ahead, then two, then four … then eight. Pawn moves up, and then he would counter with his rook, so I would have to counter that with my queen. But that would put my king in jeopardy. Move my knight? Bluff my way past his row of pawns?

I reached out to grab hold of my knight that was out in the field and then thought better of it, putting my fingers against my temple to aid my thinking. Charles looked from the board, to me, to the board. His smile was wide and brimming with pride. "Got you stuck, don't I?"

I shook my head, refusing defeat. "Not yet you don't, sir."

He leaned back from the board, crossing his arms across his chest. "Admit it. I got you beat. I'd say ... seven moves."

I scanned the board to see where he was leading. Pawn moves, taken by ... bishop? No. He wouldn't be that blatant. Damn. I can't see his plan of attack. Rubbing my eyebrow with the base of my thumb, my eyes starting to hurt from the sheer strain I was forcing down upon them, I sighed and made my move—pawn forward.

Charles clapped his hands at my move, which apparently fit right into his line of fire. He calmly reached out and took hold of his bishop and slowly slid the ebony piece directly into the path of the pawn, knocking it off its square and out of the game. I guess he would be that blatant.

A knock at the door broke the calm of the game. Both of our heads bobbed up from the board to see who it was. "Come in," Charles called out.

The door opened, and Fürl made his way into the office, a file under his arm. Closing the door behind him, he stood at attention and gave Charles a salute. I rose from my stool and saluted my superior officer. Charles gave a half-hearted salute and got up from his stool as well, walking over to his desk so that he was able to deal with the official POLICE business in a more established manor. "What can I do for you, Sergeant?"

Fürl walked past me to the opposite side of the desk, file ready to present. The file was rather thick due to being full of different colored paperwork; some of the corners of these papers were sticking out of the file. A band sealed the entire thing closed. On the outside of the file was stamped *Operation: Ant Farm—Top Secret*.

Fürl stood at attention in front of Charles, file outstretched. "You told me to come to you once I had secured proof of my theory, sir. I now present to you my proof, sir."

Charles slowly reached out to take the file and looked at him with surprise and pity. "You're still going on about that rumor from your source, Victor? I thought that was finished with," Charles remarked with a tone of irritation, no doubt thinking that he would have to rehash a conversation with Fürl he thought had been long finished.

Fürl, passing over the file, didn't flinch. "I have new information from my source regarding a new development that requires your attention. It is completely documented within the file. It includes—"

He stopped short when he recognized that the two of them were not alone in the office. Am I that invisible that I wasn't even acknowledged when he entered the office? I had saluted him, for crying out loud. Giving me a side glance that was as hard as stone, Fürl waited for me to leave. Charles, seeing that he wasn't going any further with me in the room, gave me a quick nod toward the door.

"That will be all, Corporal," he sighed.

I saluted Charles and left the office. This would probably take awhile. There was no point to me waiting around to finish the chess match. The game was pretty much done anyway. As I walked out of the building, I thought back to what had just transpired in the office. Fürl was really excited over something he discovered, that was certain. Was it to do with the meeting that Duncan had planned? Hadn't that already happened? It would explain why we hadn't seen or heard from him in the past month. Not to mention, if it was just a gathering of a few Rebells, then it would've been easy enough to complete by now. No, this was something different. And by the looks of that file folder, it was big.

With nothing else planned for the day, I figured I would give Dawn a visit. If anything, it would give me a chance to find out what "new development" Fürl was talking about.

~

William opened the door for me. "Tom. Good to see you," he smiled and shook my hand.

I smiled back. "Hello, William. Is Dawn around?"

"Nah. She's off somewhere. Gone to market or something, I think. She's always off somewhere, recently. It's hard to keep track of her nowadays."

William stepped out of the way so that I could enter his house. "Please, come in. You can wait for her if you like."

I walked into the warm house and the comfortable surroundings, content on the familiarity of the place. No matter how many times I'd come here, no matter what had happened, I always felt safe when I was in this place. William quickly closed the door behind me and waved toward the den. "C'mon. We can talk in here while we wait."

The two of us wandered into the den side by side, the fire that was crackling inside the fireplace welcoming us both upon entering the room. William eased himself into his regular chair. I sat opposite him.

"So," William sighed contently as he nuzzled himself into his chair, "what's new and exciting over at the Grounds?"

I smiled. Straight to business. "For the most part, things are pretty slow going. But there was this one thing that did catch my attention."

William's eyebrow crested over a searching eye. "Which would be?"

I leaned forward. "Has Duncan had his meeting with the other Rebells in the Zone yet, like he planned?"

"No, he put it off for a later date. Said something about needing to replan it. Why? What have you heard?"

"Nothing definite but enough to give me pause."

William looked a little concerned at that. I shook my head at my poor attempt at explaining. "Let me start at the beginning. Early in the year, there was an officer on the Grounds who had heard a rumor about something the Rebells had planned. This officer, who was fairly high ranking, organized a group of officers for specialized training in preparation to commandeer or put a stop to whatever it was that was planned. Since there was no date procured and no information as to what it was exactly that was being organized by the Rebells, the training has been generally viewed as a side factor—so the officers will be ready to be called upon at a moment's notice, but really just to keep them busy. Because no one really took it seriously, the Grounds had all but forgotten about it. According to Charles, until this rumor had more fact behind it, that's all that would happen—general training.

"When I first heard about this rumor floating around, I figured that it had something to do with Duncan's meeting, since the rumor was focused on taking the officers into the Zone. But the sheer scope of the task force meant that they were off base for where and what Duncan had planned.

Because of this, I didn't have that much concern with it and didn't really mention it to anyone."

William nodded at this and motioned for me to continue. "Something happened today, though, that caught my attention. The officer who first heard the rumor and started everything on the Grounds showed up at Charles's office with a rather thick file folder, saying that he finally had the proof he needed to take everything to the next step."

"What was inside the folder?"

"I don't know. I was asked to leave before I got a chance to take a look."

"And you think that it has something to do with the meeting that Duncan had planned?"

I waved my hands up in the air. "Your guess is as good as mine. Everything is being discussed behind closed doors, both here and on the Grounds. The only way I was able to get a straight answer from Duncan last time he was here was because you insisted that he tell me. Even then, it was the bare bones. I never got a clear answer as to what the rumor was going around on the Grounds. Again, I could only assume that it was something to do with the meeting—I could be wrong. But, then again, what else would the Rebells be doing in the Zone?"

William nodded, resting his chin inside the tips of his fingers. "So don't you think it's about time you got a straight answer?"

"And how exactly would I do that?" I asked.

"You ask, Tom. You ask."

"Ask? Ask whom, William? I told you. No one is willing to give me a straight answer. Who would I ask?"

William shrugged his shoulders. "Well, you could ask me," he pointed out, matter-of-factly.

I looked at William with utter shame. I can't believe I was that ignorant, or that proud, that I wouldn't ask him about all this. Of course William would know what was going on, at least with the Rebell's side of things.

"Okay, you got me. I'm an idiot. William, would you please tell me what is going on?"

"I thought you'd never ask," he smiled. "Here's what I know so far.... Duncan originally wanted to meet with some key members in the neighboring towns to plan an organized attack against the general on the anniversary of the war. He was hoping to meet with them in the Zone that was bordering all the towns, so no one had to travel farther than the others. The Zone was chosen to meet because it was far enough away from the POLICE so that they wouldn't bring about any suspicion, and it was in an area that no one would bother going into, so they could talk without worry of being heard. This you know. Only, when he found out from you that the general would be coming here to our town on his tour of the country, he gave word to everyone that the meeting would be postponed.

"He then disappeared for a while, going all over the place. His reasons why weren't clear. It was hard to keep track of him during that time. Personally, I haven't seen or heard from him since he left here, but a couple days ago I got word about Duncan from a Rebell who was with him on his travels. He was in the Zone with Duncan a couple days ago, taking dimensions and marking up some maps for this massive building. From the description of this domed building, it has rows and rows of seating around an internal grassy field. Apparently, it is big enough to fit all the Rebells from all the neighboring towns combined. What this has to do with anything, I don't know yet."

I perked up at the mention of the dome. "Duncan's now looking at a big building for his meeting?"

William nodded. *This is bad*, I thought. Duncan's saving grace with the meeting was that it would have been small; thus, it would have taken place inside a small building. Now Duncan was looking at the exact type of building that Fürl was preparing to invade. But the question still remained as to why Duncan was looking at the dome, or when whatever he was planning would take place. Was the dome now going to be the place where he held his meeting? It was still unclear the exact details as to what the POLICE knew about all of this or if they had the dome targeted. More importantly, why was Duncan moving from a small group to discuss plans to a huge building with a greater number of Rebells?

I took a deep breath, thinking of the work that was ahead of me. "Okay, so that's the Rebell side of things. Now I need to get the POLICE version. That's going to be a little harder," I said.

William shook his head. "Not necessarily."

"What do you mean?"

"All you need to do is ask," he pointed out.

"And what do I do when no one will answer my question?"

William simply smiled. "Then you stop asking … and start taking."

~

If I was caught, I was gonna be in a lot of trouble. Charles would not be able to stop the court martial and automatic prison sentence even if he wanted to. So far, I hadn't been seen by anyone, and I hoped my luck stayed that way. Skill and memory added to the luck, but it was luck all the same. The final question to all this was simple—was the risk worth the discovery?

The hallway that led to the reception area for the first sergeant's office was dark. Once at the corner, I risked a quick peek into the reception area. At least there were no guards outside the door at night. The coast looked clear. I crouched down and swiftly made my way to the door. The door was locked, of course. Taking a moment to look around and make sure I was still alone, I reached into my pocket and felt for the lock pick I had quickly made up—which was nothing more than a worked piece of tin to slide between the door frame and latch.

Standing in front of the door, fishing the piece of tin out of my pocket, I caught a transparent reflection of myself in a hanging picture. I looked absolutely ridiculous in the getup I was wearing: a black shirt I'd borrowed from William, black pants (also from William), black socks, a black cloth woven around my head to help cover my forehead and hair, and POLICE regulation black gloves. If anyone happened to see me, they would have probably died laughing at my cliché burglar suit.

As I worked the tin between the door and the frame, I gave myself pause in order to take in the situation. I was breaking into Charles's office. I was actually breaking into the first sergeant's office. What if the file folder wasn't there anymore? What would I do then? No, I wasn't going to second-guess things anymore. I had to stick with the plan, get it done, and get out of there.

With a flick of my wrist and a silent click, the door eased open on its well-oiled hinges, and I entered the room. I gently closed the door behind me, relocking it. I couldn't risk a light in order to allow myself to see. The guards outside the building would see the beam of light shining inside the room from the window. The moonlight that shone through the window would have to do, although it wasn't much. It was a good thing I spent a lot of time inside the office, because I had an idea where everything was.

On his desk, resting in the middle, sat the treasure that I had searched for—the folder. The security tape was broken, Charles having taken a look at the inner paperwork already. Good. That will eliminate quite a few problems. No one would suspect a break-in if the evidence didn't produce itself.

I reached out, took hold of the folder, opened it, and read the first page in the available light.

> In our fight to stop the Rebells, we have … not strong enough … stop their annoying existence once and for all. This can be done at their meeting …

My heart skipped a beat. They knew about the meeting. This confirmed it. It was no longer just a rumor—they knew! I read on.

> According to sources, they will be holding an emergency meeting inside the Dome, located in the fifth restricted Fallout Zone by the city. There, the ruler of this band of misfits, a man known only as Duncan, will announce his plan. The source has reason to believe that his plan deals with the coming of the General to Sicher Himmel. We must protect the General at all costs. Thus, my proposition: On the day of the meeting, all officers will storm the area and take all Rebell members prisoner. If resistance occurs, force must be allowed.

> Also, a few undercover POLICE officers have been placed in key areas inside the Rebell squad. We can thank these brave men and women for getting us this information.

Behind the rest of the written papers, there was a blueprint of the domed area where the meeting was to take place. All entryways were marked with a red pen and a number. My guess was that the numbers represented the number of officers that were to guard that entry. The smallest number written on the map was fifty.

I searched the blueprint for any other details. While I searched, something caught the corner of my eye. It was an old shaft—one that looked like it wasn't completely connected to the Dome. It led underneath, attached itself to the Dome for a moment, and eventually led to an open field just outside the outskirts of the Zone. I almost missed it entirely. From the scribbles on the blueprint, it looked like a ventilation shaft, laundry chute, or some type of basement storage space. Whatever it was, it looked like a good way out of there if things went bad. There was no red marker attached to the outside of it, which made it look even more promising.

I jerked my head up for a split second. All actions froze as I listened to the wind. My hearing became acute to all sounds. I could hear my own heart beating softly inside my chest, the wind outside the window, and the footsteps of someone walking toward the office. The steps were deep and heavy. That meant boots being worn by a well-built man—a guard!

Frantically, I stuffed all the paperwork I had meshed around on the desk back into the folder, slapped it closed, and tried to organize things how I found them as quickly and quietly as I could. I scanned the room to check that everything was the way that I found it. It was. That meant there was only one small problem to deal with—me!

I dove around the desk as fast as I could go while staying in control of my own feet. I moved the chair to hide myself underneath the desk in the little space the chair occupied just moments before and struggled to kick in my feet so that there was no inch of my body sticking out from under the desk. I grabbed the two closest legs that were toward me and dragged the chair back to the desk, making sure I was well out of view.

I did all of this with just enough time to gasp a lung full of air before the doorknob started to rattle. The lock clicked, and the door swung open. From where I was huddled, I could only see the back portion of the room. In order to see the front, a two-inch crack that separated the desk from the floor was my window. It was too low to get a good look at what was going on, and I didn't want to risk moving around to get a better view. I heard the door close behind whomever it was that had entered the office.

My heart crashed with each beat against the ribs in my chest. Perspiration dripped off my forehead. This was not good. The lungful of air was slowly going stale inside me. I would have to take another gasp soon. That might give me away.

The room was deathly quiet. I could start to smell the sweat on my body. My lungs were on fire. I was getting desperate for another breath. Either of these things could have signed my doom. Sight, smell, and hearing are dead giveaways for a break-in, especially if the criminal was still inside. I wrapped my arms around my legs and tried to stay perfectly still.

The person who had entered the office walked over to the desk. He had a light with him! Idiot! The light flashing around the office would call too much attention to this place and make escaping harder than it should have been. The soft flicker of the light that probably dribbled out of a lantern trickled under the desk, playing gleefully on the ground. The intruder also wore standard POLICE boots. The stranger stood in front of the desk for a total of ten seconds. I counted.

Then, he walked toward the door, opened it, walked out, and closed the door behind him. There was a soft click from the lock being set once more, and then the sound of footsteps walking away from the office could be heard faintly. I let out my breath when the footsteps couldn't be heard any longer. He hadn't seen me! But who was he?

I pushed the chair out of the way and got up. The file folder was open on the desk. I don't remember leaving the file folder open on the desk. In fact, I'm pretty sure that I didn't. Taking a second to glance through the paperwork, my heart sunk at the discovery that was awaiting me. Whoever had been in the office had taken the blueprint of the Dome. They had purposely opened up the folder, flipped through all the paperwork, and grabbed the map of the Dome. In order to do that in the short amount of time they were inside the office, they must have known what they were looking for. That means they knew the folder was here and what was inside it.

Because the stranger had been bouncing around the room with a light in full view, someone would be coming to investigate soon. I quickly left the room, making sure that the coast was clear, and tried to jerry-rig the lock back into place with my trusty piece of tin. Sneaking down the hallway, my mind raced with questions and ideas. I shook my head clear of them all. I had more important things to worry about.

The POLICE knew about the meeting.

The POLICE knew where the meeting was going to take place.

They had been training to invade the meeting for the past month.

Unless I told Duncan, the Rebells were doomed.

But, if I told Duncan, he would think that I had told the POLICE about the meeting.

What should I do?

CHAPTER 24

I<small>T WAS FIFTEEN HUNDRED HOURS</small>. He was late. The fountain splashed noisily in the afternoon sun. I was glad that the water was running, which was out of place since the spring season had just started. Normally, it wouldn't be until spring was in full effect that the water would be turned back on. For now, the water splashed contently in the basin. It would be a good cover for our voices if any prying ears happened to wander by as we talked. I slowly started to pace around the fountain, creating a small trench in the dusty ground. The water would be turned off in roughly twenty minutes. That didn't give me a lot of time. C'mon, hurry up. Where are you?

A hand grabbed my shoulder from behind me. I wheeled around from shock at the contact, ready to execute the first punch. John flung his hands up to protect himself. I lowered my hands with a sigh of relief and a smile.

"Boy, you're really uptight about something," John pointed out to me in a serious tone.

Seeing John again was a welcome relief. With his hectic schedule and my own, we hadn't seen each other in quite some time—a couple of months, actually. John had grown a little from the last time I'd seen him. Muscular wise, I meant. He was wearing his work clothes: work pants, gray shirt, dirty apron, hard boots covered in dust, and working gloves. His gloves looked well used and worn. I remembered them being his pride and joy when he first got them. He took such good care of them, making sure that they were washed and ready for the next day of work. Looking at the state that they were in now, it was clear that age and the duty of his new position had taken its toll on them. He had also not shaved for a while. John looked good with a beard.

"I'm in trouble, old friend." I sighed and sat down on the edge of the fountain.

"They found out about you and the Rebells?"

"No, no. Not yet, at least."

I rested my head inside my hands. John eased himself down beside me. "Then what is it? Has something happened to Dawn?"

I got up and started pacing again in front of John. "No, nothing has happened to Dawn."

John drew his eyebrows together. "Then do you mind telling me what's wrong?"

I sighed a long and heartfelt sigh at the situation and sat back down beside John. "You've heard about the Rebell meeting, right?"

"I've heard bits and pieces about it from William when I visit him," he replied.

"What do you know about it?"

"Well … the meeting's inside the Fallout Zone just outside of town—'bout a full day's walk or so. I think it was moved up a few days. And … all the Rebells who hear about it will attend. As far as I know, almost all of the ones I know of are going."

"Do you know the purpose of the meeting?" I asked him.

"No. Do you?"

"I have a pretty good idea. It's to let everyone know about the plan to kill the general. They will probably discuss if it's going to be inside Hauptstadt prior to him leaving on his anniversary tour or when he comes here to visit us in town."

John stared at me, taking it all in. "Are you sure?" he gasped.

I looked straight at him and put my hand over my heart. "From what I could piece together, it is."

John slunk a bit at the news. "The Rebells are planning the assassination of the general?"

"Planning and doing are two different things," I pointed out.

John sat in silence for a second or two. Then a thought came to him, and he perked back up. "Wait!" he blurted, "What has this got to do with you? Are you assigned to be his bodyguard when he arrives here?"

I brushed my hands through my hair in frustration. "No, I have to think of some way to stop the meeting," I answered him in a low voice.

John sat there, staring at me. "Why? Isn't this what all Rebells want? To get rid of the general?"

I closed my eyes and turned my back to John. "I have to stop it, because the POLICE know about the meeting. Where it is, when it is, everything."

Despite having my eyes closed, I could tell exactly what John was doing. He got up from the fountain and walked over to where I stood, stopping just behind me. "How did they find out about this, Tom? Who do you think tol—"

I turned around to face him quickly. His face was somber with a sudden realization. "Wait. Did you?"

"Of course not!" I snapped.

I started pacing around the fountain again. John just stood where he was and watched me go back and forth.

"Yesterday, I saw a folder on the desk of the first sergeant with the title 'Operation: Ant Farm' on it. Last night, I broke into the office and read the papers inside the folder. Someone told the POLICE the details about the meeting, but it wasn't me."

I had almost a pleading nature to my voice, as if I were on trial and trying to convince the jury of my innocence. John nodded.

"How many people know about this folder?" he asked.

I stood and thought for a second. "You, me, the first sergeant, Sergeant First Class Victor Fürl—I don't know—I think that's it. They might have told someone else, but I don't know."

"Can you get rid of it?"

I shook my head. "Nice idea, but I wouldn't have a chance. Charles would then ask questions dealing with the disappearance of the folder. Considering the small number of people who know of its existence, the blame would come quickly."

John walked back to the fountain and sat down, facing away from me. "That *is* a problem."

Deep below us in the ground, a gurgle and a groan escaped up from the pipes that were streaming water out into the fountain. I glanced over to the sound and watched as the flow of water started to slow and trickle. The fountain was shutting down for the day. John, still sitting away from me, gave me a shot over his shoulder.

"You have to tell Duncan," he said.

I shot John a look of mild annoyance, as if he should have come up with something better than that. "Oh, I know exactly how that's going to work out," I responded. "If I tell Duncan, he would think that it was me who told the POLICE, and 'only now am I having second thoughts about the action that I took.' Either that, or else 'I was trying to sabotage the meeting.' He never wanted me to know about it in the first place. It was only through William and Dawn that I got him to talk. Needless to say, because of my involvement with the POLICE, Duncan would be furious and take it out on me." The sarcasm was oozing out of me while I relayed my melodrama.

John got up and thumped his hands onto his hips, as if I were a small child he was belittling. "If you don't tell Duncan, then people could get hurt, maybe even killed."

"I'm fully aware of that. All the more reason to tell ... and more reasons for Duncan to yell at me."

He continued to stare at me, unblinking. "That's pretty selfish of you, Tom, worrying about your own well-being when hundreds of people are going to be walking to their doom."

I glanced at the fountain's water rippling from the light breeze, dancing without a care in the world. At that moment, I really envied the water. "Don't you think I already thought of that, John? This has me worried sick."

John smiled. "Hey. Worrying is like a game. Everyone plays it, because everyone worries over something or other. Usually, it's about something trivial or themselves, and their token goes 'round and 'round in a circle on the board. That's no way to win the game. It's knowing when not to worry about oneself when you have a problem that deals with other people as well. Try to find an answer that will benefit all people playing. That's the challenge of the game."

I nodded. In a weird way, it made sense.

"Think of Dawn," John said, his voice strong and calming.

I closed my eyes and allowed the image of Dawn to enter my mind. She was standing in a full blue dress, a wicker basket full of bits from the market latched over one of her arms. Her hair was free and winding down her back. She was smiling at me.

"And you would willingly give your life to protect her?"

"As quickly as you would have with Lydia," I replied.

My mention of Lydia only made John more determined. "Then you have to tell Duncan."

~

John and I met with Dawn halfway to her house. She was on the way back from the market, her basket loaded with all sorts of colors from the different foodstuff in hand. We told her about what I knew about the meeting in very hushed tones. Dawn looked frantic. "They found out?!"

"The scary part of this is that we don't know how they found out. Tom was in the first sergeant's office, and there was this folder on his desk explaining the entire thing," John tried to explain to Dawn, but she wasn't listening. I think she stopped listening after the whole "they found out" part.

Dawn looked as if she would faint. "What are we going to tell Duncan and Father?"

I stopped the two of them from any further travels toward Dawn's home in order to make sure I heard that last statement correctly. "Duncan's back?"

Dawn nodded. "He showed up last night. Asked if he could stay for a couple days in order to finalize a few things in town."

I took a deep breath. "We'll have to convince him to stop the meeting."

Dawn looked at me, surprised that there would be any other choice. "Of course he has to stop the meeting now that the POLICE know about it."

John smiled. "Then we're all in agreement. The meeting must be stopped at all costs."

The three of us started walking toward Dawn's house once again, a stronger and determinate pace in all our strides. Dawn led the way with John right behind her. They were talking about other things as we walked toward the house: how things were going in the Factory, what John was up to, what things Dawn was up to—general chitchat. I trailed behind the two, not wanting to disturb them catching up. I watched the two talk and laugh; Dawn hugged onto John's muscular arm as they walked. It was a good image, seeing my girlfriend and best friend walking and laughing together. I couldn't help but smile.

We made our way to Dawn's place in record time, due to our quick step. The three of us quickly wandered down the small set of stairs and entered her section of the building. The sweet smell of baking met our nostrils, no doubt from Sherry preparing dinner. A soft voice inside the den worked its way into the hallway from whence we stood. It sounded like someone was rehearsing something, saying a single line over and over in different ways.

"... celebrating the anniversary of their *victory* ... celebrating the *anniversary* of their ... hmmm."

Dawn called out to the voice that was lost in the den, stating that she had returned. Duncan slowly materialized from the den. "Dawn, did you get the—"

He stopped just short of walking into me as he turned the corner to greet Dawn. Surprised to see both John and myself standing in the hall, Duncan was quick to compose himself into the gruff and resolute leader of the Rebells.

"Oh. What are you doing here?" he mumbled.

Dawn gave me a small shove as a cue to get me going. I took a deep breath in preparation and then relayed the entire event from the start of the year to the most recent: the crates and the searching of the Zone, my future promotion, the tour of the general next year, Fürl getting a group of officers for special training over a month ago, the file folder, the map, me breaking into the office to read the folder—everything. Duncan, who was leaning against the doorframe to the den, didn't say anything during the entire speech. No reaction, no emotion. He just crossed his arms and listened.

When it got to the point of me talking about the get-together with John at the fountain mere moments ago, that's when things started to switch over from informing to convincing. John and Dawn chimed in at this point, adding their ideas and theories into the mix. It was no longer just me trying to convince Duncan to stop the meeting but all three of us. I worked off the point that the POLICE knew about the meeting, John emphasized the loss of life on both sides if things got ugly, and Dawn tried to play off of his sympathy for the amount of time he had known her and how he knew she wouldn't try to lead him astray. Duncan listened politely to us all, glancing from one person to the other.

"… and that's why you have to stop the meeting, Duncan," I pleaded with him at the end. John and Dawn stood right beside me the entire time.

Duncan looked at us all. "What? That's it?"

I looked from John to Dawn to see if they knew what he was talking about. Both were at a loss. "What do you mean 'that's it?'" I asked him. "Wasn't that enough reason?"

Duncan, straightening up and clearing his throat, towered over us all. "It's still on," he decreed.

You could have heard a pin drop inside the hallway where all four of us stood. John broke the silence with a whispered, "What?"

Duncan walked away from us and back into the den. "I'm not stopping this because a few POLICE officers happened to find out about this meeting! There's too much at risk! If we were to stop now, then that just proves to the POLICE that the Rebells would turn and flee at the littlest pressure from them. So the POLICE want to come and crash the meeting … so what! Nothing's changed. You think I wasn't prepared for this? If they push us, then we'll push back."

Dawn barely breathed. "You're willing to risk the lives of everyone going to the meeting just for the cause?"

Duncan stared at Dawn. Shaking his head at the poor girl disapprovingly, he made his way farther into the den, leaving us all inside the hallway. "Everyone who takes on the title Rebell has to risk their lives on a daily basis—from possible discovery to imprisonment and death. If they die at the meeting, then they will die doing something. They'll die trying to rebuild the ideals of freedom and democracy—exactly what the Rebells stand for. Their deaths will not be in vain," he yelled out from inside the den.

We slowly entered the den after Duncan. He was standing in front of the bookcase, head resting in his right hand, just as someone would do if he was nursing a headache. I walked to where Duncan stood. The others stayed near the entrance.

"Duncan," I tried to plead with him once more, "it's not just a few rookie officers that have figured this out. The first sergeant and Sergeant First Class Fürl know about this. They will bring every officer in the POLICE force to stop you if necessary!"

Duncan glanced at me and walked over to William's chair. He eased himself into it elegantly, as if placing himself onto a throne. "Tom, it doesn't matter if the entire force or a single SIT raids our meeting. I cannot stop it."

I glared down at him, my blood boiling in my veins. "Why are you being so stubborn?!"

He glared up at me and pulled himself out of the chair slightly so he was sitting on the edge of the cushion. "And why can't you understand? Once you go along with any of their ideals, they *own* you! You're trapped! You have to fight in order to survive! Look at them, celebrating the anniversary of the war. They're so egotistical that they actually think that the war ended over seventy years ago. It. Never. Ended! We're still fighting the good fight, and this war will not end until the POLICE regime comes crumbling down. That's what Rebells *do*! Maybe if you hadn't been so quick to join ranks with the POLICE, you'd have remembered that!"

Fire burned in my eyes. "Hey! I believe in democracy and everything else that was taught to me just as any Rebell does, but I will *not* allow you to endanger the lives of everyone just so you can continue on with your personal agenda!"

Duncan got up and walked toward the entrance of the den where John and Dawn stood watching us argue. He stopped at the entrance and turned back toward me, a concerned look on his face. When he spoke, his voice was low and calm. "I don't wish to be inside your shoes, Corporal Rebell. I don't think anyone would want to right now. You have been given the duty to protect the same people you have to betray. Yet, at the same time, you have to betray the people you trust and who trust you. How can you do that every day?"

He thought for a second. "I was wrong when I said that you shouldn't come to the meeting. Like you said before, you don't need my permission. In fact, I insist that you come. It may prove … educational for you. You might actually learn which side you're really on."

Duncan turned and walked out of view. John and Dawn entered the den and stood beside me. Dawn put her arm around me. From the hallway, Duncan yelled into the den, "Stay close to the exits, Corporal Rebell. When your friends show up, I don't think they'll be happy to see you."

CHAPTER 25

After the delivery of the file to Charles, the Grounds went into overtime in preparation for the meeting. All regular assignments had been put on hold in order to incorporate new mandatory training regiments. I tried once more to convince Duncan to stop the meeting, but he ignored me. It was happening, whether I wanted it to or not.

Now, with less than a week before the meeting, there was only one thing left for me to do. I had to figure out how, when the POLICE raided the Dome where all my friends and loved ones would be, to protect the one without betraying the other.

The door to Charles's office swung open for me, the guard making sure to stand off to the side to allow me entrance. Charles was working on some general paperwork at his desk when he looked up to see me and waved me to enter.

"I got some news that will interest you, Tom," he told me in a hushed tone as I sat down in the chair opposite him.

"You know that report that Fürl brought in for me a little while ago? The one that I had to kick you out of the office in order to discuss? Well, inside that report stated that in about two to three days, give or take a day, the people who blew up the Factory you worked at a couple years back will be holding a meeting. There's a good chance that all the members in this city and the neighboring towns will be in attendance."

I looked at Charles in mock surprise. I felt kind of bad pretending, but I had no other choice. I motioned him to continue.

"They plan on assassinating the general when he comes here," he added.

"What?" I whispered, trying to show my surprise.

Duncan eased himself closer. "Somehow, they found out that he was coming. The exact timeframe, what route he would take to come here, how long he's staying, everything."

I began to squirm at hearing that particular point for two reasons. "How many people know of the general coming here?"

Charles widened his hands apart. "At least half the Grounds by now."

I nodded and lowered my head to give off the impression I was trying to think of what to say next. I knew exactly what I was going to ask, but I had to give that false impression to him. One of the two questions was answered; the blame for the leak would not be placed on me. Too many people know about the general now.

I took a breath in preparation for the second question, to which I already had a good idea what the answer was going to be. "So, what are we going to do about this meeting?"

Charles leaned over his desk even more and talked in a very quiet tone. "There's a plan in action. Fürl has made sure of that. But I want your help for a crucial part of it."

I leaned myself in closer to Charles. He talked in almost a whisper. "I want you to go undercover to the meeting."

For a second, I thought I didn't hear him correctly. "Pardon?"

Charles held up his hands. "I know, I know, don't laugh. I'm quite serious with the idea. I want you to go undercover as a recruit for the Rebells and find out everything that you can while you're at the meeting. Find out their plans, their numbers, who's in it, when they will attack, anything you can! You'll need to keep a low profile once you're in there, of course. It's not without risks."

I leaned back in my chair. Charles had unwittingly given me a window of opportunity. I could now go to the meeting without any suspicion from either side. The Rebells would think I was there as a supporter of the Rebell's cause, and the POLICE would know I was there as a spy, as per the first sergeant's orders.

"Why me? Won't they know that I'm not a Rebell?" I asked, trying to keep as much of a straight face as I could.

"Well, I need someone who will be able to blend into the crowd, who won't stand out as an officer. You have had years of exposure with the populace from working in the Factory. They'll recognize you and naturally associate you from there. During your rather unique training regiment here, you were kept out of the general patrols of the town, so you were not paraded about in your uniform. Because of your intense work schedule and the fact that you've kept pretty much to the Grounds on your time off, not too many people outside of the Grounds area have seen you in uniform. Best of all, you're adept at thinking on your feet and coming up with solutions to problems that suddenly appear out of nowhere, which will come in handy if things get a little crazy over there. You're the best candidate for this assignment, Tom."

"Yeah, but I haven't been a part of the Factory for years. Questions will come up as to where I've been."

Charles smiled. "You'll think of something."

"And if they recognize me as POLICE and capture me?"

"Don't worry. Once the meeting gets into full swing, Sergeant First Class Fürl and a battalion of specially chosen officers will invade the meeting site. If you are captured, they shall rescue you."

I sat in my chair and stared at Charles, thinking about what luck I had. I smiled and leaned forward in my chair in order to present my hand to shake with Charles. "Of course I'll do it." I smiled with as much gusto and false bravery as I could muster.

He smiled back and shook my hand. "Good. Now, here are the rest of the details I have available to me." With that, Charles reached over and grabbed hold of a file folder that was sitting off to the side of the desk. On that folder were the words *Operation: Ant Farm.*

H. J. called out to me from across the field as I walked toward the front gate. I was on my way to go see William and Dawn in order to pass on my good fortune. I waved at him, and he started to run over to where I stood. He reached me slightly out of breath. Suddenly, I got this strange feeling of déjà vu.

"Hey. What's new?" I asked him while I continued to walk toward the gate.

He shrugged his shoulders. "Nothing important."

He started walking with me to the gate. Even though I had only known H. J. for a little while, I had learned enough about him to know that there was something he wanted to ask.

"All right. What is it?" I blurted out, stopping on the spot.

"Have you seen the first sergeant yet?"

"Just did. He liked the results of your translation process, if that's what you're wondering about."

H. J. was pleased at the news, but he was still squirming. "That's not exactly what I wanted to hear about."

"Then?" I asked, turning my head toward him.

"Did he talk to you about … the meeting?"

My heart skipped a beat. Did he just say what I thought he said? I gave the area a quick look around to make sure no one else had heard him. With no one even remotely close by, I dropped caution to the wind.

"How did you find out about that?" I asked.

He puffed out his chest a bit, trying to act smug. "I was the one who found out about the meeting in the first place."

"How?"

"I found out about it from my inside tip."

"Who?" I demanded, rather than asking.

He smiled and waved his finger at me. "I'm not going to give away my little songbird," he teased.

I glared at him.

"Uh, sir," he added. He was quick to lose the smug look on his face.

"Did you write the report that the first sergeant showed me?"

"Kind of," he shrugged and started walking back toward the field.

I grabbed his arm, rather forcefully, stopping his escape. H. J. jerked to a stop. "Kind of?" I asked.

"I originally informed Sergeant First Class Fürl when I was given the information. That's one of the reasons why I was asked on the team that went into the Zone. After being assigned to the task of translating the books we discovered, Fürl came by and asked me to do up a preliminary report on all the information I knew about the meeting, based on the scoop I'd gotten. I gave it to him, and he made it into a proper report," he stated as if this was commonplace information.

I raised my eyebrow at this, my hand still grasping his arm so he couldn't escape from my questioning. "You wrote up the report originally?"

"Yep. I used big words, too, so I could impress the first sergeant. Fürl said that he would do all the editing on the report and fix the parts that needed work. Make it more professional and official, ya know?"

"He edited your work," I interrupted, walking through the scenario inside my head. Let the lower-ranking officer do all the work, and then the higher-ranking officer can take the report and reword it slightly in order to take all the credit. It wasn't the first time that had happened, and it wouldn't be the last either.

"I even managed to find a map of the area that the meeting is supposedly taking place in. That took some real hunting, let me tell you. Had to go back to the Zone for it. It was locked up in a room on the top floor inside the Dome. I got a chance to wander around the place, take a look at things—it's a real mess in there. I don't see how the Rebells are going to clean it out in time to have the meeting."

I slowly let him go. We both started walking back into the Grounds and away from the gate. He stared at the sky, whistling some tune. I, on the other hand, was staring at the ground. I had almost forgotten about the blueprint that was inside the folder originally—the one that was taken the night I broke into the office. Charles never showed me the map during the debriefing—only the report. I don't think that Charles even knew about the map the way he went on.

"I never saw any map," I broke the cold silence between us.

H. J. laughed a little. I guess that he thought I was making a bad joke or pointing out how great his report was or being polite—or something.

I grew serious. "H. J., I was just shown the report folder. There was no map. The report was there but not a map."

He stopped. "I saw Sergeant First Class Fürl put the map into the folder before he sealed it!"

"What was the map of?" I asked, playing dumb.

"Mostly it was a general layout of the area. But it emphasized all the exits."

"Did you, personally, get a good look at the map? Enough so that you have a strong recollection of it—like you could draw what you saw?"

He thought for a while. "I don't remember exact details anymore, if that's what you're asking. But I could do a quick sketch of the place for you."

I started to grow excited at the thought. I could at least have something to show William.

"How many of the exits can you remember off the top of your head? Could you point them out on a drawing? Enough so that, if you were there, you could find and get out of the building easily?"

"Uh ... there were ... five ... six? They were basic exits. Easily found."

Easily found. He doesn't remember the exit through the tunnel—the one that I saw wasn't marked with red. He continued in silence for a few steps, deep in thought.

"I wonder why the first sergeant didn't show you the map?" H. J. pondered.

"But the first sergeant would have shown me the map *if* he had it," I pointed out to H. J., hinting that there was more to this than we could see on the surface.

"So ... he must not have it!" H. J. concluded.

"So there are two options as to what happened with the map."

"Which would be?"

I took a breath. "One: Charles accidentally lost it."

"Funny man," H. J. smirked.

I smiled as well at the thought of anything getting lost inside Charles's office. He had that room cleaned every day. He forgot where he put his cigar box once and had the entire Grounds ripped apart so he could find it. His only excuse was, "They're imported."

I brushed the image out of my head and continued with my theory work. "Two: someone took the map before the first sergeant had a chance to look at it."

"But who?" H. J. asked me, as if I would know.

I patted him on the back. "That, my friend, is what we're going to find out."

H. J. looked lost. "But, based on what you've been saying, no one really knows about the map. The only ones that know about it are you, me, maybe the first sergeant, and Sergeant First Class Fürl."

I pointed a finger at H. J. "Did you take the map?"

He looked disgusted. "No!"

I pointed at myself. "Well, I didn't take it. And the first sergeant didn't give any indication that he even saw it."

We paused, staring at each other.

"That narrows down the field a bit, don't you think?" I added, a smirk crawling onto the corners of my mouth.

I gave his shoulder a good slap as a congratulatory tribute for solving the crime, and we started to quicken our pace over toward the offices.

~

"It's *what*?!"

Fürl's voice rose as he raced around the room, cursing one nameless person after another. H. J. and I sat calmly in our chairs facing his desk as he fumed. It took two whole minutes before Victor even started to calm down. He tried to get himself under control by grasping the back of his chair, his knuckles turning white under the strain.

"Does the first sergeant know about its disappearance?" he asked us through clenched teeth.

"I don't think he even got a chance to see the map, sir," H. J. pointed out.

"Then only us three know about the map?" he asked, his eyes glaring a bit.

"I have told no one about it, sir. I really just found out about it," I lied.

"I only told him because I thought the first sergeant showed it to him," H. J. mentioned to offset the blame, jabbing a thumb toward me.

Fürl grew grim, which I had noticed was a very bad sign for the people around him. "Then we have a leak somewhere on the Grounds," he said out loud, his face growing dark and foreboding.

He turned the chair around slightly and sat down, swiveling the base so he was facing us again. "Let's narrow down the window of opportunity for this thief. Between the time I dropped off the report and the time in which the first sergeant read the report with me, no one had touched the map. It was careless of me to not point it out to him and to bury it inside the report. For that, I take partial blame. So, between the time that he and I went through the report and the following time when the first sergeant managed to go through the file in detail, someone had broken into the office, opened the report, taken the map, and left—all without being seen or heard."

Victor folded his hands on his desk and stared hard at the two of us. "The person who did that must have known what to look for. How else would he have known to go into the office?"

Victor clenched his jaw, creating a strong crease in his face as he chewed over the facts and the possible suspects. "But the question is, how did the thief know about the map in the first place? As you said, Tom, you had just found about its existence through secondary means. So, the most reasonable target for suspicion has to be someone who helped put together the report in the first place."

Victor glanced over toward H. J., an accusing eyebrow raised. H. J. gave a small gasp at the accusation. "I ... I ... I didn't do it!" he stammered, eyes wide and fearful.

Fürl glanced toward me. "He *is* the most likely suspect. Agreed, Corporal Major?"

I shifted a bit under Fürl's soul-burning gaze. "The evidence does push toward this officer being the likely candidate," I stated as I looked from Victor to H. J. He displayed a hint of hurt at my shocking betrayal. "But," I quickly added, "I can personally guarantee that it wasn't him."

H. J. relaxed a bit after my assurance to his innocence. Fürl, on the other hand, tensed. "Are you sure, Corporal Major?"

I locked eyes with Fürl. "Look at the counter-evidence. He was the one who discovered the map. If he wanted it, why submit its finding? Why not just keep it to start off with? Besides, he wrote," I started, then paused as I thought how best to reword my statement without committing career suicide, "the *pre*-edited rendition of the report. H. J. knew its importance as evidence and the need for it to stay with the paperwork. Why take it back? What benefit would there be?

"There's too much room for speculation, sir, and not enough hard evidence. I say we wait until after the meeting before we determine his guilt."

Fürl looked very uneasy at the request. Desperately, I tried to grab an idea out of the air as to how I could stop Victor from hounding H. J. "I've been told that the map has very clear diagrams of all the exits of the Dome—from easily accessible to blocked exits, right?"

Fürl nodded his head.

I continued. "And there will be POLICE officers on all the exits, even the ones that are blocked, right?"

Fürl nodded again, trying to see where I was going with this.

I continued. "So, if we capture some of the Rebells using the harder-to-access exits, then we can figure out how they got the information, along with who gave the information to them, thus getting the thief's name."

Fürl studied my face carefully while he pondered the application of strategy. I felt like a bug underneath a microscope. Finally, he nodded. "Done!"

H. J. relaxed a bit. He was off the hook—for now. H. J. started to rise to leave. I got up to leave as well.

"Corporal," Victor chirped, "before you leave. I have one last statement."

"That is?" I asked him.

"I discussed with the first sergeant about you're going undercover to the meeting. I take it that you've accepted the assignment? If any trouble occurs, leave via the subbasement storage bay. It will eventually lead into a maintenance tunnel of some sort and will take you out of the Dome. That way, you will be out of the way of the other officers who might confuse you for the Rebells and accidently cause you harm. It's very hard to find, so if you don't mind staying for a while, I'll give you directions on how to get to it. Someone will be waiting for you at the exit in order to help you. After all, we POLICE officers have to look out for each other."

Victor smiled at me as he said that last bit, trying to give off the appearance of being friendly. It only succeeded in freaking me out a bit.

CHAPTER 26

THE SKY WAS ILLUMINATED WITH the predawn light as I made my way out of the barracks. A shortened sleep made my body ache and tense as I stretched in the very early cool morning air. Waking up and getting out of bed wasn't easy—but I had to, so I did. It was the day of the meeting. As I walked out toward the gate that separated the town from the Grounds, I made some quick adjustments to the civilian clothes that had been sent to me. Casual shirt of a farmhand, work pants from the Factory—they were nothing extravagant so I would not get any unwanted attention at the meeting. I would be just another Rebell there to hear the words of Duncan.

The Grounds was completely empty except for the occasional officer doing final rounds before being relieved from the night shift. There were no morning bird songs, which I found unusual. Normally, there were at least two different birds tweeting in the air when I woke up. I guess it was too early for them as well.

By the time I got to the gate, I was already a few minutes late for meeting up with H. J. I had asked him to prep up my travel pack for me the night before, so I could spend the time going over any final details. I found him talking with the guard on duty. He was dressed in regular clothes as well, except his shirt had a hood sewn into it. There was a rather full backpack sitting by his feet. He waved at me as I walked up to the gate.

"We have to stop meeting like this," I pointed out to him, a smirk on my lips.

"You ready?" he asked me.

I looked into the early morning sky. The sun had not risen past the horizon. Only the faintest hint of sunlight glimmered in the still star-blanketed sky.

"I hope so." I sighed, grabbing the backpack that H. J. had prepped for me.

The guard opened up the gate for me, and I walked through. I was about to close it behind me when H. J. stopped the automatic backward swing of the gate and exited the Grounds as well, much to my surprise. He closed the gate behind him.

"Well, we better get going if we're going to make it there on time," he smiled, reaching out to take the backpack from my grasp.

I stared questioningly at the officer. "What the hell are *you* doing?"

Slinging the pack over one of his shoulders, he gave it a little bounce to better settle the weight on his back. "Coming with you," he pointed out to me like it should have been more than obvious.

"You're going as well?"

"Yeah. Security. A fairly high-ranking officer is going on a dangerous mission into enemy territory. You have to have someone watching your back out there. Figured it would be me," he pointed out with a smile.

"But Sergeant First Class Fürl pointed out that he would have someone at the site to help if I needed it."

H. J. shook his head. "You have to escape the structure to rendezvous with them. I'll be there right beside you in the thick of it. Also," he smiled, giving the gate a quick glance to make sure the guard was out of earshot, "you got to take a look at who's sending the help."

I stepped back a bit at the comment, eyes blinking in amazement. H. J. just blatantly disrespected a superior officer—to another superior officer! H. J., readjusting the backpack, gave me a "who cares" look at my reaction.

"What? We're dressed as civilians, we're trying to act like Rebells—that means talking trash about the POLICE. I can say anything I want about that old scarecrow, and he can't do a damn thing! I was following mission protocol."

It took a moment, but H. J.'s words started to sink in. H. J. smiled even brighter at a sudden realization.

"And if we're following mission protocol, I can't call you sir, because we're without rank. We're equals. Oh, I'm gonna enjoy this day," he exclaimed, wringing his hands in anticipation.

"Oh, this is gonna suck," I mumbled under my breath.

We started walking away from the Grounds and toward where we would eventually start our travel to the Zone. The sky was still barely visible, either due to the time or the start of cloud formation—it was hard to tell which. H. J. was busy working on a small piece of beef jerky, chewing away as happily as a cow with cud. We made our way in silence. No one was on the street; no lights were visible from the windows of buildings. It was as if the town was deserted.

We made our way to a small junction in the road; one way led into town more, and the other way would eventually lead out toward the outskirts. H. J. started to walk down the path that led out of town. I stopped walking at the fork in the road. H. J., suddenly realizing that I wasn't walking beside him, gave a quick search around him to see where I wandered. I jabbed my thumb into town.

"We ... actually need to take a little detour before we leave."

"Why?"

"We need to meet up with some people."

"Who?" he asked, making his way beside me once again.

I gave him a little nod toward the path that led inside town, and we started back up. Not too far into the trek, I switched gears and started to make my way toward one of the alleys, motioning to H. J. that he needed to follow.

"We're meeting up with my girlfriend Dawn and my best friend John," I told him over my shoulder as we walked quickly through the alley. "They're going to help with our cover story."

"Great. More people to protect," he muttered.

I gave him a shot over my shoulder. "And more people to protect us," I pointed out.

The alley crisscrossed through the town, connecting one entrance to another. If I had not traveled this route over and over again in my years, I could have easily gotten lost. I gave H. J. a side-glance to see how he was doing. He was looking around the alley, trying to get his bearing as to where he was inside the town.

"C'mon," I coaxed, "we're almost there."

H. J., skipping and jogging to keep up with me after staring at the buildings in the alley, gave my sleeve a quick tug to get my attention.

"Tom, where the hell are we? I can't tell where we are in town from in here."

That's the point, I thought to myself.

I smiled at the officer. "We're almost out of here," I added, raising my arm at the exit of the alley directly in front of us.

The two of us popped out of the alley into the open area of the fountain. Dawn and John were sitting around and talking lightly while they waited for me. John, seeing movement out of the corner of his eye, turned toward me and was about to wave when he noticed that I wasn't alone. The ready smile that would have welcomed me turned to a concerned frown. Dawn, sensing the change in the atmosphere, turned to see whom it was that John was focusing on, saw me, and waved me over. When she saw H. J., however, she stopped waving.

I walked over to the two waiting for me. H. J. stood off to the side. Dawn wrapped her arms around my waist, kissing me gently to greet me. "Have you two been waiting long?" I checked, making sure I wasn't too late.

John got up from sitting on the fountain's edge, grabbing hold of his backpack. "Nah. Not too long. So, umm ... who's the shadow?" he asked, giving H. J. a quick nod.

I looked over to H. J. and waved him over. H. J. walked over to where the three of us stood. "Everyone, this is H. J. H. J., this is Dawn," I said, giving Dawn a little squeeze in my arms, "and this is John."

H. J. nodded toward John, who nodded back. Dawn released one of her hands from around me and stretched it out toward H. J. "It's nice to meet you, H. J.," Dawn smiled.

H. J. took her hand and shook it with a simple smile. "Where are ...

the other two?" I asked Dawn and John, being careful not to give away I was talking about Duncan and William to H. J.

Dawn took hold of her backpack and adjusted it so that she was in balance. "They already left. Mother went to a friend's house."

H. J. gave John the once-over with his eyes and leaned over toward me. "Why's he coming again?" he whispered to me.

I leaned over toward H. J., playing along with the whole thing. "Security. I didn't know you were coming, so I arranged some of my own."

H. J. scanned John. "I could take him," he said plainly.

I laughed. "All right, people, let's get going."

H. J. cleared his throat, getting all of our attention. "Actually, now that I think of it, it would be best if I head toward the Dome ahead of you."

I leaned toward H. J. at this, both confused and concerned. I got the impression that I had somehow hurt his feelings. "Won't it be better if we all stay together?"

He looked from the road, and then back to me. "It would be a good idea to scope the area out before you enter it, just in case. You never know. Besides, now you got your friends to protect you on the way up. It's my job to protect you once you get there," he smiled. H. J. pulled the backpack down off of his shoulder and opened it up, being careful not to let anything spill out from the top. He started to unload some supplies that were packed and passed them over to John to carry in his pack.

I nodded, giving the sky a quick glance. The sun had just risen. A hue of red and blue scattered across the sky. No clouds in sight. It was going to be a good day, by the looks of it.

~

While walking, we passed some farmers by the side of the road, just outside of town. Despite the early hours, they were already at work. They waved at us as we walked passed them. One of the later farmers, I noticed, was a POLICE officer whom I had seen around the Grounds. He waved as well but kept his eyes on me the entire time I was in his view. He must have been one of the undercover officers I heard about. Probably set up to record everyone who was traveling out toward the Zone.

Eventually, our little group decided to stop for an early lunch about seven or so kilometers outside of town. There were a few trees sporadically covering the countryside, one of which we rested under. The small group of trees grew around a patch of green grass on a sloping hill beside a dirt road in the middle of nowhere. John reached into the pack and pulled out our lunches. He handed each of us a huge sandwich, spilling with meats and cheese, and a container of juice.

We immediately started eating. John said nothing, concentrating on his sandwich. He took out a simple switchblade from his pocket and cut his sandwich in two, so he could hold it better. He hadn't said anything during the entire trip, which I found kind of odd—not since meeting H. J. at the fountain. Dawn rested against me as she drank some juice and stared at the sky. The occasional white, puffy cloud formed inside the sea of blue above us. I, on the other hand, put my food to the side for a while and stared at the scenery in order to soak it all in. A clear, sunny spring day—beautiful.

"How long do you think we have until we reach the Zone?" I asked John.

He looked up from his sandwich and thought for a second, staring at the distance that we still had to cover. "Ummm … rough guess would be about five hours—maybe six. The towers marking the restricted area are in view, so we're not too far off, at least. The domed building is close to the entrance to the Zone, from what I understand. I think the instructions said it was just to the left of the towers, about a kilometer in. So that's the way we should head."

I glanced at Dawn. She wore a simple shirt, pale yellow pants, and regular shoes and wore her hair in a ponytail. She rested her head on my shoulder, and I stroked her bangs out of her eyes. She looked up at me and smiled. I kissed her forehead and leaned back against the tree that I was using to prop me up.

Looking off into the distance, I could just make out the towers that marked the Zone and the destroyed town beyond it. The towers stretched out into the sky like black, bony fingers. Hard to imagine that people could have lived in that area prior to the war. It must have looked quite nice once upon a time. Their houses and offices were now nothing but a heap of rubble due to time, wear, and lack of people.

The events that caused the Zone played itself out in my mind's eye. A half-visible mock-up of the city materialized in front of me. The city thrived, filled with magical technological wonders, complete with hundreds of people walking the streets. Strange vehicles flew through the town, going off wherever they needed to go. They were happy—safe. They knew that a war was going on, but this section had been taken over by the POLICE long ago so they had nothing to worry about. The war, for them at least, was far, far away.

Then, suddenly, there was a burst in the sky. The electronic gadgets that surrounded the town exploded into sparks and died around them. Panic grew. Confusion abounded. Then, faintly at first, a horn screamed through the air. With the burst, the safety parameters for the main power station in town died—a nuclear power station. With nothing to push back the radiation, the toxic air crept out into the area, making it unlivable for years and years. Those who managed to survive the first month eventually got sick. The Fallout Sickness was leeching out to everyone with whom it came into contact. The survivors branched out and made makeshift towns in the surrounding area, being careful to weed out the ones who still had the sickness. The POLICE came in and established order in the towns. The general citizens, thankful to the POLICE for their aid, never questioned the orders to sanction off the area now made unlivable by the radiation. The Zone was left to rot.

Even now, the area was still too toxic to live in for a long period, but we could visit for short bursts without getting sick. An age lost, desperate to be reborn thanks to the hopes and dreams of a few misguided Rebells. *Fitting that such an important meeting would be held in there*, I mused as I stared out at the towers. *And how fitting that the possible death of the Rebells take place inside its charcoal heart.*

John, smacking his fingers to suck off the last of the juices that managed to linger from his sandwich, gave a little hop to balance him as he stood.

"Everyone done?" he asked, referring to our lunch. Dawn, long done with her meal, leaned forward and brushed away any bits that rested on her clothes. Coming out of my waking dream, I refocused my view to my old friend and smiled.

"On our way already?" I joked.

John merely shrugged. "Hey, if we don't keep a good pace, then we won't get there in time. Remember, the meeting starts up at dusk, and we still got a lot of space to cover."

I nodded. John was right. Stretching out, I grabbed the remnants of my sandwich and juice container and started to get myself prepared to continue with my trek.

~

We arrived at the edge of the Zone right on schedule. The sun, once hanging high in the sky, was now leaning out toward the edge of the earth. Around the dead city, a high fence cut off any attempt to enter it. The wired fence was the same make and model that surrounded the Grounds. Only the amount of space that the fence needed to cover was different. I could only imagine the recourses that were needed to create a fence big enough to surround the entire area of the radiated town. Every so often, a sign was bolted to the wire mesh. About head height, the sign was bright yellow and showed off a diagram of a little stick man being zapped with multiple lightning bolts. Underneath the diagram, there was a warning: Electric Fence—Do not touch. Due to general age, some of the signs were hanging lopsided; the bolts that once secured it to the mesh had long rusted out.

I tilted my head to one side to better concentrate on listening. There was no hum. Odd. Whenever I went by the generator room in the Grounds, I heard a low hum in the air. I looked from the sign to John and Dawn. "What do you think?" I asked them.

John took a deep breath. "I don't know. Do you think it's safe?"

I looked back toward the sign in front of me. "Well, there's no electric hum, so I—"

Suddenly, I was kissing metal. John had shoved me up against the fence, my face banging up against the rusting sign. I convulsed and shook at the shock of being thrust up against the wired border. Pressing up against the mesh to get some support to push off from, I sprang away from the sign and the possible electrocution. Gasping for air, I sprawled myself out on the ground, patting myself for any sign of burnt clothes and damage. There was none. John laughed at the utter ridiculous display I gave off. Dawn was not impressed.

John, standing over me, stretched out a hand to help me up. "I think it's safe," he snickered.

I took his hand. "You, my friend, are a jerk," I growled as I climbed up from the ground, using John as a support beam.

Dawn gave John a solid swat against his arm as he helped me up. "That's not funny," she scolded the man.

John, once I was standing upright again, let go of my hand and waved out toward the inactive fence. "Oh, come on. If there were any concern from this thing, you'd think that we'd get a warning about it. 'Hey, by the way, don't touch the fence that surrounds the Zone, or else your face will melt off,'" he finished his argument by doing a bad impression of Duncan.

I brushed the dust and dirt off of my shirt and glared at my old friend. "Still wasn't funny, man."

With John's little jest long done with, I gave a moment to take in our situation. The towers, just on the inside of the fence, literally towered over us—for lack of a better word. The black stone pillars, erected to warn all nearby travelers to stay away, were covered with cracks from years of weather exposure. Just beyond the pillars, I could see the remnants of the city. Age had not been kind to the great ancient buildings. Once, shining metal and glass covered their walls. Now, rust-stained scrap littered the sides of the buildings and the streets. Buildings, with holes in them the size of John and me combined, stood out of the ground like nails in a board. There was no sound at all except the three of us breathing.

The fence that blocked our path wasn't too high—roughly ten feet tall and easily climbable. John tossed his backpack over the top of the wired mesh and watching it land with a thump on the opposite side.

That done, Dawn, John, and I traversed the blockade with little to no trouble. Resettling the pack on his back, John motioned that we should keep going into the city before making a turn toward where the domed building should be. It wasn't in view yet, the great visage blocked by the other buildings.

John led the way through the rubble-filled streets on our way to the Dome. Dawn and I followed. The streets were not exactly simple to maneuver around, with the years of debris and junk scattered throughout its expanse. Luckily, with the years of practice zooming through the alleys in town, the trek through the skeletal path of half-destroyed constructs was quick and painless.

The Dome beckoned to us, and we answered its call. Compared to all the coal surrounding us, the Dome shone like a diamond. It was old and hadn't been used in a while, but it still looked wondrous in its huge majestic form. Its white-gray sides stuck out in the darkness that hung around the Zone. A thick canvass roof, old and full of rips and holes, sort of covered and was supported by the Dome's massive shape. The remaining section of roof was made up of slabs of some sort of light metal. According to the blueprint, this part of the roof could be retracted to allow the sunlight inside. I guess they would do this to allow for natural light during events. It was huge! It easily could have held the entire town's populace, plus more. I can easily see why it had been chosen for the meeting.

As we walked toward the domed building, I could see the occasional person skitter out from the nearby rubble or crevasses in order to sprint through the open space between covered safety and the Dome. As people ran, nervous glances were cast to make sure no one spotted their actions. A single set of double doors were open from where I could see, which the cautious Rebells would scurry toward. Two men stood guard on either side of the open doors.

We quickened our pace toward the Dome. Not many people were standing outside, for obvious reasons. We walked up to the set of doors that led into the Dome and stopped just in front of a tubby man and a tall, skinny man stuck with guard duty. "C'n I-ah help yea?" the tubby man asked us, staring at us all suspiciously.

"We're here for the meeting," Dawn answered the man.

She reached her hand out toward me. I grabbed her hand in mine and gave it a small squeeze of assurance. The tubby man looked us over and smiled. "Passw'rd."

John and I looked at each other, panic settling in. Password?! When was there any mention of a password? We both glanced at Dawn, who was smiling back at the man.

"Give me liberty, or give me death."

He nodded and let us enter.

CHAPTER 27

The hallway that led out from the lobby area, which we had just entered, was long and dark despite the evenly distributed lanterns that hung along the wall to mark the direction to take. John insisted that he take the lead of our little group. "In case something goes wrong" was his excuse. There were doors and hallways that we passed that led off to darkened sections of the Dome. The smell of dust was quite strong but not overpowering. It almost felt like we were walking into the middle of the planet.

I stopped about halfway down the corridor we were traveling down, and Dawn quickly stopped at the realization I was no longer beside her.

"What's wrong?" she asked.

I looked around the hallway and tried to get my bearing as to where I was in regards to the blueprint I had glanced at so long ago. There were no markings to indicate if we were on the south side or north side of the building—or east or west. I wasn't sure which exit we had used to enter the building. If I knew that much, I could then take a guess as to where we were in relation to the emergency exit that Fürl talked about.

"I was just thinking that we should make sure the emergency exit actually exists. Last thing we need to worry about once the POLICE show up is trying to find the exit so we can escape quickly and safely," I pointed out to Dawn.

Dawn turned to John, who was now stopped a couple feet away from us, and motioned for him to come back to where we stood. John slowly made his way back, a little impatient with the delay.

"All right," he agreed. "Let's find this secret path and get back to the main meeting area. We don't want to be wandering around too much outside of the lighted areas. It might drive up too much suspicion, especially with the POLICE eventually showing up here." John spoke quietly so only the three of us could hear.

Dawn, hooking her arm around mine, smiled and turned us toward one of the darkened hallways that branched out from the one we were in. "So ... which way do we go?"

I sighed as I closed my eyes, desperate to grab some foothold of where we were. "From what I remember, if we were facing south, away from the main meeting area, then the path we should take would be ... to the left ... about five pathways down."

John looked around the area for some clue as to what I was talking about. "Five pathways down from the left? What? How did they expect you to figure out which path to take?"

I shrugged at the question. "I guess we have to get to the main meeting area first and then backtrack."

John looked ahead of us at the path we were about to take to get to the meeting area, gauging the distance we still had to travel. "It would probably look a lot less suspicious if one of us went to the area and then backtracked," he said. "Let's assume that we're in the southern part of this place. I'll go and count my way back. When I get to the—what was it, the fifth pathway?—I'll mark off the path and come get the two of you."

That said, John skipped off into a jog down the hallway. He flashed in and out of the light that hung on either side of the walls. Soon, he was gone, leaving Dawn and myself standing alone in the hallway. Dawn, still linked with my arm, gave me a quick squeeze. "What do you think is going to happen when *they* show up?"

I gave her a quick smile. "Let's hope that it won't be as bad as we're making it out to be. They could arrive late, and everyone could be gone. There was no mention on any of the reports regarding when the meeting was to start. They could miss it completely."

My words were empty, though. We both knew it. There was no chance the POLICE would be late. They would wait until the meeting started, and then they would swarm the area and take everyone prisoner—or at least those who didn't put up a fight. Why didn't Duncan just listen to reason? Why didn't he just put this off? His stubbornness was going to get a lot of people hurt.

"Hey!" John waved us down from the opposite end of the hallway. "I think I found it."

Dawn and I made our way down to where John was standing. The sound of general chatter coming from the big doors at the end of the hall gave off a good impression of how many people had arrived before us and were now waiting for the meeting to start up.

"Are you sure that we're supposed to go down this corridor?" John asked me, pointing his thumb at a short path that eventually ended with a door that stood closed. The sign on the door read "maintenance." I nodded.

John checked the handle to see if it was locked. It wasn't. Pulling the door open with a little bit of effort, he also found out that the hinges were not too stable. The door almost fell on top of the three of us as it opened. John gave it a good push toward the wall, setting it so there was no chance of it closing behind us. With the door out of the way, John walked into the room first, with the two of us following close behind him. We each held a lantern taken from the walls to help guide us as we made our way. The room that we had entered was used as an equipment storage room. Decayed equipment of a time past were scattered throughout the room in no clear pattern. John looked around the room in disgust.

"Jeez … what sloppy people!" he mused while examining the multiple styles of equipment.

There was no other way in or out of the room except how we had entered. Dawn and I started searching the walls, trying to find a door handle or a secret passageway or something indicating the opening for the exit. We looked behind shelves, under grates, under equipment— everywhere.

"Wait! I think found it," Dawn whispered.

A small trapdoor, once covered by a box holding bits of metallic parts on the ground, was squished into one of the corners of the room. Dawn opened it and took a quick look inside. The trapdoor led out into a tunnel underneath the building, pipes of all sizes sticking out in the ceiling. I guess this was the maintenance portion of the room, as the sign had mentioned. There was no ladder to climb down into the tunnel, so we would have to jump. Luckily, it wasn't that far to jump. There was just enough height for us to be able to stand inside the passage that led underneath us. There was no light inside the path, and it smelled of old, wet dirt—almost musty. Dawn closed the trapdoor and placed the box over top of it again, so we could find it easily in a rush.

"Come on," John urged us, standing beside the doorway, "let's get back to the main area. The meeting's probably about to start."

With the escape path found, we made our way through the doors at the end of the hall and into the section of the Dome that held the meeting. What a crowd! What a sight! The Dome could be broken into two sections—the floored area where everyone was gathered and the rows upon rows of chairs that surrounded us. The chairs sprawled upward toward the ceiling of the dome to no end. The ground was covered in a type of material that looked like grass, and yet it wasn't. Even after all this time, it still had a sharp green hue to it. There were all sorts of different lines marking off the areas of the grass, establishing certain zones on the ground. I could only guess that this was used for a specific sport—a widely watched sport, based on the number of seats that surrounded the playing field.

A stage stood in the middle of the arena in front of us. The stage was completely constructed by sheets of metal and stood waist-high, raised and supported by beams of fresh wood. A backdrop was attached to the stage by huge pipes that were fused to the stage. Curtains ran along the sides and back of the stage, blocking off the view so that the massive crowd could not see what was going on backstage. Torches and lanterns were scattered throughout the Dome, giving light and warmth. More warmth than needed, since the sun was clearly displayed all day and the number of people inside the Dome kept the air warm. Everything shone inside the light.

"How many people are here?" I asked as I stood in awe of the spectacle that unraveled before me.

"I assumed that about four hundred would turn out," Dawn told me.

"Four hundred just became five or six thousand, by the looks of it!" John blurted out as he shook his head at the sight.

We started walking into the crowd but tried to stay close to the hallway that we had just entered from—as well as to each other. The crowd was too thick in front of us, so we weren't able to get too close to the stage. More people walked into the Dome—old, young, middle-aged, men and women of all shapes and sizes. People rushed into the main area as if the markets were giving away free food to everyone.

I now realized why Duncan had such high hopes for this meeting. From what I overheard from the crowd, people as far as four towns over had come to hear his words. They'd probably been on the road for close to a week just to get here. When the POLICE come to storm the meeting, they would have a regular riot on their hands. They might even lose the fight! What a boost of assurance that would be! Spirits would soar! People would join the Rebells by the hundreds daily, especially with the death of the general! I could seriously see them destroying the POLICE force that would be storming into this area. This was why Duncan was not afraid of the POLICE coming to the meeting. Actually, I think he was hoping that they would come! This day—this event—it would either give the journey toward the Rebells' dream estate a huge jump-start or kill the dream completely without remorse.

"Tom!"

I searched the sea of faces to find who had called out my name. That didn't take long. H. J. made himself hard to miss by climbing up one of the poles. His entire upper torso stuck out above the countless faces, allowing him to scan the area for us. I gave a general wave toward him to show that I saw him, and he shuffled down the pole to make his way to where we stood.

"What a turn out!" he screamed at us over the common commotion as he waded through the bodies.

Once he got to where we stood, he leaned over to me so only I could hear. "I had no idea there were so many turncoats," he added, under his breath.

Dawn and John said their hello toward the undercover POLICE officer, careful not to direct too much attention toward him—especially considering the audience. I turned away from the stage to better talk with the young man. "So, did you have any trouble getting in?"

H. J. gave a quick glance around us. "I didn't enter through the main door, if that's what you mean."

"How'd you get in, then?"

"I had to run around the entire building and find an entrance that wasn't guarded. Took awhile, but I eventually found one. I don't think they know about all the doors that lead into this place."

"Did you know about the password?"

"They had a password?"

"Yeah."

H. J. raised an eyebrow in question. "There was no mention of a password. How did you get the password?"

Uh oh, I thought.

"I ... overheard the group ahead of me. Total fluke that I managed to overhear it."

H. J. thought for a second. "Wow. I never would have gotten in."

Dawn gently nudged me and pointed off toward the stage. "Look, there's father!" she told me and tried to call out to William. She waved vigorously, trying to get his attention.

William, who had just walked on stage, was fixing one of the pipes that had started to slant slightly from the weight of the fabric it was holding up. He looked ill and uncomfortable. Once he was done, he looked out onto the crowd with a sad, long look and then walked off stage and out of view.

"Why is your father here?" H. J. asked Dawn, who was still waving at William.

John's face grew into a panicked look. It was a good thing John was standing behind H. J., or else H.J. would have seen that something was wrong.

"He ... obviously was hired to do some construction work for the set," I blurted out quickly, remembering that William was fiddling around with something just moments before.

H. J. turned and looked at me, a stern expression on his face. "Doesn't he know what's going on here?"

Dawn stopped waving and turned away from the stage, presenting a sly smile for H. J.'s sake. "He was asked to complete the construction. He doesn't ask what the people are going to do with the construction once it's completed; he just quietly does his job. If it requires him to do some on-site repairs, then he will do his duty and complete his contract. Isn't that what the POLICE are always emphasizing? To do one's duty?" Dawn continued on with my lie.

H. J. was about to answer her when Duncan walked onto the stage from behind one of the curtains. The crowd rose with applause at the sight of him. He strolled up to the front of the stage, chest puffed out full of pride and air. The crowd turned their full attention to the single man on the stage. He stood tall, looking out onto the ocean of faces that stared back at him. They were all cheering him, yelling his name in unison.

"Dun-can. Dun-can. Dun-can."

He raised his hands high into the air, motioning for silence, and then lowered them once the audience calmed to a low rumble.

"I would like to thank you all for coming out," he started his speech, making sure that he was loud enough to be heard by everyone. Some of the people toward the back of the crowd started to push forward in order to hear him better. Shouts from the back made themselves known, letting everyone ahead of them aware of the fact that they couldn't see or hear what was going on. Seeing that there were people in the crowd who were having trouble hearing, Duncan turned toward the backstage area and made a quick motion to some unseen person behind the curtains. A soft murmur started to flow through the crowd as we waited for the speech to continue.

Soon, William returned on stage, carrying a megaphone for Duncan to use. He handed the cone to his friend without saying a word. Duncan quickly took the megaphone and turned back to the audience, not giving William a second glance as he wandered offstage.

"How's that? Can everyone hear me now?" he asked, holding the cone up to his mouth.

Duncan's voice boomed out clear and loud, powering through the entire area. The crowd rose back up to a cheer to show that the megaphone was exactly what was needed. Duncan repositioned himself at the front of the stage, staring out into the forest of followers and started up again.

"I thank you all for traveling here to hear my words. I know that some of you have traveled far to make it here today, so I will try to make this worth your while. There have probably been a few rumors bouncing around as to why I would risk such a meeting with all of you. Let me assure you, I would not risk it unless it was important.

"As most of you know, very soon the POLICE are going to celebrate the anniversary of the war and their grand victory. What they are really doing is celebrating their victory over the destruction of the natural world! They are celebrating the eradication of democracy! They are celebrating the *deaths of days* past!"

The crowd erupted with catcalls and hisses. "Booooo!"

"We are called *Rebells* because we think that our lives could be improved by returning to the ways of the *past* ... to *better days*!"

"Booooo!"

"We are *hunted* like *animals* in the *dark*!"

"*Booooo!*"

"Well, if we are animals, then I say we show our *claws* and *fight back*!"

The crowd exploded with the songs of angry men and women cheering Duncan on. The energy in the room was intoxicating. H. J. watched the crowd in its frenzy and slowly turned toward me to see if I was still beside him. I could see in his eyes a hint of panic and worry for his well-being. Obviously, he was no longer comfortable with being inside a crowd full of revved up, POLICE-hating Rebells.

Duncan held up his hands to grab everyone's attention once again. "I have recently found out through my many sources buried deep within the POLICE organization that the general, the leader of this unscrupulous society, is going to be taking a personal tour of his kingdom during the anniversary. That means that he's coming *here* to *your home*!"

"Booooo!"

"When the general comes to visit, let's make it so he never goes home *alive*!" Duncan shouted out into the crowd, raising his fist into the air for emphasis.

"*Wooooo!*"

"When the general comes into our town, we must attack him—we must bring him down! Now, I won't lie to you … lives will be lost. But we *will* be *triumphant*! The general. Will. *Fall*!"

"*Yeeeaaah!*"

The crowd surged once again, stirring at his words. Duncan turned toward the curtain that was outstretched behind him. With a quick gesture, a secondary sheet that was wound tight at the top fluttered and bellowed down from the pipes that held the whole production aloft. The sheet that wobbled down from its once secure position was covered with all sorts of lines and colored markers that I couldn't make out at first glance. The crowd went from an uproar of cheers to whispered and hushed tones as they tried to figure out what it was. Once the sheet settled itself, coming to a rest in front of the backstage curtain, everyone could easily see what it was Duncan had planned. A crude map of the neighboring towns was painted on the huge sheet, a single red line marking a distinct path along the roads that crisscrossed along the display.

"This is what I have planned out so far," Duncan continued, pointing toward the billboard behind him.

"The general will enter the town Sicher Himmel through one of the less-traveled side roads, so not to raise too much alarm. After all, this is an unofficial stop on the tour. He will be protected by all the sergeant majors he can afford to bring without leaving Hauptstadt unprotected, which will be a fair number. We will place ourselves by the road he will enter before the general and his henchmen arrive. I will set up an obstacle right before the parade wanders into view. At the given sign, we will swarm the general, killing as many sergeant majors as possible, and eventually killing the general himself! With him out of the way, the POLICE will *fall* and *democracy* will *live again*!"

The cries of enthusiasm poured out of the throats of the Rebells as they celebrated Duncan's plan. H. J. leaned toward me and covered his mouth a bit so that no one would overhear what he had to say to me. "*That's* the plan!? That's a horrible attempt at an ambush, if you ask me."

Looking and listening to Duncan as he continued the details of his murder attempt, I had to agree with H. J. Duncan was organizing a shoddy mob to try to take out the general and his highly trained sergeant majors. The Rebells, no matter how many Duncan might manage to secure from this meeting to try to kill the general, would all be slaughtered in the attempt. What was Duncan thinking? Why would he risk a meeting like this to tell everyone such a poorly planned form of attack? What was Duncan really trying to do here?

Duncan raised his hands up in the air again, and the audience lowered their voices. "The general is scheduled to arrive—"

The cry of a whistle screamed through the air. All heads turned from the stage to the open exit doors that surrounded them in the lower half of the arena. They were all blocked by POLICE officers; each one was displayed in a helmet and riot gear and was holding clubs. In front of one of the exits, the one directly facing the stage where Duncan stood, were three men: two holding rifles in their hands, and the third with a whistle in his mouth. The one with the whistle was Fürl.

H. J. glanced from the exit to me. He had a shocked and very scared look on his face. My heart was beating a mile a minute as well. Both of us knew that the POLICE were going to try to stop the meeting, but we didn't know that they would actually enter the building to secure everyone. The panic factor grew. The POLICE were not here to arrest the escaping Rebells—they were here to kill them all. The man with the whistle removed it from his mouth and cleared his throat. In a deep, booming, grating voice, Sergeant Fürl yelled out over the crowd to Duncan.

"Well, well, well. Long time no see, Duncan."

Duncan merely crossed his arms at the sight of Fürl. "I'm surprised you can see at all," he called out, the megaphone falling to the stage floor.

The Rebells gave off a nervous laugh at Duncan's jab. Fürl, undaunted by Duncan, took a few more steps into the area. The two officers who accompanied him followed shortly, rifles at the ready.

"Yes, I have to repay you for the parting gift you left me from the last time we met," he yelled out to the Rebell leader on the stage as he raised one hand and lightly tapped the eye patch he was wearing.

Duncan slowly unfolded his arms and reached behind him. His telltale blade that he always managed to wear with him leisurely emerged into view in his hand. The light available in the area glinted off the polished blade.

"And I'm ready to finish the job," he announced.

Fürl, keeping his eye stuck on Duncan's frame on the stage, leaned his head to the side so the officers around him could hear him easier. "Come to order!" he shouted in his gruff voice.

The officers who surrounded us stood ready for action. Leather stretched and relaxed as the gloves holding the clubs twisted and turned. The Rebells were backing up into each other as they pressed closer and closer to the stage, away from the officers surrounding them. You could smell the sweat and fear in the room, despite its size. Fürl casually raised his hand up into the air, finger outstretched.

"These people before you are traitors to the order! They have willingly given up their rights to a fair trial and due processing! They are to receive no mercy!"

The officers chimed out in unison to their commanding officer, "Yes, sir!"

Duncan, not to be undone, raised his blade up into the air to gather the Rebells' attention. "Fellow fighters! These deluded fools are trying to stop you from obtaining your right to freedom! Are you going to let them?"

The Rebells who surrounded me turned to face off against the POLICE. "*No!*" they shouted back at them. Glancing around, I could see the fury in the mob grow. Grasping hands turned into clenched fists. This was it! POLICE vs. Rebells in an all-out brawl, and I was stuck in the middle of it.

Fürl, using his upward pointed hand, lowered it so he was pointing toward Duncan on the stage. "Duncan! It's time to be cast out!"

And then, there was chaos.

CHAPTER 20

THE CROWD, ONCE UNIFIED WITH hope and cries of freedom, now fought against each other in order to escape from the POLICE. The pressure from the wave of people pushing toward the exits was unbearable. You had to yell at the person right next to you in order to be heard. Some of the Rebells in the crowd charged their way toward the officers, screaming something about honor or revenge, but most just tried to make their way to the exits.

John reached behind me and grabbed Dawn, who then grabbed me just I was reaching to grab H. J. Like a living chain, we forced our way through the doors where we had entered the arena. John's bulk helped get people out of the way so we could slither through the panicking crowd. The POLICE officers at the exit tried to stop John from escaping, but the pressure of the wave of people pressed against us aided our attempt to flee. The officers swung wildly at the ocean of lost souls in front of them, smacking random people in an attempt to beat back the wave.

One of the officers managed to lock eyes with me during the whole mess. I recognized him from the Grounds, and I knew he recognized me. He was one of the guards that stood outside Charles's office. I must have passed by him a couple dozen times a month. There was a brief moment of understanding between us. I knew he had to try to keep everyone at bay long enough for the officers outside to get properly organized for the onslaught that would befall them. He knew I had to get out of there, or else I would have been smothered in the crowd or caught by some unknowing officer. Using all of his might, the officer standing at the exit managed to grab John and everyone in the chain and threw us forward into the open area behind them. He acted like he didn't have a good enough position to stop us as we ran passed, when it was him that made out path clear. The other officers were too busy fighting off the crowd to worry about four people actually managing to sneak past them.

We reached the hallway that lead to the emergency exit at a full sprint. The noise from outside the Dome—the yelling, the gunfire, the screaming, the crying, and the many blasts of POLICE-issued whistles—could be heard from where we were. The room that held the tunnel was as it was when we left it. John grabbed the door that was still leaning against the wall outside and yanked it shut behind us all. He pulled a heavy piece of bulky equipment in front of the door, creating some protection between the hallway and us. John rested for a second against the equipment that he had just moved in front of the door as I shoved the obstruction out of the way of the trapdoor.

H. J. hit one of the walls in exasperation. "He *lied*! He was lying all along! He had no intention of arresting the Rebells at the meeting at all! That was an execution squad! He was planning on killing them from the very start. He was probably going to let you be captured and killed along with the rest of the Rebells! I bet he has some excuse readily prepared for not having someone meet us at the end of this passage."

H. J. continued to sputter and stammer his rage against Sergeant Fürl. Then, quite suddenly, he stopped and stared right at me. "What if he *has* got something planned for us at the end of the tunnel after all?"

"Now is not the time, Soldier!" I warned him, concentrating on the task at hand. Sweat dropped freely from my forehead, partially from the run.

John almost threw us into the passage when I finished getting it open. H. J. jumped down into the passage first to make sure that there were no surprises. I stood by and watched the door to make sure no one came after us. John was getting ready to lower Dawn down when she stopped him.

"Come on!" H. J. called out to her, stretching his arms out toward her to help guide her down into the tunnel.

"I can't go," she said simply.

I shot her a glance. "We don't have time for this. Let's go!"

"I can't leave without Father," she told me.

I froze in horror. William! In all the excitement, I completely forgot!

I grabbed her hand tightly and stared into her eyes. "Dawn. I'm sure that he prepared for this. A secret tunnel, like this one, perhaps? There's no way Duncan would let William get caught."

I felt like if I blinked, she would disappear on me, perhaps be carried away by the POLICE. She looked from me to the barricaded door; worry firmly etched across her face. "I … I don't know! I'm going to look for him! I'll bring him here with me!"

"I can't let you go back out there! It's a mad house!"

She looked back into my eyes. There was no fear in them at all. "Come with me."

I slackened my grip on her. "Oh, Dawn, you know I can't. It was a fluke that the officer at the exit knew me enough to let us all through. If any officers see me who don't know me or know me and don't know that I'm here through an undercover assignment, it would mean immediate death. Worse, I don't know what would happen to you, because you'd be in my company. I can't do it."

"I'm not leaving without Father," she repeated, more determined.

I stared at her for what seemed to be eternity. She slowly started walking toward the door. "Wait!" I called out to her and leaned over the trapdoor to talk to H. J., who was still inside the passage.

"What's with the holdup?" he asked me impatiently.

"How many people know that you're here undercover?" I quickly asked him.

"Almost everyone I could find. I tried to warn everyone I saw, so in case something did happen to go wrong, they would know not to attack me … or who I was with!" H. J. told me.

I sighed with relief. "H. J., you remember after the whole 'learning English' thing I said you would owe me a favor? One that I would call in and you would have to do it, no matter the reason?"

I risked a glance behind me at Dawn and then returned to H. J. "Well, I'm calling in that favor now."

I reached into the passage and offered my hand to help pull him up. "I need you to go with Dawn to help find her father."

He stared at me hard. I never dropped my gaze. "Please. Please, H. J. Help her. You're the only one who can."

He reached up and, with both hands, grabbed onto my arm. "Pull me up," he told me.

Once he was out, he brushed off the dust and debris from his clothes. Taking a glance at Dawn himself, H. J. leaned close to me in order to whisper into my ear. "No one will touch her. You have my word," he promised.

I turned toward Dawn. "H. J.'s going with you to help find William. John and I will wait for you three at the end of the passage."

H. J. took Dawn's hand and started walking toward the door. Dawn turned her head to me as she was walking and mouthed the words "I love you." I repeated the words back to her.

John had pushed the piece of equipment that had blocked the door out of the way by this time. He half-supported the door as he opened it for the two of them. As they passed, he grabbed H. J. by the shoulder. "Time to show off how good of a bodyguard you really are," John told him, more of a warning than anything else.

H. J. pointed one of his fingers at John. "I expect the corporal major back in one piece," he ordered and ran down the hallway with Dawn in tow. A moment later, and they were gone.

John shoved the door behind him, leaving it open a bit so that H. J. and Dawn could get back into the room. I grabbed one of the lanterns we had left in the area last time and leapt into the passage. John followed behind me.

～

The ceiling barely touched our heads. The musty, damp smell was worse once we were inside the passage. John grabbed for his lantern, which rested at his feet, and turned it on. I had my lantern in hand, already lit. The lights filled the tunnel, showing off the moss that was growing around us in the damp cavern. Rock and dirt and mud filled the area where metal and concrete once were. My guess was that this cavern was once built to bring equipment into the building from outside but was flooded out over time. Maybe it was a maintenance tunnel for sewage or water pipes? Whatever it was once used for, it was in need of repair and upkeep. Water dripped off the ceiling in the distance, making hollow thumps in the foreground. The lights of the lanterns bounced uncontrollably inside the cavern as John and I jogged down the path. It ran in front of us for what seemed for forever. John and I gradually slowed our jog to a steady walk.

"What was H. J. talking about back there in the room, about the lies that Fürl told?" John asked.

"Based on the impression I was given from the report, as well as all the training that was going around the Grounds, the task force Fürl was organizing was meant to capture and arrest all the Rebells at the meeting—not kill them. Also, when we confronted Sergeant Fürl, he told us that there would be someone waiting for us at the end of the tunnel to aid our escape. Somehow, I don't think that's going to happen," I told him.

John looked at the illuminated cavern in front of us. "Oh, I think he has something planned for us up ahead. We should be prepared for anything."

We walked in silence from then on. John led the way, and I was right behind him. Branches broke off from the main tunnel we were traveling along, leading off into unknown darkness. As we walked, I took a quick glance behind us at the distance we had covered. There was no way we were still underneath the building. We had to be at least two or three blocks away by now.

A turn came up ahead. John stopped and leaned against the wall. I followed his example. We inched along the wall until we got to the corner. Tension rose; my breath came in short, shallow gasps. John got ready to jump out into the open. I got ready to pull off whatever was about to jump onto John. He took a breath, let out a growl, and leapt into the opening.

Nothing.

John and I relaxed a bit as we realized nothing was going to leap out and shoot us, attack us, or eat us. We half-heartedly laughed at each other and what we must have looked like. We continued walking down the path until a shaft of light started to creep out in front of us—one that came from something other than the lanterns.

An opening, covered in vines and cobwebs, stood before us. John and I started running for the opening. We flew through the vines, exploding out from the tunnel, and readied ourselves for any style of attack. The sun was barely visible over the horizon, the sky turning a warm red and orange with the last breath of sunshine kissing its tender clouds. We were on the outskirts of the city. The door that once covered the maintenance shaft was rusting on the ground below us, covered with years of nature trying desperately to take back what was once hers. Just in front of us was the electrified fence. Grass, hills, and trees surrounded us on the opposite side of the fence; the town was behind us. It looked like we were to the east from where we had entered the city. The wide-open space called out to both John and me, but we stayed by the opening to wait for Dawn and the others.

"Well," John mused as he took a look around to get his bearing, "doesn't look like there's a welcome wagon waiting for us at least."

The echo of gunfire could still be heard in the distance, coming from the direction of the Dome. Screams too. John and I stared back at the horror we had just escaped.

"We shouldn't have left her," I whispered.

John rested his hand on my shoulder. "H. J. will protect her with his life. You know he will. We can't go back for her now. Best we can do is wait."

"Hey."

I whirled around at the sound of the disembodied voice coming from somewhere beside me. John, also at the ready, searched the area for the person who called out.

"Who's there?" he called out in a loud whisper.

A single head rose from behind a pile of rubble about fifteen feet from where we stood. It was a man, roughly thirty, dressed in dark clothes. He was covered in dust and mud from his travels.

"Did anyone else make it out with you?" he asked.

John and I relaxed a bit at the sight of the man who was obviously not POLICE. "No," I answered.

The man stood up slightly at hearing this and, being careful not to be seen by any unknown forces, ran crouched over to where we stood. When he was standing by the exit of the tunnel, only then did he stand up straight.

"How did you two manage to escape?" he asked, looking at the two of us nervously.

John jabbed a thumb up toward the path we had taken. "Service tunnel."

The man, staring down the dark shaft, nodded. "I barely made it out myself. Had to push through a whole hoard of officers to even see the outside of the building. Once outside, there was a shooting gallery. Bullets were flying all over the place. Hid in the dirt until it was clear to run. Made sure no one followed me."

He was jerking his head around at even the tiniest sound. I started to feel uneasy just being around this guy; his paranoia was rubbing off on me. I could tell that John was feeling the same. The man looked at the two of us and then to the fence.

"Which way are you two headed?" he asked.

I pointed off toward some random direction, off to the distance. "That way."

The man squinted his eyes to see where I was pointing off. "Good. Not the way I'm going."

The man started to make his way to the fence, looking over his shoulder the entire time at us and the surroundings. "If you get caught, remember— you never saw me," he called out as he started to climb the wired border. Once at the top, he leapt off onto the grassy ground and broke into a sprint toward the distance.

John waved at the back of the guy as he slowly retreated from our view. "Okay. See ya, strange little man," he said.

I returned my attention to the situation at hand. The sun was now well past its point in the horizon of giving any dependable light. I took one of the lanterns and set it just inside the exit in order to light the way out and give us sheltered light that couldn't be seen by any prying eyes. I plunked myself down against the construction that housed the opening, a simple double doorframe that eventually disappeared into the ground via a ramp. John, turning away from watching the strange man we had encountered, decided to join me on the opposite side of the opening. There we would wait for Dawn, H. J., and William.

John watched the one side for movement, I the other. Occasionally, we would take turns glancing down the tunnel for any sign of the three, but there was never any. John didn't talk while we waited. I wasn't in the mood to talk either. Worry held the best of me.

We waited for more than an hour. Dawn never showed. It was starting to get really dark. John looked over to where I sat. "Should we go back in the tunnel?" he asked me.

I sighed, staring at the passage for any glimpse of movement.

John got up and leaned against the fence. "The POLICE will be leaving the Zone soon if they haven't left already. You do know that, don't you?" he pointed out to me. "They might come this way. If they find us waiting—"

"If they see us, then they see us."

"How long are we going to wait?"

"As long as it takes," I glared at John.

"Maybe they escaped through another way. It is possible. There were quite a few other paths down that tunnel. She might have gone down another way and gotten lost or maybe came out a different hatch."

I continued to stare down the passage's mouth, hoping for some sort of sign that Dawn made it out okay. The empty shade mocked my attempt to hope. The light from the lantern streamed a few feet down the corridor, lighting the exit and the streams of vines that made their home against the opening. The rest of the path was barely visible with the light available. Other than that, nothing.

Cough.

I sat up straighter at the sound that came from the tunnel and stared down the path for some sort of glimpse of movement to match the sound. Did I just see? *Yes!* There was someone inside the passage!

"John!" I exclaimed.

John got up from his post and scuttled beside me. He saw the movement as well. We pushed the vines aside and climbed into the passage. At the first clear glance, my heart sank into despair. It wasn't Dawn. It was a man. It wasn't William, because he wouldn't have left Dawn behind. Whoever he was, he was big. That ruled out H. J. as well.

His head was down, hair matted, his clothes ripped and torn in a few places. He was limping. Blood dripped slowly from his leg. He was in obvious pain. John went to his side and hooked an arm around his waist. The man almost collapsed onto John, giving him all his weight. The man tried to take some of his own weight back, and the two stumbled toward the opening where I stood waiting to offer help. As John dragged the man closer to the exit and the light from the lantern, we could both see that the man we were helping was wearing a POLICE uniform.

John nearly let the guy go at the sight of the uniform. I rushed over to where John was standing with the injured officer and hooked myself around him opposite John. With the man between us, John and I eased the officer onto the ground just inside the exit, being careful not to aggravate any of his wounds. His head was slumped over, and his hair was covering his face, so we didn't get that good a look at him. That, and the light from the lantern didn't give off that much light to the corner we put him from where it was angled. John unraveled himself from the officer and walked uneasily away from him.

Staring at the man, a question rose inside my mind: Whom did we just help? I grabbed hold of his chin and raised his head to see who it was. The man had a black eye with an old scar that ran down one side of his face.

Vans opened his eyes.

~

"So you were undercover?" Vans asked, pointing to my civilian clothes.

"And I brought John along to help protect me in case things got out of hand," I further lied to cover up why we were there.

Vans nodded and threw a twig into the makeshift fire I had managed to throw together. The three of us sat around a small fire a short distance from the tunnel. John, under complete duress regarding the situation, helped Vans tend to his wounds. I had John's backpack in front of me and gave out to everyone what should have been our dinner on the trek back toward town. Vans shoved a piece of bread into his mouth, chewing softly and slowly, wincing from the pain it caused.

"The commanding officer did say something about trying to keep an eye out for undercover officers. Never figured you'd be one of 'em ... sir."

"So, what happened in there, exactly?" I asked Vans. "Once Fürl came in, John and I booked it out of there."

"The POLICE took quite a beating," Vans explained to us in between stuffing bread into his mouth. "At first, inside the Dome, it was a simple case of rounding up the Rebells and herding them outside so they could be properly ... interrogated. There was general panic, which made our job a whole lot easier. Once the Rebells got organized, though, we had a steady fight on our hands. They wouldn't let up, despite being completely outgunned. The size of the hoard was more than we expected, and they were quick to swarm us. I wouldn't be surprised if we lost a third of our battalion today. I just barely got here alive. It was pure luck that I managed to find that equipment room and the hatch that lead to this tunnel," Vans pointed out, stuffing another piece of bread into his mouth.

I wanted to ask him about Dawn and the others so badly. John could see my concern. He leaned toward Vans. "Did you happen to see H. J. on your way here?"

Vans looked at John puzzled. "Who?"

"He was an officer that was undercover with me. We were separated. There was someone with him," I explained to Vans.

"Was he wearing a uniform?"

"No," I answered.

Vans turned to the side so he could look toward the Zone and gave a low grunt. "Too bad. Anyone who wasn't wearing a uniform was either captured or killed. If someone recognized him, then he'll probably be all right. If not, well ..." he shrugged his shoulders at the last point, hinting toward what was not said. "One for the cause," Vans trailed off.

Vans shuffled around a bit so his back was turned toward us and continued eating. I nodded to John to keep an eye on Vans. He understood. I got up and walked away from the fire. The wind picked up a bit. There were no stars in the sky. I stood in the developing darkness. All I could think about were the people I had left behind: H. J., the tagalong who was always ready to make sure that you had everything you needed; William, my second father and favorite teacher; and Dawn ... oh, sweet Dawn. I closed my eyes, the image of Dawn resting just on the cusp of my eyelids.

Thwack.

Some sort of heavy object collided with my ribcage, knocking the wind out from under me. I fell into the darkness, landing on the grass and dirt. Something huge flung itself on top of me. A fist connected with my jaw. Sparks of pain danced in front of my eyes. Blow after blow landed on me, meeting flesh and bone with disastrous results.

I grabbed whatever was on top of me and, with some clever counterbalancing, managed to flip it. I could hear a quick yelp as whatever it was rolled off of me, completely taken by surprise by my maneuver. The thing collapsed in a heap, a little less than a meter away from me. I rolled over and stood up, fists outstretched in front of me. Vans slowly pulled himself into a kneeling position, all the while coughing into his fist.

"Not bad. The first sergeant teach you that one?" Vans scoffed as he rubbed his arm, which had landed on a rock.

I looked around, trying to find an advantage over Vans. I saw none. "Why did you attack me?"

Vans smiled and got up. "Just following orders," he bowed.

"From whom?"

Vans raised his head, so he was looking down his nose at me. "Sergeant Fürl."

That name hit me like a slap across the face. "What?!"

Vans started to circle around like a warrior would as he readied for single combat. I followed his example, countering his circle.

"You don't get it, do you?" Vans began. "In a nutshell, he found out about your 'secret life' with the Rebells. He knew everything! For years, I tried my best to point it out to him—that you were a part of the organization. He had his suspicions but never acted on it. But in the end, you were just sloppy about it. Spending so much time with *that* family, going out with the Kenneth girl—sloppy."

Vans made a jab at me. I scuffled to the side, easily dodging the blow. He was just buying time. He was playing with me. "Fürl just couldn't say anything, since the first sergeant took such a shining to you. He would've looked petty and jealous to the boss-man. It would have also looked bad to get rid of you so early. Too many questions."

Vans threw another jab my way, and again I managed to miss it with ease. Vans smiled and started to bounce around, switching his feet back and forth in some sort of boxing routine that he'd been taught during basic training. He was having fun with me. Cautiously, I gave the area where the fire was made up a glance. John was laying on his side, out cold. No doubt thanks to Vans. I cautiously paced around, eying him up and waiting for the right time to strike.

"But, with the general coming over here to promote the first sergeant to sergeant major," Vans continued, "that meant he had to move up his timetable. He had to do something to make sure you weren't in the lineup for what should have been rightfully his."

Vans made a dash out toward me, growling as he ran. I dove to the side, throwing myself into a barrel roll to avoid the coming onslaught. Vans just missed me with his charge, his arms swinging at me as I rolled for cover. Now in an uncontrolled strut, he tried to right himself out of his charge before he threw himself into something. Rocks skidded from his boots through the attempt. I scampered back to a ready stance, and we continued our encircling of each other once more. Vans sneered at me.

"As first sergeant, Fürl would be able to take this town and turn it into what it should have been in the first place. He could do whatever he wanted, including making me a corporal major. This meeting was the perfect opportunity to get rid of you."

Vans dove at me, trying again to get me unprepared. This time, I was ready for him. I leaned to the side and brought both of my fists down onto his back as he passed by me. Vans let out a roar of pain. I backed up a bit, fearing a counterattack.

"What happened to H. J. and Dawn?!" I demanded.

He looked at me in surprise. "Your girl was here? Really? How sweet. That's why you were waiting, wasn't it? You were waiting for her to come back, weren't you?"

At this, Vans began laughing. He stopped after the fourth chuckle, grabbing the side of his ribs in pain. "Forget her, Tom. She's as good as dead—"

He paused midsentence as an evil grin on his bloodstained lips formed. "Or, at least, she'll be wishing she was dead—after they finish with her."

A growl exploded from my lungs, and I leapt at Vans. He was ready for me. He grabbed my arms as I launched past him and threw me to the ground. I landed on my stomach. He stomped one of his boots onto the middle of my spine and twisted my arms behind my back, pulling them upward. A popping sound came from one of my shoulders. Intense pain flooded my brain. He grabbed the back of my neck and started hitting me on my side. I felt two ribs start to give under the onslaught … three. Then he shoved my face into the ground and got off of me.

"No … I'm not going to kill you just yet. I have to make sure that I enjoy this. Make you suffer for what you did to me," he gloated above me.

Grit and mud mixed with a coppery taste in my mouth as I coughed and sputtered on the ground. With my good arm, I rolled myself over to see him towering over me, smiling. "It's a good thing that you decided to wait for your little woman. I was supposed to be at the opening waiting for you when you first appeared. I apologize for being detained."

He kicked me on the now-bruising left side of my midsection. "I'll try and make it up to you somehow," he cackled between each strike of his boot.

Kick after unbearable kick crashed down onto me. Head, side, stomach, groin—everywhere. Blood oozed out of my mouth and nose nonstop. Vans started to slow his kicking in order to enjoy every whimper of pain that escaped me. Reaching toward his side, he unbuckled a strap and pulled out a small POLICE-issued revolver that he had hidden in one of the pouches hanging from his belt. Vans raised the revolver in the air and waved it in front of my eyes, making sure that I got a good, long look at it. Taking his time, he set me up so I was sitting on my knees. I was in no position to resist. I tried to grab the gun away from him, but he'd done too good a job on me. I had no strength left. He swatted my hand away like it was a fly.

He placed the cold gun barrel to the back of my head, right where the vertebrae met up with the base of my skull. He eased back the hammer on the gun. It clicked once and locked into position. A simple squeeze, and I would be dead.

"Any last requests?" he teased.

I closed my eyes. Tears of blood ran down my face.

"Drop dead, you bastard," I whispered.

A shot rang out.

Something hit the back of my head.

I fell into the darkness.

CHAPTER 29

A SHARP STAB TO MY SIDE jerked me out from my sleep. I felt like I was dead, but the pain told me otherwise. It took me about ten minutes to get up from the ground. I can only imagine what I must have looked like trying to flop from my prone position. My ribs were still bruised, my right eye was swollen shut, my left shoulder was dislocated—but my general cuts and scrapes were all scabbed over, so there was some sort of proof of healing.

It was morning. Vans was stretched out in the sun, face down. John was sprawled in the grass a few steps away from him, staring at the sky, his eyes were glassed over … I don't remember how I got over to John's side. All I know was that I was beside him, looking down at him. Blood, now dry, covered the left part of John's shirt. A bullet hole was neatly visible in his shirt, right over his heart. I closed John's eyes. Stumbling, I slowly made my way over to Vans. Using my good arm, I rolled him over so I could take a better look at him. There were two knife wounds showing—one in his chest and the second in his stomach. A simple knife was found underneath him—John's knife. He died with a look of fear on his face. I staggered my way back toward John. I sat beside him, staring at the numb body. Memories filled my eyes and left as tears. I wept for my friend for a long, long time.

With tear-filled eyes, I looked around the area for things that were able to burn, so I could build a funeral pyre for him. There wasn't much, at least that I could see, but I would have to make do with what was available. I was in no shape to carry John home. Easing myself up from my kneeling position beside my friend, I started up the task of gathering wood and other material to set ablaze. Walking the walk of the dead, I wandered off to the side of the area, grabbed hold of a single piece of dead brush, and began the task of dragging it back to where I decided to hold the pyre. Wander away again, return with a stick. Wander, return with a board. And so it went on. By late morning, I had enough to have a burning pyre. That was an accomplishment by itself, considering how much maneuverability I had.

Once it was complete, I gathered up my friend and tried my best to put him on the middle of the collection of wood, sticks, leafy brush, and other burnable material. I took a minute to make sure that John was in a dignified manner: arms by his side, legs straightened out, and head facing the sky. Reaching into the backpack, I grabbed the box of matches. I opened up the small box. Red-tipped sticks asleep within its bed, undisturbed by the events that had surrounded it, were soon scuttled around as I tried to grab hold of a couple in my numb hand. Using my good hand to strike the bundle of matches and ignite them, I tossed the box into the pyre to help the burn once it was lit. The lit matches soon followed.

Black smoke rose into the sky, blanketing the sun. The heat, along with the sun, was unbearable, but I couldn't bear the thought of walking away, leaving my friend. My dear, dead friend. I stood by and watched my friend as the fire soon roared around him.

"John," I whispered to my sleeping friend, "I pray you find happiness wherever you are now."

The fire was well on its way, no longer needing my attention. I gave John a final farewell and walked over to Vans. The gun was still clutched inside his fat, grubby hand. Using my boot and the weight of my body, I broke his hand in order to free the gun. A rather satisfying crackle of brittle bones chimed in with the crackle of the fire. I leaned down and took the gun. The weight of the metal contraption would be too much for me to hold as I made my way back home, I decided, so I put it into my pocket.

"May you rot!" I swore at the body of Vans.

Getting myself ready for the long trek home, I turned to the fence and started half-limping, half-jogging toward home.

~

I got into town long after the sun had gone down. The town was deserted. I couldn't see anyone walking the roads. There were no lights shining from within any of the homes. The single ray of light in the area came from my bouncing lantern that hung loosely from my backpack strap. The lantern swung with each drag of my foot, creating almost a seesaw effect as I made my way through the street. It looked like everyone was just gone. This worked to my advantage. I didn't want anyone to see me as I made my way to William's place. I had to see if they got home okay. They had to. They must have.

As I hobbled toward the home, my heart sunk into my boots. The door was broken open. The hallway inside was dark. A single painted word was splashed across the house above the door: *Aufstandiche*. Rebell. I looked cautiously into the home from the security of the doorframe.

"Hello?"

No answer.

Taking the lantern free from my backpack, I entered the place. I raised the lantern high, using my good hand so that I could easily make my way through now strange settings. Mrs. Roget's room had been ransacked by the looks of things. She was nowhere to be seen. I turned my attention to the room at the bottom of the stairs, more determined than ever.

"William! Sherry! Dawn!"

No answer.

Inside, the house was a mess. Furniture was tossed, turned, or broken altogether. The paintings that lined the hallways had huge slashes through them. The den was in turmoil. The books that used to line the bookcase, a special place marked off for each one, were now inside the fireplace. The fire had long since gone out. Pages from unknown volumes, half-burnt, were scattered around the floor of the den. William's chair was shredded. I began to frantically limp through the house for any signs of life. All objects that held any value were gone, probably taken.

"*William! Sherry! Daaawwwwn!*"

No answer.

I went to Dawn's room. Everything was broken. I began to shuffle through the discarded room. Among the discarded trash that scattered the floor, I found two crushed picture frames. One held a picture of Dawn and me, taken some time ago. A traveling carnival had been passing through the area, and Dawn wanted to go. While there, we saw a man dressed in black asking people to stand in front of this little box that he would use to take their photo. Dawn wanted a photo of us, so I paid the exuberant price to have it taken. It took a couple hours to get the photo developed, but Dawn didn't care. She was just happy that she had a photo of the two of us. The other was a picture of the entire family taken by some local friend. I took them both. As I was leaving her room, I glanced over and saw a small red ribbon that used to hold Dawn's hair back. I took that as well.

Making my way back outside, I left the house—realizing that it would probably be the last time. Walking away, I looked back toward the house and thought of all the days I had spent inside its warm embrace. The lessons I had learned. The people I loved. That's where I found my second family—my second home. Now, it stood empty and alone.

I turned my head away from the empty shell of a house and out toward the direction of the Grounds. Eyes squinted with grit, fists clenched. Weary foot after weary foot slammed into the ground as I picked up the pace. I had someone to visit ... and I didn't want to be late.

~

It was close to midnight by the time I arrived inside the Grounds. By the looks of things, the POLICE who were at the Zone had managed to get back long before I had. A garden of wounded were spread over the area I passed through. The dead lined the sides of the field as I walked farther into the Grounds. Row after row of fallen soldiers stretched out ahead of me as well as behind me. Vans was correct about losing around a third of the battalion. Medics were scurrying from one wounded soldier to the next, trying their best to help where they could. The majority of the wounded lying on the ground had been tended to. Bandages tapered in red were wrapped around every one of them. One attendant who was helping an officer with something to drink saw me as I made my way through the ocean of wounded. He quickly raced to my side.

"Come, this way," he directed me, taking a hold of my arm.

He tried to lead me off to the side, where the other wounded officer lay. I merely shrugged him off, not saying a word. My goal was not to be tended to. The attendant, shocked at my stubbornness, took a hold of my arm once again, this time more forcefully. "You're in shock, sir. You need—"

"Later," I whispered.

"But, sir, you—"

"*Later!*" I growled, shoving the man away from me.

He toppled onto the ground, not suspecting the amount of force I would implement as I threw him away. I turned away from him, not caring what state he was in. I headed straight for the first sergeant's office. No one bothered to stop me after that last display with the attendant. The officers on the Grounds just watched from where they sat as I struggled my way to the building. Inside, the place was business as usual. The receptionist was long gone, but the two guards were still there on either side of the door.

"I'm here to see the first sergeant," I managed to wheeze out.

One of the officers left his post and wandered to where I was standing and reached out an arm to help hold me up. "Sir, are you sure you should be here? You need medical attention."

"I'm here. To see. The first sergeant," I repeated.

The second officer, still remaining at his post beside the door, looked from his partner to back at me. "I'm sorry, sir. He's currently debriefing another officer."

"Who?"

"Sergeant Fürl." he answered.

Crunching my working hand into a fist, I sucker punched the guard who was trying to help hold me up. The officer doubled over from the impact, dropping his rifle. I threw him into the guard still standing at his post. The two collapsed into a pile in the corner, leaving the path to Charles's door free from obstruction. Stretching out my good arm, I grabbed the dropped rifle up off of the ground. With the weapon in hand,

I gripped it by the barrel and made my way over to the office and swung out at the two guards trying to get up.

A voice cried out from the office, asking what was going on outside. The wooden stock, thick and well made slammed against one of the officer's head, knocking it back. He slumped back onto the ground—out cold. The second officer, the one I had thrown around, looked at me in shock. He held up his hands to defend himself. Raising the weapon up again, I knocked out the officer with a single blow. When they were both out, I let go of the rifle and made my way toward the office door.

Raising a leg and countering my balance, I kicked open the door with enough force to rip it off its hinges. The door blasted into the office, slamming into the inner wall. A sudden jolt from my side reminded me of how much pain I was in from the night before, which caused me to lose my balance for a moment. Fürl, who was sitting in the chair opposite Charles, almost leapt out of his skin when he saw me standing in the doorway. Charles, his head jerking up from the desk and the documents that were stretched out on top of it, looked furious at me for the interruption.

"Surprised to see me, Victor?" I asked.

"Haroldson!" Charles barked. "What is the meaning of this?!"

I closed the door behind me, locking it as best I could with the now-nearly-broken lock, and leaned against it for support. "I'm glad that I have both of you here like this," I coughed out through a cracked smile.

Fürl jumped over the desk and stood beside Charles, who just stared at me. I cleared my throat. "Vans will not be returning to duty anytime soon. He's dead. Just thought I should warn you in case you were waiting for him to report," I mentioned to Fürl in a matter-of-fact tone, as if I were telling him that the sky was cloudy today. I stared at him the entire time.

Charles slowly stood up behind his desk and pressed his hands into the fine wooden top. "Haroldson, you better have a damn good reason for this outburst. You're walking a fine line."

I smiled at the two. "Oh, I do, sir. I'm here to debrief you on my undercover mission, sir. I'm also here to report an attempt on my life by a fellow officer."

Charles took in a deep breath. "All right. What happened to you?"

"Vans attacked me as I left the Dome," I stated as I walked into the room and leaned against the chair that Fürl had been sitting in.

Fürl walked forward a bit and uneasily sat on one of the edge of the desk, acting like he was trying to help Charles get to the bottom of this. "He always had a grudge against you. There's nothing new there. Why he would attack you now is curious, though," Victor mused, scratching his chin.

The smell of sweat rose strongly from where I stood. Fürl, I guessed, knew what he was up against. Charles looked from Victor to me. "Are you worried that we will dismiss you for his death, Tom?" Charles asked me, as a sense of concern rose in his voice.

I waved him off. "That's the least of my problems, sir. You see, before he tried to kill me, he managed to confide in me that he was *ordered* to kill me!"

"Wh-who would do such a thing?" Fürl turned and asked Charles, his rock-hard voice cracking just slightly.

I stared at Fürl. "You mean you honestly don't know?"

Charles sat back down and folded his hands on the desk. "Did you manage to find you who gave the order?"

"Yeah."

"Who gave the order, Tom?" he prodded.

"I hate pointing fingers at people who screwed up. I would prefer that Sergeant First Class Victor Fürl confess on his own."

Victor looked furious. He bounded from the desk, yelling into my face. "What lies! I've never been so insulted! Never!"

He started walking toward the door. I grabbed his arm and whipped him into the chair in front of the desk. Charles looked at the two of us very seriously. "Tom! Remember that you're handling a superior officer! Let go of him. Right now."

I eased my grip slightly around Fürl but kept him firmly planted in the chair. Charles, looking at the two of us in front of him, rubbed his eyes. "Do you have any evidence for this accusation, Tom?"

I nodded. "I remember what Vans told me."

"Speculation! It has no weight! There's no one else who can collaborate on your accusation!" Fürl cried out in a panicked tone.

I raised my eyebrow. "You want something with weight?"

I released my grip from Victor and reached into my side pocket, pulling out the gun that I had taken off of Vans. Everyone inside the room stiffened. I flipped the gun around in my hand and presented it, handle first, to Charles. He rose from his chair in order to take the gun from me, which I surrendered. Gun in hand, he examined the piece of hardware carefully, turning it around for evidence of who it belonged to. "This gun is ?" he asked, glancing at the cool metal in his hands.

"The very gun that Vans was about to shoot me with," I said, returning my grip on Victor.

Charles looked the revolver over more closely. "It's a standard-issue revolver with a bullet missing from its first chamber. What does this prove with Victor?"

"Nothing! So, if you would let me go—"

Fürl reached over to where I was holding him down into the chair and tried to remove my hand. Instead, I grabbed his hand and twisted it back behind his back, picking him up out of the chair in order to do this. Victor let out a yelp. "*Tom!*" Charles yelled.

I pointed at the gun with my free hand, still weak from the dislocation. "Look, Charles! Look at the name engraved in the bottom of the handle! All officers are to engrave their identification code numbers on the bottom of their issued weapons! Find out who the gun belongs to!"

Fürl wiggled like a worm on a hook. Charles stood there staring at the two of us, trying to decide whom to trust more. Finally—reluctantly, really—he he opened up the right-hand drawer at his desk and pulled out a file folder, brimming with a bundle of papers. On the pages Charles was flipping through were names and numbers. After a few pages, Charles looked up at the both of us; a somber expression was lost on his face.

"It belongs to Sergeant Victor Fürl."

Fürl tried to turn to look at me. "You stole it! You stole it, and you're trying to frame me!"

"Vans had it!" I yelled.

He glanced at Charles. "Charles, this boy has the weakest cry of evidence that I have ever heard. A stolen gun somehow ends up in Vans's custody, who then tries to kill a commanding officer he never liked in the first place, only to be killed himself. Before this, in order to save the embarrassment he would face from capture, Vans makes up a story saying that I gave him the gun in order to kill Tom?! Ludicrous! How do we know that he hasn't been a Rebell spy all along? I say he should be put away for good for his own safety."

Fürl tried to squirm out of my grasp again. I threw him to the ground with a thud. "You're finished here, Comrade!"

The door blasted open, hitting the other side of the wall once again. Everyone turned his attention to the open door and the figures who stood in the doorway. The two guards assigned to protect the office, now armed with clubs, stood ready. The marks from the stock of the rifle hitting them were still visible on their faces.

Victor yelled at the men, "I want you to take this man away and lock him up inside one of the bunkers until further ordered!"

Charles held up his hand toward the guards, motioning for them to stop. The guards looked at me, then to Charles for the final say on this order. Charles was completely calm and steady. "Officers, please escort Sergeant Fürl to bunker four for questioning."

Fürl twisted his face toward Charles. "What side are you on?!" he bellowed.

The guards marched up to Fürl, making me step aside, to secure him into custody. With clubs at the ready, they reached down and pulled the officer up off of the ground. Fürl, kicking and thrusting his body in every which way to avoid being taken, was no match against the well-trained officers. The two guards turned, with Victor locked between them, and left the room.

Fürl screamed out as he was being carted away. "I'm not the traitor! He is! He's the traitor! I was doing my duty! He's the traitor!!"

"Tom," Charles calmly called out to get my attention.

I turned back toward him. Charles was hunched over his desk, his face downcast and eyes burning into mine. He glared at me, yet his voice was quiet and steady, like it took all of his effort to keep it that way. "I want you here tomorrow. Noon. No later. You and I are going to have a long talk about what just went on inside here."

I suddenly got a very bad feeling that I had lost all trust Charles had put in me.

I nodded and somberly walked out of the room. I closed the door behind me, the door barely able to fit against the frame from the two destructive kicks against it. The weight of the day was setting in. I dragged my feet out of the building toward the open air and almost collided into someone trying to make his way in. I was about to tell whoever had crashed into me what to do and where to go, when that person spoke.

"*Tom!*"

H. J. stood in front of me, arms outstretched to help steady me from the collision. I picked him up and swung him around inside my arms. In half swing, I nearly dropped him from the sharp intake of pain I received from my injuries.

"How did you know I was here?" I asked him

H. J. looked at me like I was crazy. "You kidding? The entire Grounds is abuzz with rumors of this one half-dead officer marching into the first sergeant's office and yelling at him. I knew it had to be you the minute I heard."

"What happened to you at the meeting? John and I waited for you for over an hour. Where's Dawn? I passed by her house, but—"

H. J. sobered up at that. "I have something to tell you."

~

We made our way out of the office building and wandered over to where the officers were being treated for their wounds. The night air was brisk, and our breath came out in cold, white puffs. There was no wind, but clouds hung overhead. The attendant had just finished bandaging me up and left the two of us where we sat to gather up more supplies. Once we were alone, H. J. took a deep breath and started his tale.

"We ran through the Dome like it was on fire. Dawn was frantic. There was no way we could get to the stage. It was too chaotic. So, then we went outside. Everyone was there—the POLICE and the Rebells. It looked like they were trying to join together and become one giant person. They piled on top of each other and threw people into people—fighting, yelling. The Rebells tried anything to escape.

"Dawn ran into the thick of it all, trying to find her father. I tried to stay as close as I could to her, like I said I would. We got into a few confrontations with officers, but once they saw who I was, they let us go."

H. J. looked into the distance. He stared into a puddle on the ground, like he was watching the events through the ripples and splashes in the water. "She found her father, finally. He was cornered by two big POLICE officers who were swinging clubs. They were not being easy on him. Dawn burst into a run and leapt onto the nearer of the two. I tried to break the two apart while explaining the problem to the other officer. Whoever said 'you can never do two things at the same time' was right."

At this, H. J. lifted up his left pant leg. There, just below his shin, a bandage was wrapped around his leg. "Five stitches."

"The officer and Dawn fought each other like crazed animals. They wrestled, bit, kicked … Dawn was taking this guy to town."

He turned toward me. "They wouldn't listen to me, Dawn, or her father. They saw us as Rebells, so we had to be taken down. Since we wouldn't go down peacefully, they used force. Dawn and the officer wouldn't stop fighting. The other one had his hands full with her father and me. A rifle expert saw us. He saw how poorly the two officers were fighting against the three of us. He decided to help the officers…. He … the officer … Dawn … she—she was thrown off…. The rifle … she … I tried, Tom! I really tried."

He collapsed into my arms, sobbing like a child. The news never affected me. I just sat there, staring out into the darkness of the sky. I was completely numb, dumbfounded. H. J. squeezed me, like I would have fallen apart if he had let go of me.

I stared at the puddle at our feet. The stars had no reflection inside the water. There was no light in the sky.

Finding my voice, I whispered, over and over again. "I lost Dawn…. I lost my Dawn…. I lost my Dawn…."

I lost my Dawn.

PART 3:
GENERAL PROBLEM, TOUGH SOLUTION

CHAPTER 30

"You're sitting at my table."

I looked up from the meager breakfast I was in the midst of eating while sitting at the outside café to see who was speaking. In front of me stood a very elderly gentleman, looking somewhat cross at the issue at hand. He was dressed quite casually and had a few layers on, despite the light morning warmth that was coming off the sun when it was able to peek through the clouds. The thin frame and the wrinkled brow showed off the many years that this man had been privy to. And yet, his eyes were quite lively, darting around the area to take in all that there was. One of his hands grasped a finely crafted wooden cane. It looked like it was whittled from an oak branch or some sort of heavy tree. The handle, somewhat lost in his grasp, had an ivory glint to it. Some craftsmanship had definitely gone into the construction of that cane.

"I'm sorry?" I asked for clarification regarding his statement.

"What, ya deaf? I thought I was supposed to have hearing problems, not a young guy like you," he snapped at me.

I looked around at the nearby tables. There were five of them, set up in a hexagonal shape around me. Each one was void of any people. "There are others."

"Yeah, but this is *my* table. I sit here every morning. Have been for months. Ask anyone. You're in my spot," he affirmed his predicament.

The other patrons eating in the outside café along with me were starting to stop and stare. Soft whispers and gossip were exchanged between the occasional customers, eyes steadily watching what was about to transpire. Too much attention was being brought to me. I had to end this quickly.

"I'm sorry. I didn't realize that this table was taken," I finally answered, grabbing my plate as I prepared to leave the table and move to another one.

The old man raised his bushy white eyebrows at my response, which looked like it took much more effort than it should. "Manners. Ahhh. Rare nowadays," he smiled and started to ease himself into a chair beside me.

He took his time easing himself into the wooden apparatus, leaning heavily on the cane he was using to help him get around. I stretched out my arm to help him finish his journey into the chair. Wrapping my hand softly around his arm to help carry his burden, I was shocked by his strong pull away from me—he merely shrugged me off. With a final grunt and a sigh, he plunked himself into the chair, content that the journey was at an end.

"Well, I guess there's no reason why we can't share, now is there?" he winked.

I stopped gathering my things and placed the plate with the eggs and sausage back onto the table. He looked around the area at the other patrons, who were back to whatever they were doing, before he returned his attention to me. "Richard," he said, introducing himself, and leaning deep into the chair that he sat in.

"Tom."

Richard adjusted his cane so that the ivory handle hooked itself against the edge of the table; the white boned extension secured the wooden shaft from wobbling and rolling onto the ground.

"So," he started up his inquisition, "breakfast, huh?"

I picked at the remaining scrambled pile of yellow on the plate with my fork. With each jab into the fluffy meal, I got more and more uncomfortable having this man sitting with me. He was the type of person who demanded attention—whether you gave it to him or not. And attention was not exactly what I was after at the moment.

"Yep. First meal of the day," I answered politely.

"Been here long?"

"'Bout half an hour," I answered, my mouth filling with a slice of sausage.

He smiled at my remark, the wrinkles creasing into well-known crevasses in his face. "Smart-ass. I meant in town."

"Just passing through."

He nodded simply. Looking over his shoulder, he waved at the young brunette who was gathering up some discarded plates at one of the tables just behind him. The girl, seeing the wave, gave Richard a quick nod and continued to load up her arms with the dirty plates. Turning around once again, Richard smiled at me. "You don't say much, do you?"

I shrugged at his last question; the eggs were now close to mush from my constant berating them with the fork. "Don't have much to say."

Richard harrumphed at me. "Now that, I don't buy. You look like a guy with a story behind him."

I looked up from the plate at the old man. "How's that?"

He folded his arms across a once-powerful chest. "You're at my table," he answered matter-of-factly, as if the answer should have been self-evident.

"I don't follow."

"Take a look around you. Not a single other patron is anywhere near ya. You coulda chosen a table closer to the other people around here having breakfast, but instead you chose the table that had absolutely no one near it. That just proves that you have some sort of secret locked up there in your noggin."

I began to slice off another chunk of sausage from the link on my plate, the knife cutting through the cooked meat easily. "Maybe it just means that I didn't want to be near anyone."

"And if all the tables had someone at them? Then what?"

I shrugged, starting to get annoyed at the old man who had invaded my space. "I'd probably have to sit beside someone. Look, what's the point of all this?"

He held up his hands. "Nothing. Nothing. Just making conversation. That's all."

We sat in silence for a second or two, Richard sitting comfortably in his chair while I continued to eat my breakfast. The waitress whom Richard had called over before finally reemerged from wherever it was that she took the dirty dishes and wandered by the table. She was a slightly plump young girl, her thick hair tied back in a ponytail in order to keep it out of her face. She looked a little frazzled from her workload, despite the fact that it was very early in the morning and her shift was probably far from being over. She looked down at the old man sitting beside me and gave him a wink.

"All right, ya old coot. What'll it be this time?" she teased.

Richard smiled at the young girl. "Now is that any way to talk your better?"

He turned his attention from the girl to me. "Ya see what I mean about manners?" Richard grumbled, giving me a swat on my arm for emphasis.

I rolled my eyes at the whole ordeal and returned back to my breakfast, fast becoming cold in the not-too-warm morning. Richard stretched around so that he could see the menu that was posted from a sign hook at the entrance of the café.

"Has Hammond gotten that new shipment of steaks yet?" he asked the waitress, still staring at the menu.

"It's breakfast, Richard. You don't have steak for breakfast."

He quickly turned around and stared with utter shock at the young girl who was helping us. "What? Since when? I've always had a steak for breakfast. Ask my boys. Steak and eggs. Good for you. Put meat on your bones."

The woman gave Richard a sassy look and pulled out a small pad of paper and a pencil from one of her pockets in the half-apron that hung around her ample waist. Tapping the pencil against the pad in rhythm with the light tapping she began to do with her foot, she stared down at the old man at my table.

"Well, we don't have any. It won't be coming till the afternoon. So you're stuck with sausage with your eggs, if you want it. Or you could have pancakes. Or bacon. Or you could always go with what you always order: tea and toast."

Richard mumbled and waved her off. The young waitress, putting her pad and pencil back into the small pouch in her apron, turned on her heel and started to wander back to the kitchen area. "Tea and toast it is," she grumbled.

With the girl gone, Richard moped for a second in his chair. He folded his hands on the table, ancient fingers interlinking themselves with each other, and pursed his lips together. "Always had steak for breakfast—" he mumbled out loud.

Seeing that I wasn't going to get any peace with this man sitting beside me, I decided to hurry with what was left of my breakfast, pay, and leave him to his day. There were about five good forkfuls of food left, and I was going to need every last bit of it for the long walk ahead of me. Richard, after his bit of moping, freed his hands from each other and reached out toward me. He rested his hand gently onto my arm; the control of his action was deliberate and sure.

"So, ya defecting?" he asked.

I dropped my fork at the bluntness of the question, the metallic instrument clanking against the plate. "I beg your pardon?"

"Your jacket. It's POLICE issue. But there are no insignias anywhere on it, and it's in horrible condition. That means one of two things: one—you found the jacket, and now you're trying to hide the fact that it's POLICE issue because ya don't want people to associate ya with them or have 'em think you stole it. I don't think that's the case. You wear it too well, like you're used to wearing something like that. That leaves two—you *are* POLICE, and you don't want people to recognize you *as* POLICE for some reason. So, ya defecting?" he asked again, his tone quieter than before.

I adjusted myself in my chair. "It's just … something I picked up during my travels," I stuttered out, my free hand reaching down to where my pack rested beside me in case I needed to grab it and make a quick getaway.

He smirked, pulling his hand away from me. "Tsk. Ya, right. An' I'm gonna believe that."

"Look. I don't want to get into it, all right? Just leave it be."

Richard smiled and clasped his hands. "Ah ha! There we go. You do have a story."

I sighed and returned to what was left of my breakfast. Richard leaned forward, scooting his chair over slightly so that we could talk in a more hushed tone. "So, what's the deal? Finally had enough? You kill your neighbor in a jealous rage after finding him with your sweetie?"

I scoffed at his accusations. "No ... and no."

He gave a sly glance around to see if anyone else was listening. "There's gotta be some reason why you're wearing your jacket all muddied and disheveled."

"How did you know it was a POLICE jacket?" I asked the man, giving the jacket a quick glance. There were no discerning markings of any kind that would distinguish it as POLICE issue—I made sure of that. The dried mud and the months on the road had definitely put their wear on the fabric. Yet he was able to pick it out, clear as day.

"Simple," Richard smiled. "It's the cut. You can try to hide it by changing its appearance, you can cover it with mud trying to mask its color, but you can't change its cut."

He ran his finger around the sleeve of the jacket, pointing out the sewing and style that went into its design. "My pap, when I was quite young, was a tailor. Used to work in a store that built suits for upper businessmen from scratch. They'd come into the store fresh from some sort of meeting, smelling like money, and my father would start to take their measurements for a new suit. I'd help out on the weekend and the summer. My father got it in his head that I would take over the store when I was old enough. Too bad the war came in and ruined that idea."

This last topic caught my attention. "You were alive before the war?"

He gave a general nod. I leaned forward in my chair, careful first to move the near-empty plate off to the side. "Richard, could you tell me what life was like before the war?"

Richard thought for a second. "That was awhile ago. I was just a young kid back then. Um ... I remember not being old enough to fight in the war. My father was happy over that—I wasn't. Ahhh ... I remember that things were a lot more complicated back then. Everyone was angry over something or other. Kids were angry over being in school for so long, teenagers were angry over not being able to drive until they were older, men were angry with each other for all sorts of reasons, and older men were angry with the government for—well, for being the government. Still, we could do a lot more back then. Had the ability to communicate with anyone we wanted to, no matter where they were in the world. We could travel the world in a blink of an eye—the technology that we had at our disposal—yeah, things were good."

Richard leaned forward a bit, waving me closer to him to hear what he had to say. "Ya know what I miss the most from back then? Ice cream … maybe a big chocolate bar." He closed his eyes and smiled. "Man, what I wouldn't give for a heaping bowl of chocolate mint and an Oh Henry right about now. Mmmmm."

The waitress came by once again, this time holding onto a small saucer and cup full of steaming water. She placed it down in front of the old man. Seeing that I was done with my breakfast, the young woman took it up and glanced over at Richard. "Toast will be right up," she chirped and left once again.

Richard, seeing the cup of tea in front of him, smiled and clasped it in both of his hands. Raising the tiny cup up to his face, he bathed in the steam that rose from the basin in his hands, smiling even deeper.

He sipped the tea lightly, and the warm liquid slid out of the cup into his mouth with a rather loud slurp. Suddenly, he jerked away from the cup with a strong grimace and crushed one of his eyelids shut. Soft gurgling sounds came from his twitching form as he tried to cope with the liquid that had entered his body. It looked like he was having a stroke.

Richard put the cup of putrid liquid down in front of him in disgust and turned in his chair to face the covered kitchen area. "Hammond. Hammond!"

The stout man behind the counter didn't bother to look up from his cleaning as Richard called out to him. "Yes, Richard," he responded in a tired, singsong tone like he was used to Richard's interruptions.

"Have you been letting Mr. Whiskers use the tea bags as his litter again?" Richard called out loudly, holding up his teacup.

Hammond, still cleaning the area he was busy with, refused to show any emotion to the claim. "And I save them strictly for you, Richard," he responded to the accusation, again in his singsong tone.

Richard turned from Hammond and gave off a grunt while he waved him off. I smiled at the old man. "Well, looks like I'm done," referring to the now-gone plate of breakfast.

With one hand, I tossed out a few coins onto the table and reached over to my side with my other hand to grab my pack, full to bursting with new supplies that jostled around as I lifted it up from the ground. Richard, seeing that I was about to go on my way, tried to forcefully push himself up out of the chair to wish me off. Half standing, he stretched out a hand for me to take.

"Nice meeting ya," he said. "The next time you're in town, you're welcome to sit at my table anytime ya want."

I shook his hand and started on my way once more. Taking a look around the area, I tried to remember the direction I had come from so that I wouldn't backtrack too much into town. Slinging my pack onto my back once more, I felt my journal slam against my spine. It's a good thing I opted not to write anything while I was sitting at the café, or else Richard would have never let me leave. As I made my way out from the confining tables of the café, I tried to plan out what I would write down the next time I had the chance. Before leaving the café well behind, I could hear Richard behind me.

"Hammond, damnit! Ya burnt the toast again!"

~

After the night of the meeting, the mood inside the Grounds was stagnant. There was no jubilation from the steadfast victory over the Rebells. There was no cheering—no victory lap around the Grounds. Those who were not inside the battalion against the meeting were eerily quiet around those who were—almost like the officers were a witness to something truly horrifying, and the others did not want to bring up any kind of terrifying memories for the poor bastards.

Charles, good to his word, made sure that I was at his office the next morning in time to explain my behavior—no matter what the medics might have said regarding my condition. He wanted answers, and anyone standing in his way be damned. The meeting between Charles and me ran most of the day.

As I was standing in front of Charles, still bandaged, bleeding, and bruised, I admitted that I had no true excuse for my overall presentation of the evidence against Fürl. Despite my emotional position at the moment, I was still a POLICE officer and should have responded as such. Charles took it with a grain of salt and then allowed me to enter my side of the story: The meeting, Dawn, Vans—everything. He didn't say a word the entire time I gave my report. I was dismissed when he was satisfied with the answers.

When it was over, I returned to the medics. I was laid up mending my wounds for about a month. Maybe a little longer. While I lay in the medical ward, it was like I was cut off from the rest of the world. There was no news passed on to me, despite asking about what had happened to Fürl. Didn't get any visitors, either. Not even H. J. came by to see how I was doing, which was kind of odd. When I was allowed to get up and start my recuperation physiotherapy, I found out that there was a set of guards placed outside my room. Charles actually put a set of guards on my room! I assume he did this to make sure that I would not get any visitors to finish the job that Vans started—or to make sure I wouldn't get the idea to escape. Didn't find out which.

When I was well enough to start wandering around again, I managed to pick up what I had missed through general comments and eavesdropping in on careless conversations. Fürl had been interrogated for a long time regarding the meeting and what happened afterward. So were all the other officers who were a part of it. No detail was left out. Charles made up a special group to oversee the investigation. I was told that they received a special note stating that they had "governing rank," or something like that, making them free from discipline regarding their methods for obtaining information.

Fürl, despite his many years of valued service, was stripped of rank and removed from the Grounds. Charles made a rather public ceremony of it too. The entire Grounds was called out to bear witness.

He gave a speech to the officers directly afterward, announcing that the same would happen to anyone who would dare try to diminish the good visage of the POLICE. There was a lot of talk over the attempt on my life, the resulting loss of life from the brutal attack against the Rebells, and how that was not the way to go about trying to get rid of them—how we were better that that.

Rumors of what I did inside the office flew around the Grounds like wildfire. Most were highly exaggerated. My favorite rumor was the one where I tried to rip out Fürl's good eye with my thumb while fighting off four guards who were trying to subdue me. Had a good laugh when I heard that one.

The bad side of the rumor mill was regarding my relationship to William. With William being captured at the meeting and me going out with his daughter, there was a lot of speculation regarding my loyalty and if William was just using his daughter to get information from me. H. J. quickly put an end to those rumors on my behalf. He made it clear to everyone that I had brought Dawn with me to help with my undercover posting. The fact that William was there was strictly through work-related activities. Charles, having had William already investigated because of my relationship with Dawn, took the whole scenario as a huge misunderstanding.

There was mention that William had been released shortly afterward, but nothing was confirmed. I feel kind of bad that I never did find out what happened to William and Sherry once I was better. Never bothered to hunt them down and find out how they were. Figured that even if I managed to find them, they would want nothing to do with me. I did put out a general inquiry with a few Rebell merchants that I knew, but they never saw them again.

Duncan had managed to escape from the meeting. No one saw him after he left the stage. No one had heard from him. He just ... disappeared.

When I was finally released from medical and returned to active duty, things were—well, different for me. I found that as the months went on, I was not invited to the office as often. I guess

Charles figured that he needed to separate himself from me. The whole Grounds was still churning over the events that had gone on during and after the meeting.

Perhaps he didn't believe the whole cover story about William after all. Either that, or I needed to prove myself to him once more—especially after that whole debacle. I also found that I went into town less and less often. There wasn't a need for me to wander off the Grounds anymore. By the time summer hit, I was living on the Grounds 24/7.

Yet, despite spending every living moment on the Grounds, I found myself actively avoiding interacting with others. I sat by myself during meals. I went straight to and from the communications building and the barracks and avoided going to the social areas. H. J. made it his mission to try to get me out of the slump I was in, but he had one hell of a battle to fight.

This was how things went. Days faded into weeks … into months. Summer came and went. Soon, the new year was upon us. Charles gave me the occasional mission to keep me busy, but they were nothing in the category that I used to get. Before, every mission led to my advancement. Now, they were routine and dull.

The anniversary of the war was quickly coming. There was no party planned—no parade. There were probably going to be small celebrations throughout the town but nothing that one would expect. The general public was probably confused as to why the POLICE didn't have anything prepped up. The officers, on the other hand, knew exactly what was coming. There was one thing that churned over and over inside everyone's mind.

The general would arrive in Sicher Himmel soon.

CHAPTER 31

It was February 24, 2116. The seventy-fifth anniversary of the war had finally arrived. Felt like any other day to me. The sun didn't rise with fanfare but rose in the cool late winter air like it always did. There was no trumpet flare cascading across the wind, but the sound of birds waking to the morning. No confetti explosions bursting with every new step. Nope—it was a day like any other.

I brought the rag across my boot with a regulated earnestness as I polished it to a shine, my hand flying across the strong leather in a steady back-and-forth motion from many years of practice. I was staring off through the window into nothingness, the act of polishing my boot holding no focus over me. Out the window stood the beauty of the Grounds in the early morning air. My eyes glazed over. All I could hear was the thum-pa, thum-pa as rag was swept across my boot over and over again.

Knock, knock.

Taking a moment to glance down at the boot I had spent time buffing, I saw the effect of daydreaming on my attempt at polishing—the area I was brushing over and over again had started to wear through the shined leather, a thin patch of rough hide had lost its polish and luster. Giving the boot a grimace, I carelessly dropped the two objects I was holding and got up to see who had rescued me from having to purchase a new set of footwear.

Knock, knock.

I opened the door to find an officer standing with a satchel on his side.

Mail. In his hand was a letter, which he gave me quickly, saluted, and left. Closing the door behind me, I held onto the letter and gave it a good stare. It was in the first sergeant's handwriting, which was a good sign. It could have been written by my new department head in the communications building: Corporal Major Biggins. Biggins and I didn't exactly get along for some reason. It could be due to the fact that he was fifteen years older than I was, yet we held the same rank. It could have something to do with the fact that I was able to complete any and all assignments that were given to me within record time, yet he was unable to complete things in an acceptable time period. It could be a bunch of reasons. Needless to say, I've been trying to avoid him for the past few weeks. I just wasn't in the mood to deal with his pettiness. Inside the letter was a simple card. On it, Charles wrote, "Come immediately."

Charles has finally decided to let me grace him with my presence again. The last time Charles had asked me to his office it had been New Year's Day. I had passed by it now and again, but it wasn't like it was before the meeting. Not at all. The familiarity that was once there seemed to have seeped out of the place. The camaraderie hadn't felt genuine for a while. It probably had something to do with the meeting aftermath, but who could tell. I quickly brushed off the boots any polish that wasn't buffed away and got myself ready to see Charles.

The walk over to the office felt long. I wasn't taking a new route, I didn't get stopped by anyone or anything, and I wasn't purposefully dragging my feet or slowing my way for any reason—It just felt like it took a long time to get to the office. The Grounds was clear of any major traffic that morning. Everyone was sleeping in, I guess. Due to the anniversary, there were no huge assignments or projects on the go for the day. Everyone wanted to have the day off to have some sort of attempt at celebration. I occasionally saw an officer on guard duty wandering around the area, either coming or going to his station in a relaxed march. I didn't wave at them, though. I had other things on my mind.

The office stood empty in front of me. Normally, there would be a few officers standing around outside or just within the doors ready to run off to another building with some sort of important message handed to them by a receptionist or sergeant. Today, there was no one. Odd. I opened the door that led into the building and entered. The building was eerily quiet, which made me stiffen up in response. Something was wrong.

I made my way down the hallway that led to the reception area for the office. Turning the very familiar corner, I was greeted by the receptionist and guards. The guards stiffened up at seeing me, as they always did whenever someone came into view. The receptionist, however, also stiffened up, which was quite unlike her. Her desk was a mash of folders and paperwork. It was as if she suddenly decided to do a year's worth of work in a week's time.

"Can I help you?" she asked pleasantly.

Being stopped by the receptionist like that was the final key point that proved that something was up. She was alert, responsive, and actively working—not like her at all. She was also polite to me, which had never happened before. I held up the letter that Charles sent my way. "I've been ordered to see the first sergeant."

The receptionist nodded and turned to the guards. "Please inform the first sergeant that Corporal Major Haroldson is ready to see him."

I looked around the reception area, trying to figure out if I had entered the right building. What was going on? One of the guards rapped on the door gently and then opened it just enough to poke his head in. He said something to the first sergeant that I couldn't hear properly, since it had been addressed toward the office and the guard spoke in a hushed tone. While I waited to be let in, I looked over at the other guard standing in front of the door. He was eyeing me closely, gripping the rifle that was slung across his chest and shoulder. At first glance, the scene looked as it had all the other times I had entered the office previously—but today it felt different. There was something different about it all that I couldn't put my finger on.

The guard who had just introduced me turned out from the office and nodded, showing that I could enter. I started for the door when the second guard took a step forward and held out his hand, blocking my way.

"Please stand at ease and submit for a search for any weapons or contraband, sir," he ordered.

I stopped dead in my tracks, my freshly polished boots skidded along the carpeted floor in midstep. *Submit for what?* I thought to myself in shock. Seriously? It's come down to this? I now have to be searched for weapons before I can go in to see Charles? Has he lost *all* trust in me? I have to submit to this degradation? Shaking my head at the ludicrousness of it all, I stood at ease before the two guards and allowed them to search my person for any hidden weaponry.

While one guard patted me down carefully for the contraband, I glared at the other one who stood before me with gun at the ready. A flash of metallic glint caught my eye as I was staring at the guard, the gun's stock firmly planted against his shoulder. These were not the regular guns that the guards carried. The barrel was pointed down to the ground, allowing me to see the overlay of the rifle clearly. The makeup of the rifle was not the standard design that the guards had carried in previous times. The clip locked in the rifle was darker, thicker—not the fake empty ones normally loaded into the nonworking rifles. These rifles were real—loaded with real bullets.

The guard who was searching me down gave me a pat on the shoulder, proving that he was done. "You're clear, sir," he said, giving the other guard the head's up that I could pass.

The guard standing before me took a strong step to the side, allowing me passage into the office. I carefully walked over to the barely open door and stepped inside. The lights were not on in the office, which made the room quite dark, despite the morning light coming in through the window. There were two people inside the room talking in hushed tones. Charles was behind his desk, masked by the shadow of the chair cascading over him due to the lack of light. The second person in the room was in the chair facing the desk. I wasn't able to see who it was.

Charles looked up and waved for me to come closer into the room. I did as I was told and closed the door behind me, which cut off the only other light source to the shade-covered office. Taking in the room quickly, the first thing I wondered was why all the lights were off. I started to enter the room more, so I could get my bearings as to what was going on inside the office, but Charles held up his hand once more for me to stop.

"That's far enough, Corporal Major," Charles ordered me in a controlled voice.

I stopped where I stood as a rather uneasy feeling sunk into the pit of my stomach. Charles was acting very serious—more so than what was usual for our general meetings. He lowered his hand and placed it back onto the desk beside a box. From what I could see of it, the box was metallic in nature and had a simple latch. It was unlocked. Charles looked from me to the box, then to the man who was still hidden from view in the chair.

"Corporal Major, stand at attention and await orders," the first sergeant firmly order me as he straightened up from his hunched position.

Slowly, I positioned myself into attention, placing my arms by my sides and straightening up to my full height. My boot heels softly clicked together in assurance of my stance. My eyes were still looking at Charles, trying to figure out what he was up to, but my body showed off a position of duty and readiness. Charles turned his focus to the man sitting in the chair and nodded once. The mystery figure rose up from the chair to greet me.

The first thing I noticed was the boots—shining black, hard, well-used boots with the symbol of the POLICE along the side. A neatly pressed uniform clung to a muscular form that had no real need for exercises, his muscle structure looking all natural. A club and revolver holster, complemented with a rather finely instrumented revolver handle protruding from it, hung from a leather belt around his waist. Stripes and medals of honor, loyalty, and bravery extended themselves from his jacket, adorning practically the full left side of his torso. A thin, black mustache covered his upper lip. Despite the youthful appearance of the face, the fiftyish-year-old man had deep, aged eyes, which stared into mine and filled me with awe and surprise. The general was a man with presence.

The general, lightly brushing out a crease from his jacket that had developed as he sat, looked me up and down in a quick inspection. I hardened my stance at the realization that I was standing in front of the commander of the entire POLICE force. He was here—in the room with me. But he was early! The general was not supposed to be here for another couple months.

The general, stepping around the chair that sat in front of the desk, made his way until he was standing directly in front of me, his boots making a hollow thump against the flooring. He searched my face for something, I couldn't tell what he was looking for.

"Are you Corporal Major Thomas Haroldson?" he asked me, his voice powerful and demanding, yet softly spoken.

I didn't move. "Yes, sir," I said, voice sure and steady.

The general, nodding at my answer, started to pace around me leisurely. "I take it you are aware of who I am?"

"Yes, sir."

The general nodded a second time. "Good. I've been informed by the first sergeant that he has put you in for recommendation for taking over POLICE Grounds number one-zero-four, founded inside the town Sicher Himmel, upon my immediate transfer of the first sergeant to sergeant major. Have you been made aware of this?"

"Yes, sir."

The general made his way back in front of me, his hands clasped behind his back as he calmly paced around where I stood. "The first sergeant has surrendered your file to me, and I've had time to look it over in detail. Do you know what I have found, Corporal Major?"

Uh oh.

"No, sir."

His eyes bore into my own, staring deep into me. "Based on my review, Corporal Major, I've found some rather interesting things that ... stick out. Things that need to be answered."

At this, the general turned from me and made his way toward Charles. The first sergeant opened up the drawer in his desk where he kept all of his paperwork and files and pulled out one file in particular. On the file, my name was written in big, black letters. He handed the file over to the general, not bothering to close the drawer after removing the file. The general, taking the file coolly in his hands, opened it and started to casually flip through the pages marked off within. Charles, still standing behind his desk at ease, looked from the general to me, a concerned expression on his face. This did not bode well.

The general, squinting hard at the words found within the file, turned to Charles briefly. "First Sergeant, if you wouldn't mind?" he politely asked, pointing at the lamp on his desk.

Charles, nodding slightly, leaned over and turned on the lamp. The lamp, with its single electronic bulb, gave off a soft hue of light, just enough to lighten up the room and to illuminate the immediate area around the desk. Happy with the amount of light, the general went back to the file and started to read once more.

The general, finding what he was searching for, positioned himself on the desk so that he was half leaning and half standing in front of me. "It says here that you joined on your birthday. Is that correct?"

"Yes, sir."

The general nodded and pursed his lips at my answer. "Hmmm ... you seem ... young to me, for a man your age."

"Yes, sir."

He returned his attention to the file open in front of him, careening for some other lost point that had caught his attention. "It also states that you recently went undercover to the local Rebell meeting in the radiated Zone nearby. There, you were in a confrontation with another POLICE officer, which evidently led to his death. Correct?"

"Yes, sir."

"This confrontation also led to the dismissal of a very highly ranked officer within this Grounds. Correct?" he asked.

"Yes, sir."

"Yet, upon returning from the meeting, your presentation of information to the first sergeant and the treatment of said superior officer was concerning."

"Yes, sir."

"And there was also rumored connection between your deceased civilian friend and girlfriend, whom you escorted to the meeting, and that of her entire family to the Rebell faction."

My jaw started to tighten at that last point. "This was both speculation and hearsay, sir. Both were proven clear of any association to the Rebells by an investigation, sir. I brought them along for added eyes, ears, and to help portray my undercover position, sir. They were no more Rebells than I am, sir."

The general returned his attention to the file in his hands, flipping a page over to read the information written on its back. He took a moment to scan through the information and then pointed at some clear fact and nodded in affirmation. "Yes. Right. As mentioned. Well, there's just one other point that I am having trouble with in regards to the first sergeant's recommendation, though."

At this, the general tossed the file onto the desk behind him and looked at me with a puzzled thinking expression. "You're too low of rank to start the proper training for the head officer of a Grounds. You would need to have at least the rank of sergeant to even be considered. Then, of course, there are the years of training in Hauptstadt before you would be granted approval and officially be given power over the Grounds."

Charles looked down at his desk at the announcement. I can only imagine what he was thinking at that moment. I refused to show any reaction, despite what I felt at the news. That's that, I guess. There goes my chance at making a difference around this place. "I understand, sir," I replied simply, trying my best not to show off any emotion or remorse.

The general got up from his position on the desk and turned toward Charles and the box. "No, Corporal Major, I don't think you do."

Charles reached down and picked up the simple metallic box up off of the desk and held it out for the general, who then opened the latch and pulled back the lid. All I could see from the position I was standing at was the red velvet lining within the box. The contents were too deep within. The general reached into the box, picked up two things, and closed the box once more. Charles put the box back down.

Holding onto the contents tightly so that I could not see what it was, the general turned his attention back to me. Charles snapped into attention behind the general, his entire body growing stiff and strong. The general walked up to where I stood.

"Corporal Major Thomas Haroldson, for your outstanding dedication and actions in times of service, I hereby promote you to the rank and station of sergeant."

The general held up his hand and showed off the contents that he had taken out of the box. There in his hand sat two pins. One of them was the symbol of the POLICE, which he reached out and attached to my lapel. The second one was a soft, velvet strip. On it, there were two more pins, each one in the design of the sergeant rank. The general, taking the pins off of the velvet strip, attached them onto my uniform while removing the old pins that took their spot.

Once the general was done putting the pins on me, he stepped back a step to get a better look at me. "Officers, salute!" he ordered, more for himself and Charles than for me. Charles snapped into a salute behind the general, his salute more casual but still strong and firm. I saluted the two of them and returned to my stance of attention. They did the same. The general smiled at me and stuck out his hand. "You can stand at ease now, Haroldson."

I reached out and took the hand of the general, shaking it lightly. "Thank you, sir."

"It's I who should be thanking you. The report only touched the surface of what really went on during and after the meeting. I spent a good, long while with your first sergeant in order to get the full story of what went on. Taking down the corruption that was poisoning this Grounds, as well as facing off against a fellow officer in an assassination attempt. That's something to be proud of, son. It's too bad about your friend and your girl. I'm sorry for your loss."

The general really sounded sincere. "I ... appreciate your words, sir."

Charles, relaxing his stance, walked out from behind the desk and shook my hand. "Congratulations, kid. I always had a feeling that you'd go far."

There was the Charles I once knew. The weight of the room seemed to disappear as soon as the short ceremony was over. With the seriousness taken care of, the three of us entered into general chitchat and talked about the upcoming days ahead. A quick thought popped into my head.

"I just have two questions that I need to ask," I chimed in.

Charles, who was sitting back down in his chair and lighting up one of his cigars, raised an eyebrow. The general, back to leaning against the desk, gave off a big smile.

"Let me guess. What am I doing here, and … who's going to be left in charge of the Grounds when the first sergeant leaves with me when I return to Hauptstadt? Am I close?"

I smiled. "Actually … no. The first sergeant … heard a rumor that you were coming, sir. We just figured that it wouldn't be for another couple months."

The general gave Charles a quick glance over his shoulder for confirmation. "Really?" he asked, more amused than surprised.

Charles shrugged his answer, still trying to ignite the cigar that was latched between his lips.

"I see. Someone in my office has been busy," he smirked as he returned his gaze to me. "I assume you thought me being here had something to do with my tour? As I was telling the first sergeant, he's not the only officer who I'm collecting up for training. There are two other officers that I'm moving to sergeant major who resided in a few towns southeast of here. I figured that it would be best to gather everyone up prior to going on my tour rather than picking him up during. Then, of course, there's the question of your training to first sergeant. You need to go to Hauptstadt for that. Might as well come with us. That way, you'd be training while the tour went on. I'd hoped that we'd be back in Hauptstadt before the anniversary date, but there was a … delay in the last town I was in."

I nodded. Made sense. "Did I at least get the second question right?" the general inquired, a playful tone in his voice.

"Well—" I stammered, not wanting to hurt his feelings, "I was going to ask what was with the receptionist being so polite and why the room was so dark?"

The general leaned back and laughed a hearty laugh.

~

The entire Grounds was called out to the fields. It was actually impressive how quickly everyone was able to come out and organize. Rows upon rows of officers, lined according to rank and placement, covered the area. There was a general lull over the crowd as to what the impromptu address might be about. We'd had addresses by Charles before, but these were on rare occasions. Charles was more of a man who liked to send out memos to people as opposed to making huge speeches in front of everyone. I'm going to take a quick guess that it had something to do with the general showing up early. I caught sight of H. J. briefly in the group sectioned off for the communications building. He gave me a quick nod, and I responded in kind.

A single officer walked out into the middle of the area and turned toward us all. I immediately recognized him as the new officer that Charles chose to replace Fürl: Staff Sergeant Mayer. He was an okay guy. I'd only met up with him on a few occasions. From what I got out of Charles, he was a real stickler for the rules. I even heard that he was the only man on the Grounds who could not only quote directly from the manual but could tell you the page number and paragraph. Definitely someone to balance Charles as he tried to come up with stuff that might be considered questionable by some.

"Officers, stand at attention and await orders!" he yelled out over top of the quiet conversations and general movement. As one, the entire Grounds stomped and slid into attention.

The officer, stiff with stern practice, tapped his right foot behind him and turned ninety degrees toward the office. He stomped back into attention and gave the building a salute.

"Officers awaiting orders, sir" he shouted out toward the building. Apparently waiting for his cue, Charles, in full regalia, opened the doors and wandered out from the office, the other higher-ranking sergeants in tow.

The small parade of officers marched out to the center of the area, each of them in order of rank and placement. The mob made their way directly to Mayer, who had not moved since returning from his salute. Once they were in the center, they fell into line.

Charles stood for a moment, looking the entire Grounds over. His eyes searched the crowd in front and beside him, making sure that everyone was giving him their full attention. Charles stood in front of us all straight and proud, taking a moment to fully absorb the task that was placed in front of him. Softly, he cleared his throat and addressed the officers under his command.

"I'm sure that the majority of you know what day it is today, so I won't bother going into the general history of the day or the reasons why it is important that we take a moment to remember why today is so important. Rather, I will jump right into the grit of it all.

"We have been honored to have among us a special guest. One that has traveled far to be with us today. I expect you all to be on your best behavior and to show pride in your Grounds as you hear what this man has to say. Officers, I give you ... your General."

As a flowing wave across a barren sea, everyone on the Grounds spontaneously broke into a salute.

The door to the offices was opened by one of the sergeant majors. He walked out of the door and held it open, hastily standing at attention. A few other sergeant majors exited the building, streaming out from the building like water out of a tap. They calmly marched out onto the Grounds and took position up around the area where the general was about to address the crowd. Once they were in position, the general appeared from the building. He was also in full regalia, medals and awards hanging off of every inch of his jacket. The sergeant major who was holding the door open for him fell into line behind his commander as they made their way from the building. He strode out quickly and strongly into the middle of the Grounds where Charles stood awaiting him.

The general, as he stood in front of us all, lightly brushed his eyebrows as he stared across the sea of faces before him. We were like a vast forest, unmoving and silent. The general leaned over to Charles and whispered a few words to him, giving a quick gesture toward the overpowering mass of officers who were awaiting his words. Charles nodded briefly to whatever was said and then took a step back in order to give the general the full authority of the floor. He stood at attention toward us all and saluted. Only when he finished the salute did we, the entire Grounds as one, lower our hands back to our side.

"Greeting, my fellow officers," the general called out to us all, his voice carrying strong and powerfully over us.

"I am honored to be here with you today. A day like no other. For today is the day when we celebrate seventy-five years of peace. Seventy-five years of order. Seventy-five years of POLICE rule."

All the officers on the Grounds, as a collective mind, shouted out a single hoo-rah at the general's words and then fell silent. The general began to lightly pace back and forth as he continued his speech, making sure to look into the eyes of all the soldiers who stood before him.

"I wish to celebrate this day by honoring those who have given their lives for their duty and to honor those of you who still uphold what we all treasure dearly. I want to do this by doing three things. First, I want to declare that there will be a monument created on every Grounds that will hold the names of every POLICE officer who has lost his life in the act of duty. This monument, this symbol of bravery and sacrifice, will not only be made up of the officers from this point on but will also hold the names of the warriors who eagerly fought during the war to make sure that you would be standing here today."

The crowd hoo-rahed at the declaration and then fell silent.

"Secondly, there is an officer here who has demonstrated superior leading abilities. An officer who has made this Grounds one of the shining stars in our world. I am here today to honor his abilities by asking him to come with me back to Hauptstadt to train as my next sergeant major. First Sergeant, please step forward."

As requested by his commander in chief, Charles stepped forward and stood in front of the general at attention. The general turned and faced Charles. He reached into one of his pockets and pulled out a single pin, which the general held out toward Charles. The early afternoon sun glinted off the shiny metal in the general's hand.

"Do you accept my offer of your own free will?" he asked.

"I do," replied Charles.

The general reached out and put the pin on his lapel, adjusting it a little after it was securely on. They saluted each other, and then Charles stepped back to where he once stood. The crowd gave off a hoo-rah and fell silent.

"Lastly, it has come to my attention that this particular Grounds was key in the takedown of the local tribe of Rebells. In fact, according to the report that I was given, the leader Duncan was at that meeting. Now, he might have escaped and run hiding with his tail between his legs, escaping us for now … but he will not hide for long. In order to show my deep appreciation for all of your hard work, dedication, and risk of life and limb in the name of the POLICE, as well as to celebrate this day, I have a gift for you all."

At this, the general waved off to the side where a pair of sergeant majors were standing. In between them rested an oaken barrel, towering up from the ground like a gigantic anthill. At the signal from the general, the two turned sharply in unison and maneuvered the barrel so that they were each holding a part of it. Lifting it up effortlessly, the two overbearing men carried the barrel to where the general stood and put it gently in front of him.

The general turned back to the officers. "In my possession, I have twenty-six barrels of ale that I was forced to confiscate from a couple towns south of here. Apparently, the ale master was smuggling his alcoholic wares to the general public for profit, which is against POLICE law. Since I had not planned on taking on such a commodity, I am faced with a dilemma—one that can be easily remedied."

The officers, eager to hear what would come to pass regarding the many barrels of ale, started to glance out of the corners of their eyes at their neighboring members, each one grinning sheepishly from ear to ear. The general made a grand sweeping gesture to the entire Grounds with his proclamation.

"Thus, in honor of your great sacrifice and in honor of the day, I hereby present these confiscated barrels to the Grounds. I expect not to see a single drop of ale by morning!"

The crowd, completely forgetting protocol and order, roared to life in hoots and hollers in favor of the general.

CHAPTER 32

A COOL, CRISP BREEZE KEPT ME company as I took my nightly stroll around the Grounds. After the long meeting with Charles and the general, as well as the gathering for the speech, I decided that I would take an extra long walk in order to clear my mind. The Grounds was generally clear of officers, the majority of the men were in the barracks swilling down the beer that the sergeant majors were unloading out of the cart that had been brought onto the Grounds by the general. Everyone else was gone.

Good. I preferred to walk alone tonight, my thoughts being my only companion. The moon, just starting its long trek through the sky, was along its last phase before plunging into darkness. A sliver of silver shone through the partly clouded sky above. The occasional star blinked hello from the heavens.

"Nice night," someone announced from the darkness.

I turned around to see the general walking up behind me. He had a walking stick with him. On the top of the stick was a fairly large jewel of some kind that his hand was clutched around. I saluted. He nodded. We continued our walk together.

"What brings you out here, if I may ask, sir?" I tried to start up a conversation.

The general took a deep breath, filling his lungs with the shrill air, taking in the night. "It got too stuffy in my quarters."

I nodded. As we walked, the two of us broke into general chitchat

348

and light conversation. We talked about simple things: the weather, recent events, future goals, our personal lives. We even shared a few jokes. The general emphasized to me during our general wander that he "was off duty and should be treated as such."

"Ya know," he smiled, "this is the first time in—wow, I can't even remember the last time that I've spent a good length by myself," he mused.

I glanced over at the general. "Sir?"

The general stopped for a moment. "I mean, not having some sort of huge entourage following me around. Do you know how many guards I had to bring with me before it was even considered safe enough to leave Hauptstadt?"

I shook my head. The general continued his trek around the Grounds, me in tow. "Twenty," he answered his own question, a tinge of bitterness in his voice. "Twenty sergeant majors were made to come with me on this simple grab-and-run trip to three different towns. The towns weren't even that far away in the whole scheme of things. Just imagine how many I'll have to bring on my tour."

"But it's for your own safety, sir. No one can risk you being attacked by the Rebells, sir."

"Attacked? The Rebells in this area have all but been decimated. You were a part of that endeavor. What are they protecting me from?"

The general waved his walking stick at the surrounding area while he continued. "Besides, part of the point of the tour to all the places I want to go to is to observe the inner workings of each town—to see what it is about them that makes them work so well. Why is it that one town is able to maintain order so much better than another? How can I do that with twenty sergeant majors clamoring around me? And let's not forget—the last thing I need is to wander around the place with some officer wanting to make a mark for himself by playing tour guide and pointing out 'important building A, B, C, not to mention the new extensions on building D over there.'"

I smiled at the man and his overexaggerated display of some guy giving him a tour. The general smiled and turned his attention back to me. "Your turn. Why aren't you with the rest getting rid of all that ale for me?"

I shrugged. "The walks help take my mind off my troubles."

He nodded. "The night will do that."

We walked for a bit in silence. The buildings that surrounded us were as dark as the night sky with everyone off at the barracks. "So, out of curiosity, when you went undercover to the meeting ... were you able to see Duncan personally?" the general asked.

"Yes, sir."

"How'd he look?"

"Umm ... he looked sure of himself and what he was doing."

"And while he was ranting on the stage, did he happen to mention what his 'great plan' was to eradicate me?"

I was a little surprised that the general had not already heard of the plan that Duncan had come up with. "Was that not in the report that you were given?"

"The report that was sent to Hauptstadt was so full of holes you could've hidden a house in it. Even when I asked for an undistorted report from your first sergeant, he never went into any real detail in regards to the assassination plan—only that there was one organized for my eventual arrival at Sicher Himmel."

I squished my eyebrows in concern over this bit of news. "Why would—"

"Because they didn't want me to worry over it," the general interrupted. "I can kind of understand why. What with the number of times the Rebells have tried to kill me."

"How many times *have* they tried?"

The general stared up at the starry sky for a moment. "I think the total's up to ... nine? And that's only against me. They went after my father a lot worse."

I wondered for a second if I should tell him. Everyone else had spent so much effort trying to keep it away from him; I should probably do the same. But he does have a right to know. Anyway, it was a horrible plan to begin with. And so, I gave the general the full story, right down to the diagram that was on the huge sheet behind Duncan. I even tried to draw it in the dirt ground with his walking stick, which I borrowed in order to draw. The general listened carefully to the details as I poured over the event and how it happened the best my memory would allow. He studied the ground as I drew the map of the overall area and the path that he was expected to take, right down to the ambush markings and what would be his eventual downfall.

When I finished drawing and marking up the ground, I gave back the sturdy and expensive-looking walking stick back to the general. He took the staff back from me without looking up from the drawing, his eyes following along the seated route in the dirt and the markings I made up for the Rebells. The general finally straightened up, his back, making a simple crick as he stretched himself out to his full height.

"That's it?" he asked.

I simply nodded my head. The general merely shook his head at the diagram. "That has got to be the shoddiest plan I have ever seen. I'm shocked that this is what Duncan brought forward. He's usually much more cunning than this."

That last bit caught my attention. More cunning than this? Just how well does the general know Duncan? "Sir?" I asked, hoping that the general would go into more detail.

The general pointed down at the ground with his stick, the point a natural extension of his finger. "In his previous plans against me, there has always been a plan within a plan. An option B, as it were. With this scenario, as it's laid out, there is no route for a secondary venue of attack. It's an all-out, last-ditch effort. Victory or death. That's not Duncan's style. He has always had some means to modify his plans on the fly, in case the unexpected showed up. Not to mention, he's too exposed in this. It just … looks wrong."

I looked from the diagram to the general, who was still pouring over the plan in the dirt. "You know Duncan? Personally?" I asked

The general shot me a side glance. "Um … it's … complicated."

Giving the ground a quick kick, the general scattered a bunch of loose dirt up and over the drawing that I had made of the battle plan. I glanced over toward him.

"Sir … may I ask a personal question?"

He looked over at me. "Depends how personal."

I thought for a second as how to best word my question without sounding too much like an idiot or giving myself away to the commander in chief of the POLICE.

"What made your father start the POLICE? How did he ever think of something like this organization, sir? More importantly, why is it that there's so much hostility between the POLICE and the Rebells?"

He tilted his head at the question, his eyebrows scrunching together slightly as he searched his mind for an answer. "Don't you know? I thought everyone knew that. The history of the POLICE is written inside some instruction booklet that everyone has to read when you join ... can't remember which one, but it's all in there: how it was formed, how the war started, how it was finished ... blah, blah, blah."

"Well, yeah. There are official reports and stories from people who have heard this point from you or heard that point from a reliable source ... but what I want to know is the full story. No editing for security reasons or—no, that came out wrong. I was wondering if you could explain it to me through your own thoughts and opinions."

He smiled. "No one has ever asked me for the 'story behind the story' before. I'm not sure where to even begin."

He stared at the sky, around the Grounds, and back to me. "You know a place where we can sit and talk without being disturbed?"

I smiled. "I know just the place, sir."

⌒

I decided to take the general to the fountain. The only thing stopping us was getting off the Grounds and getting past the sergeant majors who now made up the nightly patrols and the guards at the gates. Getting to a gate was simple enough. Everyone was getting drunk in the barracks, so there was no one to stop us while we zipped from building to building. The general was having a bit too much fun with it, acting like it was a training run for some sort of secret mission. He would throw himself up against a building and then creep up to the corner to see if the coast was clear. When he saw that there was no one in the path or cross street that we needed to get to, he gave me a coded hand gesture reserved for on-field situations to inform me that "area was clear" and "advance with caution."

If Charles ever found out about this, he would have both our heads on report. That was a funny thought—putting the general on report.

The gate that the two of us arrived at was guarded by a single sergeant major. He looked quite foreboding standing there, eyes searching the night air for movement. The general and I hunkered down behind a trash bin beside the building we zipped to in order to figure out a plan. "This might be a problem," he whispered to me, referring to the major.

The general could have order the sergeant major to stand aside and let us pass, but then the sergeant major would also insist that he accompany the general, which was not what he wanted. I glanced around the area to see if there was anything we could use as a distraction. Unfortunately, the Grounds was clear of any useful material. We sat for a minute and gauged our situation. I tapped my fingers against the rather bulky trash bin as I tried to figure out a plan. The general, looking at my hand quietly rapping against the bin, smiled at me.

"Good idea," he smirked.

I was at a loss as to what he thought my plan was. He fished in his pockets for something, turning them inside out to see what he was holding. Small pieces of paper and whatnot fell from the inner lining of his pockets onto the ground. He nodded for me to do the same. I quickly emptied what I had on me—a small ball of lint and a note that I'd made for myself as a reminder to talk to Charles regarding scheduling. Not very helpful.

The general took up the pieces of paper form the ground and reached into his breast pocket with his free hand. He pulled out a small metallic box, finely ordained with the symbol of the POLICE on the outside of it. It had a cut all around it, which was blocked on the side by a simple latch. Giving the metallic box a flick in his hand, the latch caught the lid and flung it open, revealing a wick and flint combination. Giving me a wink, he brushed down on the flint and lit the pieces of paper in his hand. Once the papers were ignited, he snapped the lid shut and put the lighter back into his breast pocket. Careful not to shed too much light around the area, the general stretched his arm up and flicked the burning papers into the bin.

With the papers safely smoldering inside the trash bin we were facing, the two of us sprinted around the building and into position to see if our distraction would work. I crashed into the corner of the building, the general right by my side, and the two of us slid along the brick surface to a crouching position. I risked slowly craning my head out to see if the sergeant major had moved. He had not. He was still standing in front of the gate at attention. It had been at least two minutes since the general had thrown the burning papers into the bin. If there were anything flammable inside the bin, surely it would have caught by now.

I looked back at the general, who was watching me for a sign that it had worked. I merely shrugged my shoulders. The general looked a bit downcast that his plan didn't work, giving off a deep sigh.

"Hey! *Fire!*"

I perked up at the sound of the sergeant major around the corner. Giving another shot, I eased my head around the corner. He was gone. I motioned behind me for the general to follow and slowly made my way around the corner. Staying low and pressed up against the brick wall, I sidestepped toward the mesh gate and freedom from the Grounds. The two of us quickly made our way to the opposite corner of the building. Around where the bin sat, I could hear the sergeant major cursing and fumbling around with something. Risking a glance, I peeked my head around to see. The sergeant major was in front of the bin, which was now totally engulfed in flames and belching out black, putrid smoke. He was flapping his jacket at the flames, trying desperately to smother it.

I think we did too good a job.

I signaled to the general to make a break for it, and the two of us ran straight for the gate. Grabbing hold of the handle, I gave it a twist and swung the gate wide for the general to get through. The gate, its hinges well oiled and cared for, barely made a sound as I handled it roughly in the chaos. Twisting myself through the opening, I pulled the gate closed, and the two of us sprinted out into the open path away from the Grounds. With legs pumping and lungs screaming for air, the two of us didn't look back as we rocketed down one path and another. I quickly took lead and started to direct the general out toward our destination.

As we started to get closer to the fountain, I slowed from a breakneck sprint to a light jog to a walk. The general followed suit. Once we were far, far away from the Grounds, only then did we stop. Holding onto my side from the sharp cramp that was developing there, I breathed in and out in controlled breaths in an attempt to slow my pounding heart. The general, a few feet from me, was leaning on his knees in a half-hunched position.

"I can't believe that actually worked," I wheezed.

The general, hooking his hands on either side of his waist, flipped his head back and stared hard at the blackened sky above. "Yeah," he gasped, "but the real trick will be to get back in."

He was more right that he knew. The gate's locking mechanism was on the inside of the Grounds. The handle inside the Grounds was always unlocked, while the outside was always locked and required someone to open the gate for you. That meant that we would need someone to let us back in. Either that, or we'd have to hop the fence, which would be very interesting.

The two of us, once we caught our breaths, continued down the road and alleys until we eventually made it to the fountain. The general looked at the fountain with appreciation.

"Nice spot," he offered.

I sat down on the cold mixture of stone and cement, glad to be sitting after our little adventure. The general followed my lead. He looked around the area, taking in every detail. The fountain was long turned off for the winter, but there were still jets within the fixture that made the water available within the basin churn on top of it. That way, the water kept moving, and it would have less of a chance to freeze during the winter.

The general smiled. "This is more of the reason why I'm on tour. I get a chance to see how the countryside is holding up, how I can improve it, and what to remove."

I leaned back a bit. "I come here quite a bit. I find it refreshing. Also, it's a good place to talk. Seats are built in, wonderful view, and the splashing of the water muffles voices from prying ears."

The general nodded. "I should have one of these put in all the towns. It would make a nice community gathering place, as well as a nicer spot to get water than those ugly hand-pumping wells."

The two of us talked for a bit about John and me growing up inside the town and how important the fountain was. I told him the occasional story about some of the mischief that we would get into. The more I talked, the more the general relaxed into the surroundings. Eventually, he cleared his throat and began his tale.

⁓

"From what I remember my father telling me, he thought up the idea for the POLICE, really, when he was about ten. My grandparents—well, apparently they were not the easiest people to get along with. They were always fighting with each other, or else they were away on some trip. Don't remember what it was that my grandparents did, exactly. All I remember is that their job took them all over the world, which left my father alone with his guardian. The same could be said about the country that my father was living in at the time. The fighting part, that is. There was always news of one country battling another country for who-knows-what reason. I guess he just got tired of the fighting in general.

"By the time he was thirteen, he decided enough was enough and took matters into his own hands. He went about gathering up his friends and school buddies and made up a local gang. He figured since he couldn't stop his parents from fighting and he couldn't stop his country from fighting, he would try to gain some sense of order around his neighborhood. Maybe then people would take notice and follow suit. You can understand that no one took a bunch of thirteen-year-olds very seriously. But, my father was a very stubborn person—even at that young age. That made him fight even harder.

"When he was fourteen, he was the leader of a fairly big gang whose members ranged in age from eight to eighteen. He allowed one adult to join the gang early in its formation. Apparently, the guy tried to take over the gang and make them his slaves, trying to make 'em do all of these horrid, illegal things. My father, seeing that the gang was moving away from his original design, again took charge. The adult—not sure what happened to him, but I was told he never came around again. From then on, until my father became an adult himself, he decided not to allow any more adults into the gang.

"In the beginning, they would walk around the neighborhood, help people out, and try their best to stop local crime. They didn't go after bank robbers or terrorists or anything, just snatch-and-grab stuff. Sometimes, they were successful. Other times, they just got in the way. That's where the POLICE originally got the name: Publicly Operated Law-enforcement Instigating Crime Eradication. My father's gang became a real presence in his town. 'The Protectors.' 'The Law-enforcers.' 'The Heroes.' The cops in his town were taking a real shine toward his gang. With the POLICE, general crime was starting to decline. They were all made deputies once they reached a certain age. His picture was up on all the walls over town to remind people, 'Hey, look out! We're watching you.'

"His POLICE gang grew by leaps and bounds. What started as four boys grew to forty and then to four hundred. When he reached the age of eighteen, there were close to one thousand members. Eighteen! He was ruling a small army when he was eighteen!

"He made an old factory the official POLICE headquarters. They needed one. There were too many people to organize without one. The place was donated to them by the town as a way of saying thanks. It took them about two summer days to have it 'Grounds' ready. The place was broken into different wings: barracks, where you could sleep or just relax; communications, where all the battle plans were made; law and order, where there was a permanent cop administrator to help oversee everything between the gang and the local law (and to make sure that they weren't doing anything outside of the law as they tried to uphold it); and the Grounds, where a mock gym and training area was constructed. My father moved into the barracks at that point, since he was old enough to leave home. He said it was so that he could be close by in case he was needed. It was just an excuse to get away from his parents, I'm guessing.

"The POLICE, along with the combined efforts of the cops, reduced crime to almost nothing. Everyone in town loved them! There were all these endorsements from the mayor of the town, and the community really went out of their way to support them. Since they were working so well together, the cops eventually built a second POLICE headquarters as an add-on to their own station, officially joining the two groups together. Given, my father was still solely in charge of the POLICE, but now he officially had the full backing of the cops. He was one of them now. My father finally felt like he had a true sense of purpose—like he was actually making a difference! I remember him telling me that he felt like he had a true home now—with a really big family.

"The chief of the cops and my father had become good friends by then. He taught my dad pretty much all he knew. My father told me that the chief was a retired officer in the army, so he taught my father all sorts of military strategies, tactics, and insights. My father would then bring all the training over to the POLICE for everyone else to learn. The guy was a brilliant strategist, and my father was a fast learner. Soon, to test everyone's skills, the two organizations started to have these friendly contests against each other: the cops versus the POLICE. They had these Olympic events to see which side was faster, better, stronger.... The POLICE usually lost but only during the beginning years.

"At age twenty, my father took on the nickname General, since he was in charge of this little militia. It stuck. There was a local artist inside the POLICE, whom he asked to make up the symbol for the organization. That stuck, as well.

"My father soon thought that the group needed something else to strive for, since crime was almost eradicated inside the town. Thus, the different levels of rank inside the POLICE and the jobs associated with them became established. I think that the chief had something to do with that. Then came a young officer with a fresh idea: since the program was doing so much good for this one town, wouldn't it be a good idea to make this program worldwide?

"Well, my father took up the idea like it was liquid lightning! Banners, signs, newspapers, speeches, and advertising of all kind was used. He gave the four sergeants, the ones who started the gang with him, their own towns to start up a POLICE Grounds. The cops thought it was a good idea and helped out where they could. I mean, the statistics spoke for themselves regarding all the good they were doing. In a few months, there were POLICE Grounds all over the map. All of them were collecting recruits daily. *All* of them! There was nothing stopping them.

"After taking conquest after conquest, my father decided it was time to take his idea to the United Nations. If the entire world had POLICE protection, there would be no more wars, no fighting…. All that wasted money put toward finding some sense of order could then be put toward the betterment of mankind: medicine, food, all going toward aid and helping lesser-developed countries. It was an ambitious goal, but my father refused to accept anything less.

"It took a lot of convincing, a lot of talking, and a lot of planning, but somehow my father won out. The UN decided to give the organization a trial run under a few strict conditions: one being that he share control over the POLICE with those inside the UN. He stupidly agreed, not realizing the error in judgment at that point in time.

"The POLICE became official. All over the world, people joined up with the organization. With every new POLICE Grounds that popped up around the globe, crime slowly but surely went down. With every successful story that went up on the news praising the endeavors of the POLICE, people flocked to join. My father toured the world, talking to all the different officers inside the different Grounds. Everything was going wonderfully! Terrorism and death became as low as the need for food and water. For once in recorded history, everyone was happy—except the people at the UN. They got greedy.

"They started making demands to my father, ridiculous demands. Day by day, they tried to add the world's problems into the organization: race identification and making it mandatory that a given percentage of members be of a certain creed or background, thus pushing aside better qualified candidates in order to fill a quota; religious dress codes replacing standard uniforms, thus segregating from within; cultural standpoints being integrated into policies, thus further separating the recruits; language barriers breaking down communication, due to refusal from different countries to speak a single language; unions and pay differentiation for higher positions. It makes my head spin just thinking about it! And if my father refused to incorporate their orders, the UN would go over his head and hold a secret vote. When that happened, the general rule would be that the vote would pass, and the rule would be implemented.

"All of the sudden the chaos was starting to creep back into the world. POLICE officials started to become corrupt due to bribes, allowing greed to factor into orders. Animosity between countries and racial tension within the Grounds became rampant. Internal politics took precedent over getting out onto the street and stopping crime. Officers didn't get proper punishment for derelict of duty, because they were protected by the union. It was the final straw! My father marched into the United Nations and demanded full power over the POLICE so that he could annul all votes made by them. Do you know what they did? They kicked him out!

"My father realized then that as long as people like those inside the UN governed the world, no one could be happy. That day, he wired all the sergeants, telling them that the POLICE had broken away from the UN, and none of their orders should be acknowledged or followed.

"Once that happened, the UN tried every sleazy trick in the book to close the POLICE organization down. And in order to keep the organization alive, the POLICE were forced to fight back with everything they had. After a few heated discussions, the UN brought in their army to shut him down. So, in order to defend his dream and everything that he had worked so hard for, my father was forced to bring in his army. World War III commenced right there on the UN steps.

"There were some long years ahead with all the fighting. Some of the things that happened—well, I'd rather not get into it. Needless to say, the POLICE eventually prevailed in making the world realize what it was that the POLICE organization was providing. The world came to its senses. Once the war was over, Father really went to work at cleaning up the place. He tried to get rid of everything that caused turmoil and fighting in the world before. He got rid of all the governments and borders, so there wasn't a need to fight each other over land or politics. He outlawed all other languages, so there were no excuses regarding miscommunication or misunderstandings. He abolished the religions, so there was no need to prove which deity was more powerful. He wiped the slate clean for everyone. There was finally a true chance for peace.

"And yet, despite all the efforts and sacrifices, there are still people … *still* … who insist that the old ways are better. Ya know, sometimes I'll be in my office, and I'll read some sort of report about this attack or that attack by the Rebells, and I'll stop and think of what my father would have done if he were here."

~

The general trailed off at the end, musing over how the Rebells kept trying to usurp the power of the POLICE and their constant attempts to bring the general down. I looked out at the area, taking in everything that I had just heard. Knowing what I already knew about the POLICE took on a whole different meaning after actually hearing the tale from the general. This made me take a moment to ponder what it was that I was actually doing. Can the Rebells' ideals and their dream of democracy and the POLICE actually coexist? Is it possible? Have I been fooling myself all this time? The POLICE and the concepts that the Rebells have been fighting for tried to live together once before, and it ended up in a world war. How can I even attempt to try to bring the two together?

The sun's rays started to poke through the clouds that had formed overnight as we talked at the fountain. The general glanced up at the partly covered sky, the sudden growth of light in the area catching his attention. I looked up as well, content in the sight of the light blue dome that surrounded us.

"Hey," the general called out to me to get my attention. I turned my head so that I was looking at him. The general was still looking up into the sky, taking in the sunrise as it streaked across the sky. "I just want to thank you," he smiled.

"Thank me? For what?"

The general waved around the area. "For this. For giving me a night off. I haven't had a night off in years. This was the first time in a long time where I wasn't hassled by anyone or surrounded by the sergeant majors—just allowed to sit back, relax, and ... just talk."

I smiled at the compliment and then realized something that the general mentioned, which brought the situation ramming back to the front of my attention: the sergeant majors. With a jolt that shook me to the core, I suddenly realized that the general and I had been sitting at the fountain for a good portion of the night. The sun rising in the sky was a key giveaway. Everyone at the Grounds would no doubt have realized by now that the general wasn't there. We were in so much trouble.

I sternly cleared my throat to get the general's attention. "Um, sir ... I think it would be a good idea if we made our way back now," I suggested, a hint of panic in my voice.

The general, catching my sudden unease, took hold of the situation and nodded. The two of us got up off of the edge of the fountain, our legs not used to the act of movement from the long hours sitting on the cold cement and rock. With stiff joints and aching muscles, the general and I started to run back to the Grounds—like kids way past their curfew.

CHAPTER 33

The General and I got back to the Grounds without any trouble. When we arrived at the gate, there were a couple officers leaning up against the fence, totally plastered from drinking all that ale. They were singing and swaying back and forth, totally oblivious of the two Sergeant Majors who were trying to get them to stand up and leave the area. The General and I stayed put while the events unfolded. Only when the Sergeant Majors left the area to get more help did we move forward and get one of the drunken officers to let us in. I figured that the odds were in our favor that they wouldn't remember anything. Later on that day, I found out from the General that no one even knew he was gone. We got lucky.

Over the next two days, I personally showed the General the Grounds and the town from my point of view rather than doing a proper, boring tour of the place. I would tell stories about some old experience that I'd had at each and every place we went. We ended up spending a lot of time hanging out with Charles as well. The three of us would hide away inside the office, drink brandy, and talk about whatever topic happened to come up. The General actually insisted on this endeavor but made sure that all the Sergeant Majors knew he was "in a meeting and couldn't be disturbed." I guess that the General got a taste of freedom and wanted to hold onto it for as long as he could. He was having a great time. During these

363

conversations, I learned some stories about the organization that I had never heard.

The General, Charles, and I got a going away party from the entire Grounds the night before we left. H. J. made a speech to us. Nothing too classy. After the party, we three went to Charles's office for cigars.

~

"I'm going to miss this place," Charles mused as he leaned back in his chair. A small smoke ring was lazily hovering in the air directly above him. The desk that Charles had been locked behind for years was now gone from the office. Most of the collection of awards and memorabilia that lined the office shelves was packed away and ready for shipment to Hauptstadt. All that remained were the three chairs that we were sitting in, a small table where the brandy and glasses sat, and the box of cigars that were at my feet. It felt weird being in the room in such a state. I wasn't used to all the space and lack of stuff. The general, chomping down on his cigar, stretched out and grabbed a hold of the carafe of brandy and gave his near-empty glass another healthy shot.

I took a long pull on the cigar in my hand and exhaled a plume of smoke out into the air above me. The cloud of tobacco swirled in the empty office, snaking slowly toward the open window. The act of smoking one of the cigars from the stash that Charles kept on his desk felt almost weird. He'd never let me have one before, let alone sip on his private collection of brandy. I guess with his moving on, he no longer had need of these things.

"Don't worry, Charles. The Grounds will be well looked after. The door will always be open for you," I assured him.

The general sipped on his brandy before speaking. "Is everyone ready to leave tomorrow? I have to stay on schedule."

Charles took a sip on his brandy. "How long do you think we will be on the road?"

The general thought for a second before answering. "Should be roughly ten days to travel to Hauptstadt, but we're going to need to stop at the towns Stadt von Prozessen and Blaues Wunder to replenish supplies, so about two weeks."

Charles took a draw on his cigar. With a wrinkled brow, he released the lingering smoke from his lips. "Two weeks to get to Hauptstadt? Are you sure? Won't it take longer?"

The general smirked at the newly made sergeant major. "Not the way we're traveling," he grinned as he put his cigar between his teeth.

Charles and I took a glance at each other, neither one of us knowing exactly what he meant by that. When the general arrived at the Grounds, he just walked up to the gates and asked to be let in, his twenty or so sergeant majors in tow. We both knew there was no way that he walked to the Grounds from Hauptstadt, or whatever town he'd gone to first, but nothing was mentioned as to how he'd gotten here. The general scrunched his brow together.

"There is one small problem that must be addressed before we leave, though," He began.

Charles and I looked at each other again and then back to the general. He answered our unasked question. "The sergeant major who had been assigned to be my personal guard on the trip has fallen ill and will have to stay here until he's better. I can't wait for him, so I have need for a new personal guard for the return trip back to Hauptstadt. I'm already going to be down one sergeant major, due to leaving him here to take care of the Grounds until Haroldson's return from training."

I took a quick sip from my glass of brandy, the dark drink trickling down my throat in a lava-like cascade to my stomach. The general casually looked toward me, cigar clamped firmly in place between his teeth.

"Interested?" he asked.

What?

I sat up from my chair at this. "What about the other sergeant majors? What about Charles? He's of higher rank than me, as well as way more experienced."

Charles looked over at me with a scowl. "You saying I'm old?"

The general smiled and gave Charles a quick shot out the corner of his eye. "I'm sure that he meant it another way."

Charles waved off the general, the brandy making his actions a little too bold for my taste in regards to his casualness. The general, not paying any mind to Charles, turned his attention back to me. "I'm sorry, Tom. Can't use him. Charles will be starting his training with the other recently promoted sergeant majors on the way back to Hauptstadt."

"Excuse me, sir?" Charles asked while clearing his throat, his eyes growing at the news.

The general shrugged simply at the man. "Didn't I mention this already? As soon as we leave, your training begins. I'm going to be putting you under the order of Sergeant Major Holgam. He's one of my best trainers and will be in charge of every aspect of turning you into a sergeant major. I specifically brought him along for you and the others whom I picked up."

Charles looked a little downcast at the news, his shoulders slumping into his frame. The general turned his attention back to me. "You, on the other hand, won't begin your training until we get back to Hauptstadt. And, since I don't think you have any pressing matters while you're on the trip, you'd be perfect for the position."

"What would I have to do?" I asked him.

"Do what you have been doing for the past couple days. Just make sure that I'm safe, make sure that I don't get into any trouble, make sure that I don't get myself killed—or have anyone else kill me—and you'll do fine."

The general swallowed the rest of his brandy with a gulp and a wheeze. "Which reminds me … I need to get one last thing for the trip," he casually mentioned as he got up and walked toward the door.

Grabbing hold of the handle to the door, he gave it a gentle turn and swung the old wooden frame open. Just before stepping through the opening, he gave a quick glance back toward the two of us. "Be out in the yard at seven hundred hours tomorrow morning … and be ready to move."

He closed the door behind him, and he was gone. Charles and I just sat there in the empty office, staring off at the closed door that the general had used to exit. Neither of us said a word.

We never even got a chance to salute him.

"You're going to be what?!" H. J. blurted out, his eyes nearly bugging out of his skull at the shock of hearing my words.

"I've been asked to be the general's personal bodyguard on the return trip back to Hauptstadt, since the other guard is sick and has to stay here," I explained to my comrade a second time.

The two of us were inside a small room in the communications building assigned to H. J., so he could complete some secret-style project. Some general material rested out in front of him on the table separating us. H. J. slumped into the chair. He slapped his face with his hands in exasperation.

"What is it with you? Why do you get all the lucky breaks?!" he exclaimed.

I looked at him from behind a sly grin. "Maybe it's fate."

He glared at me. "Fate, my eye! Being in the right place at the right time—that's fate. Being the only person able to do something from within a huge crowd—that's fate. But your quicker-than-average rise in ranks, your constant good luck, and your new assignment with the general? That's way more than just fate. That's … that's … I … I have no idea what to call that. It's almost like there's some … unseen person watching out for you and shoving these good fortunes right in your lap!"

"Oh, yeah, I've had nothing but good fortune thrown my way. I practically started out in life with great luck, what with my family all but dying right there in front of me. Then there was that period where I lived by myself for years on end. Oh, and let's not forget my constant bullying by Vans throughout my younger life. John's fiancé being killed in the Factory explosion was a throw of luck. Then, of course, there's the more recent loss of my best friend and girlfriend … or do I need to remind you of that one?"

H. J. was about to respond to my attack but only turned away, his jaw tense and teeth grinding behind his cheeks. I hit him hard with that last point. He still had not forgiven himself for allowing Dawn to be killed. Reminding him of it was a low blow. I regretted saying it the moment the words left my mouth. We sat in silence for a little while.

Eventually, I asked him, "What are you doing for the next hour or so?"

H. J. breathed deeply. "Nothing."

I got up from my chair. "Come on. Help me pack?"

H. J. slumped out of his chair reluctantly.

～

I walked into the courtyard at six fifty in the morning. H. J. was behind me, carrying my luggage. Charles and the general stood in full dress inside the middle of the field, along with two other officers whom I didn't recognize at first. They were surrounded with boxes and bags of all shapes and sizes. I can only assume they were the effects that Charles was bringing to Hauptstadt with him and some general supplies for our trip. The general had a box under his arm, tucked comfortably against his ribs. I saluted them both when they noticed me. Charles waved me over to where they were standing.

The general smiled at the two of us walking toward him and took the small box from under his arm. "I was beginning to think you weren't going to show."

"Had to make sure that I got everything, sir. Didn't want to have to make a trip back."

The general nodded and turned to the other two officers who were standing with him and Charles. One of the officers, standing closest to the general, was a taller man than most of the party there. Very thin, but still powerful looking in nature. Thin black hair covered the sides of his balding head, balanced also by his wire-framed glasses. The second officer, standing beside Charles, was the more stereotypical POLICE officer. He looked like the type of man who was used to giving orders rather than receiving them. He was short and stocky, which gave off the impression of many hard hours of training, but he also had a rather staunch belly, which showed off his lack of athleticism for the past years.

"Sergeant Thomas Haroldson, I would like to introduce you to future Sergeant Major Stockgran and future Sergeant Major Van der Hoit."

The two men nodded and saluted at the calling of their names; I followed suit. Stockgran, the taller of the two, adjusted his glasses to a more comfortable position and smiled at me. Van der Hoit, after receiving my salute, returned to his staring off to the distance impatiently, like he was expecting something to pop around the corner.

The general held out the box in his arms toward me. "Since you're going to be my personal guard during the remainder of this trip, I figured you'd need one of these."

Van der Hoit perked up at this. He looked back toward the general with a very disapproving scowl on his brow. "Sir, with all due respect, I must—"

The general rolled his eyes. "First Sergeant," the general started up, as if this was the umpteenth time he's uttered these words, "I have made my position quite clear."

Van der Hoit shrank away from the general, knowing that his battle was over. "Yes, sir," he mumbled as he reluctantly bowed down to the general's wisdom. I took the box from the general and held it in my hands. It had some weight to it, so I had to adjust the box a bit in order to open it without having whatever it was inside tumble out. Inside the box was a POLICE-issued six-shot revolver and a holster, which could attach itself onto a standard POLICE-issued belt. I looked from the gun to the general, not sure what to say. "Th-thank you."

The general smiled. "I take it you've had small arms training?" he asked, taking a quick shot at Charles for confirmation.

Charles and I both nodded. Before I had a chance to even try to take the gun out from the box, a whistle blew from the corner of the courtyard just behind a building. The general looked over toward the distance from where the sound came from with a bit of excitement.

"Good. Right on time," he smiled.

From behind the building, a rather big carriage made its way into the yard, led by four horses. There was a small roof, which gave it a royal look. The side doors had the design of the POLICE etched on them. Wide, wooden wheels covered with a layer of rubber spun around and around as the coach came closer and closer. When it was close enough, the driver pulled back on the reins that connected all the horses together, and it stopped in front of us. The horses never made a sound out of protest or otherwise. They stood, majestic and calm, waiting for their next order. I can only guess at the training those animals had received. The driver, in standard POLICE uniform, climbed down from his seat in order to help with the loading of the baggage and to aid everyone onto the vehicle. He reached down to the door constructed into the side and pulled on a handle that was buried deep in the refineries that adorned the carriage. A drawer that was modified as a stepping platform materialized.

I stared hard at the majestic contraption in front of me. "Where were you hiding this thing?" I asked the general, giving the carriage a general wave.

The general turned and gave me a knowing wink just before stepping up onto the pulled-out step. The general entered the carriage first, of course. Charles and I followed him. The other first sergeants followed after that. The driver took the pieces of luggage from the ground and placed them on the back of the carriage as we got ourselves comfortable inside.

The carriage interior was nothing glamorous, but it was the first one I had ever been in, so it was exciting for me. Plush seats made of some sort of soft fabric greeted us inside. There were thick curtains drawn back that could cover the windows surrounding the carriage. I positioned myself beside the general, whereas Charles and the other two future sergeant majors sat opposite us. Inside, off to the side, sat a bucket with some ice and a single bottle of wine chilling. A box of cigars sat beside the wine.

"My contributions to the trip. The best of what's left of my stock," Charles pointed out proudly to the others.

One of the other officers opened up the box and started to pass around the cigars, gladly taking one for himself before moving them along. The second officer gave Charles a curious glance at the fineries that he was giving up so freely. Charles saw this and smiled.

"You didn't think I was going to leave them behind for the others, did you?" he joked.

I leaned out the window and waved H. J. over to the hulking carriage. He walked over to the side where I was hanging out the window and looked up at me. "I guess this is it." I sighed as I stretched out my hand to shake farewell to my fellow officer and friend.

H. J. grabbed hold of my hand and shook it firmly, smiling all the while. "It's not like you're never coming back here. A couple years are nothing. You'll be back running the show in no time."

Before H. J. let go of my hand, he gave me a little tug to pull me closer. "I bet you a case of brandy I'll be a corporal major before you get back," he winked.

The driver, who had made his way back atop his bench, leaned over the side and stared down at the two of us from where he was perched. "We're about to be on our way. Please stand clear."

H. J. nodded and backed away. With a light rap of the reins, the horses pulled on their harnesses and the carriage delicately lurched into motion. I continued to stare out in wonder from the window. The Grounds washed past me like I was watching a flipbook in action. Building after building passed us by as we skillfully weaved between them on our way toward the main double gate.

Out in front of the opened gate were the rest of the sergeant majors and a second coach. The other carriage was a bit smaller but looked identical. Eight of the officers were on powerful-looking horses, all of them layered with simple supplies and a saddle. When we came into view, a good number of the officers quickly clambered into the waiting coach. Our carriage quietly came to a halt just behind the other carriage, and the officers on horseback made their way into position. Three of them rode out in front of the first carriage. Two rode to the space between the carriages, and the remaining three rode to the rear. One officer in particular made his way to our carriage and stood just outside the door.

The general positioned himself so that he was looking out the open window of the door at the sergeant major outside. "Officer, I relinquish control of the Grounds to you until the promotion and return of Officer Thomas Haroldson."

The sergeant major gave the general a snappy salute. "Yes, sir!"

The officer now in charge of the Grounds stepped back away from the parade of horses and carriages and stood off to the side to watch us leave. The remaining four officers went to either side of both carriages and leapt up onto a small ledge on the outside of them, perfectly designed for a single person to stand on as it traveled along. Their hands gripped onto a metallic handle for added support and security, so they didn't fall off at the first bump in the road.

The general gave a final look around to see if everything was in order and then gave the head sergeant major a wave from outside the window. The sergeant major, seeing the signal, gave the horse he was on a little nudge to get moving. "Officers. Forward."

The parade of sergeant majors and the carriages rolled forward at a simple pace, being careful to maneuver through the metallic gate and the rows of obstacles that were in the way just outside the Grounds. The sergeant major in charge of the Grounds, once everyone was clear and past the gate, moved from his position at the side and started to push against the open gateway.

The gate clanked in the distance behind us.

As we rolled through the town, I noticed something strange. Perhaps it was the view from the carriage. I don't know. When the parade went through the streets, everyone who was there before—the people who had been on the street before us—left. No, *left* was a bad choice of words. They fled. First, I assumed it was to get out of the way of the horses and the carriages, so they wouldn't be run over. But when they looked at the huge parade from the safety of wherever they managed to clamber to, I could see on their faces why they had run: fear.

Once we got to the edge of the town, the carriage started to slow significantly. One of the sergeant majors who was leading the two carriages rode by and maneuvered his horse beside us, matching our speed. Once we came to a stop, the sergeant major gave a wide swooping motion and dismounted, being careful to keep his horse under control. He passed off the reins that he was still holding onto to one of the other sergeant majors and walked straight for the door. The general opened the door for the sergeant major.

"Are we far enough outside the town?" he asked the officer outside.

The sergeant major gave a quick nod. "Should be far enough, sir."

The general, leaning back into the little room, looked at the three first sergeants who sat across from him. "Well, Gentlemen. I believe that this is your stop."

Charles, along with Stockgran and Van der Hoit, looked at the sergeant major waiting outside with unsure eyes. Stockgran, the bravest of the three, cleared his throat as he tried to muster up the strength to ask what the other two were obviously thinking. "Um ... sir? I thought we were coming with you?"

The general smiled. "You are. You are. But, like I've told each of you, your training will start up on the trip back. That means now."

Stockgran looked outside the carriage at the waiting sergeant major, then back to his finely pressed and adorned uniform. "Shouldn't we change out of our dress uniforms, sir?"

The sergeant major took a single step forward toward the carriage, making sure to stay out of the way of the door so they three could exit. "You're holding up the procession, Officers. Exit the carriage now."

With a disgruntled grunt, Van der Hoit was the first to leave, quickly followed by an unsure Charles and Stockgran. The three left the confines of the carriage and stood out in front of the sergeant major at attention. The sergeant major, looking back into the carriage, gave the general a quick nod and closed the door behind him. Turning on his heel to address the officers in front of him, the sergeant major straightened up to give out his orders.

"Since it's my duty to get you three up to where you need to be physically for your future position, I will expect the same dedication, if not more, then what you deemed necessary from all those officers who have trained under your control. Is that understood?"

The three of them, in true POLICE fashion, barked back their response. "Yes, sir!"

"Good," the sergeant major nodded. "The three of you will be leading the party, but we will be setting the pace. Get out in front."

Charles, giving the other two a quick glance out of the corner of his eye, raised his hand to get the sergeant major's attention. "You want us to *march* all the way to Hauptstadt?"

The sergeant major reached out his hand to the officer who was holding onto his horse and took back the reins. Hooking his boot into the hanging foothold, he gave a little hop to give himself enough momentum to swing back onto the patient beast. Giving himself a small jostle to get himself comfortable in the saddle, he gave the horse a soft nudge to start moving. The horse, quick to obey, clopped over to where the three still stood.

"Oh no, I don't expect you to march," the sergeant major answered Charles from on top of his horse. "I expect you to run."

CHAPTER 34

The parade traveled nonstop from morning until early afternoon, when we stopped to let the horses rest and have a quick bite to eat. Shortly afterward, we were back on the road. I never got a chance to see Charles and the others after they sprinted up toward the front of the caravan at the start of the trek, the sergeant major on horseback right behind them. With no one else inside the carriage, the general and I talked up a storm, taking full advantage of the cigars and wine that Charles was so kind to leave for us.

"I have to be truthful with you. The man you replaced wasn't sick. I sent him on ahead, so he could scout for any possible trouble during this trip."

I took a long drag on the finely crafted cigar that I had between my teeth as I listened to the general relay his battle plan. Confused, I leaned forward to address the man. "But, sir, the Rebells' forces are all but disbanded in this part. You pointed that out yourself a couple days ago. What trouble are you expecting?"

The general looked at me a little disappointed, as if I should have seen this a mile away. "When someone is at their weakest, that's when you should watch them the closest. That's when they will try something daring and foolish. I received a report recently that the Rebells in this area have concentrated their forces—rather, those who remain active from the meeting. The Rebells' influence also goes farther than just this one area, and there's no doubt that they sent word of what happened at the meeting across the country and have requested reinforcements. This leads me to believe that there is something in the mix. Not to mention, Duncan escaped capture. That man, by himself, is reason alone to be extra careful. I know how that man thinks. With him on the loose collecting all of the strays, the Rebells should be considerable trouble—if not now, then soon."

That's twice that the general mentioned some sort of understanding of how Duncan thinks. "Sir," I thought for a second to properly word my inquiry, "how is it that you know Duncan? I mean, I know that he has attempted to assassinate you on multiple times, you've said so yourself, but I get the impression that there's more to it."

The general sat there opposite me, his glass of wine resting against his knee. He turned his attention to the countryside that wafted past the window, staring off at the early signs of spring found amongst the trees. He gave a heartfelt sigh. "It's—"

"Complicated. I know, sir," I finished his sentence for him, remembering what he said to me the last time I'd asked about his past relationship with Duncan.

The general shot me a glance out from the corner of his eye; a sly gleam glinted from it. "And what do you know of this man?"

I put the cigar inside a simple tray by the box of cigars, being careful so it wouldn't roll out at the slightest bump and letting it rest against the ashes that it held. Thoughts of my time with Duncan at William's house ran through my mind: my first meeting with the man, brief encounters I had, and the last time I saw him. Then, my thoughts fell back on more pressing matters: how he treated me every time I was in his presence, how he viewed me as a threat and a spy, and how he deserted everyone at the meeting in order to finalize his escape. My jaw started to twinge at the very image of it.

"I know that he's very determined. Pigheaded, even. Once he makes up his mind, there's nothing that will dissuade him. And that he's willing to do anything to achieve his goal, including leaving his most dear friends and comrades to escape."

The general slowly turned his head from the window toward me, a rather surprised and impressed expression on his face. "Looks like I'm not the only one who has come face-to-face with this man."

I looked down at the floor of the carriage, the hot images of what Duncan had done still fresh inside my mind. "I was there at the meeting, if you recall. I listened to his speech, I saw his face, and I bore witness to his lack of action against the slaughter of Rebells at the POLICE's hand."

The general nodded. "True. That you did. So you have a better understanding than most as to what we're up against."

I looked up from the floor slightly and stared upward so that I could see the general just past my brow. "But the more that I know about my enemy, the better I would be able to protect you. I'd be able to anticipate his actions, as you have. How am I supposed to protect you by going off of the little information I have been able to observe, sir?"

The general puffed a smirk across his face. "Fair enough, then. But what I'm about to say will not go past these walls, am I clear on that note? I don't like others knowing about this little part of my life."

"Yes, sir."

The general gave off a quick toss of his head as he looked through the maze of his memory. "Ahhh … okay. I'm going to need to backtrack a bit in order to properly explain Duncan. You remember what I told you beside the fountain, about how the POLICE was formed …"

~

"I didn't enter the story until a good twenty plus years after the end of the war. Duncan came much later than that. I was born into my position. Rather, there was no option for me other than to become the general of the POLICE. That was my sole purpose for being born. My father, now in his early fifties, knew that he would need to retire from his position soon and that if the POLICE were to continue on, he would need a son. The first child born to my father was a daughter. Yeah, I have an older sister.

My dad was happy to have a daughter, don't get me wrong, but he needed a son to lead the POLICE. Thus ... ta da—here I am.

"My training began as soon as I was able to crawl. The POLICE doctrine was drilled into me from day one. I lived and breathed the ways of the POLICE during my younger days. Never had time for anything else. My education came first—always. I was given private tutors, personal trainers—anything and everything that contributed to my preparation and advancement to the ultimate goal. I guess you could say that I never had what you would consider a natural childhood.

"Did you know that I didn't really even want to lead the POLICE at first? Yeah, no kidding. I never really took my training that seriously, much to my father's frustration. I actually wanted to become a painter. When I was given some free time, I would lose myself in some sort of doodle or drawing, using whatever I could find at the time. Charcoal sketches on the back of reports, crayon designs on loose papers, water paints of landscapes—whatever I could imagine at the time with whatever supplies I could use. My father eventually found out about my desires and quickly put a stop to that nonsense.

"Eventually, I had learned all that I could from my old man and his closest advisors. It was now time to send me off to the rest of the world to learn from other experts of their fields. My father sent word to all of these strange people, stating that I would come looking for them and that they were to become my new educators. My first stop was to Shensheng de Deng, where I learned all about a rather unique form of hand-to-hand combat. Next, to Pollice di Efesto for sword training under the great Alessandro. I went all over the place, learning all sorts of unique styles and techniques to aid me in my future position. Eventually, I was sent to La Tower, where I met up with this older gentleman named Marceau who was going to teach me about urban tactics: sabotage, street fighting, interrogation, gang mentality, bomb construction, the ability to travel the streets without being noticed—those sorts of things.

"The first unofficial assignment he gave me was to actually find him. He wasn't the type of person who had a regular storefront and advertised his talent. No, if you wanted to learn from him, you had to find him first.

That way, he would gauge what he still had to teach you. I asked around, did some general recon of the area; all I had to go off of was a name and a quick description. When I finally found him, though, he was reluctant to make me his pupil. Said that he let me find him, and that was only because of who my father was.

"Marceau was already in the midst of teaching this other young guy too. Tall, strong, smart—incredibly smart. He'd found Marceau about two weeks prior to me showing up. While I was being trained under Marceau because of my father's influence, this other young guy became a pupil the old fashioned way: he paid Marceau. This young man had a mind for tactics like I'd never seen before. He was always one step ahead of me, no matter what I tried. He called himself Duncan.

"That was lesson number two—to come up with a new name. Duncan was not the kid's real name, but a name that he had come up with. As Marceau put it, 'the purpose of deception is to allow your enemy to think they have weight over you, when in truth it is you who holds power. The most powerful tool in this endeavor is your name. Create one of stealth and espionage to hide your real one.' I chose the name Linden.

"As Duncan and I trained under Marceau, we started up this unspoken competition between the two of us. It was a game that we were locked into. When we were given an assignment, we would work feverishly to see who would win the round. No one was actually keeping score, of course, and there was no true prize at the end, but that didn't stop us. It was a matter of pride. Sometimes Duncan would arrive at the goal first; sometimes I would win. I almost imagined that this was what it was like to play with someone. When we weren't beating heads in some heated training assignment, the two of us would terrorize the town in some mock contest. We made real names for ourselves.

"Toward the end, the game changed. I had met this girl at a local café. She was gorgeous. We really hit it off. I would come and meet with her every second day or so, and the two of us would sit there and talk—among other things. When it came time for proper introductions, I told her my real name. I figured that since she wasn't a part of the training regime, what would be the harm of it? I only ended up scaring her off. Only then did

Marceau's second lesson hit home. Apparently, my name held a lot more
weight than I first thought—my father being in charge of the POLICE
and all.

"That was the start of the end for me.

"Duncan soon managed to find out who I actually was. That's when
things really changed between us. Apparently, Duncan's father and my
father were thinking along the same path, and he sent his son to Marceau
to further his training to prepare him for his future career. Actually, it
was more of a final trial preparation to see if he was capable of leading
the Rebells after his father was gone. Once his training was finished,
Duncan was supposed to take what he had learned and try to kill my
father. Duncan, now that he knew who I really was, decided instead to
make me his first official target. Of course, I didn't find all this out until
much, much later.

"So, there we were, the future leader of the POLICE and the future
leader of the Rebells—sitting mere feet away from each other for close to a
year. Finally, we were given our final assignment: capture the flag. Each of
us had a base of operations on either side of the town. Our own pickings
for location. It was up to us to manage defenses and whatnot. The goal,
of course, was to take the opponent's flag by destroying the base with a
single timed charge we had to make prior to the start. The trick, however,
was that we could only rely on ourselves—no outside help, and no other
weapons or tools to aid us. If you lost or damaged your timed charge, then
that was it. You lost.

"During our last assignment, when Duncan thought he had an
opportunity to strike, he took it. His father had given him a hunter's
knife, which he used to try to assassinate me. He almost succeeded, too.
He somehow managed to find out what building I'd chosen for my base.
Don't know how he figured it out. Maybe he followed me one day. When
I entered my base, he was there. Duncan jumped me without a word, blade
out. Missed my heart by an inch, maybe less. Got my lung, though. As I
lay there, choking on my own blood, he took back his knife and left me
for dead. It was sheer luck that an older woman happened to pass by after
Duncan left and saw me. She saved my life, going for help like she did.

"That's what sealed the deal for me. Ya know how I said I wanted to become a painter? Well, after that brush with death, I realized what type of a threat the Rebells were and what my role was in this world. In a way, it's because of Duncan that I am who I am now and where I am today. Strange, eh?

"Anyway, Duncan and I eventually became the people in charge, and we've been fighting each other ever since."

~

There came a light rap from the roof of the carriage, which brought the general out from his tale. We both stared up at the sound. The general scooted along the cushioned seats so he was able to stick his head out one of the windows to see what it was. The driver called out from his position at the front, "The other majors are wondering if you would like to stop for dinner, sir."

"Fine then. Let's stop for a moment and give the horses a chance to rest up," the general responded and returned back into the carriage. The driver could be heard calling out to the horses for them to slow, and the carriage crawled to an eventual stop. A general commotion started to grow from outside the carriage, where the other majors were starting to disembark from their horses and the sides of the carriages to help secure the area. The general, once the carriage was at a full stop, reached out toward the door, opened it, and left the security of the roaming room. I quickly followed.

There was a flood of movement around the area. Three or four of the sergeant majors were gathering the horses toward a small pond to allow them to drink. The general waved four majors to each corner of our caravan to stand guard as we stopped, and they quickly ran off toward their positions. The driver was busy searching the crates of supplies atop the carriage to find our dinner, while the driver on the carriage ahead of us was pulling off rolls of fabric from his collection of supplies for us to sit on.

Charles soon joined the general and me by the carriage. Sweat trickled down his face unchallenged.

"Getting quite the exercise, First Sergeant?" the general teased.

Charles smiled in response. "I guess, over the last little while, I've had one too many cigars behind my desk and not enough exercise with the other officers," Charles wheezed.

The driver called out to me and handed down a basket of food. One of the sergeant majors walked over to where we were all standing, a blanket taken from the carriage ahead of us under his arm. With a flick of his arms, the roll became a flying, flat border of cotton that slowly descended onto the grassy ground. Charles collapsed onto the blanket as soon as it hit the ground, his entire body covering one full side of the fabric. Everyone had a good laugh at the display.

The other first sergeants were not doing any better. Stockgran plopped himself against one of the wheels of the carriages, using it as a back brace. The glasses that once covered his face when I first met him were long gone. His jacket, once pressed and ordered, was folded under his arm. Darkened patches of fabric showed off collections of perspiration from his run. Van der Hoit was not showing off any better, bent over and clutching his knees in an attempt to catch his breath.

Once everyone was sitting, or lying down in Charles's case, I handed out the food from inside the basket.

"So, Charles," I asked, trying to start up a conversation, "how's your first day of training?"

"Taxing," Charles answered, while stretching out some of his sore muscles.

"Have you figured out which of the seven lessons you're supposed to learn today?" the general asked Charles.

He shook his head, which took a little more effort than it should have. I gave the general an inquiring glance.

The general explained. "The first sergeants, in order to become sergeant majors, must first pass seven tests. Today, with all the marching and endurance and extra work that we're giving them, they're to learn about loyalty."

Charles looked at the general like he was talking nonsense. In a way, so did I.

"But, sir," I asked the general, "how does all this reemphasize loyalty?

All they're doing is being thrown into hard labor. They're being treated like first-year recruits—"

The general lowered his head, giving me another one of his you-should-know-better looks. I stopped midsentence before I embarrassed myself further. "Or have I just answered my own question?"

Charles rolled onto his back and stared at the sky. "How much more loyalty will I have to learn?"

The general smiled at Charles. "Ask the head major in charge of your training. You're under his command."

Charles moaned and rolled onto his side, facing away from us. "He hates me. I'll never finish with him on my back."

I laughed at Charles. "How do you think the recruits felt with you in their face during their training? You made them go through hell and back just to make sure that they were capable of taking responsibility. If they failed, and I'm quoting you here, 'You were just wasting your time trying to join the POLICE.' You should know that, Charles. I'm ashamed of you," I teased.

Charles turned to look at me. "You're enjoying this, aren't you?"

I smiled. "Immensely. Every wheeze and gasp of air. Don't forget, you pushed me harder than the rest of the SITs, and then you pushed me harder than the other officers I was of equal rank to. They're just doing the same to you in order to turn you into a major officer."

Charles flopped back onto his back. "But when I was doing it to you … I was on the giving side."

∽

The stones that I managed to find throughout the area made a nice ringed border around the small fire that crackled and danced in front of me. We all got comfortable for the night. The general ordered the two carriages off the road toward nightfall, deciding that it was better to secure a spot for the night than to risk traveling on. The drivers were put in charge of securing and caring for the horses, while the sergeant majors went about to secure the area and start setting up camp with the help of the first sergeants. Once camp was set, a routine was organized as to who would be on watch while the rest of us started picking out spots for ourselves. I chose a place close to the general, just in case.

The general was sitting in front of his fire pit, leaning up against his bedroll, flipping through a book of some sort. I couldn't see what the title was. Charles and the other first sergeants were sitting together in front of a small, glinting fire pit a few makeshift bunks over. Most of the sergeant majors were either finishing up their spots or wandering around the area, marking off the patrol round that they would be taking during the night.

"Your fire is too high," came a deep voice from behind me.

I glanced up to see the head sergeant major in charge of training Charles and the others standing behind me. He had two bowls in his hands; steam rose happily from the hidden contents within. He offered one of the bowls to me, being careful not to spill anything as he passed it down to where I sat. I reached up and gladly took the metallic bowl from the man, nodding my appreciation for dinner. Inside the bowl was a mixture of meats, potato, carrots, onion, celery, and some sort of bean broth. The smell that wafted up from the bowl was intoxicating. After taking a spoonful of the meaty mixture, I could detect a hint of rum in the concoction as well.

The major, with a tired grunt, eased himself down onto the ground in front my fire and joined me as I ate. The officer, clearly past his prime but far from out of shape, looked like he had seen quite a few battles in his years. His hair was leaning more toward gray than brown, but he still held onto his strength and demeanor. He nodded toward my fire, which was burning brightly in front of the two of us.

"You made your fire too strong. Right now, there's too much new fuel in there, which is why it's giving off too much light. It's giving away our position. You need to balance the fuel between giving off heat and light. It has to burn out a bit before you add anything else, and when you do, only one log."

I nodded to the man. "Yes, sir. Thank you, sir."

The major took another spoonful of the hash in his bowl, slurping up the remaining juice that lingered on the spoon. "So," he smiled, "you're the super soldier I've been hearing about for the past few days."

I was about to take another bite of food when I stopped my spoon midscoop. "Pardon?"

The major gave a general toss with his spoon to the rest of the party. "It's all anyone's been talking about. The youngest man to ever become a sergeant in POLICE history. Hell, you're eventually gonna be the youngest officer in charge of a Grounds. That's gotta say something about your abilities."

I stirred the meat combo with my spoon slowly. "Thank you, sir."

The major continued on, giving the general's direction a quick nod. "And let's not forget having the general pick you out to be his personal guard on this little trip. He's taken a real shine to ya, putting you under his wing like that."

I gave the general a glance to see if he heard the major talking. He was locked in his reading, oblivious to the world and the conversations around him. I returned my attention back to the major. "It is indeed a great honor to serve the general."

The major leaned forward at that point, almost meeting me nose to nose. His eyes gripped a hold of my own. I was unable to look away, both from surprise at the sudden movement and the intensity of the major's mesmerizing gaze. His voice was quiet and deep, like a low growl from a wild animal.

"Which is why I'm here to remind you that this isn't some sort of pleasure cruise you're on. You're here to make sure that the general makes it to Hauptstadt without as much as a mosquito bite. If anything happens otherwise, I will be very, *very* upset."

The major leaned back and casually returned to eating his dinner, as if his sudden, stern warning was nothing more than two friends telling a dirty joke to one another. The man leaned back and set his hand on the ground in order to push off and stand once more. Stuffing another spoonful of the meal into his mouth, he nodded toward the fire in front of me.

"Wait another hour before feeding your fire," he muffled through full cheeks before he wandered away to rejoin the other sergeant majors.

I sat alone for a moment, staring off into the crackling fire, unable to breathe. The intensity of the major's warning was still fresh in front of my eyes.

The general's voice called out to me from where he was sitting. "You have to excuse the sergeant major. He's just reestablishing himself as the alpha male of the pack."

I glanced over to the general, who had briefly stopped reading his book and was now sitting and poking at the small fire to stoke it.

"I'm sorry?" I asked.

The general came over and sat down beside my fire. His thumb was carefully nudged inside the book he was reading, marking off which passage he left off on. "He sees you as a threat to his authority. Take no mind of him, but I wouldn't go out of my way to spend any time by him for the rest of the trip," the general smiled, looking over at the sergeant majors sitting and joking around their bonfire.

"How long will Charles have to be trained before he's a sergeant major?" I asked the general, staring out at the big man who had just a few moments ago threatened my very existence. I suddenly felt really bad for Charles for having to put up with him the entire trip.

The general thought for a second, the shadows from the fire playing with the lines on his face. "He has six more lessons to go through: will, strength, knowledge, courage, control, and leadership. As to how long that will be, I guess it will take as long as it takes."

I nodded. "How long have we to go until we're at the next town?"

"Less than a day, I think," he replied, looking up from the fire, a raised eyebrow on his face.

I nodded. We sat in silence for a while. I stirred the spoon inside the meal I was holding without thinking, the mush of meats and veggies creating a small vortex inside the broth. The general sighed a deep sigh, took out a ribbon from his breast pocket and carefully laid it down between the pages that were being pushed apart by this thumb. Once he marked where he had stopped reading, he closed the book and put it off to the side.

"Want to talk?" he asked casually.

I awoke from my haze and looked toward the general. "What?"

He just sat, staring at me. "There's something on your mind that's disturbing you. What is it?"

I put off his question, but he insisted on knowing. Finally, I gave in. "I was thinking about my old gir ... Dawn. I was thinking of how one of the last memories I have of her was inside a big open field, which had a few trees in it—just like the one we're in. This place reminds me of her."

The general put his hand on my shoulder, his touch calm. "You have to stop punishing yourself. It wasn't your fault that she died."

The general sat for a second, staring off into the fire to aid him in collecting his thoughts. With a sigh, he returned to me and spoke. "Between our talks and reading your file, Tom, I like to think I've learned a lot about you. Not that many people have had to live through the things that you've had to. Your family died early in your life, your girlfriend was killed, her family mistakenly taken away—now lost—your best friend murdered while trying to protect you, and *he* lost someone dear to him. Your life is a collection of death. Most people would have collapsed from the pressure by now. Not you, though. You've taken everything that life has thrown at you and not only surpassed all expectations, but you ... you've blown them out of the water. That's what's impressed me the most about you, Tom. Your ability to take tragedy and turn it into virtue."

He bent toward me. "Tom, can I give you some advice? Leave the past in its place. That's the only way to survive in this world. The past is done. Look toward the future. Move on to bigger and better things."

I looked toward the darkened road off in the distance. "The future isn't what it used to be."

"Tom, I'm serious! If something doesn't work—an idea, for example— you try to fix it so it is possible to work. For example, the world was in turmoil, so my father fixed it. It was rough going for a while, but he fixed it for the better. You have to get rid of your fixation on the past. Work toward the future, Tom. Work at making your life better than what it is now."

"Thank you, sir." I smiled.

He gave me a sturdy slap on the back and picked back up his book. "We wake at sunrise, so you better get some rest."

CHAPTER 35

I SAT SILENTLY ON A SIMPLE wooden chair. Everything was pitch black around me, and yet I could see perfectly. I was wearing my POLICE uniform, sergeant rank on my shoulder. I sat there alone in the darkness. There was nothing to indicate where I was. I couldn't even tell if there was an actual ground, the darkness encompassed everything. As I sat there, in the darkness, I started to think about my friends, family, and everyone who had made a great impact on my life. I envisioned them all standing in front of me, staring back at me.

They all started to appear to me in the murky blackness as I had pictured them: Father in his work clothes, Mother looking deathly pale from the disease, my sister holding onto that little rag doll she always had with her, Dawn being the vision she always was, H. J. smiling and holding onto a list of contents from the crates we had categorized so long ago, Sherry in her apron that she always wore, Charles proudly displaying a sergeant major rank, Duncan with his knife gleaming from some unseen light, John and Lydia, William, and the general. They all stood in front of me in a row, staring and waiting for me to do something.

I got up and walked toward them. I looked the group up and down, as I would if I were inspecting a group of officers. I stood in the middle of the line, five paces from everyone. I focused on my father's face.

"You died," I told him.

The image of my father started to fade. Soon, he was nothing but an outline showing off his former shape, and then he was gone. Next, I focused on my mother and my sister. "You two died as well."

They vanished, just as my father had. I turned toward John and Lydia. They were holding hands, staring back at me. Lydia was in her work clothes, her hair tied back with a bandana. John had that stupid smirk on his face, as if he knew what was going on but wasn't going to tell me anything. I looked at the two of them—they were so happy.

"I miss you two," I softly spoke to them.

As if on cue, they reached out to try to hug me as one. As they stretched out their arms to take me into their embrace, they started to fade off into the darkness. By the time their hands made contact with my own, they were gone.

I focused on Dawn for a long time. She was dressed in the clothes that she'd worn to the meeting. She stared back at me, a huge smile on her lips. She was smiling because of the warmth of the sun that had glowed that day under the tree where we had lunch. I could almost hear the birds in the background. A small breeze brushed her bangs out of her eyes. I closed my eyes and bit my bottom lip.

"You're dead," I whispered.

When I opened my eyes, she was gone—forever.

Left standing in front of me were H. J., Charles, Sherry, William, Duncan, and the general. I looked at the general. "You will leave on your tour, once we reach Hauptstadt."

He nodded low toward me and walked off to the right. As he wandered, the darkness seemed to envelop him, but he was still barely visible. Once he was out of view, I focused onto Charles.

"You will stay in Hauptstadt to continue your position when I return home."

Charles nodded at me and walked over to where the general had disappeared. I focused on H. J., trying to suppress a smile.

"You. I'm not going to be free of you for quite some time."

H. J. nodded and walked off to the left, only he stopped quite a bit sooner than the other two. From where H. J. stopped, I could see him quite clearly. He turned around and again faced toward me, waiting for some sort of direction as to what to do next. Sherry and William stood together, arms linked around each other. I looked at the two, despair deeply set in my heart at seeing them again.

"I'm sorry about what happened to Dawn. I know you blame me, and I'm not surprised you never want to see me again. I just hope that, someday you can forgive me."

William and Sherry nodded toward me and wandered off into the darkness, their silhouettes the only thing remaining to let me know of their presence. I looked back at the row once brimming with familiar faces. Now, only one person was left in the row—Duncan.

Duncan stood by himself in front of me. He was wearing a uniform that I had never seen him wear before. Other than its odd color scheme, it was the same as the POLICE's uniform in every way. Medals shone on his chest. His knife hung loosely on his belt, yet it was unsheathed. I walked toward him and stood two paces away. He stared hard at me, waiting for his order.

"I don't know about you," I told him.

He smirked at me. "I'm not surprised."

His voice was hollow and metallic, as if he were speaking to me through an empty can. I stood in front of him, unmoving, my eyebrows scrunched in thought.

"So, Duncan, what are you? My past? My present? My future?"

"Haven't you guessed that one already?"

I shook my head. He looked discouraged. "No, I suppose you won't know until you see me again. I know one thing, though—I won't be happy to see you."

"Why's that?" I asked him.

Duncan began to pace around where I stood, encircling me as if he were interrogating me. "Ah, come on. Think, Tom! The last time I saw you the POLICE were bursting into my meeting and killing all the Rebells. Before then, you turned your back on everything that William had given you. You even took his daughter away from him. Do you honestly think the next time I see you that there would be hugs and kisses? That there would be a single chance of me believing anything you say, let alone trusting you?"

I pointed a finger at him. "I told you not to go through with the meeting, but you insisted! Now, because of that damn thing, Dawn's dead! You should've known better!"

He stopped pacing and glared at me. "True, the Rebells have suffered a great shortage in members around here because of my ... tactics. But it was the POLICE who shed the blood. So, the next time I appear to you, I'll be attacking with a vengeance. You can be sure of that."

With Duncan frozen in place, I started to pace around him. My mind was racing with possible scenarios that he would or could implement. I started to piece together the evidence in front of me: the lack of Rebell traffic, Duncan not making a single appearance anywhere since the meeting, and then it hit me.

"You're still going to attack the tour, aren't you?" I asked.

He turned so that he was always facing me as I continued to walk around him. "You know me well enough to know that I would, even if it's just by myself. I have tried over and over again to bring back the past ideals. Why not? Your general has made our lives a living hell! Your life hasn't gone all too smoothly either, has it? And do you know whose fault it is? Think back! Just remember ... the POLICE called your father away, and the next time you saw him he had the Fallout Plague. Soon, both your sister and mother had it. Did you ever ask yourself why your father got the disease? Where he got it? How he got it? Do you remember how they writhed in pain as their insides liquefied? Just how many days did they try to hold on?"

The image of Duncan started to grow in size as I wandered around him. First, he was only a head higher, but the more he talked, the taller he grew.

"But that was years ago, wasn't it?" he continued. "Easy to let slip from your mind. Only, your parents and sister weren't the only ones to be taken away. How many have been taken away in the past year? Two years? Three? You've lost Dawn, William, Sherry, Lydia, and John to those butchers! They've destroyed your entire life, Tom! Yet, you honor them by wearing their uniform! You're even protecting the main threat to your happiness—the general!"

The giant Duncan jabbed a finger out toward the area where the general had wandered away to. A huge beam of light shot out from his pointed finger, blasting the area with a white-hot glare. The shaft of light cut through the sea of darkness leading directly to where the general stood. Under the illuminated cone, the general started to sizzle and twitch.

"*Stop this!*" I screamed out.

Duncan turned toward me. As he twisted around, he shrank back down to normal size. The light that escaped from his finger doused back into the darkness.

Duncan's face turned hopeful suddenly, his hands grasping my shoulders in a vice-tight embrace. "Help me, Tom."

I looked toward my feet. "I can't. I don't even know where you are."

Duncan slowly let go of me. We stood in front of each other for a moment or two silently, him staring at me; me staring at my feet in shame. Slowly, he turned and started to walk away into the darkness. As he wandered away, the dark shade that surrounded us started to encompass him.

"You know this lifestyle can't survive. Help me bring back the old ways, Tom...."

Duncan was almost completely invisible from where he stood. He turned back toward me. "... or die with its defeat."

$$\sim$$

I awoke with a start, my eyes flashing open. The light from the rising sun passed through the leaves of the tree beside me, helping to shadow my sleepy eyes from its bright wake-up call. The camp was bustling with general activity as everyone was quickly packing things in order to get back onto the trip. Stockgran and Van der Hoit were putting material back onto the top of one of the carriages. The sergeant majors were wandering the area in order to mask any clues that we had been there, such as scattering the ashes from the multiple fires and brushing the area with branches they'd ripped off the nearby trees. The general was standing by our carriage and supervising the teardown of the camp.

Charles wandered over to where I lay on the ground, a cup in his hand. "Good morning. Didn't think you were going to wake up in time. I was afraid we might have to leave you here," he smirked.

As I pushed myself up to a sitting position, the thin blanket had that covered me during the night fell into a lump near my legs. Brushing the sleep from my head, I drew my hand across my face to wipe away any dust that had collected. "What time is it?" I asked Charles, blinking my way to some sort of sense of what was going on.

Charles crouched down to my level and handed me the cup he was holding. The strong smell of coffee wafted past my nose, the warmth of the mist that seeped out caressing my face.

"Time for you to get up and start helping out," he warned.

~

We rode on in silence for the rest of the day. The general chose this time to catch up on some of the paperwork that he'd fallen behind on during the past few days. Seeing that the man was busy, I chose to stare off out one of the windows. Hills rolled past us as we continued on our trip. Trees swayed in a light breeze. The occasional person came into view beside the road. They stood unmoving, watching us pass with eyes that could have burnt through the carriage. Some looked on in horror, some in awe, and some in anger. But, no matter how they stared at us, not one looked away. Even far away from us, the continued to watch us go.

We stopped for a quick lunch, the town we were riding toward clearly in view off in the distance. Charles looked content, although he was sweating up a storm. The head major talked privately with the general in order to give his report on the first sergeants' activities and progression for the day. After lunch, we finished the distance to the next town in record speed.

Looks like I'll be sleeping in a bed tonight, I happily thought to myself.

When viewed from a distance, the town looked like any other town. It looked quite a bit smaller than Sicher Himmel—probably only held about six thousand people, maybe seven.

As the caravan came closer to the town, we started to pass through the local farm fields. Row upon row of wheat, corn, or greeneries just starting their growth spurt dotted the landscape. I watched contently as the carriage rolled past, eager to get to some sort of sense of civilization. The general was oblivious to the events outside the window, his nose stuck in a report of some sort. Just another town on the way to Hauptstadt, I guess.

As I looked out the window at the fields, I started to get a rather uneasy feeling about it all. There was something off about it, although I couldn't put my finger on it specifically. I tried to think back to the other farms I had seen, such as the ones that Dawn, John, H. J., and I passed by on our way to the meeting on the outskirts of Sicher Himmel. I closed my eyes to better imagine the scene: the wide, open fields, the farmers working hard on the soil, the smell in the air—and that's when it hit me.

"Sir?" I called out to the general.

"Are we there yet?" he asked.

"I think you should take a look, sir."

The general smiled. "I've seen farms and farmers before, Sergeant. Trust me, I'm not missing anything."

I glanced back at the general. "That's the thing, sir. The farmers are missing."

The general lowered the form that he was going over and took a look out the window on his side of the carriage. Outside there were great big fields, covered with all sorts of trees, bushes, and growing foodstuff. But there were no workers on the fields. There were no working animals either. There was no one on, by, or near the roads. Everything outside the town looked and felt absolutely empty.

The general, staring out the window in my direction, grew serious at the signs. He banged on the roof of the carriage and stuck his head outside to address the driver and sergeant major who was riding on the little platform attached to the carriage.

"Send a rider up ahead to scout. All others will slow and await report," he ordered.

The majors, at hearing the order from the general, removed their weapons from their sides and pulled in closer to the carriages. I unbuttoned the strap that held my revolver inside its holster also, just to be on the safe side. The general became deathly silent and scanned the area around us. The carriage slowed down to a crawl, the horses reacting in protest to the sudden change of pace they were forced to endure.

The entire party was on edge. All eyes were searching the distance for some sign as to why we were on alert. There was no sound made by anyone, neither horse nor human, as we waited for a report back from the major who had ridden on ahead. The driver shooed the animals quietly, desperate to calm them. They could smell the stress that danced around the area. Everyone was on high alert.

A horse's hoof hitting the ground could be heard from the direction of the town; it was coming toward us. I risked a quick glance by sticking my head outside the carriage to see what was going on. The major who had ridden ahead to scout the town was returning at a hard gallop. He rose past everyone else in the party and reined the beast just outside the carriage. Dust and dirt kicked up from the hoofs of the horse, panting deeply from the short sprint. The general again looked outside from where he sat.

"Report," he ordered.

The major looked white from shock. "They're … gone. The entire town … gone! You … you need to see it for yourself, sir."

The general looked back inside the carriage for a moment in order to weigh his options, his brow scrunching together in concern and thought. His eyes squinted as he stared off into nothing. A small vein in his temple pulsed in beat with his heart as he concentrated on what to do. With a nod, he looked out toward the major outside.

"Continue forward in V formation, half speed, and weapons ready. Be prepared for immediate retreat," the general ordered.

The major turned his horse around so he was facing the front of the caravan once more. "Sir!" he responded, kicking the horse forward.

From outside, I could hear the major giving orders to the others. The carriage lurched back into motion once again, but at a much slower pace than before. The majors who were on the platforms on either side of the carriage moved forward a bit so that they were blocking the back windows with their bodies, their arms hooked over the bar that ran across the top to help steady themselves as they aimed their revolvers out toward the landscape. I gave a quick hand gesture toward the general, asking him to go back from the window. He nodded and sank into the seat a bit, removing himself from view. I continued to watch through the window. The town crept toward us, ever so slowly. Still, no one was to be seen.

There were no guards at the entrance to the town. No one came to greet us. Upon seeing this, all majors cocked and readied their weapons. The formation that they had made around the two carriages became more confined on the narrow road within town. The natural V that once consumed the carriages now turned into an arrowhead at the front and back of either vehicle.

The group continued to march through the deserted town. Not a sound echoed through the area, except that which we made. Nothing emerged to see the group pass by. Nothing—except for the occasional cat that peeked its head out from an alley nearby or a bird that flew overhead.

Doors were left wide open in the houses we passed or were removed completely from their hinges. Windows were broken. Shelters were in disarray, destroyed, or burnt to the ground. Objects of all shapes and descriptions were scattered across the road. The city was in ruins.

We continued on toward the center of town where there should have been a rather substantial area to park the carriages and set up some sort of command center while we tried to figure out what had happened here. As the road started to open up for us, the majors on horseback moved back into a V formation around the carriages. The head major, who was at the front of the pack leading us through the town, held up his hand for everyone to stop. Everyone immediately did as they were told.

The wide-open space of the area allowed us to spread out a bit more and take in the eerie presence of the totally deserted town. The head major waved at the other mounted majors to make a secured perimeter within the area. They calmly rode out from their positions around the carriages to the nearby outskirts of the center, giving a wide berth to any building or obstacle that blocked their point of view. The general risked a quick glance from the window he was beside. There was no other sound around us but our unified breathing.

When it looked like the area was secure, the head major dismounted from his horse and started to take a better look around. He first examined to see if there had been any recent foot traffic on the ground and then looked to see if there was any evidence as to how long ago this disappearance happened. The other majors stood their ground, continually scanning the surrounding area with their eagle-sharp eyes.

The general motioned for me to come close. "Check in with the head major. Find out what you can from him and then report back to me."

I nodded and reached for the door. Opening it slightly, the major standing directly outside the carriage slid along the little foothold so that I could open it more and leave the safety of the carriage house. Once I was outside, the major slid back into position to block the doorway. With revolver in hand, I crouched on the ground, giving the area a quick scan for movement. Not seeing anything out of the corners of my eyes, I started to make my way over to where the major was continuing with his investigation.

"What do you think happened to this place?" I asked him in a hushed tone once I stood beside him.

He scanned the area thoughtfully. "It looks like this place was in some type of a massive fight," he pointed out to me, nodding toward a broken barrel on the ground by one of the buildings. On the splintered pieces was dried blood.

His voice was deep with concern. I looked at the still chaos around us. "What should we do?"

"We should go to the POLICE Grounds inside this town. Maybe we can get a few clues to explain all this. If anything, we'll be in a more secure position to act," he said, searching the town uncertainly—like he was waiting for something to jump out at him at any moment.

"I'll tell the general your idea," I whispered to the major and quickly started walking back to the safety of the carriage.

I passed by Charles. He whispered to me as I walked passed him, "I don't like this."

I knocked on the door of the carriage. The door barely opened, but there was just enough room to allow a gun barrel through, which was pointed straight at my head. Seeing that it was me, the general jerked the gun back away from my head, all the while holding up a hand to show he was sorry for the rude greeting. I sat down inside the coach and tried to ease my nerves from the shock of having a gun pointed at me.

The general eased forward. "Well?"

"The head major thinks that the town was in some type of fight. He suggested that we go to the Grounds inside town in order to get a better idea as to what happened here," I explained.

The general nodded. "Do it."

I leaned my head out of the window. The head major was watching from where I had left him. I waved him forward. At seeing the signal, he gave three distinct gestures to the other majors, silently informing them that they were about to go on the move again.

The trip to the Grounds was slow and cautious. All eyes were open and alert. Nerves were very itchy. Everyone was jumping at ghosts and shadows as we made our way through the streets. As soon as we reached the Grounds, everyone inside the tour knew that there was something very wrong with this place. The main gate to the Grounds demanded that some type of guard was to protect it. There was none. There was no evidence of anyone inside the Grounds either. One of the majors left the security of the caravan by dismounting and taking up the little ground there was to the gate itself. He rested his hand against the gate as he tried to search his pockets for some sort of object he could use to try to pick the lock. With the simple force from the major trying to lean up against it, the gate swung open a bit. This made the major have to catch himself and rebalance before he toppled down onto the ground. Everyone in the party gave a unified gasp inward at the sight. The gate was unlocked!

The group entered the Grounds at an even slower pace, guns raised. As we entered the courtyard of the Grounds, the carriage jerked to a stop. The horses cried out in protest to where they were supposed to go. The general and I could hear the driver trying to calm the horses, as well as an occasional breathy curse that came from one of the majors. The general peeped his head out of one side of the carriage. I looked outside the other window.

We stared out onto a giant grave. Bodies on top of bodies were scattered through the courtyard, some partially buried. The occasional fly buzzed around a corpse, trying to better position itself for its feast. Others were sprawled in hastily dug pits. Most of the bodies were wearing POLICE uniforms. Less than a third were not.

I quickly turned away from the sight, my stomach turning from the sight now forever imprinted inside my mind. There were hundreds of them! Thousands! A cold sweat erupted from my pores. My hands started shaking uncontrollably, the metal gun inside my hand shaking along with it. I glanced at the general to see how he was taking the grisly sight. His back was to me. He was still staring out the window, out onto the nightmare that stretched out just inches from us.

"Sir?" I squeaked.

Silence.

"What should we do?" I asked him quietly.

The general, unmoving from his spot, let out a single breath in a hiss.

"Gather all the bodies together. Go through the charts inside the office for roll. Do a sweep of the Grounds for survivors. I want to know who's here, who's missing, and who survived. Get me a count."

~

"One thousand, nine hundred, and fourteen dead, sir," reported one of the majors, a piece of paper in his hand. "Thirteen hundred and sixty-one POLICE officers, including Sergeant Major Grolhaven, whom you sent to scout ahead. Five hundred and twenty townsfolk, thirty-three children. Causes of death are a mixture of bladed weaponry, club, … and gunfire. Based on deterioration of the bodies, I'd say they've only been dead for a few days. Evidence of bodies being moved to the Grounds is apparent. Four hundred and seventy-two officers are unaccounted for. Still no toll on the populace of the town or new information on what happened to them, sir."

The major who took the report gave it to the general, who was sitting on the ground beside the carriage. The general stared at the piece of paper that he held out in front of him.

"What should we do now?" the major asked the general.

The general looked up toward the major. "Find and issue out shovels to everyone. Give the higher-ranking officers a proper funeral in accordance to their placement. Burn the bodies of the townsfolk and children. The private- and corporal-ranking officers, as well."

The major paused, not sure that he had heard the order correctly. "Sir? You want us to—"

The general turned on the major sharply, irritation strong inside his voice. "I don't want this place to become a breeding ground for disease. We'll bury whom we can, but we don't have the manpower to bury everyone. I want to be back on the road as soon as humanly possible."

The major nodded solemnly toward the commander in chief. "Yes, sir."

Before the major had a chance to leave, the general reached out to stop the man. "Send one to take stock of the armory. I want everyone to arm themselves with rifles from now on until we reach Hauptstadt."

The general returned his attention back to the list in front of him. The major saluted and walked toward the rest of the majors, who were standing together talking. The general looked over to where I was standing by the carriage and motioned me closer.

I slowly eased myself down and sat beside the general. "Yes, sir?" I asked.

The general looked up from the sheet toward me; a very tired look had managed to crawl its way onto his face. "What a mess, eh?"

I nodded, unsure as to what I could've said that might have changed anything.

The general leaned back against the carriage, his head bouncing off of the wheel that he was propped up against. "What possessed these people to revolt against us?"

"Revolt, sir?"

He waved his hands at the destruction that faced us both. "Take a look around this town. The evidence is right in front of us. All the officers who were reported to be inside this area are killed or missing. There's supposed to be almost nine thousand people inside this town, yet we find a scratch of that number lying around us. No … two scenarios are playing themselves out here.

One, the town rioted over some unknown event and overwhelmed the POLICE, at which point they fled in order to avoid retaliation from the survivors, who are now searching the area for them. The other possible scenario is that this was carefully planned out. They had help from the missing POLICE officers when they stormed the Grounds and then ransacked their homes for supplies before they abandoned the area—going who-knows where. But why? What's the reason?"

The general stood up and stretched his back. He looked out at the majors hard at work piling the bodies on top of each other in the center of the Grounds, getting ready for the bonfire. Some of the majors had started digging graves for the dead officers, tearing into the ground in order to quickly get their assignment done.

The general shook his head. "Such a waste!"

He took off his jacket and put in inside the carriage, laying it down flat so that it wouldn't get creased. Rolling up the sleeves on his shirt, showing off the substantial muscle structure of his arms, he then walked over to where some of the majors were digging graves and started helping them with their chore. I got up and was about to start helping as well when Charles walked up to me.

"How are you holding up?" he asked.

I turned to Charles. "I'm okay, I guess. The general is taking this kind of hard. He blames himself for this."

Charles looked over to where the general was digging inside the courtyard. "Why?"

"The general thinks that this was due to a revolt."

Charles leaned up against the carriage. "A revolt? Against the POLICE? What would possess this town to go up against the POLICE?"

I stared at the increasing pile of bodies five of the majors were working with.

"I don't know," I said. "The general seems to think that they did this either deliberately or at the spur of the moment. Needless to say, something or someone sure spurred the townsfolk into action."

Charles gave a rather long sigh at the thought of it all. Eventually, he placed a hand on my shoulder and led me toward the other sergeant majors who were working hard on creating plots for the fallen officers.

"C'mon … let's help out," he suggested.

CHAPTER 36

The fire could have been seen for miles. Flames fled into the open sky, belching up huge plumes of ash and smoke. We all stood around the bonfire of the dead and gave a private prayer to all who had died. The General held a sermon during the night, talking about the past deeds of the Grounds, those who were stationed there, and how their deaths would be avenged.

The funeral pyre burned all through the night. No one got any sleep. The smell of smoke and the burning of flesh were too much for anyone to sleep through. Also, despite how tired everyone was from all the manual labor we had done that day, the general atmosphere of the empty Grounds was too much. No one could relax enough to go to sleep.

When the dawn broke through the clouds, we were ready to continue on. The morning was cold, showing off the slow transitional shift in season. There was no joking, no smiles, nothing like the past morning had brought. Everyone's spirit was focused on last night. We didn't prepare breakfast. I think everyone was content with that. I got the impression that no one wanted to stay inside the town any longer than we had to.

I had just entered the carriage when I caught myself on the door handle. I looked to see what had caught me. It was the ring that I found inside the communications bunker so long ago. I found it the day I'd met H. J. After Dawn's death, I started wearing it. I guess it gave me comfort. I unhooked myself and continued into the carriage. The driver got the horses started, and the carriage jerked into motion. The occasional shift of weight of the carriage was rocking me to sleep. Even the general's eyes started to droop. The events of last night were starting to show on us all.

As we got to the edge of town, I opened the window and looked back toward the Grounds. The faint trickle of smoke sprayed itself against the sky, tarnishing the cherry red sunrise. A bright ball making up the sun could be seen through the smoke, trying to push its rays through its thickness. Slowly, the smoke faded and the sun shone through, lighting the area's cold from the night before with its warmth.

I continued to watch this as we exited the town. I stared down at my hand after a thought. Deciding, I reached over with my other hand and took off the ring. Leaning out the window in order to give myself enough room, I gave the ring a good heave. The golden pebble flew through the sky, glinting in the sunlight, and disappeared somewhere in the dead town. I closed the window.

It wasn't mine anyway.

~

We stopped about two hours after starting out. We were somewhere outside of town up a small hill. The order was given for us to make camp. The majors had no energy to move farther. Breakfast was made for those who wanted to eat. As breakfast went on, the general decided to stay the morning inside the tree-covered area instead of riding on as soon as we were finished. The group agreed on a heavy rotation for guarding the site. That way, everyone would be given a chance to rest and recoup from the traumatic events of the previous night.

The general walked over to the head major, said something to him, and then climbed into the carriage and went to sleep, thus giving me some free time. The head major walked to where all the other majors were standing or sitting and told them what the general told him. There were a few nods. I went over to where Charles was sitting, eating his breakfast. He offered me a seat, which I took.

"How's training?" I asked him.

Charles waved his fork at the head major. "Today, there's not going to be any training for us first sergeants. The head major said so. We all have leave for the morning. After last night, everyone needs one. Of course, you're still expected to be ready for your turn on rounds."

I nodded my head in agreement. Charles returned his attention back to his food, so I looked around the area. Everyone was spread out into little groups. The head major and two others were sitting by a tree playing a game of cards. Four other officers were watching them and giving their advice to the card players. A few officers were stretched out in the grass by the road, sleeping inside the sun. The carriages were off to the side of the road. The drivers were caring for the horses, giving them a brush. Everyone was trying their best to relax and enjoy their time off. All, but one.

I noticed one major, a younger man in comparison to the others, sitting by himself near the edges of the trees that began to line the road on one side. It was the one who had given the general the report in town. He was concentrating on the single dribble of smoke that came from the town off in the distance. I left Charles's side and walked toward him. He didn't notice me, or tried not to.

I looked toward the town. "Depressing, isn't it?" I asked him.

He looked up at me. "I had to bury my brother."

I bent down beside him. "Your brother was there?"

He nodded and looked back toward the spiral of smoke in the sky. "I remember how he wanted to join with me that very day when I signed with the POLICE. He wasn't old enough, so he had to wait. But when he became proper age, he joined and worked hard to make me proud of him. He just turned sergeant a couple months ago. Yvan. That's his … was … his name. He almost blew a gut when he found out that I'd become a sergeant major. We had dinner together the night before I went off to be trained. That was the last time I saw him alive. I was supposed to go see him there, at the Grounds, when we passed through the town. We were going to have dinner and talk about the old—"

He hung his head down onto his chest and started to weep quietly. I rested my hand on his back and stood by as the major mourned for his lost loved one. Soon the major tried to compose himself, brushing his face with the corner of his sleeve.

"Don't you need to check on the general, Sergeant?" he asked. I caught the hint and gave him a quick reassuring pat on the shoulder, leaving him to privately continue his process.

Instead of immediately returning to the carriage where I'd seen the general go, I opted to wander through the area where we were camped. I wanted to be by myself to think for a bit. Before I wandered too far off, I managed to catch the eye of one of the majors. Giving a quick hand gesture, I motioned that I was going to take a look around. He nodded toward me, letting me know that he understood. Best to let them know what I was doing in case anyone need to get hold of me.

Along the edge of the road, trees sprung up out of the ground that covered the entire area. It's as if civilization stopped, and nature preserved itself inside this one spot. A few paces away from the camp, I found a path through the light forest. It was a path that looked like it had not been used for quite some time. Some brush stretched out their branches in order to block my way through the path. They failed.

Birds sang in the distance, warning their bird friends of my intrusion. The smell of pine, fresh leaves covered in dew, and sap flew through the forest. All shades of green were just starting to make their presence known. An overwhelming awe of peace fell over me. All my worries and pangs escaped my imprisoned shoulders. A deep breath, and I was in paradise.

I wandered on the path for some time. I don't know how long, exactly. The occasional shot of the road could be seen through the trees. *At least I know where I'm going*, I thought to myself. Continuing down the path, I was so much as ease that I didn't hear someone sneaking up behind me.

"Hello, nature boy," Charles called out to me.

I spun around to see his smiling face. A spasm of fright shot through me. "Charles! Don't do that!"

Charles wandered to where I was standing. "What did you think of your hike?"

I stood, hands on my hips, staring at the leaf-covered sky. "Peaceful, enjoyable, quiet."

"Come on. I was told to bring you back. We're going to move on in about an hour," Charles told me.

He slapped my shoulder and started walking back down the path from which he came. I followed but at a slower pace. Charles soon went out of view, and I continued my walk in blissful silence with only the birds and the wind for company.

⁓

After taking the much-needed respite, everyone seemed to be in better spirits. All we needed was a half-day break, and we were ready for the trek onward.

"How long is it to the next town?" I asked the general once the carriage was moving again.

The general leaned over to where a small compartment stuck out inside the carriage, opened it, pulled out a folded piece of paper, and closed the compartment. He opened the map and gave me a corner to hold onto. We quickly found the town we had just left and followed the road to the next town on the list. It was estimated to be about three days ahead of us. He folded the map and put it away without saying anything more. I sighed inwardly. The slow travel toward Hauptstadt was starting to grind on me. How long had I been traveling for now? How must the general feel? He'd been traveling much longer than I had. I stared out the window at the trees as they passed by the carriage.

The carriage bounced along the trail as we wandered our way through the area toward our eventual destination. The general went about trying to busy himself within the coach, working on paperwork or reading from his book. I continued to stare off outside the window at the world as it traveled by me. Boredom quickly took its toll on my sanity. I started to envision myself running alongside the coach, zipping between the trees that we passed, or running through the open fields. I smiled at myself in the open air, running and leaping over the obstacles that managed to creep up.

We continued to travel in silence until it was almost dark. The driver called down from his seat that there wasn't any space that was big enough for the carriages to park, so we were forced to continue traveling. Everyone's concern was now put toward trying to find a nice place to camp. One of the major problems we faced was that the forest that once covered one side of the road now covered both sides with its thick protection.

The moon started to climb in the sky. It was on its way to becoming full, thankfully. Its slight light guided us down the otherwise dark path. The branches made interesting and spooky shadows on the ground and the side of the carriage. One of the majors up ahead of the carriage made a mocking howl of a wolf, which carried its way through the caravan. That eased everyone into a light laughter.

The general was starting to fall asleep inside the carriage. He had grabbed his jacket and was wrapped up in it like a blanket. I was starting to nod off as well. The smooth motion of the carriage's rocking back and forth, the exhausting night before, as well as the lack of entertainment throughout the afternoon's trek added to the deprivation and my determined desire to fall asleep.

There was a call from outside. The carriage suddenly stopped, which jerked us both out of our sleeping stupors. I guessed that they had found a spot to camp. I leaned out one of the windows in order to see what was happening outside. Just ahead of the group of majors who rode out in front of the lead carriage, a single man stood in the middle of the road. He was waving for us to stop.

"Have we found a place to stop?" the general asked me, taking his jacket off of him and sliding his arms into its sleeves.

I turned to face him. "No. A man is standing in the middle of the road."

The general nodded and grew serious. I could easily see what was on the general's mind. 'What is a man doing here, in the middle of nowhere, in the middle of the night?'

After unbuckling the safety strap on my holster, I returned my attention to the events outside. The general reached out and took hold of one of the rifles that was tucked away underneath the seats. He pulled back on the bolt along the side of the rifle, readying himself for anything. A single bullet was heard sliding into the chamber. With a slap, the general knocked down the bolt and rested the weapon in his arms, looking outside cautiously.

I stuck my head back out the window in order to see what was going on. The head major had ridden up to where the man was standing and was talking to him. The man looked about forty, but with the available light and the space between us, it was hard to tell. I could see that he was a farmer by the style of his clothes and the hoe that he carried. On the hoe was a piece of white cloth, limply sagging from the metallic shunt on the top. The man and the head major talked for a while. Bits and pieces of their conversation carried to me on the cool night air, but I couldn't make it out fully.

I leaned out more in order to address the driver. "Can you hear what's going on?"

The driver leaned over toward me, keeping his head out toward the action in front. "It seems that the man escaped the onslaught that occurred at the town just past. He wants a ride into the next town, so he can start a new life. Right now, the sergeant major is grilling him for more details."

I popped my head into the carriage where the general was awaiting news. "Looks like we might get some answers as to what happened at the town after all."

The general, not wanting to remove his hands from the rifle, risked a glance outside to see what state the events were. "How did he make it out here already?" the general mused out loud as he stared off toward the stranger and the sergeant major.

I looked from the window to the general. "Should we take him along?"

The general bit down on the bottom of his lip, churning the scenario over in his mind. Finally, after much deliberation, the general shook his head. "No. Can't risk it. He can stay with us for the night once we find a place to camp. He'll need to be guarded, though—just in case. Unfortunately, once morning breaks, he's on his own."

The general removed himself from the window and sat back into his seat, the rifle resting on his lap. I stuck my head back out the window to see how things had progressed. By the looks of things, the head major wanted nothing to do with the man. His voice was starting to rise to the point that I could understand what he was saying clearly.

The major was trying to explain to the man that he didn't want any more people to look after than he already had and that we were on an important mission that didn't need the complication of civilian problems. He waved the farmer off, yelling at him to stand aside, and turned the horse back toward the group.

What happened next—I won't soon forget.

The farmer reached toward his back for something hidden. All majors toward the front saw this and started waving and pointing—anything to get the head major's attention to the action behind him. The farmer pulled his hand away from his back, a POLICE-issued revolver catching the glint of light that shot out from the lantern on the front carriage. One of the majors tried to race the farmer by unstrapping his own revolver and pulling it out of his holster. The head major had just enough time to turn toward the man in order to see the revolver pointed at him.

The major who had pulled out his revolver fired his gun. Seconds later, the farmer's revolver went off. The head major jerked back violently, jumped backward off of the horse, and landed on the ground with a squishy thump. The farmer violently flinched to the side, jerked forward clutching the side of his chest, and collapsed into the dusty road.

The forest, and everything within it, fell silent. Everyone froze. The lead caravan's driver grabbed and focused a lamp that hung outside the carriage at the head major on the ground. Blood leaked out of his still chest unimpeded.

I turned toward the general, who had heard the gunshots and was gripping the rifle more tightly. "Stay down!" I ordered him.

One of the majors screamed out, "Ambush!"

The forest around us exploded with cries of ferocity and battle. People sprang up from the bushy foliage and raced toward the entrapped caravan. The sergeant majors, well trained for events such as these, immediately took action by grasping their rifles that either hung from their backs or were tucked aside among their possessions within their saddles. The majors who were stationed just outside the carriages yanked upward on their pistols and opened fire into the crowd storming toward them. I pulled up the window and stared out onto the world through a protective seethe of glass, revolver in hand. The forest erupted with people of all classes: merchants, farmers, mine workers, women—all the people normally found inside a community or town.

The Revolt!

The sergeant majors tried to organize themselves and circled the carriages as best they could, all the while shouting and strategically firing into the oncoming wave. The sound of horses whinnying and the majors trying their best to control the massive animals could be heard over the blasts of gunpowder and yells.

The townspeople kept coming. The sergeant majors, despite being grossly outnumbered, were somehow managing to keep the hoard from getting anywhere near the carriages. The front carriage, the one that was used to house all the officers on foot, split open on either side, releasing the sergeant majors hidden within. One managed to make his way on top of the carriage and started to peg off people with his uncanny marksmanship. The general, all the while, dug out the other rifles hidden underneath the seat he was once resting on.

"Damnit!" he swore to himself while he organized the pile in a makeshift order of use for me. "Should've seen this … Knew better … Walked right in …"

One of the majors who guarded the door of the carriage started banging on it desperately, trying to get in. I quickly opened the door and let him in, slamming the door shut behind him and locking it. It was the major who had taken my place guarding the general when I talked to the head major inside the town yesterday.

The general turned his attention to him, locking the bolt into place on the rifle he was holding onto at the time. "What's the situation?" he asked.

The major sat for a second, trying to catch his breath. He rested against

one of the pair of leg rests used to support the seats. "Surrounded....
Driver's dead ... shot.... No way ... to expect something like this. They're
coming from all sides. Not sure the number we're up against. When one
man runs out of the forest, three more are right behind him, and five after
that. All are armed with POLICE weaponry. Mostly clubs and batons ...
few are carrying revolvers. No rifles. Guessing they couldn't get into the
armory back at the Grounds."

While the major sat explaining the events outside to us, the gunshots
from those weapons echoed inside the carriage. One bullet dove through
the window of the door I was closest to, the one I had been looking
through just moments ago. Glass ruptured from the destroyed pane onto
the three of us, scattering everywhere within the carriage.

I chanced a glance outside. The battle had turned into a street-brawl.
Teams of Rebells threw themselves onto a single POLICE officer, only to
be shot or removed by reinforcements, only to be mobbed by a new wave of
Rebells. The officers on horseback were riding in circles, firing haphazardly
into the crowd. One horse, minus its rider, was in the midst of bucking off
a Rebell who tried to mount it.

In the chaos, blood flowed freely. So did fists, feet, and teeth. I returned
my attention to the matter at hand: to protect the general. He was stretched
down on the floor, eyes dancing around the area for any sign of movement,
a single rifle notched against his shoulder and cocked ready to fire. The
major was squatting down, aiming his revolver at the door opposite of
where I stood ready. Obviously, this was not the first time he had been
tossed into a gunfight while in the presence of the general.

Two Rebells tried storming into the carriage from either side. I called
to the major to warn him just in time to see one man above me reaching
for my shirt through the destroyed window. I grabbed the hand that
stretched out to me with my own free hand. We both swayed from the loss
of balance. Remembering that I had a revolver, I tried to get a shot at him,
but there was no way I could do it—the positioning was too awkward. My
gun was pinned between me and the door. The Rebell somehow managed
to retake his footing and was pulling me outside.

Twisting my body, I managed to free my arm, and I fired. The bullet exited the cylinder, exited the gun barrel, entered the door, went through the door, and entered the man who was holding me. I felt him jerk. His grip tightened on me for a second. His eyes grew wide with shock and pain. He slowly let go of me. As he started to fall, I let go of his lifeless body. Truthfully, I gave his dying husk a nudge to help him on his way.

The other man, while I was busy, tried to climb through one of the still-open windows on the opposite side. The major didn't waste any time like I had. He aimed and shot a bullet straight into the intruder's head. He was flung out of the carriage by the force of the bullet and landed on the dirt below.

Outside the carriage, the battle raged on. The main force of the fleet against the POLICE was ignoring the carriages completely. They were more concerned with the ground force, which was killing the intruders faster than they could compensate. What started out as a battle against around five hundred was decimated to a mere two hundred fifty-some-odd townsmen within minutes. But still, two hundred fifty versus twenty-plus officers was a lost cause—no matter how well they were trained.

I leaned toward the general and the major. "We have to get out of here," I exclaimed.

"But we're surrounded." the major pointed out, as if I was blind to the fact.

I shook my head. "There's a path by the forest. I wandered along it when we were camped earlier today. If I'm right, it should've continued to where we are now. It will lead us back to the town and out of this blood bath."

The major shook his head in disagreement. "There's too much of a chance that the general will get hurt out there."

"The general could just as easily get hurt in here," I screamed above the noise, pointing out the glass and blood splatters within the protective housing we were huddled in.

The general rolled toward the door with the empty space for a window. He fumbled around a side drawer beside the door, tossing different trinkets and whatnots from the wooden basin onto the ground. Finding what he was madly searching for, he took out a pocket mirror and held it up above his head in order to look outside. We stared at the general, watching his every move. The general soon brought the mirror down to his chest.

The general nodded toward the action outside. "There are too many people against us. We'll be overtaken soon. I say we go for the forest and the path and take our chances there."

The major, obviously upset with the decision, nodded his head in agreement. He leaned against the door opposite me with the window still intact. He looked out, checking to see if it was okay for us to make a break for it. "When I say, we run. I lead. The general follows. You stay close behind the general and, above all else, get rid of anyone who tries to stop us. Got it?"

I agreed. The three of us crouched into position. The major grabbed the doorknob. Gun raised, he eased the knob sideways very slowly so the door was unlocked, but he didn't open the door. We waited there, with baited breath, ready to run. The major never left the view of the window. He took a breath.

"Now!"

The door burst open with a sudden push, and the major was outside. The general quickly followed the major. I followed the general, revolver in hand. People were fighting everywhere. Officers and Rebells alike were flying into each other, determined to see each dead and gone. We didn't bother trying to come to anyone's aid. Our combined focus was the tree line and finding the path. The three of us sprinted toward the forest with all we had. We didn't stop for anything! Objects flew through the air, just missing the three of us. We grew closer and closer to the forest. Screams of pain and anguish blasted behind us.

The major leapt into the underbrush like a scared deer fleeing a hunter. The general pushed his way through the forest, knocking branches off of trees. I reached the brush shortly afterward. The major zoomed through the trees and flashed through the underbrush, leading us deeper and deeper away from the road. The general was close on his heels, the rifle he was clenching now nothing but a prop to help avoid oncoming branches. I grabbed onto a single branch in order to push it out of my way as I continued to run at a breakneck speed. At least, that was the idea.

Someone tackled me from behind. The stranger and I rolled and flopped into the trees and down a slight hill. We landed at the bottom of the hill in tangles. I couldn't see whom I was fighting against, only that he was bigger than me. I needed to get back to the general. We wrestled for control of the fight. We both knew that whoever had control of the fight would be destined to live. A punch to the kidneys gave the winning flag to the stranger.

The light inside the forest was low. All I could see was leaves, mud, and the shadow of the man who was on top of me. I got twisted onto my front, my arm pinned behind me almost to the breaking point.

"Thought you could get away, didn't you?" a voice spat into my ear, out of breath from the run and the fight.

I lifted my head a bit at the sound of the voice. "Duncan?" I asked.

CHAPTER 37

~

M<small>Y ARM SLACKENED BUT REMAINED</small> secure inside his hands. "Tom?"

I relaxed myself. "Yeah, Duncan. It's me, Tom."

My arm screamed with pain. He tightened his grip on me and twisted my arm even farther behind my back. "Get up," he growled.

I was forced to my feet. He threw me against a nearby tree, knocking the breath out of me. Feeling me go limp in his hands, the fight literally knocked out of me, Duncan then let go of my arm and twisted me around so I could face him. For good measure, he brought his knee swiftly into my stomach. I doubled over in pain, my good arm jutting out to stop myself from collapsing onto the ground once again.

"What are you doing here?" he demanded.

I gasped desperately to try to fill my lungs with air. "I … am here … to guard … the gen—"

He kicked me in the back with enough force to break my spine. I felt one of my ribs go from the hard heel of Duncan's boot—one of the ribs that I'd needed wrapped from my last fight with Vans. A spasm of pain shook my system. It didn't' feel like the rib broke, but it was probably close to it. Duncan towered over me.

"So that *was* the general I saw you racing after."

He stood above me, staring off into the direction of the forest where the two before me disappeared. He looked from the trees to me. Duncan smiled. "You're about to do your good deed for the day, Corporal Ma—Sergeant now. So this was the price for your betrayal?"

He dragged me to my feet again. It took another fist to my side for me to get my footing straight. He half led, half dragged me back to where we slid down the small inclined hill. There, lying patently for me, was my revolver. He bent down and picked it up. After checking to see how many bullets it had, we started our journey through the forest in search of the two lost POLICE officers.

"I'm glad William's dead for this reason only, Tom," he whispered into my ear as we walked along the forest trail.

What? William's not dead. He was released, I thought to myself.

"I'm glad he didn't survive in order to see how you had betrayed him," Duncan continued. "How you betrayed Dawn. How you betrayed everyone you ever cared about!" Duncan spat as he dragged me along.

I tried to stop Duncan from walking. "Duncan, you don't under—"

He pulled the gun on me, stuffing the barrel just under my jaw. I could feel the cold metallic tube jutting into the soft flesh under my chin. "It's only because I knew how dedicated you were to my old friend that I don't kill you right now. Keep moving."

That said, we jerked into motion again. Duncan led the trek through the forest, almost dragging me behind him. I couldn't tell where we were going, because of the poor light and the fact that my mind was shorting out from the pain.

Images of the past few years flashed across my eyes, sparking into view and disappearing as quickly as they came. I tried to focus on them rather than the stagnant forest that I was being jostled through. The first image was of the day I met William. How I had to beat up Vans in order to save them. I remembered how kind that family was. Then came John's reaction at finding out that they were Rebells. The many talks between John and me at the fountain. Dawn ... the letter. The first day as a SIT for the POLICE. The armband. Duncan—when I first met him in the den. The meeting.

"Why?" I whispered.

Duncan gave me a tug, making me lose my balance for a second.

"Shut up," he warned me, giving the revolver in his hands a brush in front of my face. I was not going to be daunted by the man.

"Why ... meeting?"

Duncan, still leading me through the maze of trees and brush, gave me another jab. "I said be quiet."

My focus was starting to come back to me, probably from the huge amount of adrenaline in my system. "Duncan, why did you go ahead with that meeting? I warned you that it was going to be a disaster."

Duncan slowed, pulling me to a stop in front of him. "A disaster? Is that what you thought? No, it went better than I could have dreamt."

I flew from confusion to anger to bewilderment in seconds. Duncan slowly started to form a smirk, the realization finally dawning on him. "Wait a minute.... You thought the point of the damn thing was so I could talk about trying to take down the general?"

Duncan, seeing I had absolutely no idea what he was talking about, just shook his head and pushed me back into walking out in front of him. "The meeting was nothing more than a means to an end, Tom. It was supposed to be a massive recruitment drive," he tried to explain to me.

"But you said—"

"That was at the start, when it was nothing more than a few of us. With the amount of people gathering for the meeting, I saw it for what it could be," Duncan interrupted me, knowing full well what I was about to say.

"But the plan you gave—"

I could hear the smile in his voice. "They were expecting me to say something. I had to make something up."

I tried to look back at Duncan as I stumbled through the brush. "How did you think—"

Duncan waved at the bigger picture forming before him. "Get the POLICE to capture and interrogate a bunch of innocent civilians from a collection of neighboring towns? This would get some much-needed sympathy for the cause. This was the general plan. Yeah, it would hurt at first, and it would take time to rebuild. But the result would have been worth it, and I'm a patient man. But to have the POLICE come in guns blazing and slaughter men and women who had no hope of defending themselves? To show everyone exactly what the POLICE are capable of? To get those townsfolk left behind riled up to the brink of rioting for revenge over their lost loved ones? I gotta say … Fürl did more for the Rebells in one night than I have done in ten years. He opened the floodgates."

I was dumbfounded. "So you were willingly giving up everyone who went to the meeting? Just so that you could get sympathy toward the cause?"

"People have finally woken up, Tom. They've had enough and are now at the moment when they're starting to take action. Blind submission and fear have given way to frustration and anger. It was amazing how quickly I could whip up a mob mentality in the last town. The days of the POLICE are coming to an end, Sergeant Rebell."

He was gone. The man I once knew was gone—replaced by this crazed hooligan.

He said Rebell like it was poison on his tongue. We were beside a small clearing somewhere deep in the forest. Through the brush, I could just make out the major standing and looking down at something. I couldn't see the general.

Duncan put the barrel of the gun to my temple and held me close as he forced me to walk slowly ahead of him. He was going to use me as a shield in case the major opened fire at the sudden movement. We walked into the clearing. The major pulled out his revolver as soon as he saw me. He moved it from me to Duncan when he emerged behind me.

The general was sitting down on the ground, a rushed makeshift fire composed of a single torch staked into the ground in front of him to give the area a little bit of light. He was trying to shake out some pebble or obstruction from a boot in his hand, the other boot sitting beside him. The general's gun was beside the boot. He looked up at me with utter shock, not expecting me to walk out of the forest after being missing for so long. The general then saw Duncan behind me, and his look turned to disgust. He stood up, dropping the boot.

"Tell your guy here to drop the gun, Linden!" Duncan yelled at the general.

The major did not bat an eye. Neither did the general. Everyone just froze where he stood. All muscles were tense. I looked from the major to the general, seeing if they were going to take action against Duncan.

The general stared hard at Duncan. "Let the lad go. He has no place in this. You know that as much as I do. He's suffered enough by your hands."

Duncan tensed up more. I could hear the trigger go farther back, forcing the hammer to rise with a click-click-click. "My hands? *My* hands?! It's your damn project that got him mixed up in the first place! He was perfectly happy with us until that first sergeant stuck his nose into things that didn't concern him."

The general's jaw almost dropped. You could see that Duncan's words hit the general off guard. Duncan eased up a bit, setting the hammer back to its resting place. He knew he had hit a nerve.

"You didn't know. You didn't know that this runt was a Rebell?"

At this, Duncan burst out laughing—a teasing, annoying, got-the-better-of-you laugh. The major stood still, gun still aimed at the two of us. One word, and we both would have been shot. That didn't even faze Duncan in the slightest.

He grew serious again. "Your boy over there is still holding that gun. I want him to drop it."

Duncan then pointed the gun at the major. He didn't flinch. The major stood still, as if he were carved out of marble. The general bounced from looking at the major to us, as if deciding whether or not to give the order.

"Tell him to drop it. Final warning," Duncan ordered.

The general turned to the major. "N—"

Duncan never let the general finish his command. He fired the gun at the major, and the bullet dug deep into the officer's skull. The major dropped his gun and fell to the earth dead.

The general stood extremely still. He looked from his fallen soldier to the pair of us, a bead of sweat resting on his forehead. "He was a good officer," the general cursed at Duncan.

Duncan brought the gun down to a resting position at his side. I thought he was going to point it at me again. But, instead of placing it back against my temple, he jammed the metallic weapon in the back of his pants within easy reach. He then started pushing on my shoulders, forcing me to support myself by locking my legs. I shouldn't have done that. He raised his boot up a bit and brought it crashing down on the outside of my knee. I fell without a word, landing in a lump. Once on the ground, Duncan repeated the action, but on the front of my kneecap this time. I could feel the bone crack under the impact.

I tried not to black out from the pain. He set me up against a tree, so I had an impartial view of the clearing. Once satisfied that I couldn't move or interfere, he got up and returned his attention to the general. The general had not moved a muscle, except for putting on his boots. His gun still rested on the ground.

"You always were the dramatic one," the general smiled at Duncan.

Duncan steadied himself, walking out into the clearing. The general walked out from behind the torch and started to circle around the area. "I suppose this is to the death?"

Duncan went to one knee, ready to pounce. "You assume right."

The general slowed his pace, keeping his attention solely locked on Duncan. "One question…. Does the winner get dibs on him?" The general shook his head toward me.

Duncan continued his dance around the torch, being careful not to step on it. "Added bonus," he offered.

The general stopped pacing and stood upright. "What are the rules this time?"

Duncan stood as well. He put his hands on his hips. "I think the average rules apply: no weapons, no help. Just you and me, like it's always been."

The general held up a hand to his chest, scratching at a long-ago healed wound. "Where's the knife?"

Duncan risked a quick check, looking down at the empty holster where his hunting knife normally hung. He gave off a general nod off into the forest. "One of your sergeant majors is holding onto it for me."

Despite the pain I was in, I watched the two of them encircle each other discussing the eventual battle like they were discussing ground rules for a game. The general walked around the torch to meet Duncan. Duncan stood still, waiting for the general to meet him on the other side of the fire. They stood toe-to-toe, staring into each other's face.

"Who threw the first punch last time?" the general asked.

Duncan was about to reply when the general threw a quick jab to Duncan's midsection. Duncan, unprepared for the blow, buckled a bit. That gave room for a few quicker, harder hits from the general. Duncan went to his knees but not out of pain.

He grabbed the general's closest leg and pulled it out from under him. The general went down like a sack of potatoes. He landed hard onto the torch that stuck out from the ground, catching a few embers in the dark jacket he was wearing. The general quickly rolled onto his side, smothering the embers. Duncan leapt on top of the general, hands placed firmly around his neck. The general tried to gurgle out a curse, but all that came out of his mouth was a wheezed haze.

The general gave a hard fist to Duncan's side, but he still wouldn't let go. It took four more hits before Duncan gave in and released his grip. They separated by rolling on the ground in opposite directions, allowing themselves a little breather. Duncan, recovering first, rolled and brought his heel onto the general's chest. The general purposefully wrapped himself around Duncan's foot to stop him from delivering any more cheap shots.

Duncan brought his other heel down onto the general's head. The general, recovering quickly from the blow, started twisting Duncan's foot until a crunching noise filled the clearing. Duncan let loose a scream from deep within him.

I looked on at the pathetic display between the two from where sat. It didn't matter who won. I was going to have to deal with the winner. Odds were, it wasn't going to be good.

I looked around for something to use in order to protect myself once the fight was over. I couldn't run with my broken knee. I couldn't crawl away, that would take too long. I was stuck. The dead major lying on the ground away from the fight caught my attention. I started to muse about how much time I had left in this fight before I would eventually end up joining him. I stared at the man—and the gun that was still visible under his body!

Being careful not to draw attention to myself, I watched the two continue to fight as I dragged myself over to the dead major. Duncan was sitting up with the general inside a headlock. He slowly let go of the general, who managed to get away. With great effort, Duncan got up himself together and pulled himself up. He was carefully balancing himself on his remaining foot, teetering as he tried to steady himself.

I continued crawling while I watched. The general took a running jump at Duncan. They connected and tumbled back onto the ground inside a tumble of arms and legs. They reminded me of two boys playing in the mud.

They were insane-both of them.

The general gave a left jab, connecting with Duncan's jaw. Blood shot out of the Rebell's open mouth. The general continued with a few more jabs to the face. Duncan brought the leg with the wounded foot up and into the general, pushing the man off balance and off of Duncan.

I was almost in reach of the gun.

Duncan climbed on top of the downed general. He started delivering jab after jab to the general, tenderizing his face. The general waved his arms, trying to get a good grip on his opponent.

I grabbed the gun. Opening the cylinder, I checked to see how many bullets were left. Two bullets. Fitting. I closed the cylinder and cocked the gun, locking one of the two bullets into place.

They both crouched in front of each other, staring intently and countering each position. Blood trickled untouched out of Duncan's mouth. The general's right eye was starting to puff shut. Duncan took a deep breath and cringed slightly at the pain that it caused him.

"The future—your future—is doomed to fail!" Duncan began. "The people … are tired of your … dictatorship! Listen to them! Give them what … what they want! Give them their freedom! As long … as people are under your rule, they will … rebel. They will fight … you all the way to your death. It's time … to bring back the old ways."

The general turned his head to the side and spat out blood. "The past is dead, Duncan. Leave it buried! You cannot resurrect it. It's done. My father stopped your precious 'democracy,' because it was causing more trouble than it was worth. There's no room for your past in my country. Just as there is no longer room for you."

The general reached toward his back. His hand disappeared within the folds of his jacket, now disheveled and missing many of the ornaments that once covered the fabric. His hand slowly rematerialized, a dust-covered revolver resting firmly within his grip. Duncan quickly checked to see if he still had the revolver he'd taken off of me. It was gone.

"Lose something?" the general asked, trying to smile through cracked, bleeding lips.

Duncan, grimacing at his carelessness, slowly pulled his hand back out in front of his body. The general held the gun out for Duncan to see, turning it from side to side in order to better admire it in the little light that managed to creep into the clearing. From where I sat, I could see that it was the revolver that the general had given me—the one that Duncan had taken. The general must have taken it off of him.

"It's amazing what one can lose inside a struggle," the general pointed out.

The general set the revolver's sights to his good eye. Duncan sat up straight. "That's the only way you could have won this—by cheating," he spat.

The general cocked the gun. "I didn't cheat. I just changed the rules."

The gun fired. The shot echoed inside the small area, like the bullet was shot from a cannon. Duncan closed his eyes as the bullet entered his chest. He shuddered, convulsed, and collapsed to one side. Blood eased itself from the fresh wound. Duncan took in one last breath and then stopped moving.

He never made a sound.

I was frozen. Duncan was dead? I couldn't think. Duncan was dead! I should've done something. I owed it to the others. Duncan was dead. With him gone, for the first time in a long time, the POLICE would have absolute power. Nothing could stop them. No one would dare stand in their way. The remaining factions of the Rebells, without Duncan to lead them, would fall in a matter of months. With the Rebell's gone, the general would rule supreme by the year's end.

I came out of my haze. The general was sitting exactly as he was when he shot Duncan. He dropped the gun, letting the smoking barrel bury itself into the ground. The general stood up and looked around the area for me. Finding me beside the dead major, he walked toward me.

The general stood over me and smiled. "The nightmare is finally over."

I stared back at him, unmoving, as he continued to gloat to the rest of the clearing. "The Rebells are now as dead as Duncan is. Nothing will hold them together ..." The general slowly turned toward where I was stretched out on the ground. "... except for a new Duncan."

He bent down onto his knees in order to look me in the eyes. I hid the gun that I had taken off the dead major behind me as best I could. He smiled at me. "Duncan was lying when he said you were a Rebell. Right, Tom? He was just trying to goad me?"

I didn't say a word. I just returned his gaze. I felt a single droplet of sweat run from my temple to my jaw.

The general got up from his hunched position, stretching weary muscles as he grew in stature in front of me, and walked away from me. "I'm very disappointed," he called out to me as he casually made his way back to the revolver on the ground. "You had such high possibilities. I could've pictured you earning the rank of sergeant major in about six years from now. If only you kept on the path you were on. I guess we'll never know. Tragic how Duncan shot you while you tried to run away from the fight. Left me all defenseless. Why, other officers would consider that ... traitorous."

He reached down and picked up his gun, lightly clearing off the dust that had settled on it. Panicked, I stuck my gun out in front of me and aimed it at the general. He didn't notice it until he returned his gaze back to me. There was no reaction—at first. Then the general started to slowly applaud, clapping his empty hand against the wrist of the hand that held the gun.

"You remembered that the major had a gun. So, while Duncan and I had our little fight, you snuck around us and picked it up. The question now is—are you prepared to use it?"

He stared walking back toward me nice and slow, like he didn't have a care in the world. His gun rested inside his hand, which rested by his side so as not to intimidate me. He stopped a few paces away from me.

In a mocking pose, he held out his hands to his sides in an attempt to surrender. "You got me."

"Duncan never shot me," I pointed out to the general, trying my best to sound confident. The level of concentration I was exerting to keep the gun level and aimed at the general was excruciating. My eyes started to blur slightly from the constant pounding and throbbing that came from both my ribs and my knee.

The general smiled. "Well, that's your opinion. See, I have to make up some excuse for those who are gonna miss you. What I don't get is why you didn't want to live life like an honorable POLICE officer, like we all thought you were? You could have lived a happy, successful life. But *no....* Ya had to throw it all away. Since you were involved with those nasty Rebells—well, not much of a choice left, is there? With Duncan gone, they're going to be looking for a new leader.... Someone who is capable of dragging them back from the brink. I can't have you picking up where he left off."

I sat dumbfounded and tried to get my mind to work. Tried to find a way to stall or trick the general. "Duncan was right. The people are tired. They are also scared."

The general bent down to my level and rested himself on the balls of his feet so that it looked like he was perched on some invisible branch. He folded his arms slightly to help keep himself balanced in this semiawkward position and rested his gun on his knee. "How can you say that?"

"Didn't you watch the scenery as we traveled here? The people that we passed? They were scared of that carriage. They were scared of you," I pointed out.

"They're supposed to be," the general retaliated, as if this was common knowledge. "We need to establish ourselves as a force that no one can stand against. We have to push down hard on the common man in order to make sure that there is a strong sense of order. Any attempt otherwise would show weakness, and the POLICE are not weak! If they don't fear us, they won't listen to us, and chaos will rear its ugly head once more. They'll start to question what we're doing. They'll start to demand equality. They'll flock to the Rebells and their fight to bring back the old ways. I can't ever allow that to happen. I will not let my father's dream die because of some ignorant Rebells. So any attempt to cause disorder is dealt with—swift, strong, and without mercy. It's stated clear as day in the handbook: Obey and survive."

I gave off a quiet huff with the sudden realization of what the POLICE were all about under the general's rule. This wasn't an organization set out to bring order to the world. It might have been at one point in time. It wasn't anymore. The POLICE were no longer about law and order. They were about oppression and fear. It was about establishing themselves as better than the common man.

What about the foodstuffs that I was privy to as an officer, while flatly denied for the merchant to sell? How many innocent people were dragged away or killed in the name of "preserving order"? How many times had I just passed by the report after report of officers spying on the average townsmen, like the bunker's purpose inside the Factory? This was a group that wanted to make everyone so scared out of their minds that they wouldn't even dream of fighting back. The Rebells were just an excuse to further push the populace down under their boot. Why did it take me so long to realize it?

I stared long and hard at the general through the sights of the gun. "The past is dead. You're correct in saying that," I finally spoke.

The general stood up to his full height. "Well now. It's nice to see that there are some brains in that head."

I raised the gun to match up the sights with the general's head. "But you're also wrong to think that the future is yours. Your future is coming down around your heels. That town was proof enough."

The general cocked his head to the side, not liking how the conversation had turned. The grip on the revolver in his hands, I could see, was tightening. "Just what are you trying to say?"

Through much effort and strain, I stumbled to a standing position and balanced myself on my good leg. All the while, I kept the gun in my hand aimed at him. "The world you created; this is not the dream that your father wanted. Your father strived for a world that emphasized unification—to stop all the disorder that was running rampant around the world. And, in a way, he succeeded. But the way you're trying to rule the POLICE—segregation, bullying, oppression—it's causing everyone to turn against you. The meeting at the Dome, the town, your constant hunting the Rebells—it's just fuel toward your downfall. If something doesn't change soon, then a revolution will occur, and it will be the war all over again. You have to—"

The general glared at me, his grip tightening around the gun. "How *dare* you! How dare you accuse me of tearing down what my father built. You think you know better, you ignorant child?"

I didn't flinch. "I've seen both sides, General: POLICE *and* Rebells. I've seen what it is that you're fighting for and what they're fighting for. And if you think that your view is the better one, then you're fooling yourself. Theirs isn't perfect either, but at least it gives everyone a better chance to work toward fixing this situation instead of trying desperately to keep the status quo. You need to step down, General. You need to let this world start healing itself."

The general slowly raised his gun toward me. "I'd rather die, traitor."

"So be it."

The general growled at me, his smirk long gone from his cut and bruised face. Time slowed to the point where I could see every action as it took place.

I pulled the trigger.

The blast of the gunpowder ignited.

The bullet rocketed out of the chamber.

The general's eyes bulged.

The gun jerked from the push of the bullet.

His arm, holding the gun, continued to rise.

He screamed his frustrations out at me.

The bullet targeted his eye.

He fired his gun.

The bullet struck the side of his head, slicing his ear.

His bullet flew passed me.

He dropped his gun.

His ear was a fountain of blood.

He raised his hand to his face.

His screams turned from anguish to rage.

The general turned away from me.

He bent to one knee.

I lowered the gun.

I aimed at the back of his skull.

I pulled the trigger again.

The bullet rocketed across the small distance between us.

Lead met up with bone and brain.

The general fell dead to the ground.

The area fell silent. The air came to me in long gulps. The gun, now empty, felt heavy in my hand. I stared at the dead bodies that were scattered around the area. A loyal soldier and two dreamers—dreams that were facing the opposite ways.

The weight of everything suddenly hit me hard, and I let the gun fall from my hand to the ground. The sounds of the gunfire would attract someone eventually. They would see the bodies of the two leading factions and the major—and me. Questions would need to be answered—answers I couldn't give. I had to avoid everyone and go into hiding. There was no telling how much time I had left.

Taking a look around the clearing, I tried to search for something I could use for a crutch. The immediate vicinity was sparse of thick, longer-limbed trees and fallen branches. I hobbled awkwardly toward the edge of the clearing and grabbed one of the pieces of wood, setting it firmly against my wounded knee. Gritting my teeth, I did so again on the opposite side with another thick branch from the ground. Making sure that my leg was as straight as possible, I ripped off a good length of fabric from the bottom of my shirt and tied the two pieces of wood together tightly. I soon realized that I should've gotten myself some sort of brace for my mouth as I almost bit right through my tongue from the sheer agony of the action.

With my leg in support, I was able to barely put weight onto it. I was still in no shape to make my escape yet, though. I needed a cane. I limped over to a tree and pulled off a good size branch. *I'm going to need this*, I told myself. I gave the clearing a final look over. *I have a long walk ahead of me.*

I started walking out of the clearing when a soft chill crept up my spine. The adrenalin of the recent events had worn itself out. I suddenly started to feel the coolness of the air more readily. A thought came to mind. Taking a few steps back into the clearing, I moved beside the body of the general and bent down. His jacket was simple enough to pull off of him. He didn't put up a fight over losing it. With a swing, I flung the jacket on top of my shoulders and gave it a quick shakedown until it settled on my form, sliding my arms down through its sleeves.

I looked down at my uniform. There were patches of all types decorating me, medals hanging loosely from the struggle between Duncan and the general, as well as other special gifts given from unknown presenters. With a renewed vigor, I grabbed at all the memorabilia, patches, and symbol-pressed buttons that adorned both my shirt and the jacket I had just stolen. Anything that distinguished me as an officer needed to go.

I never was one.

EPILOGUE

... and I walked away, never looking back at the misery that I had just left.

My name is Thomas Haroldson.
I am not a POLICE officer.
I am not a Rebell.
I am a man ... one of many who have lost their way.
All I ask is that you leave me so that I can try to find it again.

I closed the book. The leather binding and the golden words on the cover sparkled and twinkled in the sun. This book cost me a pretty penny, but I had to do it. For the memory of all who had died, I had to do it.

Leaning hard on the pack that sat innocently beside me, I lurched myself off the flat rock that I had used for a stool so I could write my final words in my new grail. Pins and needles poked and prodded without mercy at both my legs as I took my first step; the length of time I'd been sitting on the hard surface had taken its toll on me. I shook my legs, desperate to get the blood circulating back into them. I suddenly remembered, with a sharp jolt, the entire reason why I stopped in the first place: there was a rock in my boot.

Easing myself down again, I untied my boot and shook out the rock. While tying my boot back up, I stared out onto the sky. A bowl of blue wonder stretched out over the wild grass field in front of me, speckled with white mist and fluffy folds. Birds sang from the trees; insects sang from the grass. The gravel road that I was traveling separated the fields. Up ahead, a small patch of trees spanned out and disappeared. That's where I was headed.

I got up and returned to my pilgrimage down the road. My leg, though far from completely healed, no longer needed a stick or cane to help me support myself. Hadn't needed one for some time. Not since the farm. I shook my head as I thought back to the farm and its tenants. That wasn't too long ago, I figured, yet it felt like a lifetime. Looking at the sun, I saw that it was almost time for dinner. I smiled as I looked back at my comfortable stool and my ignorance of time. I'd wasted away too much time as it is.

I'll eat when I get hungry, I told myself.

The road, rocky with the occasional hole, rolled out in front of me like a gray carpet. I felt like a king or someone important entering a fine entranceway. I imagined guards holding open the door so I could enter. Inside, there would be tables upon tables, seated among them my friends and family. They all looked well and happy. I smiled at them all. In the center of the room stood a king's throne just for me.

I blinked.

The gravel poured out in front of me, almost forever. The carpet was as long as the countryside. I laughed quietly to myself.

A noise caught my attention, coming from behind me. A quick glance told me that a wagon was coming up the road. Three people were inside. Farmers, by the looks of them. The wagon slowed down beside me. The driver, a man in his midforties, called out to me.

"Evening."

"Hello." I smiled.

"Where ya headed?" he asked me.

I slowed my pace and stopped beside the wagon. I lifted my hand in order to block the sun from my eyes. "Down the road."

"You in a hurry?"

I smiled at the man. "I got some friends waiting for me," I lied.

"Want a ride?"

I looked down the road. It was a long walk ahead of me to any sense of civilization. I looked back at the man in the driver's seat. "Sure."

He offered me his hand to help me up. I took it. The wagon started rolling again. The two in the back of the wagon were young. One was about ten, the other ... seven, maybe eight. They were both boys. His sons, I guessed.

"My name's Milton. The two in the back are Angel and Marcus."

"Thoma—"

My throat was dry, which caused my voice to wither up and die midphrase. Good thing, too. I couldn't believe I almost gave him my name. I had to be more careful. He offered a small jug of water to me. I took a deep pull on the jug and gave it back to him.

"Sakes alive, you're thirsty. When was the last time you had a proper meal?"

I stared down the road. "Awhile ago."

The man glanced from the road to me. "When are your friends expecting you?"

I smiled. "Not for a while."

"Good. You're coming to my place for a hot meal and some drink afterward," he ordered.

I looked at him, half surprised. He smiled. "What? Never had a stranger offer you a meal before?"

"No. It's just ... I ... uh."

He glanced toward the rocky road in front to make sure he was driving it straight and then turned back to me. "In these days, ya have ta help each other, or else none of us will survive. Well? How about it?"

I stared into his eyes. They were bright and full of life.

I agreed.

"My name is Tom Hill. Glad to meet you."

We continued talking as the wagon rolled down the road.

LITERATURE CIRCLE QUESTIONS

1. **(Novel)** Which side do you favor: Le Rebells or the POLICE? Remember—by siding with a specific faction, you are providing support towards their actions... both good AND bad. Does the bad outweigh the good, or vice versa, when examining their cause (POLICE—going to war with the world, obliterating the known establishment, in order to obtain ultimate peace and order. Rebells—committing terrorist actions and killing innocent people to bring about freedom from the totalitarian organization in power).

2. **(*Novel*)** What will happen to the POLICE without the general? Le Rebells without Duncan?

3. **(*Novel*)** After the epilogue, what will happen to Tom?

   Or

   (*Novel*) Are you satisfied with the ending of the novel, with having Tom ride off into the distance? Do events play out as you hoped it would, or did something happen that didn't quite fit with what you had hoped? In your opinion, was there something left unfinished?

4. **(*Ch. 30*)** Do you think William was actually released by the POLICE, or did something else "happen" to him?

5. (*Novel*) Was the use of the journal throughout the book effective? Did you wish the events described in the journal narration to be played out within the novel (in full detail) instead of being summarized in journal format, or was the quick summary better for the flow of the novel?

6. (*Novel*) Could the POLICE, in your opinion, actually exist within our world, or is the construction of the organization too 'far fetched'? Why/ Why not? What about the overall world that Tom lives in? Could it actually come to be?

7. (*Ch. 4* + *Ch. 15*) Do you think it was the right move for the Rebells to blow up the Factory, or was there a more effective way to obtain the desired goal (destroy the files & strike a blow against the POLICE)?

8. (*Ch. 21—28* + *37*) Should Duncan have stayed true to his original plan for the meeting (small group to plan the assassination of the General in Hauptstadt), or do you agree with his changed plan to have the meeting in the Dome (gather support for the Rebell movement)? Why/why not? Do you agree with Duncan letting the meeting happen, despite the POLICE finding out about it, or do you think he should have cancelled it?

9. (*Novel*) If you could rewrite history within the novel and rescue one of the characters from death, who would it be (General, Duncan, Dawn, Lydia, John, Vans, Tom's parents, etc.)? Why choose that character? With the rescue of that character, how would the rest of the story change, based on the decisions that the other characters made due to the death?

10. (*Ch. 28*) How did Fürl figure out that Tom was not as loyal towards the POLICE as he should be? Why send Vans after him? Why not approach Charles with it?

11. (*Novel*) Which character do you best relate to? Why?

12. (*Novel*) How would the story change if Tom took favor with a particular side from the very beginning, instead of choosing to play both sides in

order to protect the Kenneth family? How would the story play out if he sided with the POLICE from the start? The Rebells?

13. (*Part 3*) During the first two parts of the novel, Tom tried to play both sides in order to protect the Kenneth family. Yet in Part 3, with the family gone, this was no longer an issue. In your opinion, with the loss of the Kenneth family, did Tom finally choose a side or was he still trying his best to stay neutral? Explain.

14. (*Novel*) Examine the title of the book. What's the significance of the title? What does it mean? How does it relate to some of the themes/images/symbols present within the novel?

15. (*Novel*) In the journal, Tom insists that he's writing it in order to keep a non-biased documentation of the events as how they played out, since "history is written by the winners" and can 'muddy' events to favor them. Does he truly write a non-biased version of events? If the POLICE were to write the events that transpired in their history books, how might it be written? How would the Rebells write the events of the novel in their history books?

16. (*Ch. 17 + 19*) Discuss the relevance of the books found within the crates from the 'Zone or discussed by Tom and HJ in comparison to the novel: Hard Times (including the selected passage), 1984, Peter Pan, Around the World in 80 Days, Robin Hood.

17. (*Ch. 9*) Why do you think William chose Animal Farm specifically to better demonstrate his thoughts on the POLICE? In your opinion, is there a different novel—a better choice—that he could have chosen? Look at his analysis of the novel. Clearly, it's a skewed interpretation, since he did not have the prior knowledge of Orwell's opinion on Marxism. Does his interpretation still work?

18. (*Ch. 18 + 36*) What is the significance of the ring found within the bunker where Tom and H.J. inventoried the crates from the 'Zone? What

might its story be? [Hint: See Ch. 10] Why did Tom toss the ring away at the beginning of Ch. 36 when he leaves the town caught in the revolt?

19. (*Novel*) How many hidden references to the World Wars (dates, associations to famous people, etc) were you able to find within the novel? [Hint: There's quite a few. Look at the numbers used in the book—what significant event happened in that year? Look at character traits, hobbies, history lessons, locations, names, events...]

20. (*Ch. 1 + 32*) Inside the novel, the general and Tom refers to 4 main categories as the overall reasoning behind all the battles and wars in the world: Politics, Land, Religion, and Miscommunication. Do you agree with these categories? Should there be different ones? Why/why not?

21. (*Ch. 11*) Charles tells Tom that he was right to be suspicious regarding the secretary, Betty Nikle. What do you think the POLICE found?

22. (*Novel*) Did you enjoy the story? Do you want the saga to continue?